W9-ARE-810

PRAISE FOR *YOU LUCKY DOG*

"Full of laugh-out-loud charm." —*Woman's World*

"Julia London's hilarious and sweet romance *You Lucky Dog* begins with an accidental dog-swapping, which quickly leads to puppy love between two very different dog owners. Trust us, even if you're a cat person, you won't be able to resist this story's charms." —PopSugar

"I laughed, I teared up, and I rooted for these characters every misstep of the way. . . . A perfect choice this summer." —Fresh Fiction

"Comedic and fast-paced. It is filled with an offbeat cast, zany coincidences and romantic moments, and mishaps that will leave readers giggling in amusement." —Shelf Awareness

"A canine mix-up leads to unexpected love in this bright, bubbly rom-com. . . . There's heady chemistry between the optimistic Carly and the slightly nerdy Max as they stumble into co-parenting the pooches, with the fabulous four-legged supporting characters providing both laugh-out-loud hilarity and some touching moments. Readers will be in doggie heaven." —*Publishers Weekly*

"Once again, London proves she is a master of deliciously snarky dialogue and delectable sexual chemistry, both of which are expertly infused in a delightful love story that not only joyfully celebrates the special bond between humans and dogs but also doesn't shy away from exploring some of life's more serious challenges."
—*Booklist* (starred review)

"[An] affecting and ebullient romantic comedy. . . . London's loose and limber comedic writing amplifies Max and Carly's appeal, filling each voice with a unique perspective and personality." —*BookPage*

PRAISE FOR THE NOVELS OF JULIA LONDON

"A passionate, arresting story that you wish would never end."

—*New York Times* bestselling author Robyn Carr

"Julia London writes vibrant, emotional stories and sexy, richly drawn characters." —*New York Times* bestselling author Madeline Hunter

"Julia London strikes gold again."

—#1 *New York Times* bestselling author Stephanie Laurens

"London's characters come alive on every page and will steal your heart." —*The Atlanta Journal-Constitution*

"Entertaining. . . . The reader is pleasantly carried along by the author's instinctive narrative gifts." —*The New York Times*

"Few authors can write a book that pulls you into the love story the way Julia London can." —*The Oakland Press*

JOVE
New York

It Started with a Dog

Julia London

A JOVE BOOK
Published by Berkley
An imprint of Penguin Random House LLC
penguinrandomhouse.com

Library of Congress Cataloging-in-Publication Data

Names: London, Julia, author.
Title: It started with a dog / Julia London.
Description: First edition. | New York: Jove, 2021. | Series: Lucky dog
Identifiers: LCCN 2021012827 (print) | LCCN 2021012828 (ebook) |
ISBN 9780593100400 (trade paperback) | ISBN 9780593100417 (ebook)
Subjects: GSAFD: Love stories.
Classification: LCC PS3562.O48745 I85 2021 (print) |
LCC PS3562.O48745 (ebook) | DDC 813/.54—dc23
LC record available at https://lccn.loc.gov/2021012827
LC ebook record available at https://lccn.loc.gov/2021012828

First Edition: September 2021

Printed in the United States of America
1st Printing

Book design by Laura K. Corless

I dedicated my last book to all the dogs that have shaped my life. I was horrified to realize I had forgotten Sun, an Irish setter with a fun-loving spirit who went on every adventure that my brother and I ever set out on as country kids.

This book is dedicated to Sun.

Since my last book, we had to say a tearful goodbye to Sonny. But then we welcomed a new puppy, Lily.

This book is also dedicated to all the dogs who will come to our family in the years ahead. We will never be without dogs.

A Mardi Gras Festival in Austin

Winter rains that have pummeled Austin finally clear to reveal azure blue skies. It is Mardi Gras, and a cool breeze wafts down Congress Avenue. It's been a long day of parades and parties, but the diehard revelers aren't leaving before the crowning event.

The star of the show appears at the entrance to the cordoned-off street between two men assigned to escort her. She doesn't walk, she glides. She's had a blowout, and her flaxen hair lifts on the breeze, a streamer of silk. She is calm. She's in no rush. Why should she be? Look at all these people who have come here to see her, from all corners of town, from as far away as San Antonio and Dallas and Houston. They have come to celebrate her rapid rise to the top.

She doesn't look right or left, but straight ahead. She seems almost bored, as if she's seen so many crowds in her life that she can't be bothered to be awed by another one.

She is one cool cucumber.

She is simply the best.

She has stolen all their hearts.

The onlookers part like the Red Sea as she moves down the avenue on her way to the stage. Some of them have kids on their shoulders who point and shout with delight. Some have dogs on leashes who search the ground for dropped food or strain at their tethers, eager to meet and greet. Some of the onlookers have drinks in hand, or giant globs of cotton candy. Some of them have even set up camping chairs as if they think this might take a while.

The men escort the star onto a stage where a young woman waits, almost levitating with excitement. She has a colorful tattoo sleeve on one arm and has arranged her hair into a curious array of four haphazard buns around her head. She is wearing shorts sheared so short that the crowd can see all of London and all of France.

The star steps gracefully over the wires and cables left behind by the band that will return to the stage to close things out. She elegantly takes her place atop the dais.

Four Bun girl bounces to the front of the stage. She turns a grin to the star one last time before facing the crowd. She leans into the mic. "Can you hear me?"

The crowd roars in the affirmative.

"I am so excited to be here today! It is my very great pleasure to introduce you to Sheeba!"

Sheeba, Sheeba! The crowd chants. Someone throws a tennis ball on the stage.

Sheeba gives it a disdainful look but does not move from the dais. She stares straight ahead, her nose tilted upward, as if she is sniffing her own rarified air.

"On behalf of the Austin Canine Coalition and our participating sponsors, H-E-B, the *Austin American-Statesman*, and Covert Ford, I am so pleased to introduce you to the winner of the Annual Mardi Gras King Mutt competition!"

The crowd goes wild. Sheeba's ears flatten. Four Buns whips around, clapping enthusiastically in the dog's direction. Sheeba stares at Four Buns blankly.

Good girl, good girl, the crowd begins to chant. Sheeba lifts her back leg and scratches her ear.

"Thank you, Austin!" Four Buns shouts into the mic. "Sixteen dogs entered our annual King Mutt and raised a collective sixty-two thousand dollars for local animal rescue organizations!"

Sheeba yawns, then slides ever so gracefully down onto her belly, one paw crossed beguilingly over the other.

"Thank you for participating! And now, the crown!" Four Buns picks up a plastic gold crown with purple bobbles on the points. She tries to settle the crown on Sheeba's head, but the Afghan hound's head is too narrow and long. "That's weird," Four Buns says to one of the handlers. "It's supposed to fit."

"Yeah, I think they had to get a new one after the Lab chewed it up last year."

Four Buns vaguely remembers it. She has to use some of Sheeba's mane to anchor it, but she manages to perch the crown on the dog's head.

Sheeba, Sheeba, Sheeba! the crowd thunders.

Sheeba thumps her tail once or twice on the dais in acknowledgment of their adoration. Four Buns returns to the mic. "Planning is already underway for next year," she announces. "We hope to expand beyond the Mardi Gras business crawl so that we can add more dogs to compete for the coveted crown of the Most Popular Rescue Dog in Austin!"

Sheeba lowers her head, pillowing it on her paws, and with a long sigh, closes her eyes.

The crowd applauds enthusiastically.

"One hundred percent of the proceeds will go to support the Austin Canine Coalition, so please remember to vote with your dollars next year."

Sheeba rolls onto her side. The crown falls off her head and rolls off the stage. Somewhere, the Steve Martin song "King Tut" begins to play, and dogs up and down the street begin to bark.

One

Ten months later

This shared ride had the distinct vibe of a horror movie, and Harper should know, because she had seen practically every horror movie ever made. *Girl enters dark interior of nondescript van. Girl is smashed up against a guy with an uncompromising manspread, only slightly preferable to the other guy with the guitar case wedged between his legs. Girl is barked at by dog in pet carrier in front seat, held by a woman with a shower cap on her head. Girl is confused by driver, who is chatting like rain isn't coming down in torrents, like he can see just fine out the front windshield when they all know he can't, like it's a good idea to keep looking in the rearview mirror to gauge the effect of his speech on the passengers in back when road conditions are treacherous. Eyes on the road!*

The only thing missing from this scene was the alien creature that should be splatting on the windshield any minute now.

This was a Rain Event to be sure, coming very inconveniently on the eve of Christmas Eve, which, Harper's driver informed them, was the busiest travel day of the year. She wished she'd known that before she'd purchased her ticket home for the holidays. She'd meant to leave a day or two earlier, but as usual, her boss, Soren Wilder (yes, his real name), threw some stuff at her last minute. And as usual, she didn't say no. Harper Thompson didn't turn away from a challenge, no matter how small or inconsiderate.

Plus, she'd wanted to pay a visit to Bob. Bob was old and crotchety and didn't have many friends, and she couldn't bear to think of him alone for the holidays. So she'd gone round to see him one last time, like she did every Saturday, and he'd sighed and looked away, and then she'd snagged what was possibly the last ticket out of town. On the Megabus, no less, a monstrosity of steel and rubber and cushy seats and decent Wi-Fi that would whisk her the three and some-odd hours to Houston.

Predictably, because it was raining, it stood to follow that she'd had to wait on a street corner for the Lyft van to inch toward her in the crazy traffic. Her cheap umbrella had turned inside out on the first strong gust of wind. When the van pulled up, she'd stepped off the curb and into a river of gutter water that filled her bootie. She'd had to stuff her suitcase into the back hatch with the other bags. And now she was squeezed between the van door and a large man, and rain was still trickling down her back and she was pretty sure she was not going to make her bus.

At least her seatmate smelled good. Spicy and a hint of evergreen. But his knee kept bumping her.

"First stop, Megabus!" Amal, the driver, announced cheerfully over the blast of his music.

The dog growled.

"*Megabus?*" the man next to Harper repeated under his breath in a tone that suggested he couldn't quite grasp the concept of a giant double-decker bus. What, was he taking a private jet or something? It happened to be a very quick way to get to Houston, thank you.

"Hush, Beanie," the woman in the shower cap said. Presumably to the dog. She reached into her pocket, then shoved something through the wires of the carrier. "Excuse me, can you turn that down?"

"We're going to be late, man!" the guy with the guitar shouted over the music. "Seriously, can you turn it down?"

"Your wish is my command," Amal said, and turned down the music. "I don't have a five-star rating by accident. I'm very good at my job," he said, jabbing a finger upward. "Everyone will get to their destinations on time, trust me." And then he turned left when he should have turned right. "You will not find another driver with ratings as high as mine. Five stars, every time. Trust."

No one said a word as they sat at a light, watching cars move at a snail's pace through the intersection.

Harper was increasingly aware of the press of her body against the long-limbed, hard-bodied man, mainly because he kept shifting, like he couldn't quite fit between her and Guitar Guy. His knee bumped against her leg again.

God, her feet were prunes. If she did make her bus, which she would bet one hundred bucks she would not, it would be a miserable ride to Houston.

"You sure you want to go this way?" Guitar Guy asked. "The Megabus station is over by the capitol, isn't it? If you go up Lamar, you can flip around to Gaudalupe."

"The app is telling me to go this way," Amal insisted, and pointed at the screen of his phone, perched like a lighthouse beacon squarely in the middle of the dash.

Harper managed to dislodge her arm from underneath the giant next to her and look at her watch. Amal's five-star rating for on-time deliveries notwithstanding, she was going to be late.

She tried to put her arm back where it went, but that was impossible. So she sat forward, curved like a banana over her overstuffed tote bag.

"Come on, man," Guitar Guy whined. "This is seriously the wrong way. I can't miss my flight."

"Well, I can't miss mine, either," the grandma in front said, as if Guitar Guy had somehow implied he was the only one who couldn't miss a flight.

"Problem is," Amal said, "the rain. Climate change is doing this. Never saw rain like this in Austin before global warming."

"That's a bunch of bullcrap," the woman in the front seat said. "There's no such thing as global warming."

The man next to Harper sighed softly under his breath. Harper felt his pain and would have sighed, too, had breathing not been so difficult in her current position.

"This traffic is worse than it is during South by Southwest," Amal said, referring to the annual arts festival. "I drove the Killers to their gig last year. Nice guys. Really nice guys. They had a guitar, too. It's kind of weird when you think about it, like, maybe, people should leave earlier."

What?

Harper glanced around the interior of the vehicle in the dark. Guitar Guy was staring out the window. Grandma was keeping a steady stream of treats going into the pet carrier. The guy in the middle kept shifting around, trying to get comfortable. She wished she could get a look at him, to see what face went with those thighs, but it was dark, and it would be very obvious if she did turn to look at him, because it would require the use of her entire body.

Amal and Grandma kept up their argument about climate change as they crawled toward the bus depot. Harper glanced at her watch again. *Was this worth it? The long hours? The completion of project after project with the hope that something would happen? Was Soren really going to promote her like he'd hinted, or was she a chump for believing him?* She could almost hear the voice of her best friend, Olivia, in her head. *"You're such a chump, Harper."*

They were only three blocks from the bus depot now. Dammit, she was going to have to hoof it to make the bus and her boots were already squishy and her suitcase was heavy. The light turned green, and Amal turned onto the depot street. And stopped. Just up ahead were the red brake lights of many more cars. "This isn't good," he opined.

"Dude—turn around and come in from the east," Guitar Guy said.

"Yeah, I don't know," Amal said uncertainly. "The app says this way."

"I'm telling you, there is another way," Guitar Guy said, and pulled out his phone.

Harper silently agreed—there had to be another way. She reached into her tote and pulled out her phone, too. The guy in the middle dug his elbow into her side as he fished his phone out of his pocket. "Sorry," he muttered.

The three of them pulled up Google Maps and began searching for an alternative route.

"I'm turning around before the cops block off the whole street!" Amal suddenly shouted, and like a general taking charge, he gunned it, veering into the next lane. The two men smashed into Harper with the force of the car swinging left. And then Amal slammed on the brakes and they all lurched forward and phones went flying into the inky black of that van's interior.

"If you kill us, that's going to seriously fuck your five-star rating, man," Guitar Guy snapped. He shoved his guitar into the face of the guy in the middle so he could lean over and search for his phone.

The guy in the middle and Harper both reached down, groping around for phones on the floorboard, their elbows knocking into each other, their hands colliding more than once. Amal gassed the car again, tossing them backward, then sped up and tore around a corner. Beanie barked frantically for all of them.

"That's how you do it," Amal announced triumphantly over the dog.

"That is *not* how you do it," Grandma shouted. "We're all lucky to be alive right now!"

Harper's fingers touched something hard and square. She held it up—it was white. Her phone. The man next to her had found one, too, and was handing another one to Guitar Guy.

"Hey, Megabus, can you walk from here?" Amal asked, looking at Harper in his rearview. She quickly weighed her options: a block of unrelenting rain, or a block in Amal's van. "*Yes*."

He braked hard again, and the door panel slid open.

"Need help?" the man sitting next to her asked.

"Don't offer!" Guitar Guy said frantically. "We don't have time for chivalry."

"I've got it," Harper said into the dark. She emerged from the van like popcorn from a hot pan, grabbed her tote, and left her useless umbrella. She ran to the back and yanked her bag free of its wedge, hit the close button, and sprinted down the street, her tote bag and suitcase banging hard against her leg, rain slipping in her collar.

She reached the depot just as the Megabus was preparing to pull out. She threw herself into the opening before the driver could close the door. "I'm here!" she shouted triumphantly and handed over a soggy paper ticket. He scanned the bar code. "Your seat is on top."

Which had seemed like a great idea when she'd booked it. She'd imagined a leisurely drive high above the highway. Harper hauled herself up the stairs, dragging her bags, her ankle booties squishing with each step, her coat dripping. People grimaced and shot her dark looks as she tried to fit down the narrow aisle. "Sorry," she muttered more than once. "So sorry."

Her seat was near the back, because she had also thought that would be more relaxing. And she'd booked a window seat and now had the problem of a large woman as a seat mate who did not appear to want to stand to let her pass.

"Excuse me." Harper wiped a rivulet of rain from the side of her face. "That's my seat."

The woman looked at the seat, then at Harper. She tried to scooch her knees to one side. "Just climb over."

Was she kidding? Harper hadn't been on a jungle gym in close to thirty years. "I don't think I can." She winced apologetically and, with her head, indicated her bags.

This irritated the woman. She sighed loudly, grabbed onto the seat in front of her, and hauled herself up. She stepped into the aisle, knocking into Harper when she did.

Harper moved quickly. She shoved both bags onto the floorboard and fell into her seat. She managed to partially wedge one bag underneath her, feet propped on top of it. But the tote wouldn't fit, so she had to haul it up and hold it in her lap. The lady cast a look of disapproval over her, then climbed back into her seat, buckled herself in, and took the middle armrest.

Dammit. Now Harper had to pee. But she leaned back, resting against the headrest, and closed her eyes.

She should have waited until tomorrow. It wasn't as if her parents were eagerly anticipating her arrival. In fact, when Harper had texted her dad to tell him she'd been held up and couldn't come until tonight, he'd responded with one word. Great! When she texted them earlier and gave a time to expect her, her mother replied, We've gone out to dinner. You know where the key is.

Or maybe she should have left when she'd planned. Olivia thought Soren was amazingly good at always finding a last-minute emergency only Harper could handle.

"Why do you let him do you like that?" Olivia had asked her, annoyed that Harper was arriving a full day later than she'd promised. Olivia didn't understand how busy Harper's life had become since moving to Austin four years ago. She'd known when she accepted the position that it would be crazy and sacrifices would need to be made. Not that she minded—she had a goal and she was willing to work for it, which she'd tried to explain to Olivia.

"A goal shouldn't consume your life," Olivia had said, pouting.

Maybe. But it was her life to consume, and setting goals and achieving them made her happy. It blocked out all the other noise in life—every day was focused. Harper had ambition. She'd worked her way up at StreetSweets, Inc., and she planned on going the distance—chief executive officer. All she had to do was convince Soren he could leave the running of the company to her. She was miles from that, but she was gaining ground.

StreetSweets franchised food trucks specializing in coffee and pastries, like a Starbucks on wheels. But in the past couple of years, Soren had ventured into the fixed restaurant side of the ledger and had built three upscale coffeehouses in Austin.

Harper had started with the company six years ago. After graduating from Rice University with a degree in social sciences and business administration, she'd held a series of assistant management jobs, then had lucked into the position of district manager overseeing the StreetSweets food trucks in Houston. Her job had been to place the trailers for commerce, move them as necessary, and most important, turn a profit. She'd done more than turn a profit—the demand for StreetSweets food trucks was so good that Soren eventually added two more to the Houston fleet.

And then he'd offered her a job as vice president of development in Austin, a totally manufactured title to entice her to move. It had worked.

They'd opened two Deja Brew Coffeehouses in Austin, but the flagship Deja Brew was slated to open after the holidays. It was on South Congress, near a stretch of the avenue that saw heavy tourist traffic. With the successful opening and launch of this store, the plan was to expand nationwide. Harper wanted in on that expansion. She wanted to run this company. Her first step was to make herself indispensable. She was always the first one to volunteer, always the one who went above and beyond what was expected. Which was why she'd volunteered to plan the grand opening of their flagship store. Soren had wanted to hire an event planner, but Harper convinced him they didn't need to spend that money.

"But why?" Olivia had asked once. "Why is it such a big deal to be in upper management?"

"I don't know," Harper said. "More money. More responsibility. More opportunities to create new things."

"Less free time. Less opportunity to date. Less time with your *friends*," Olivia had countered. "Don't you want a life? Don't you want to get married or have kids or travel?"

Olivia was still mad that Harper had bailed on the girls' trip to Cabo San Lucas last fall. Olivia was a journalist for the *Houston Chronicle*, so it wasn't like she didn't work long hours, too. But what she did not have was the drive to climb like Harper did. Olivia's philosophy was to work to live, not the other way around.

Harper would concede that her goals were always ambitious and sometimes she worked so hard to meet them that she did miss out on life. She wanted a dog but had no time for one, so she'd settled for walking rescue dogs on the weekends at the Austin Canine Coalition. That's where she'd met Bob, the crankiest bulldog in America. She wouldn't mind a boyfriend, but with her hours, finding someone to date was not going well. And she was tired all the time. Like now. And with the gentle rocking of the bus as it pulled out of Austin, she dozed off.

She was awakened when the woman next to her pushed Harper's tote bag off the armrest. "Sorry," Harper said groggily, and righted herself and the bag. She dragged her fingers through hair that was still damp from the rain, then shifted her gaze out the window. She'd more than dozed off—they were close to an hour out of town, and the rain had turned to mist.

Harper yawned, then dug into her tote for a snack. She pulled out a small bag of nuts and her phone. She righted the thing, and when she did, the phone came to life. But her phone's lock screen confused her—she didn't know the photo that appeared. She couldn't remember even taking it. Staring up at her was a big white dog with a coal black nose. It looked like a golden retriever or a husky or some cross between dog and polar bear. It was dressed in a red bandanna with green Christmas trees and wore a headband with reindeer antlers. It looked like it was smiling, its long pink tongue hanging out of one side of its mouth.

Where had this dog come from? She racked her memory. It was entirely possible she had taken the photo. For one, the dog was adorable, and she often took snaps of adorable dogs. For two, she was often at the ACC, where many adorable dogs passed through. But it also felt impossible that she would not remember meeting this beautiful hunk of dog. And anyway, even if she had taken it, how had it become her wallpaper?

A black banner across the dog's chest proclaimed she had new texts.

She switched on the little light overhead and turned the phone over, examining it, and as she did, a slight bit of nausea waved through her. There was a crack on the back that hadn't been there before. Maybe she'd cracked it when Amal had slammed on the brakes and their phones had gone flying. Or maybe—and this was far more likely—she'd picked up the wrong phone. Holy shit. *She had the wrong damn phone.*

The phone suddenly vibrated, startling her, and she dropped it into her tote. She quickly dug it out again to see a new text message notification. She slid her finger across the screen, and miraculously, it was not locked.

You have my phone, the text message read.

She gasped loudly and craned her neck to see around her. Was this person nearby? Had she fallen asleep and this person had switched phones? How did anyone know she had the wrong phone?

She looked at the texts before the last one and read several more that said pretty much the same thing: You have my phone. We got our phones mixed up. HELLO? She scrolled through them, counting fourteen texts in all announcing that she was in possession of the wrong phone. "Are you fucking kidding me right now?" she muttered.

The woman next to her shot Harper a disapproving look.

Come on, I need my phone. You can text me—I'm an idiot, I don't have any security set up. Are you the (he inserted an emoji of a dancing girl) or the (he inserted an emoji of a guitar).

This could not be happening. Harper suddenly thought of all the texts Soren would send her this week. Of the terribly inappropriate texts Olivia would send her. "*Nonononono.*"

She texted back the emoji of the woman.

The text bubble instantly popped up. I have to be honest, I was hoping it was you and not the guitar guy. BTW, lucky you, getting out of that damn van when you did—you missed the debate about the upcoming election. If I could have figured out how to open that door, I would have thrown myself out.

She smiled, surprised by the friendly nature of his text. So you're . . . She inserted the emoji of a man in a bowler hat because it was the first man emoji she ran across.

?? I'm not a detective. I'm more like (he inserted a picture of a man shrugging).

Harper's smile widened.

Where are you, he texted. Is it possible to get my phone back?

Was he kidding? I'm on a bus, remember? Where are you?

Waiting for a plane to take off . . .

"For heaven's sake," she muttered. What now? She typed, I guess we're stuck.

Unless you know how to teleport?

She sighed and texted, Alas I do not. She ended it with the crying emoji.

Is that a literal or ironic emoji? I don't want to say the wrong thing.

She grinned. A little of both.

Totally get that. By the way, thanks for also not having a secure phone. I would have lost my mind.

I guess I'm an idiot, too. But the security thing takes too much time. I want to pick up my phone and go to what I want without swiping or showing my face. It skeeved her out a little that technology could read her *face*.

Right?

Wait a second. She needed a phone this week. Maybe they could meet up and exchange phones. Where are you headed?

Chicago.

Ugh, Chicago, clear across the country. I'm going to Houston. When will you be back in Austin?

New Year's Day.

So no meet-up. Wow. I guess we are really stuck.

Looks like.

She considered this a minute. Is it all right if I use your phone to make calls?

Knock yourself out. Mind if I use yours?

Not at all.

Then, she remembered Soren. Her boss was not for everyone. He was . . . different. You might get some weird texts. I have kind of an insane boss.

How insane? Like, on a scale. 1 being just regular insane and 10 being pictures no one should ever have on their phone insane.

A 5-ish. Probably has dicey pics but not so insane as to send them. I don't think. Am I going to get any weird pics from anyone?

Not unless you ask me. Ha.

She had to appreciate a man with a sense of humor, particularly in the midst of this colossal mix-up. Whereas she was starting to freak out a little. How was she going to manage without her phone? Her entire life was on that thing.

BTW, my family is chatty. They blow up my phone sometimes.

Ah, the ubiquitous family group texts. Olivia got them, too. Thanks for the heads-up. I think I can deal with chatty.

You say that now. He followed that with a row of laughing emojis. I'll give you a call at the end of the week and we can figure out when to exchange phones. Merry Christmas. Or Happy Holidays. Happy Hannukah. Feliz Navidad.

Merry Christmas, she wrote.

He replied with a thumbs-up.

Harper had almost dropped the phone into her bag when she thought of something and quickly texted once more. Hey, what's your name?

Jonah. Yours?

Harper.

Hi Harper. Gotta jet (literally). The flight attendant looks like someone's Russian grandmother and she means business. Happy Holidays.

Harper clicked the phone off, took one last look at the dog, then slipped the phone into her tote bag with a smile.

At least she wouldn't be getting texts from Soren Wilder, the "original Bohemian" as he liked to introduce himself (whatever that meant).

Two

Jonah Rogers arrived at Chicago's Midway Airport, and the moment he had cell service, he texted Amy, the manager at the Lucky Star Coffee Shop. He told her he was going to video-call her from a strange number.

He got an immediate reply. New phone, who dis?

"Very funny," he muttered, and put in the video call.

Amy's face suddenly appeared on his screen. She'd piled her red hair on top of her head and had tied a colorful scarf around it. She'd changed her nose ring to gold, he noticed, probably in honor of the holiday season, and of course she was wearing glasses that looked like two candy canes had been welded together. "Whose number is this?"

"A stranger's. That's why I'm calling. I need you to do me a favor," Jonah said as he strode in the direction of baggage claim.

"Sure, Joe. I'm already doing you a huge favor and working your shifts over the holidays. What's one more?"

"Aww, so sorry that you have to make an occasional cup of coffee for double pay this week. Anyway, this is a tiny favor. Just text my parents and my aunt and uncle and tell them I lost my phone and someone else has it, so don't text me."

"But who has it?"

"A woman. There was a mix-up in the ride share to the airport."

Amy frowned with suspicion. "I don't get it. How do you mix up a phone on a ride share?"

"You just can and I did." He jogged down the escalator, squeezing past travelers who stood in the middle of the stairs with their bags.

"But how are you going to get it back? What about your contacts? And your photos?" She suddenly gasped. "What about your *banking* app?"

Why had he called Amy, again? She'd been working at the family business for so long that she was like a kid sister to him and acted like it. "When I get back to Austin, I'll meet up with her and we'll exchange phones. She can't get into my banking app because it needs my face. Anyway, please don't blow up my phone while I'm gone because I won't be the one to see what a nerd you are. And tell Mom and Dad and Marty and Belinda."

Amy snorted. "You think they're going to remember not to text or call you on your number? Here, you tell them."

She swung her phone around so that Jonah could see his mom and dad and Aunt Belinda and Uncle Marty sitting around a table in a private dining room. There was a half-completed jigsaw puzzle in the middle of the table. Some empty dishes were stacked in the corners, a few books in front of his dad, and Aunt Belinda was knitting. Behind them, through the open doorway, Jonah could see some of the regular patrons of the Lucky Star, and the top of the cook's head, wrapped in a red bandanna, behind the counter.

"Hi, Joe!" his parents and aunt and uncle shouted. They were drinking beer and wine, and Jonah watched as a man suddenly appeared in view with two pizza boxes. "Pizza's here," he announced.

"Thanks, Kev!" Amy said.

Hadn't he talked to them about bringing in food from competitors? Why, yes—yes, he had, and on more than one occasion. "Why let customers know there is a better place down the street?" he'd demanded of the four of them.

"It's good pizza," Uncle Marty had said.

"Joe lost his phone," Amy announced as the pizza delivery guy went out.

"What?" Aunt Belinda exclaimed. "Then how is he calling you?" Uncle Marty took charge of carefully laying the pizza boxes on top of the puzzle.

"He mixed up his phone with someone else's, and he is using that phone to call."

"Why didn't he just give it back?" Jonah's dad asked.

"He won't say," Amy said. "He's being kind of secretive about it."

"I'm not being secretive!" Jonah shouted so that the four seniors would hear him. That was Amy for you, always tossing a little Tabasco into any situation. The seniors didn't hear him, because they were discussing how annoying it would be to lose a phone as they grabbed for slices of pizza. "Mom! Dad!" They were not listening to him. Typical. "Amy? Can you help here?"

"Joe, honey, how did you lose your phone?" his mother asked.

"It's a long story, Mom. I don't have time to get into it right now."

"Why? Are you in a big rush to go caroling?" Amy asked.

Everyone in the store laughed. *Everyone*, including Robert and Lloyd, the two old guys in Marine ball caps sitting next to the enormous Christmas tree. And the six members of the Little Stacy Neighborhood Book Club, who met every third week to discuss books, and then every other week to discuss their kids and husbands and crafts. They were having their holiday party under the string of oversized ornaments Aunt Belinda had made Uncle Marty hang across the ceiling. Jonah could even hear Bing Crosby crooning in the background, *Ho Ho Ho-ing* along with the chorus.

In the corner of the dining room, standing sentry, was the life-size cutout of Roy Rogers, his father's namesake. That cutout had been there longer than Jonah had been alive. He'd been refurbished a time or two in the last thirty years, but he was always there, wearing something indicative of the season. Today, he was wearing a Santa hat over the crown of his cowboy hat, and someone had wrapped a garland around his neck.

This was the Lucky Star Coffee Shop. His family's business. Correction—his family's failing business, the one that was leaking money. Which reminded him, and he asked hopefully of Amy, "Hey, did you sell any of the Christmas trees?"

"Are you kidding? In this rain? No one is hauling a tree in this rain."

He glanced down the pickup lane, looking for his cousin's vehicle. "They're small trees. Tabletop trees. People should be able to carry them. That was the whole point."

"I'm just saying, no one is buying trees in this weather."

They hadn't bought the trees in any weather. Jonah didn't get it. Didn't millennials put up trees? He'd had the brilliant idea that they'd stop in for a tree and stay for a burger or a coffee. But they didn't.

A familiar black SUV made the curve in the road and flashed lights at him.

"Listen, Allen and Andy are here. Merry Christmas, squirt. And remember—don't blow up my phone. Promise me you'll make sure my family understands that."

"Have fun, Joe!" his mother called from somewhere behind Amy.

"I'm not blowing up anything. Bye, stupid," Amy said, and clicked off.

The SUV pulled to a halt beside the curb, and the back door popped open. Jonah tossed his suitcase inside and followed with his body. A male voice from the front demanded, "Dude . . . why aren't you answering your texts?"

He wasn't sure which twin had asked that, Allen or Andy. His cousins were identical in appearance. They were both doctors—Andy a pediatrician, Allen a gynecologist—and they were so stinking good-looking that any man who went along as their third wheel was going to get some residual attention from women. Jonah had always enjoyed that perk of being their cousin.

The only difference between them was that Allen had married Naomi two years ago, and they'd just had their first baby, little Lena. Allen and Naomi were moving into a bigger house over the holidays in anticipation of a growing family, and in a couple of months, Uncle Marty and Aunt Belinda were moving to Chicago and into the in-law suite of the house to help out with childcare and to be close to their sons.

Jonah had come to help with the move. At least that's what he'd said to everyone who asked. But he'd really come because he needed a break. Living around and working with his parents and aunt and uncle had a way of putting a guy in front of the five o'clock news and a prompt bedtime. He felt like he'd gone straight from young club stud to lining up for early bird specials.

Plus, he had a lot to think about and needed some time away from everything to do just that. Sometimes, it was very difficult to think in Austin.

He leaned forward, put his hands on Allen's shoulders, and jostled him around. "It's a phone mix-up. Long story. Where's Naomi?"

"Spending the night at her parents' house with the baby. She said she doesn't want to see what I become around you two."

"Smart girl. Where are we going?"

"O'Riley's," Andy said into the rearview mirror. "It's very important that we start this holiday off with a bang."

Start it off with a bang they did. Jonah woke up the next morning to the birdsong chirping in time to his throbbing headache. His mouth tasted like he'd eaten part of an alley dumpster, and his neck was stiff from sleeping on the sunroom couch in Andy's house. Allen had taken the spare bedroom.

Jonah winced; the bright sunlight reflecting off old snow was shooting daggers through the sliding glass doors and directly into his brain. "*Christ*," he groaned, and rolled onto his back.

That's when he saw Allen and Andy seated on stools at the kitchen bar. They were showered and dressed. They each had a cup of coffee. And they each watched him as if he were a strange creature they'd discovered wandering around their living room.

"What?" Jonah asked irritably.

"It's Christmas Eve," Andy said.

"I know." Jonah closed his eyes.

"We're going to the *Christkindlmarket* today."

"What is that and why are we going?" Jonah croaked. He opened his eyes and forced himself to prop up on his elbows.

"Because we are going to be guests in the home of my in-laws and we need to take a proper gift. Didn't Aunt Darlene and Uncle Roy teach you anything?" He picked up a folded towel from the kitchen bar and threw it on Jonah's face. Then he set a steaming mug of coffee on the end table next to him. "You know where the shower is, and dude, you reek of whiskey."

"Whose fault is that?" Jonah pushed the towel off him, forced himself to sit up, and lunged for the coffee.

"You really tied one on last night," Andy said with a grin. "Trouble at home?"

"Hilarious," Jonah grumbled. There was trouble at home, all right, but not the kind his cousin meant. He hadn't told them yet. He hadn't told anyone how bad it was. He wasn't ready to talk about it. Frankly, he didn't want to think about it today.

"Hurry up," Allen said. "I'm starving."

Jonah gulped down the coffee, picked up the towel, and carefully stood, testing to see if he still had functioning legs before he stumbled his way to the shower. When he was assured that he could make

it without face-planting on the way, he grabbed his phone and started
shuffling in that direction. With a yawn, he looked at the screen . . .
and at a picture of a flower shop taken through open weathered
wooden doors.

Right.

He had someone else's phone. What was her name? *Harper.*

Harper had a text message. Jonah's first thought was that he
should definitely not tap on the screen to read the text because that
was a total invasion of privacy and it was none of his business. He
would not like to think she was scrolling through his text messages.

His second thought was that he should totally read the text. What
if it was important? What if someone had died? Okay, if someone
had died, the news probably wouldn't come in a text. Okay . . . what
if someone had used her credit card? And hadn't she said to let her
know about texts?

He tapped on the screen.

Her text message was from someone she had marked in her contacts as SW:

Harper, greetings and felicitous felicitations given with genuine felicity.

Jonah stumbled mentally over that and had to read it again.

As the year draws to a close—a bounteous year, for which we were truly
blessed—I am reflecting on our goals and contemplating some changes.
You were right to tell me that you deserve better. I have sought higher guid-
ance through meditation, and I am ready to share my thoughts with you
when you come back. I hope the holidays bring you peace and light. Soren.

Well, hello, this was some boyfriend she had for herself. Or girlfriend. For the sake of his own curiosity, Jonah wished he'd gotten a
better look at the woman sitting next to him in the ride share yesterday. All he really remembered was that she smelled like wet clothes
and lavender, and she had light brown hair with gold highlights. But
that was all he could recall, because at the time he'd been straddling
a nonexistent middle seat and bracing himself for impact.

He decided he ought to forward the text. He didn't want to

bother her on Christmas Eve, but if this was a boyfriend-girlfriend text, she would probably want to know. He would want to know if he had a girlfriend, which, hello, he did not, because . . . honestly, he didn't know why. Maybe because he was essentially dating an old coffee shop.

He continued on to the guest bath. He stepped inside and closed the door, and forwarded the text to his number. He added, Good morning. I thought you might like to know that your boyfriend or girlfriend sent a text. Should we have a rule about texts? Read or don't read? Anyway, hope I'm not interrupting holiday plans. J.

He left the phone on the counter and turned on the shower. He stood under the stream of water long enough that one of his cousins banged on the door. He got out, wiped down the steamed mirror, and shaved.

He felt much better after the shower. He wrapped the towel around his waist and picked up the phone. Harper had replied.

Definitely read!

And then, OMG SO NOT my boyfriend, followed by the vomit emoji. That's my boss. But thanks for sending it along, because between you and me, it's a Christmas miracle that he agreed I was right and that I deserve better. Now, if only I knew what he was talking about, because I do love it when I'm right. I like to hang on to being right and wear it like Joseph's Technicolor dream coat for a few days. She inserted a smiley face and a Christmas tree to end the text. Merry Christmas.

Jonah liked this girl.

At the Christmas market, Jonah and his cousins found a suitable holiday gift for Naomi's parents, then wandered around the stalls for the afternoon. Later, they went out for a steak dinner and talked. Their conversation covered the usual ground—women and sports. But eventually Allen asked about Jonah's aerospace engineering job. "Your employer is still cool with you helping out at the Star?"

He sounded a bit incredulous, as if it was beyond the realm of reason that an employer would give an employee a few months off to deal with a family problem.

The family problem was the coffee shop on the corner of Mary Street and South Congress Avenue that had been there since what felt like the beginning of time. They all knew the story—their grandparents, Juanita and Howell, had opened the coffee shop in the mid-fifties and had named it the Lucky Star Coffee Shop after an episode of the old weekly *Roy Rogers* television series. They'd obviously been huge fans.

The Star, as they called it, was a squat and plain red brick building, and through the years, as buildings had been torn down and new ones put up all along the avenue, the coffee shop had remained exactly the same. In the late seventies, Juanita and Howell sold the Star to their sons, Roy and Marty. Marty and Belinda (Allen and Andy's parents), and Roy and Darlene (Jonah's parents) added more baked goods to the menu. Jonah's mother had become a self-proclaimed master pie baker, but most of Austin had agreed with her—the Star became the place known for homemade cakes and pies and a cup of joe.

Over the years, a hodgepodge of items had been added to the menu. Big salads. Burgers and sandwiches. Chicken potpies. Basic comfort food that any cook with a spatula could make. But the pies were the draw, and the Star developed a loyal following from the surrounding neighborhoods, including the book club, Vietnam War veterans Robert and Lloyd, a Bible study class from Mt. Zion Baptist Church on the east side, a Mother's Day Out group, and more.

Like their fathers before them, Jonah, Allen, and Andy had been raised in the coffee shop. During summer breaks and holidays, they all had jobs as busboys. Jonah experienced his first kiss there. And his first breakup—in the back booth with the cracked vinyl seating, Crystal Mendoza told him she didn't want to date him anymore a week before their high school graduation. Allen broke his arm there, jumping off a ladder. Uncle Marty confessed to Aunt Belinda that he'd kissed Mrs. Sanderson beneath some mistletoe there. And when Jonah's older sister, Jolie, died of leukemia, his parents had retreated with their grief into work there.

Jolie had died when Jonah was a preschooler. He really didn't remember much about her—she was a ghost of a memory, a sickly-looking girl with dark circles under her eyes. A few of the regulars remembered her. Lloyd had once told him she'd sit quietly in the back booth with coloring books, never wanting to eat or drink much.

When Jonah was older, and the bus dropped him off from school at the Star, he and his mother would paint the store windows with sketches he'd made. There was no rhyme or reason to them—he just thought of pictures that were cool to his thirteen-year-old self, and his mother helped him paint them on the windows. His parents had never cared if dinosaurs walked across the front windows, or space-ships crashed into the brick. All they ever cared about was that Jonah was close by and safe. He'd always intuitively sensed that they were afraid of losing him, too. And he'd always felt compelled to assure them that he was there for them.

The Lucky Star was one of those places that old-timers pointed to with great fondness, but in the last decade, old Austin was slowly consumed by new Austin, with designer coffeehouses and trendy shops and people flocking in from California to live in high-rises. Property values in what was once a fading section south of downtown had skyrocketed with the ongoing gentrification. The Rogers family struggled to pay the property taxes on the coffee shop. The only reason they'd survived as long as they had, outlasting other mom-and-pop shops, was because Juanita and Howell had bought the building. Otherwise, astronomical rents would have forced them out long ago.

Two Christmases ago, the Rogers family held a meeting. The profit margins had shrunk, and they'd had to let some longtime staff go. But still, they'd all imagined that the Lucky Star would find a way to carry on as it always had.

Seven months ago, there had been another family meeting. Jonah's father, who was the business end of the Star, announced he had cancer of the bladder. The treatment was brutal, and Jonah had helped as much as he could, dropping by after work, filling in for his dad, taking him to doctors' appointments.

Three months ago, Jonah realized that he couldn't help as much as they needed him and do his day job at the same time. So he'd taken a sabbatical from his aerospace engineering job at Neptune Industries to help. It was the only thing that made sense to him. His mother was the baker. Uncle Marty did all the maintenance. And Aunt Belinda helped Amy run the storefront. None of them were suited or wanted to take on the business aspects.

Jonah's boss, Edgar, was supportive of his request, given the circumstances. He called to check in with Jonah every couple of weeks.

Last week, he'd called with news.

NASA had contracted with Neptune Industries to develop a long-range, deep space satellite. The project would include six months of training at NASA's deep space communications facility in Madrid, Spain. And a substantial raise. They needed someone to lead the project, and Edgar said the partners wanted Jonah. He'd earned it. He was their best guy. What was not to love? A cool job and more money. Was it possible he could cut short his sabbatical?

Jonah desperately wanted to jump at the opportunity. This was the sort of project that people like him spent an entire career working toward. Why hadn't he just jumped? No one would blame him. And yet, he'd told Edgar he needed to think about it.

Edgar said he could take a little time, that he'd check in with him after the New Year, but they'd need an answer then.

Jonah's hesitation was complicated and began with his parents. By Christmas, his dad had completed his treatments, but he'd not yet returned to full-time work. He didn't look so great, to be honest. But it was more than that. When Jonah had taken over, he'd discovered that the Star was lagging in more ways than one behind the latest coffeehouse trends. He'd tried to explain it to his parents and aunt and uncle, but they didn't seem to get that for some coffee aficionados, there was a distinct difference between a coffee shop and a coffeehouse.

"That's the dumbest thing I ever heard!" Jonah's mother had scoffed, and the two sets of parents had laughed.

"Well, Mom, some people think a coffeehouse or a coffee bar is where you get artisan coffees, and a coffee shop is where you get drip coffee and a piece of pie."

"So? What's wrong with that?"

"That's my point. There is nothing wrong with it, but some people would rather get their joe in a coffeehouse."

His parents and aunt and uncle had just looked at one another, probably marveling at the dumb kid they'd raised. Sometimes, getting them to listen felt a little like flipping tractor tires—they seemed to think that the more things changed, the more things ought to stay the same inside the Lucky Star. Just like the good ol' days.

That was the crux of the problem—the Star had remained exactly the same for seventy years because the regulars liked it that way. And so did the owners. But many of the regulars were dying or had been pushed out of central Austin by rising costs, and the new people moving in were not coming into the shop to take their place. The new people were young and hip and biked to work and took spin classes and cared about the environment and marched for social causes on weekends. They were used to technological conveniences, they didn't eat a lot of pie and cake because of the carbs, they refused food that wasn't free of GMOs, and why would they ever stop in at the Lucky Star for a cup of coffee when they could order ahead to a ubiquitous Starbucks?

Jonah had optimistically believed they could reinvent themselves and remain an Austin institution. That all it took was some understanding of their market. He'd tried different things, like improving the Wi-Fi. He'd tried to get the word out using social media—he and

Amy had opened accounts and she tried to keep up with them, but it was hard to do on top of her job. They advertised fun pastries, like their twist on Taco Tuesday—taco-shaped fried pies. Nothing worked. The verdict rolled in every month when he did the books— he had not saved the Lucky Star. Not even close.

Jonah did not see a way out. After the holidays, it was his intention to recommend to the family that they sell. The land they were sitting on was so valuable that they could all live comfortably for the rest of their lives. Why worry about the shop when they didn't have to?

When Allen asked him how it was going, Jonah thought of the holiday, of the good time he was having, and of the great job offer he'd just gotten, and how he'd really just rather have more wine and forget about it. Unfortunately, he couldn't forget about it.

He said, "You know Billie Salazar? She owns that vintage clothing store up the block from the Star?"

Allen and Andy nodded in unison.

"She said the new building they are finishing up across the street from our place is a Deja Brew flagship store."

Allen and Andy dropped their jaws at the same moment.

"I know, right?" Jonah didn't have to tell them what that meant— the New Age coffeehouse, a Starbucks on steroids, was relatively new in Austin. They had every coffee gadget one could imagine, and even a couple he couldn't imagine any use for. Even their seating was trendy—instead of the usual setup of bistro tables and chairs, they had egg-shaped basket seating suspended from the ceiling.

They had an actual lending library at each of their stores. They featured the work of local artists on their walls and functioned like a local art gallery. They had garden seating at all locations, strung with lights, dotted with flowers and small Zen garden fountains, and on weekends, they featured local musicians. Their coffee was fair trade, and Jonah couldn't even think about their pastries—all locally sourced ingredients, no GMOs, gluten free, and keto friendly.

"If a Deja Brew is going in across the street, we're sunk. No way we can compete with that."

"We need an order-ahead app," Andy suggested.

They needed a whole lot more than a single app. "There isn't any money for that sort of thing. The bottom line is that there is just too much competition for the millennials—every gym and bank has a coffee shop now, and all of them are cooler than the Star." Jonah paused and looked at his plate. "I think we ought to talk about selling. The land is worth so much, we'd all be set for life."

"*Sell* it?" Andy seemed dumbstruck.

"Think about it. Your parents are moving to Chicago to be near you. Dad's been sick. Mom can't keep making pies all her life."

The brothers looked at each other, then at Jonah. "What did Mom and Dad say?" Allen asked.

"I haven't told them. I wanted to talk to you first."

"Your parents aren't going to sell, Joe," Allen said. "It's in their blood. Not to mention they associate Jolie with the Star."

Jonah was on the verge of saying that Jolie had been dead for more than twenty years, but his phone buzzed. "Sorry," he said, and pulled it out of his pocket as the waiter picked up their plates. It was a text from Harper.

Sorry to be a pain . . .

"I can't imagine *selling* it," Andy said. "That seems too drastic."

But you got what looks like a very important message from someone in your contacts named . . . Boobs?

"Oh hell," Jonah muttered.

"What?" Andy asked.

Jonah showed his cousins the text.

Allen stared at the screen. "*Boobs?* You put a woman in your phone as Boobs?"

"No, she did." It had been a private joke that he couldn't remember anymore.

"Where is this Boobs? Why haven't we ever met her?" Andy wanted to know.

"Because she was no one to me and it was a long time ago. I met her at a party. She was a little drunk, unnaturally endowed, and proud of it. We hung out that night and I told her I'd help her move, and she put her number in my phone like that."

"Why are you always helping people move, man?" Allen asked.

Jonah ignored him and typed a response to Harper. Well, this is totally embarrassing. What is the message?

A picture of the text in question popped up: a string of purple eggplants and a Hope to see you in the new year tag. Unbelievable. Jonah hadn't talked to or seen Tamara in a couple of years, and honestly, he'd never done anything but help her move. Well, and help her get her car fixed. And find her cat a new home because the new place wouldn't take cats. Now he remembered—their very brief acquaintance had been a lot.

Heartwarming. In my defense, she is just an acquaintance, he texted. But the moment he sent it, he knew that made him sound like a jerk. I mean, she entered her contact info into my phone. She thought it was funny.

And now he sounded defensive.

And I thought it wasn't any big deal because . . . What was he doing? He backed up, deleting that. He sighed and texted, Curious—how deep is the hole I'm digging here?

The balloon with the three dots popped up at the bottom of the screen. I'm going to say about a foot so far. I'm actually more concerned with this. She inserted a smiley face emoji and then forwarded a picture of him from last Halloween that she'd obviously taken off his photo roll. He and Amy had gone to work as the Duke and Duchess of Cambridge, complete with crowns and sashes. Only he was the duchess and Amy was the duke, and his enormous dog, Truck, wore a plume like a horse.

I'm pretty sure this must be you because that dog is your lock screen.

I've grown very fond of your dog, by the way. I like looking at him when I pick up your phone. It makes me happy. I love him.

That picture of Truck made him happy, too. That's Truck. And there's an explanation for this photo, too.

She responded with a few laughing emojis. Pretty self-explanatory! Anyway, sorry to disrupt your Christmas Eve. I just thought you'd want to know that Boobs misses you and thought maybe you'd want to let her know that you don't have your phone right now. I figured if I said it, she'd think she was getting the old heave-ho.

A likelier guess was that Tamara had texted him by mistake. Appreciate it.

Once again, Merry Christmas. She sent a GIF of dancing Santas.

Yes, he liked this girl.

"Hello?" Allen said, leaning across the table.

"Yep, sorry," Jonah said, and slipped the phone into his pocket. "Okay, the Star." He took a long drink of his wine and tried to explain to his cousins that the family was facing a seismic change whether they liked it or not.

Three

On Christmas morning, Harper was startled awake by a foghorn ring tone. "What the hell?" Oh, right. She had someone else's phone. She kept forgetting.

She groped around for it on the bed. When she located it, she could see that it was a video text and tapped the screen. Four people popped into view who looked to be about seventy or so and wearing Santa hats and reindeer antlers. "Merry Christmas, Joe! And Andy and Allen!" they said in an attempt at unison, but one of the men switched the names around. "And Naomi and Lena!" They were laughing and immediately burst into a rendition of the old familiar "We Wish You a Merry Christmas."

Her mother's cat, Mr. Snuggles, crawled onto half of her face. He began to purr and stretched his claws into her scalp, and that was the reason Harper was a dog person. "Okay, all right." She pushed him off and he gave her a perturbed meow, then lifted his tail and presented his butt to her. "You are so *obnoxious*," she said to Mr. Snuggles, and put him on the floor. "You should be like this guy," she said, and showed the picture of Truck to the cat.

He pranced out of the room.

Harper glanced at the clock on the bedside table of her old room at home. Seven o'clock—too damn early for anyone to text singing videos.

She closed her eyes, determined to get a few more minutes. But the phone pinged again. And kept pinging. Halfway through her second cup of coffee, Harper figured out that the woman who kept texting was Jonah's mother. She'd texted fuzzy pictures of a Christmas tree. And then a fuzzier picture of a pile of presents. She'd texted a picture of a Christmas sweater, her eyes peeking up over the top of it as she held it up. See what you're missing?

Harper saw what she was missing, all right. It looked like a lot of fun and a lot of libations would be drunk. But it was still too early to get that party started.

Harper turned off the phone and went back to sleep.

Later, when she was dressed and ready for the day, she walked through a very quiet house on her way to the kitchen. Her father and his mother, Mimi, were seated in the area off the kitchen. He insisted on calling it a den. Harper's mother insisted on calling it a keeping room.

Dad and Mimi were reading. Her mother was in the kitchen, bent over, looking for something in the fridge.

"Merry Christmas," Harper said.

"Oh, Merry Christmas, lovely!" her mother chirped. "You're just in time. I was about to start heating the food I picked up from Whole Foods."

This was how Harper's small family celebrated the holidays. Which was to say, not at all. There were no sweaters and piles of gifts. There wasn't even a tree. Her parents weren't religious or secular or, really, anything that she knew of. But in a bow to the nation's obsession with Christmas, Harper's mother generally picked something up at Whole Foods that had to be heated, and they would sit at the kitchen bar, and they would discuss which movie to watch later, until one of her parents would remark that, really, they'd rather read, and then they would opt for that, and Harper would scroll through Instagram and dream of fabulous trips and count the hours until the holiday was over.

It was no secret that Dr. Edward and Mrs. Marlena Thompson had been surprised by a pregnancy at the age of forty. They were quite open about the fact that they'd never wanted kids. "But we are so happy we have you," one of them would invariably add. The two of them had never managed to get into the child-rearing mindset. Instead, they'd cheerfully allowed Harper to exist in their sphere. She'd had a good childhood, and she had no complaints—but now that she was an adult, they seemed even less inclined to put on any act of parenting.

Harper's mother had bought ham, mashed cauliflower, green beans, and wine. For dessert, a towering chocolate cake from their favorite bakery. There were only a few gifts. Harper had something for each of them: a new e-reader for her mother. A box of fancy cigars for her father. A wine club membership for Mimi—she lived in a senior village and liked to entertain. In return, her parents had handed her an envelope stuffed with money and a thin gold chain from Tiffany's. Mimi had given her a pair of sweatpants.

By seven that evening, Harper's father was snoring in the easy chair in the TV room, and her mother and Mimi were reading. Her father was awakened by a call on the landline at eight. Harper was in the kitchen when he finally stumbled in and handed her the phone. "Hello?"

"What the hell?" It was Olivia, from next door. "Why aren't you answering the phone number you gave me? I had to call your parents' house phone and then I had to talk to your dad, Harper."

"Oh, right," Harper said. "I had to silence it, because the guy's mom was blowing up his phone."

"His *mother*? Not Boobs? I'm coming over. I mean, if that's okay."

"Get over here," Harper said.

Harper loved Olivia like a sister. And Olivia could definitely annoy her like a sister. When Harper was six, she had moved with her parents into this neighborhood. It had been maybe a day before Olivia was on the doorstep demanding to know how old she was. Harper had been a little intimidated—Olivia had the warm glow of olive skin and sleek dark hair. She was beautiful, and she'd grown into what the magazines confirmed was a perfect figure. Harper's hair was the color stuck somewhere between blond and brunette, and she was two inches taller than all the other girls. When they were teens, Olivia was always the one in a string bikini at the neighborhood pool, and Harper the one in the modestly cut one-piece.

Every time Harper saw Olivia, she was reminded that she had lived in the shadow of a truly beautiful friend all her life. Boys who showed any interest in her usually wanted to meet Olivia. Men fell over themselves trying to open doors for Olivia, then forgot Harper was there and would let the door slam in her face.

Olivia could be completely natural with men, whereas Harper was a little stiff and took a while to warm up. Olivia had brothers and therefore rode a skateboard and played video games. That Harper never played a Mario Brothers video game or a game console, or tried to skateboard, was the most scandalous thing of all to Olivia.

Now, Olivia loved to travel and shop and flirt. She worked as a journalist, and she saved her money to buy outfits to wear on her many dates. She was secretly planning her wedding even though she had no candidates. It annoyed her to no end that Harper didn't spend all her money on outfits and seemed to want to work instead.

Olivia turned up on Christmas night at the kitchen door like she had done their entire childhood. She was wearing a Santa T-shirt, and her dark hair was piled on top of her head. "Merry Christmas, Mr. Thompson!" Olivia said to Harper's dad. "Merry Christmas, Mommy!" she said to Harper's mother. "Merry Christmas, Mimi," she said to Harper's grandmother.

"Now, you're the girl who is friends with Harper," Mimi said, as if she'd seen Olivia only once.

Olivia was not offended. "Don't you remember, Mimi? You've met me, like, five thousand times."

"You know, I think I have," Mimi agreed, finally realizing the grown woman before her was Olivia, and earned herself a kiss on the cheek from Olivia for it.

They went to the living room so as not to disturb the readers. "Don't look at me," Olivia said to Harper, even though Harper wasn't looking at her. "I ate a house today." She fell onto the couch and kicked off her shoes. "How long are you in town?"

"Until New Year's Day." Harper settled onto the couch beside Olivia, her legs tucked under her.

"That is not enough time. I never get to see you anymore."

"That's not true. You were in Austin last month."

"And you worked the whole time." Olivia rubbed her eyes and yawned.

Her complaint about Harper was getting old. Harper worked too much, she never wanted to do anything fun. But to Olivia, doing something fun meant hitting the clubs and being universally admired while Harper nursed a drink. Not fun.

"Okay, I can't stand it another minute. Let's see this phone guy and his mom."

Harper pulled out the phone. "First, you have to see this dog."

Unfortunately, Truck was covered up by several more text messages from Jonah's mother. Harper swiped open the phone to a barrage of them, including pictures of a cooked turkey, a table full of plates scraped clean, and a cobbler that made Harper's mouth water. Your favorite!

"It's weird," Harper said as they scrolled through the texts. "I know this guy got a sweater for Christmas and his favorite is peach cobbler and his family is all jolly and happy and I've never even met him."

"Can we finally see what he looks like?" Olivia was impatient.

"Girls?" Harper's mother popped her head into her room. "Don't stay up too late."

"We won't, Mommy!" Olivia assured her. Harper's mother walked on and Olivia whispered, "Does she think we're thirteen?"

Harper's father was right behind her mother. He wandered into the living room with a pint of ice cream. He consumed a couple of healthy spoonfuls as they watched. "Dad?" Harper asked.

"Yep. Turn the lights off, Harper, will you?" he asked. "We've got to get up early tomorrow. We're going to drop Mimi off then do some shopping before our big trip."

"Big trip? What big trip? I haven't heard about a big trip."

"Didn't your mother tell you? We're leaving for a Mediterranean cruise on Thursday. Two full weeks. Then we're home for about a week and off to China with our travel group."

They were leaving a full three days before she'd planned to return to Austin and wouldn't be home until when? Why was it so hard for them to keep her in the loop?

"Night," her father said, and wandered back into the hall.

"They're going again, huh?" Olivia said. "No one travels as much as your parents."

"I know." Harper tried not to sound bitter, but . . . why couldn't they just tell her these things?

"Phone guy," Olivia reminded her.

"Okay, but first, phone dog," Harper said. She picked up the phone, but just then it suddenly pinged, startling them. A calendar reminder popped up on the screen. Ed was all it said.

"Suspicious," Olivia said.

"An appointment reminder is suspicious?"

"Forget the dog, let's see him."

Harper opened the phone and tapped on the photo box. Dozens of photos popped up and she scrolled through them, landing on the Halloween costume first. Olivia laughed. She pointed to another of the photo squares. "That one."

Harper tapped on it to bring it to full screen. It was the same man from the Halloween photo, but in this one, he was dressed in street clothes and had his arm around a woman. He was grinning at the camera.

"Oh my God, Harper! He's *hot*."

He *was* hot. And he was charming in his texts. And online, because of course she'd checked out his Instagram and Twitter accounts (both tame) and had looked to see what he was streaming on Netflix (*The Office*—points for having a sense of humor). She had not, however, opened his e-mail. That was definitely an invasion of privacy, and she had to draw the line somewhere or question everything she thought she knew about herself.

The man smiling at them in this photo was tall and dark-haired, gray-eyed, and fit. He had a lovely smile, all white teeth and a single dimple. In the photo, his arm was draped lazily around the woman's shoulders, his hand dangling just above her breast.

"Girlfriend?" Olivia mused. "Must be. Look how his arm is around her—that's not a casual acquaintance."

No, it didn't seem so. How disappointing.

"But just because he has a girlfriend—"

"Or a wife," Harper said.

"A girlfriend," Olivia continued, "doesn't mean he's not open to meeting other people, you know."

Harper sputtered a laugh. "That's *exactly* what a girlfriend means. It means you have committed, that you are not open to meeting other girls. And second, why are we having this conversation? It's not like I have time to even think about him."

"No one is that busy. Literally no one!"

Harper groaned. "I know, I know, I don't date enough, I don't want a boyfriend enough, I'm not like you."

"You don't have to be like me. But what about sex?" Olivia demanded. "Surely you're into that."

It wasn't that Harper lacked desire. But it wasn't at the forefront of her mind all the time—at least not like it seemed to be at the forefront of Olivia's. She talked about it like she thought about it ten times a day. "Fair point," Harper said. "But there are tools to help with that if necessary."

"First of all, TMI," Olivia said, holding up one perfectly manicured finger. "And two, it's not the same, Harper. It's just not."

It really wasn't the same.

The phone suddenly pinged. This was a text that included a picture of a newspaper spread open to the ads section. Sweetie, Kohl's is having an after Xmas sale starting tomorrow. Do you need some underwear or socks? 75% off. I'll pick some up for you but need to know sizes. Don't ignore me, Joe—you cannot beat these prices.

Harper and Olivia looked at the screen. Then at each other. And burst into howls of laughter.

"Does he have, like, an unhealthy attachment to his mother?" Olivia asked, gasping for air from laughing so hard. "Which is only okay because he is so cute. Anyway, I'm bored now that I've seen him. Let's go out."

"It's Christmas night," Harper complained. "Nothing is open."

"You'd be surprised." Olivia pulled out her phone and turned on the camera to check herself out.

Harper had no doubt that she would be surprised. She clicked the phone shut and got up to get ready.

The next morning, Harper was doing what felt like a month's worth of laundry when the phone pinged. It was a text from Jonah.

Hope you had a great Christmas. Mine was pretty good until my cousin found that bottle of scotch he'd been saving for a special occasion. Wanted you to know that Oakwood Gynecology and Obstetrics thought it imperative to remind you at 6:15 this a.m. that you have an appointment on the 15th. Shall I press Y to confirm or N to reschedule?

Lord. Y to confirm, please.

Shall any emojis accompany this reply?

Ah, so he'd noticed her overreliance on emojis. Yes. Obviously the doctor emoji and the smiley face with the mask.

Obviously.

She smiled. This is great timing! Because you got a text from your mom. She is going to shop the sales at Kohl's and would like to know what size underwear you need. Boxers or briefs? The last question had not come from his mother, but Harper had a burning curiosity.

The question was met with silence. Harper held her breath. Had she gone too far? Dammit, she'd gone too far. This was her problem— she never understood the rules of the game. Which annoyed her, as she really liked Jonah and she hadn't meant to insult his mother and she really, *really* wanted to see his dog.

She began to type out a profuse apology, but a text suddenly pinged. Sorry—I died for about a minute and only the urgent need to tell you my mother does not buy my underwear brought me back to life.

Harper laughed.

This is so awkward, he texted. My mom can be a little out there. I told her I didn't have my phone.

Harper turned on the dryer and leaned against it. I don't think she got the message. She texted several times yesterday. Mostly with pictures of presents (you got a sweater) and food (she made your favorite cobbler).

Jonah sent an emoji of exasperation. Damn. I do love that cobbler. So I don't know how to say this, especially since I don't know you, but I really need you to understand that I am not as weird as my phone must make me seem. I swear I'm a normal kind of guy and really need us to be on the same page about that, so I submit exhibit A from your phone as a friendly reminder that we all have stuff. What followed was a picture Olivia had taken of her during a girls' trip to New York a couple of years ago. Harper had awakened in borrowed, too small, onesie pajamas (she'd forgot to bring her own), and after tossing and turning in a bed as hard as a slab of marble, she'd had some serious bed head and mascara smeared under her eyes.

Harper burst out in laughter. Yes, everyone had stuff. That is so unfair, she texted. At least you can blame your stuff on your mom.

Are we even?

Harper was still grinning. We are even. Still, I think you should let your mother know your underwear needs. It seemed really important to her.

A laughing emoji. Moms, amiright? Let me know if she sends anything else and in the meantime, I'll give her a call and REMIND her that I don't have my phone. Boxer briefs, BTW. Smiley face.

That made her blush. Yessir, Harper was definitely looking forward to meeting this guy.

She put the phone down and carried on with the laundry until the phone pinged again. She had to laugh—this was a text from "Dad" in Jonah's contacts list. Cowboys play Philadelphia Monday Night Football. You coming? She forwarded the text to Jonah.

Oh my GOD, he texted back, along with an exploding head emoji. Do they listen to anything I say?

And so it continued.

When someone named Caden texted him about girlfriend troubles, she forwarded that, too, with her own take. I'm no expert, but I have to say that if a guy gave me a fishing rod for Christmas, I would not be happy. Not gonna lie.

He texted back, AGREED.

He texted her with news about a New Year's Eve party from Allison Mitchell, an acquaintance of hers. Harper asked him: Can you text her and tell her I can't make it with a suitable sad face emoji? Not the teardrop one, just the usual frown. We're not that good of friends, lol.

He texted her a range of sad faces to choose from, and after some discussion, they jointly agreed just a regular down-turned smile was the right one for the occasion.

Harper's parents left for their cruise midweek and told her to be sure and leave the envelope on the kitchen bar for the cat sitter. Harper decided it was time to go back to Austin. She was packing up to leave the next morning when she got a text from Jonah. I'm heading back to town tomorrow to get my new socks and underwear. Can't wait. When are you back?

In the morning, she texted. What part of town do you live in? Maybe we could meet for a drink and exchange phones. She hit Send before she could talk herself out of the invitation. She'd enjoyed this banter between them, and she really did want to meet the dog, but he probably did have a girlfriend or a wife and she held her breath, already kicking herself for asking and making it sound like a date. For heaven's sake, she hadn't even realized she had so much riding on this, but she felt stupid and hopeful and . . .

I'm in Crestview. What about you?

She squealed softly with delight. The Triangle.

Got it. Hope this doesn't come across as show-offy, but how about the Dive Bar and Lounge on Guadalupe? First Lone Star beer (happy hour, 99c) is on me!

Harper grinned. A dive bar AND a Lone Star? Are you trying to impress me? How does 5 sound?

Sounds like happy hour to me. See you there New Year's Day.

Any chance your dog can come?

He responded with a line of laughing emojis.

She texted, P.S. You may not recognize me because I will have combed my hair.

I'm pretty sure I will recognize you after seeing all the mirror selfies.

Harper cringed. Nooo! I had forgotten about those!

Harper . . . never forget about the mirror selfies.

Wide-eyed emoji, laughing emoji.

Four

Jonah had never imagined that the highlight of his break would come from text-flirting with a woman he had yet to actually meet. It was like one of those dating reality shows, where you talk first and meet later. But after a frustrating, tangled slog of a year, it had been a very pleasant surprise. Most of his days were filled with the dread of what bills were owed, or depression at looking at the day's receipts and knowing that the latest effort to bring in business had failed. The switch in phones had been initially frustrating, but had turned into something new and different. It was nice to have something to look forward to, and he'd looked forward to every text from her.

Harper was funny. He liked people who made him laugh, and he especially liked women who made him laugh. And she was cute, too, from what he'd seen between her Instagram and mirror selfies and the picture of her with the wild hair and raccoon eyes.

To say he was excited to meet her in person was an understatement.

He positioned himself outside the Dive Bar and Lounge and watched people on the street. Would he recognize her? People used so many photo filters online that sometimes they didn't look quite the same in real life.

He needn't have worried—he knew her the moment he saw her. She wore boots over tights, a T-shirt beneath a chunky cardigan, and the enormous tote he recalled from the night in the Lyft van. She was seriously cute. She reminded him of the girl you'd lived next door to all your life and then one day she was suddenly all grown up and hot.

She fairly blew in his direction on a strong gust of northern wind. "Hey!" she called, waving. She recognized him, too.

Jonah pushed away from the wall he was leaning against and waved back. She grinned, and picked up her step like she was running to meet an old friend. She had a long braid of light coppery brown hair over one shoulder, and when she got closer, he noticed the smile in her big, Coke bottle green eyes. They actually sparkled. Maybe he was seeing things, and maybe the sun hit her just right, but that looked like a sparkle to him, and it made him feel warm all over.

"You must be Harper." Who else would she be? He could really sound like a dolt sometimes, and act like it, too, because he leaned in without thinking, his instinct to kiss her cheek because he felt like he knew her. He instantly realized his mistake and reared back with a strange pat to her shoulder.

She laughed. "You must be Jonah." She peered up at him.

"Not what you were expecting?" he asked with a bit of a nervous laugh. Did he look different? Did she like what she saw?

"You are *totally* what I was expecting," she assured him. "It's just weird to actually see you in person."

"Oh. Ah . . ."

"I mean, you're bigger than I thought. Taller." She lifted a hand overhead. "And . . . like, *realer*. Which is not a word, obviously, but, you know."

He *did* know. "You look realer, too." He almost said *prettier*.

"It's really great to meet you, Harper. I am excited to treat you to that 99 cent Lone Star beer." He gestured to the door of the bar.

"You better treat me. I slogged all the way here for it."

"What was that, a full ten-minute drive from The Triangle?"

"Seven! No traffic." She grinned.

So did he. He opened the door to the establishment.

They took two seats at the bar, away from the pinball machine. The place was fairly empty but still had the musty smell of booze from the night before. A bartender appeared and tossed down two coasters on the bar in front of them. "Happy New Year. What are you having?"

"And a Happy New Year to you," Jonah said. Jesus, he sounded like Uncle Marty walking through the store. "This is a big day for us, so we're going to celebrate with a couple of Lone Stars. Cans, not bottles, of course." He looked to Harper for confirmation.

"Of course. I must have the metallic taste of can in my beer."

The bartender opened a cooler just beneath the bar. "What are you celebrating? An engagement?"

They both laughed so loudly and shook their heads so adamantly that the few people in the bar turned to see what was going on. "We don't even *know* each other," Harper said. "Honestly, had it not been for a dog, I'm not sure I would have come."

"I get that a lot," Jonah said. "Truck is a very appealing dog. In theory."

"He's adorable! And I have to confess, I feel safe meeting the guy who put a dog like that in reindeer antlers. That guy can't be an ax murderer, am I right?" she asked the bartender.

"Odds would be against it. You two like anything besides the beer?" He opened one can and set it in front of Harper, and then the other, which he set in front of Jonah.

"Just a sec." Harper held up a finger and turned to Jonah. "Beers are great, but . . . are we maybe selling this occasion short?"

He didn't know what she meant at first, but then he recalled her

Instagram account. "I think I know where you're going with this. Want to take it up a notch?"

The sparkle exploded in Harper's eyes again. "Just so there's no confusion, what does 'take it up a notch' mean to you?"

He snorted. "Chips and salsa, obviously."

"Yes! How did you know?"

Harper's laugh of delight tickled all of his senses. "I'm no amateur, ma'am. Plus, your Instagram account is full of pictures of food and none of it healthy."

"That's because I'm a human garbage disposal. Smother something in cheese and I will devour it."

Jonah said to the bartender, "A basket of chips. And a couple of glasses for the beer, if you don't mind. First impressions and all that."

"Coming right up."

Harper twisted on her stool to face Jonah. "Isn't this strange? I mean, I feel like I know you, and yet you're a complete stranger."

"It's strange and awesome. What did you figure out about me?"

"Well, obviously, you have a dog you love a lot. You have only a few pictures on Instagram and most are of him. My favorite picture is him floating on a yellow duckie float in the lake."

"Truck does enjoy his leisure time."

"And because you don't have a lot of pictures, I have surmised you are not into social media."

He had to laugh. "Busted. What else?"

"Your mother buys your underwear at Kohl's—"

"Correction," he said, putting a hand up. "I was very clear that I do my own underwear shopping."

"True. Allow me to rephrase—I know your mom is desperate to buy you some underwear and that your parents are a hoot. Those videos!" She giggled.

He liked her mouth. Full lips, expressive smiles. "*Hoot* is definitely not the word that I'm usually reaching for when I think of my parents, but I can see how they might appear that way to others.

What else?" And he liked the way her brows arched perfectly above her eyes. They were supposed to do that, yes, but they looked really cool on her, especially the one that seemed to rise above the other when she was making a point.

"You have a couple of friends, Boobs and Caden, and you are totally into weather notifications because you get them *all* the *time*."

He had to laugh at that. "What can I say? I like a good, solid forecast."

"And now I know that your hair is a dark brown that women will pay top dollar to get, and your eyes are really slate colored, and not blue or the freaky red laser dots they are in the picture of you at Halloween. And you like horror movies."

Jonah paused. "Wait . . . how did you—"

"Instagram. The picture of your dog floating on the yellow duckie? You captioned it *You'll float too*, which is totally from *It Chapter Two*."

He was impressed. "You've seen it?"

"Twice."

Lord, he was a smitten kitten right now. The woman looked like this, laughed liked this, smiled like this, and she watched his favorite genre of movies?

The bartender arrived with the two beer glasses and a basket of chips and salsa. They each poured their beer into a glass. Harper held hers up for a toast. "Happy New Year."

Jonah tapped his glass against hers. "Happy New Year, Harper."

Their eyes met, and for a moment that seemed unusually long, they took each other in. And it felt nice, a warm, happy thing sliding through him like a bit of honey. But then he started to feel a little too warm and broke the spell. "I feel like I know you, too."

"Tell me." She picked up a chip.

"You like to eat, for one." He pointed at the chip she popped into her mouth.

Harper nodded. "Too easy. I'm a big foodie and it's all over my phone and I've already told you I'm a garbage disposal."

"Street tacos?"

"*Definitely* street tacos."

He held out his fist, and she bumped it.

"Okay. I know when your next gynecology appointment is, and by the way, if you have any changes in your insurance, you need to arrive fifteen minutes early."

She laughed.

"I know you take spin classes, because your phone notified me of a monthly payment. I know you're a heavy sleeper because of the picture I found that I sent you. I know that Mimi, who I take it is your grandmother, loves you, and has the habit of commenting on all your Instagram photos . . . and all the comments on all your Instagram photos."

"Oh no," Harper said.

He nodded. "A Happy New Year text was sent out to what looked like five people? And to every Happy New Year, Mimi said, 'Happy New Year to you, too, honey.'"

Harper winced playfully. "She's still getting the hang of texting. And she thinks Instagram is just between us."

"I also know that you really like to take selfies in the mirror."

Color crept into Harper's cheeks and she gave a charming, self-conscious laugh of surprise. "Did you go through my *entire* photo roll?"

"I would need more than a week to scroll through the thousands of photos on your phone. But I did complete a cursory inspection. Didn't you?"

The color in her cheeks deepened to an enticing shade of pink. "I might have skimmed them."

Well, Jonah had done more than skim. He liked her mirror selfies and had scrolled looking for them. There were other pictures on her phone, too, pictures that allowed him to imagine her life, like the ones she'd taken with friends at recognizable sites around Austin and Houston. Or the selfie in front of the Paramount Theater in Austin for the Moontower Comedy Festival. With a beautiful, dark-haired woman in front of NASA in Houston. In a bar with several women, all of them in sparkly dresses and plastic tiaras. And there were photos of food trucks. And dogs, seemingly at random.

What he didn't know was her job, which was not apparent in any of the photos. He never took work photos, either, not at his real job, and certainly not in the dingy office at the Lucky Star. But she did seem to be in and around the Domain a lot, an area of town where residences were intermixed with shopping, restaurants, and high-tech industry. He guessed her job was something in technology.

"So? Should we do it?" Harper asked between chips.

Jonah blinked. "Excuse me?"

"Exchange phones."

"Oh. Right." How quickly he'd forgotten the reason for being here. He reached in his coat pocket for her phone, laid it down on the bar, and slid it across to her. "No weird texts or pictures—well, I think my cousins might have taken a picture or two of me one night, but you knew that was going to happen. No unauthorized purchases. All the phone numbers associated with my family have been blocked because none of them listen and they definitely don't take instruction well. I return this to you as I found it, minus the mint that was stuck to it from the floor of that van."

"Gross. Thank you." She reached into her bag for his phone and put it on the bar before him. "Thank you so much for the generous use of your phone. I sincerely hope you have an unlimited plan."

That brought his gaze up.

She laughed, and the sparkle in her eyes charmed him. "Just kidding. Sort of. Oh, and likewise, no weird pictures or unauthorized photos on your phone, either."

He slid the phone into his pocket. She dropped hers into her tote. "Now that the great phone caper is over, how was your holiday?"

"Good. I helped my cousin move. What about yours?"

"It was quiet. My parents left on a cruise, sooo . . ." She looked away, shrugging a little. "Oh, hey! You got a great new sweater. Izod. My dad wears them all the time."

"So does mine. Bet you know where it came from."

"Kohl's, definitely."

They laughed together, and Jonah wondered when had it ever been this easy? "Thanks for sending me a picture of the present, by the way. I needed that heads-up so I can get my happy face on by the time I see my parents."

"I completely understand. My grandmother got me some sweats. But not cute joggers like everyone wears. I mean *sweats,* the kind you wear when you're training for an Olympic weight-lifting championship. You know, thick and utilitarian."

Jonah pictured her in thick utilitarian sweats. He imagined that she'd pair them with an old, oversized college sweatshirt and fuzzy socks, and tie her hair up in a messy bun on top of her head. He would like to see that. "What do you think happens to our parents when they get older? It's like they think if you wouldn't wear it when you were twelve, they must have a shot at it again twenty years later."

She laughed.

"What's the best Christmas present you've ever received?" he asked curiously.

"Oh wow, I have to think." She ate a couple of chips as she pondered it. "It's not very sexy, but the Christmas after I graduated college, my parents paid off my student loans. Now *that* was a great gift."

So she'd gone to college. "No kidding," he agreed. He was still paying his loans. "Where'd you go to school?"

"Rice. You?"

He jerked his thumb over his shoulder in the direction of the University of Texas campus. "UT."

She took another chip. "What was your best Christmas gift?"

"Truck," he said instantly. "Truck the dog, I mean. I finished graduate school one December and I guess I'd been talking about wanting a dog. And then, one day, my mom found him wandering the street. He was just a puppy, but he didn't have a collar and he wasn't chipped. And the rest, as they say, is history."

"That is so awesome. It sounds like a Christmas miracle! He looks like an amazing dog."

Jonah had to laugh. Truck was one hundred and twenty pounds of undisciplined goofball. He loved him. "He is . . . but he's not well behaved."

"No?"

"He's horrible," Jonah said, and he wasn't exaggerating. Two weeks ago he'd come home from work and found the pantry door chewed and an empty bag of chips in the living room.

"Here's a question," Jonah said. "What do you do for work?"

She tilted her head as if trying to decide what exactly she did. "A better question is, what do I not do? My job is kind of hard to explain. I work for a guy who has a lot of irons in the fire."

For some reason, that description reinforced Jonah's idea of the tech world with office space at the Domain. He imagined a Jeff Bezos–type boss.

"For example, he e-mailed me over the holidays to tell me he was thinking of making candles. Like, manufacturing them with his favorite incense scent. Where did that come from? And why? Is there great money to be made in candles?" She shook her head, apparently still flummoxed by it. "Anyway, I'm in management. I help him manage some of his investments."

Ah. A financial person in the tech industry. Jonah suddenly remembered that text her boss had sent. "Have you found out what you were right about?"

"I have not. But I'll see him tomorrow and I will get to the bottom of *that*."

He felt fondness for her waving through him.

"What do you do?" she asked.

"I'm an aerospace engineer."

Her eyes widened with surprise. "That's awesome! You design rocket ships?"

"Not rocket ships, although I would not be opposed. Satellites."

"No way! Here in Austin?"

"Yeah," he said. "Neptune Industries." He didn't mention that he was on a sabbatical to help out his parents. Frankly, he was enjoying this meeting so much that the last thing he wanted to think about was the Lucky Star.

They ordered another round of beers and talked about Austin. It was growing so fast, she said. She was taking spin classes at Soul-Cycle in the Domain, but they were expensive, and she'd started running when the weather had cooled. Jonah said he often ran on the Butler Hike and Bike Trail around Lady Bird Lake, and they should go for a run sometime.

She said a new horror movie was coming out soon, and he knew all about it. She said her favorite restaurant was the Knotty Deck & Bar, because she liked the rooftop and the cushy furniture they had in addition to the food. He said he was more of an old-school diner and his favorite restaurant was Matt's El Rancho.

Harper gasped. "The *cheese enchiladas*."

"To die for," Jonah agreed.

Somewhere during the course of working their way to the bottom of the chip basket, Harper glanced at her watch. "*Oof*, I'm going to have to go," she said. "I have a couple of things I need to do before work tomorrow."

Jonah reluctantly looked at his watch, too. He'd told his parents he would swing by tonight. "Yeah, me too."

"Hey, want a commemorative photo?" Harper asked, pointing to the photo booth. "Someday you can tell your kids about the time you lost your phone with actual evidence."

They took photos of themselves holding up their phones, pretending surprise and then despair. They laughed in the photo booth until their eyes teared. They took the thin paper photos and tucked them away.

As they were leaving, she said her one regret was that she did not get to meet Truck. Jonah jumped at the chance. "Would you like to meet him after work sometime? We could take him for a late run down by the lake if you're up for it."

"Yes!" she said, her eyes sparkling again. "You have my number, right?"

Jonah laughed. "I do."

They made arrangements to meet under the Loop 1 Bridge in a couple of days after Jonah checked his weather app and gave the all clear on the forecast.

On his way home, Jonah got a text. You're even better IRL. Looking forward to making Truck's acquaintance.

He texted back. You're better in real life, too. I'm going to give that driver Amal five stars.

You know he didn't get his five-star rating by accident.

Jonah laughed at the memory of that night in the van. Trust, he responded, and received a line of laughing emojis for it.

In a funny way, Harper was the best Christmas present he'd gotten in a very long time. "Sorry, Truck," he said aloud, and grinned like a fool all the way across town.

Five

The Lucky Star was closed for the day, even though Jonah's parents, his aunt and uncle, and even Amy were there. That they were not open New Year's Day had been another point of contention between him and his parents—Jonah thought the store ought to be doing business. The Starbucks three blocks down was definitely open. The restaurants around them were open. People would be walking up and down South Congress enjoying a day off. Was there a better day to visit a coffee shop?

"But we've always closed New Year's Day for inventory," Uncle Marty had said, appearing almost bewildered by the conversation. "Our staff deserves a day off, Joe. And we have to do inventory."

"But we can do it just as easily on a Monday sometime. And our staff might like the overtime," Jonah had pointed out.

"But we like to have a cocktail when we do inventory." This, from Aunt Belinda, who liked to have a cocktail with everything she did.

"Let's table this discussion for now," his dad had said. He'd looked exhausted, and Jonah had let it drop. And then, before he knew it, one of the four had announced to their staff members that New Year's Day was a well-deserved holiday for them all and that, as they say, was that.

On his way to the Star, Jonah imagined them all with their legal pads and cocktails and pencils so short, it didn't seem to make sense to keep them. Truck would be there, too—Amy had kept him while Jonah was gone.

He parked in the lot in back and let himself in with a key, shouting his arrival so as not to startle anyone. He was immediately assaulted by Truck, that enormous mix of husky and Great Pyrenees (at least that was the vet's best guess as to what exactly Truck was). The dog was so excited to see Jonah that he slammed into a metal baking rack in his haste, almost toppling it, then twisted his huge body into a knot before launching at Jonah, paws to chest, trying to lick his face. Jonah stumbled backward into the door.

Truck was the worst-trained dog ever. Amy said that was Jonah's fault. Jonah thought Truck was unusually resistant to command, but *tomay-toe tamah-toe.* Truck tried to lick Jonah's face again, but this time, he caught the dog's legs before he could knock him onto his ass. He answered Truck's enthusiastic greeting with a vigorous scratch of ears and chest. "Hey, buddy! I'm happy to see you, too."

He managed to get Truck off him and walked into the kitchen. He could hear Willie Nelson drifting over the restaurant from the speakers.

"Happy New Year!" His mother appeared from the big walk-in storage area. She was wearing a leather apron over her jeans and a long-sleeved T-shirt. She looked like she was conducting some chemical experiment in the back. "How was Chicago?" She came forward, her arms out, and wrapped him in a tight hug.

"Great," he said into her hair.

"Did you see the photos I sent?"

"I did eventually," he said as she let go of him. "Did you forget I didn't have my phone?"

"What?" She smiled and patted his cheek. "That was a week ago, wasn't it?"

It was just as he'd told Harper—they didn't listen. "How would I have gotten my phone back while I was in Chicago?"

She cocked her head to one side, her blue eyes searching the ceiling for an answer. And finding none, she said cheerfully, "Good point."

"Oh. It's only you."

Jonah turned to see that Amy had entered the kitchen area. Her red hair was once again piled on her head, but she'd changed out her candy cane glasses for glitter frames. "Back so soon?"

At the sound of her voice, Truck rushed to her, hopeful for a treat. She petted his head while she gave Jonah a good once-over.

"You are, like, always here. Are you an orphan?" Jonah asked, leaning over Truck to put an arm around her and give her a quick hug.

"If I was an orphan, I'd adopt your parents. News flash—they like me better than you."

"Oh, Amy, that's not true." His mother winked at her. "It's a very close tie between the two of you."

"There's no inheritance if that's your angle," Jonah warned Amy.

She snorted. "Like you had to tell me that. Are you almost done, Darlene? I'm about ready to make a pitcher of my famous margaritas."

"Famous! Then I'm finishing up right now."

"Come on, Jonah, be my taste-tester," Amy suggested.

A margarita sounded pretty good. They didn't serve alcohol at the Lucky Star, but it was definitely an option on Jonah's list of last-ditch efforts. Somewhere along the way, they'd gotten the license for it. If it brought people in, he was for it.

He followed Amy out into the restaurant seating area. Truck stayed on his heels so closely that he kept bumping into Jonah, his paws catching the backs of his shoes.

The main dining room, awash in Christmas lights and ornaments, had remained unchanged for decades. With its scarred wooden tables and chairs, the three window booths, and the framed, autographed pictures of Roy Rogers and Dale Evans, as well as framed photos of old Austin, the place looked dusty and tired to him, particularly after going in and out of trendy bars and restaurants in Chicago all week.

Someone had rounded up his tabletop Christmas trees and stuffed them into a corner. They were bunched together like some dystopian landscape. What the hell was he going to do with all those trees?

"Joe, buddy. How are my sons?" Uncle Marty stood up from a table near the coffee bar. He had a ledger spread before him, entering the inventory. By hand, of course, because heaven forbid these guys invest in technology. There was still a push button cash register on the counter.

"Your sons were horrible. Bastards, the both of them."

Marty laughed.

"Aren't they the best?" Aunt Belinda walked out from behind the coffee bar and gave Jonah a hug. Truck tried to shove his enormous body in between them. "For heaven's sake, Truck!" Belinda said, and kneed his panting, slobbering snout out of the way. "He's not going to let you leave again, Joe." She bent over to give proper attention to Truck. "How is my grandbaby? And the new house? Tell us everything."

"Lena is very cute. And your house is big and roomy. I think you will like it. Naomi has already started painting the walls."

"She is just the best. One of these days, that will be you, Joe."

"I'll be Naomi?"

"I mean you'll find someone special to marry."

"Belinda," Uncle Marty said, sounding disgusted. "Don't say that. Jonah marches to his own drummer."

"What?" Jonah turned to his uncle, unsure what to make of that comment.

"Happy New Year, Joe."

Jonah's dad had appeared. He was wearing a gray sweater that made him look even gaunter than usual. He had a highball glass in his hand with an amber-colored liquid over ice.

"Happy New Year, Dad."

His father looked as if he meant to hug him, but Truck began wagging his tail so hard that his dad could see what was coming and changed course.

"So!" Jonah glanced at his watch then looked around the room. It looked a bit on the side of ransacked. "Doors open at six in the morning. Are we ready for that?"

"Yep," Amy said, sailing by with an armful of ketchup bottles, his mother right behind her.

"Does everyone remember we have a new contest for January?" Jonah pointed to an enormous crossword puzzle that was attached to the wall near the front door. The thing was four by four and featured a crossword puzzle from the archives of the *New Yorker*.

Everyone paused what they were doing to look with varying expressions of understanding at the giant puzzle. None of them looked very positive. This had been Jonah's idea—solve a clue, get a free coffee. It had seemed like such a great idea at the time, but now it seemed dumb. The printing had been expensive in logistics and cost, and then the rules for the contest had sparked an argument between the six of them that had ended when Jonah shouted that nothing could ever be accomplished by committee.

Amy had decided to make the puzzle her mission. She'd written instructions that were tacked next to the puzzle. "Contestants" were allowed to solve only one word, and there was one drink per correct answer. If a word was solved by a table, say, only one free coffee would be doled out. Jonah said that seemed a little cheap. Amy asked if he was ready to give all of Austin free coffee. Jonah said they were already losing money on the deal, what was a little more?

"Everyone is on board with this, right?" Jonah asked. "Point to it. Get people to play."

"I know the answer to 1-across," his mother said. "It's ICON."

"I think it's IDOL," Belinda said.

Jonah shifted his gaze to the windows and happened to notice that someone had left the lights on in the building across the street. He walked to the window to have a look. Since he'd been out of town, the signage had started to go up. Giant gold letters merrily spelled D-E-J-A. A steaming cup of coffee was positioned next to the A. The letters were affixed over the entry, but not centered, because of course they would need to add B-R-E-W. Billie was right—that monstrosity was a Deja Brew Coffeehouse.

Through the windows, even at this distance, he could see that many of the iconic egg baskets had been installed. The coffee bar on the first floor was so shiny, he wondered how people could sit in there without sunglasses. The coffee apparatus was all chrome and futuristic. Was that necessary to sell coffee?

He looked to his right, at the giant crossword puzzle. It looked ridiculous in comparison.

Amy was putting markers in a box beneath the instructions.

"I looked it up," he heard Belinda say. "It's IDOL."

Jonah turned around. "You looked it up where?"

"Google. You type in the clue and it pops up."

Amy paused. "You mean people can google the answer and get a free coffee?"

"Yep," Belinda said.

"Great," Amy muttered, and looked accusingly at Jonah.

"How was I supposed to know? Okay, everyone, listen up," Jonah said. "We need to talk." All heads turned toward him. Except for Truck. Truck was licking something on the table. Jonah made a mental note to get some sanitizer and clean that up.

"Is this a team meeting? Because I have to pick my brother up," Amy said, looking at her watch.

"Yes, this is a team meeting. Look. We have to get real about our situation, guys. We have to do something to pull in business or Deja Brew over there is going to eat our lunch."

"What are you talking about?" his dad scoffed. "They're a coffee shop. We're more than just coffee."

Marty lifted his glass for a toast to his brother. Jonah's dad tapped his against Marty's.

"First, they are a coffee*house*. We talked about this. And second, are we really more than just coffee? Because the name of the family business is the Lucky Star Coffee Shop. We have to be smart about how we put ourselves out there. We need to be competitive."

Five sets of eyes stared at him like he was speaking Greek. Except Truck, who always stared at him adoringly, no matter what. "You look so serious, Joe," his mother said. "Have a margarita."

"We don't have any money," he said to them. "We're not bringing in any money, either, as you all know. We are losing business because we're not hip, we're not fun, and now we have Deja Brew going in across the street, and they *are* fun, and Starbucks a few blocks down, and they are fast. Do you see what I mean?"

"No," Uncle Marty said, his brow furrowed with confusion.

Why was this so hard? Jonah resisted the urge to scrub his face with his fingers. "C'mere," he said, motioning for them all to join him at the window. There was a scrape of wooden chair legs on tile floor, a bit of muttering that he thought came from his father, and then they joined him at the window. Truck pushed in between Jonah and his mother and began to lick the glass.

"See that?" Jonah pointed to the building across the street. To the baskets, the shiny coffee machine. "The seating is cool and probably a lot more comfortable than wooden chairs. See the bookshelves? I hear there's an actual lending library. Honor system, but still. Notice this is a two-level store? Two separate coffee bars and fair trade coffee."

"Oh my God," Amy whispered. "They're going to *destroy* us."

"No, they're not," Marty scoffed. "No artsy-fartsy coffee shop is going to hurt us."

"Coffeehouse. And I think it could, Marty. We have to come up with something to get people in the door. Once they're in, maybe they'll stay for the food and the old-town feel. But chances are really good that they are going to walk past us and go across the street."

They all stood silently for a moment, staring across the street, no sound but Truck's sudden chewing of his back leg.

"And?" his mother asked.

"And . . ." Jonah looked across the street. "We could take what I think would be an insane amount of money developers would offer us for this land and move on with our lives."

The room fell silent. No one spoke until Jonah's father sank into a chair and said, "What in the hell are you talking about? We're not selling."

He sounded angry.

"Our parents opened this shop. Marty and I have spent our lives here. You think it's that easy just to walk away and watch some asshole tear it down?"

"No, of course not," Jonah said. "But do you want to hold on to a business that's going to drive you into the ground?"

"Hey, that's not going to happen," Marty said.

Jonah tried to change course. "Then we have to come up with a way of having your Average Joe turn away from that door and into this one if we're going to have a fighting chance."

Marty looked at the crossword puzzle. "Well . . . I know you were pretty proud of that, Joe, but I don't think that's going to do it."

"Yeah." Jonah sighed. "Me either."

"We could update the menu," Amy said.

"Oh, sure," Jonah's mother said with a roll of her eyes. "Burt will be okay with that."

Burt, their cook, could be a little rough around the edges. He'd been a homeless Iraq War veteran when Jonah had hired him. Honestly, Burt wasn't his first choice, but the Star couldn't afford anyone else. Burt had turned out to be a godsend. He'd never missed a shift. He'd saved his money and Jonah had helped him get into a small trailer at Community First! Village east of Austin. Burt had made many strides . . . just not in the area of social graces.

"I have a better idea," his mother said. "What if we offered a slice of pie with each cup of coffee?"

"People are health conscious now," Jonah said.

"Not to mention, that's a lot of pies," Amy added. "You know what we need to do? We need to find out what *they're* doing." She looked at Jonah. "We need to go to a Deja Brew and spy on them."

Jonah smiled lopsidedly. "I think we can just walk in and look around."

"I mean we need to hang out like we are supposed to be there and figure out how to one-up them." Amy yanked her phone out of her back pocket and started scrolling. "I can't go tomorrow. My brother's band is playing—hey!" She looked up from her phone, her blue eyes bright with her idea. "What if—"

"Nope. Not your brother's band," Jonah said, cutting her off before she could suggest they play here.

"But they—"

"Are heavy metal. We are not a heavy metal establishment."

She huffed. "Fine." She looked at her phone. "Let's go spying day after tomorrow."

That was when he was meeting Harper. "I have plans. How about Friday?"

"What plans?" Amy asked without looking up from her phone.

"Just plans."

Amy looked up. He intentionally avoided her gaze by petting Truck. "Why are your plans a secret?" Amy demanded as Truck melted down onto the floor, all four legs in the air, a not-so-subtle invitation for a belly rub. "Do you have a date?"

Jonah's hesitation proved fatal.

"You have a *date*?" Amy shouted.

"Is that really necessary?" Jonah asked. Good God, he was thirty-four years old. "Why are you acting like I've never had a date before?"

"Because you haven't," Belinda said.

"What are you talking about? I've had plenty of dates."

"Not recently," his mother said. "Belinda and I were talking about it just the other day."

"You were talking about my lack of dates?" Jonah didn't know how insulted he ought to be. "All right, before you start analyzing me, maybe I haven't dated in a while, but that's because I've been trying to pull our collective bacon out of the fire. But I *date*. I had a girlfriend for two years, remember?"

"Yeah, yeah," Amy said, waving her hand as if Megan had been a childhood friend instead of the woman he'd dated until a couple of years ago. "Who's your date?"

He glared at her, hoping she would get the message. "No one you know."

"Then where did you meet her?" Mom asked.

"Did you meet her here?" Uncle Marty asked. "Or on the plane? I bet he met her on the plane or in the airport. I read that's one of the number one places to meet singles because you can always pick them out—"

"Okay." Jonah threw up both hands. Truck leapt to attention, his tail hitting the window so hard that Jonah feared it would shatter. "That's enough of the third degree if you don't mind. I met someone, I have a date, it is no big deal, and don't you think we have much bigger fish to fry?" He gestured to Deja Brew across the street. He did not miss, nor did he appreciate, how all the women in this room were smiling at him. Like he was the last kid to get a date to the prom.

"And with that, I am taking my dog and going home. I have the morning shift. Come on, Truck."

"You should get a trim of that mop before your date," his mother advised. "You're looking a little scruffy."

"Oh my God," Jonah muttered to himself as he walked to the door. "Good night, everyone! Start thinking of what we can do to get some traffic in this joint!"

"Good *night*, Romeo!" Amy called after him, and all of them laughed at his departing back.

He put the dog in his truck, then climbed into the driver's seat. He stared blankly out the windshield a moment and marveled at how quickly his life had morphed into one that was not his own. They'd be all over him this week with their questions, and not one of them would think of what they could do to drive traffic into the Star.

He pulled out his phone. Hey. I must have had a great time tonight because I'm still thinking about it.

A moment later, his phone pinged. Me too. Looking forward to that run around the lake. I think. You might smoke me.

He smiled. Only if he was a fool. Doubt it. And besides, Truck is never in a hurry. He likes to chase dicks. "Holy shit," Jonah muttered when he saw what he'd typed, and quickly tried to amend it.

DICKS!

"Noo," he moaned. He typed D U C K S. Truck chases CUCKS. He dropped his phone in his lap like it was a burning coal. "Stop it," he said to the phone.

A string of laughing emojis popped up. Stop while you're ahead.

Am I ahead? Really not sure at the moment.

You're ahead, trust me. Winky face. See you Thursday at the lake.

He sent back a thumbs-up, because he didn't trust himself.

Six

Kendal, Soren's assistant, was sitting at reception and opening Soren's mail when Harper arrived at work the next day. He was a tall, slender man with brown skin, meticulously groomed, not a hair out of place, his goatee neatly trimmed, and his clothing ironed to perfection. He was the exact opposite of Soren. One other thing about Kendal—he did not like Harper.

Maybe because she had mistaken him for a receptionist on his first day of work and asked him to fax something for her. In her defense, he was sitting at the receptionist desk, and they didn't have a receptionist, and no one had told her otherwise.

Kendal was the office administrator. Or the administrative officer. His exact job was still unknown to her.

"Happy New Year," Harper said.

"Happy New Year to you." He flicked his gaze over her.

"Did you have a good holiday?"

"The best."

Kendal was as efficient with his words as he was with his duties.

He did not offer any explanation of "the best," and honestly, if it didn't entail skydiving over the Arctic and then surviving alone on berries for a week, it had probably been about the same as hers. She looked in the direction of the closed door to the interior office. "Is he in there?"

"Yep. It's yoga time." Kendal scanned the contents of an envelope, put the letter aside, and glanced up at the wall clock. "He should be hitting Shavasana about now. Help yourself to some coffee."

Harper winced a little. "No thanks." Soren liked his coffee strong enough that she was surprised it didn't melt spoons. She took a seat and began to scroll through her phone.

"Anything exciting happen while you were away?" Kendal asked.

Harper glanced at the string of text messages between her and Jonah. Yes, something exciting had happened while she was away, but she was keeping it to herself for now. She had this weird idea that somewhere Kendal had a little notebook to write down all the details about her. He'd done absolutely nothing to give her that impression. And yet she had the distinct feeling they were competing for . . . something. To be determined. "Not much."

A gong sounded from inside Soren's office. That was followed by the opening of the door, and her forty-year-old boss emerged wearing a Mexican poncho, skinny jeans, and some insanely expensive ostrich leather cowboy boots into which he had tucked his jeans. He had thinning wavy hair, which he wore to his shoulders, and a vague shadow where a beard would grow in during those months he was inclined to grow one. Harper had to hand it to him—Soren Wilder managed to be endlessly fascinating in a variety of ways.

His brown-eyed gaze moved over her, as if looking for damage from shipping. Finding none, he placed his hands together at heart center and bowed. "Harper, you're looking well."

"Thank you." In stark contrast to his choice of work wear, she had on a black skirt and jacket, and a crisp white blouse. She could never be sure whom she was going to meet on any given day working for Soren, and since he often looked like he'd just driven in from the farm, she thought it best to balance him with regular, normal clothes.

"Coffee?" Soren offered.

"No thanks."

"Bad choice. Kendal?"

Kendal was already there with a cup of coffee for Soren. So was he a receptionist or not?

"Thank you. See that, Harper? Here's a young man who knows his job and knows how to do it well."

Kendal made a flourish with his hand and bowed before returning to his desk.

"Come in," Soren said, gesturing for her to follow.

The moment she stepped inside, she was hit with an overpowering scent of incense and sneezed. She couldn't see where the incense was burning to perhaps avoid immediate proximity, because Soren had turned down the fluorescent lights and had turned up his mood lighting. Soft, velvety streams of lavender light drifted around the room and skimmed the ceiling, then melted down the walls and floors.

He walked over to a large cushion on the floor and sat carefully with his cup of coffee, crisscrossing his legs like a yogi. He gestured to the two floor pillows near him. "Care to participate in a circumstantial rejoinder of conversation?"

That was another thing about Soren that fascinated Harper—he really enjoyed throwing words together that made no sense to anyone but him. She didn't know if it was intentional, a speech tic, or if he truly thought he was saying something profound. "Not today," she said, and gestured at her skirt. "Can we maybe turn the lights on?"

He gave her a look of disapproval. "Harsh fluorescent light will interrupt the flow of your chi."

"Yes . . . but it also makes it a lot easier to see."

Soren snorted. He got up off his cushion. "Fine." He stalked to his desk as if she'd insulted him and flipped on the overhead lights. Harper took it upon herself to open the heavy drapes and let in the weak winter sunlight.

"There we are, much better. How was your holiday, Soren? Make any New Year's resolutions?" That was a trick question because she knew he hadn't. Soren thought every day deserved a resolution, not just once a year. But even knowing his Very Strong Views on resolutions didn't mean she would resist the opportunity to nettle him when she could. And true to form, he sat back in his chair, steepled his fingers, and stared at her. "Holidays are a capitalist creation born of abusive economic constructs."

"Well, of course," she said. "But it's also family time. I thought you went to see your mom."

"I did."

"And? Did she have a tree? Hot cocoa?"

"No, she did not have a pagan tree." He picked up a pen and tapped it against the desk. "She had a menorah, thank you."

"Ah. Happy Hanukkah."

"I am not Jewish, but I will pass your felicitously solicitous greeting along to my mother."

He'd stumped her, as he often did. "You're not Jewish?"

"I align with Buddhists. Mostly, I spent the week meditating."

"That sounds like a blast."

Soren smiled a little. "I know you're being sarcastic, but maybe you should give it a go."

"Too busy."

"Mmm. About that."

"About what?"

"Have a seat," he said, gesturing to one of two orange plastic chairs at his desk. He'd once told her he liked them because they were uncomfortable and people tended to say what they wanted and get out. He was right—with their scooped-out, unyielding seats, they were so extraordinarily uncomfortable, she had to wonder why they even existed.

But she sat—she'd learned how to arrange herself on one hip. She had about ten minutes before some part of her began to go numb.

Soren took off his poncho and laid it carefully on one end of his desk. He was wearing a black John Lennon T-shirt underneath it. He dragged his fingers through his shaggy, dishwater blond hair, then put his elbows against the desk and leaned forward, peering intently at her.

"Yes?"

"While I was meditating—the multitudinous benefits of which you will hopefully discover—I felt as if you were sending me a message."

"You did?" *Hate to burst your bubble there, cowboy, but I was specifically* not *sending you messages. I made a concerted effort not to think about you at all.*

"The message I received said that you are ready for the next phase of our journey." One of his dark brows rose high above the other.

"Whose journey?" she asked, not understanding.

"Yours and mine."

"We're on a journey?" She debated telling him that she was not on a journey with him. That this was a job.

"Let me expand on the postulating postulation. You are aware that I like to hire people who are capable of doing many things. Look at Kendal—he is my administrative director and my accountant."

Harper inadvertently choked on what was going to be either a laugh or cry of alarm. "Kendal is your *accountant*?"

"My personal watchdog. My raison d' job. My point, madame," he said, accented as if he were actually speaking French, "is that Kendal is a man of many talents. And you are a woman of many talents. From many talents comes the potential for change and growth. I have built a company unsurpassed in its extaordinariandom and many talents. I started with a single food truck selling funnel cakes at the state fair, and look at what I've become," he said, casting his arms wide. "I've taken the rambunctious challenges and made myself a global being."

A global being? They hadn't made it out of Texas yet. "Mmm . . . sort of?" she said, with a ticktock of her head. "Maybe a regional being."

He suddenly leaned forward, his hand in a fist. "But an *important* regionality," he said. "First it was food trucks. Then it was coffeehouses. Next it will be restaurants. Do you see?"

She did not see. This was the first she was hearing this. "Obviously, I knew about the food trucks and coffeehouses. But the restaurants are new."

"New is only as good as the moment, Harper."

"Umm . . ."

"You are an important part of this entity. You've been working diligently on the South Congress Avenue store."

"Yes, I have." She had been working harder than she thought he even understood, and if she did say so herself, the new flagship looked really good. A couple of weeks ago, she'd gone down to check it out with Veronica Sousa, who was responsible for building the physical assets for the company. "It looks great," Veronica had said with much enthusiasm. It was a two-story coffeehouse, with a coffee bar and stage on both levels. It was all chrome and mahogany and fancy coffee machines, egg basket seating, library, and a quiet room. Austinites were going to flock there.

"We must make a splash, Harper," Soren said, drawing her back to the present. "That store must be the featured contralto of the opera."

Meaning, in Soren-speak, that it really needed to stand out.

"I want you to take the helm of the grand opening. Finish what you started with implementing the design. I want you to make that coffeehouse the best coffeehouse in Austin. I want the grand opening to be the sort of performance that puts the indescribable arousal for conversance at an all-time high."

There was no translation for that. "Got it."

Soren pinned her with an intent look. "The sky is the limit for you, my friend. If this goes well, we'll be launching in other cities that have the *in toto* mindset of harmony. On a grander scale, of course."

"What?" A grander scale than . . . the store? Austin?

"And you could be entirely responsible for that expansion."

"What cities?" she asked, trying to catch up. Her breathing had quickened, like she was gearing up for a run. "How *many* cities? And what exactly are we doing in these cities?"

"All to be determined with alacrity," he said with a flick of his wrist. "Upscale coffee bistros."

"More than one city?" She should be focused on the grand opening instead of this new expansion, but she would really like to understand the stakes here.

"Definitely more than one."

"Here's a question—does it mean more money for me?"

Soren tilted his head to one side. "The evidence of your pleonexia notwithstanding, yes. Significantly more. Thirty thousand more."

Harper was so shocked, she couldn't draw a breath. She stared at him, tried to read something in his unreadable brown eyes. What was going on here? "Are you kidding?"

He clucked his tongue. "The lucky winner will receive a raise of thirty thousand per annum."

Wait just a minute. "The lucky winner," she repeated slowly. "Which implies more than one candidate."

"Well," Soren said with a careless shrug. "I have two talented prodigies. One, or both, or some emerging amalgamation will be named the lucky winner."

He'd only mentioned one other "talented prodigy," and it wasn't Veronica. "Are you saying that Kendal and I are going for the same job?"

"You will both be demonstrating your adroit capabilities, yes."

Oh no. *No, no, no.* She *knew* there was some competitive undercurrent between her and Kendal. She'd worked too hard for this, and

Kendal had shown up two months ago and taken a seat at the receptionist's desk! This infuriated her. She had just set up the new store and completed interviews for staff hires all on her own. She had worked her butt off for Soren. What had Kendal done?

She needed to get out of here. She needed to think. "What is the budget for the grand opening?" she asked, the slight shake in her voice betraying her fury. "And how long do I have to plan it?"

"Unlimited budget. And three weeks."

"Three weeks? That's it?"

Soren picked up a bell from his desktop and rang it several times. Moments later, Kendal popped in. "You rang?"

"I was just explaining to Miss Thompson here that we have an unlimited budget for the opening of the South Congress store and a subsequent three months of operation."

Kendal looked at Harper. "Well . . . it's not *unlimited*."

Was he really Soren's accountant? Since when? "Soren said unlimited." She shrugged in a too-bad, so-sad manner.

"I defer to Kendal."

Soren smiled at Kendal in a way that shot a shiver down Harper's spine. Like Kendal was his son. Her fury ratcheted. "How much?"

"We'll make available what you need," Soren said.

"Within reason," Kendal amended. "If you can give me your final budget, I'll see if we have any wiggle room. I feel certain we can accommodate what you want to do. Within reason."

There were those words again.

Soren had come out of his chair and had wandered over to the window to stare out at the sea of glass and metal buildings that populated the Domain.

"I'll give you some ballparks on your way out," Kendal said.

"I just bet you will," Harper muttered.

Kendal pretended he hadn't heard her.

Harper turned back to Soren. "May I go now?" she asked. "I apparently have a lot to do."

Soren turned from the window and gave her a rare smile. "You're very good at your job, Harper. I hope to see you soar to heights you've not even imagined."

Oh, but she'd imagined her heights.

"One more thing—I don't want anyone getting wind of our plans. The grand opening should be a plethora of exhilaration and unbridled covet. Do you understand?"

"In other words, he wants to make a big splash," Kendal translated.

Like she needed anyone to translate Soren to her. "Yeah, I got it," Harper said with a withering look for her competition.

"Now, I should like to see your progress," Soren said, and walked back to the desk and picked up his poncho. "We'll come have a look at the facility tomorrow. Kendal, summon a transport from the intransient pool of ride shares for the occasion."

Yes! Bring them a transport from the intransient pool! Harper was going to make this the mother of all grand openings, and Kendal had better stay out of her lane.

Seven

Jonah and Truck were the first to arrive at the trailhead where he'd arranged to meet Harper. Truck was full of Big Dopey Dog Energy, excited about the number of people and dogs around him. They couldn't have picked a better day—the sky was a pale winter blue, the air dry and cool.

He didn't see Harper until she was upon them. She'd tucked her long copper brown hair under a knit cap. She was wearing running tights that fit so well that for a moment Jonah couldn't remember his name. She had a thin waterproof vest over a long-sleeved shirt, and her running shoes were neon green.

Jonah lifted his hand in greeting, but Harper wasn't looking at him—she was looking at his dog, her sunny smile for that lunkhead. "Look at *you*, Truck!" she exclaimed.

That was a mistake. In a feat that belied both his size and physics in general, Truck took a flying leap in the air for Harper so fast that Jonah wasn't able to grab the leash tightly enough—it came right off his wrist. Harper was obviously not expecting such a greeting, and down she and the dog went, one of them landing with an *oof*, and he was pretty sure it wasn't Truck. A collective *Oh!* went up from the people who'd seen it. Several people stopped.

"Oh my gosh, are you all right?" one woman asked as Harper fought off Truck's tongue on her face.

"I'm fine!" Harper said, but she sort of shouted it, which made Jonah think maybe she wasn't fine.

"Truck!" He most definitely shouted and grabbed Truck by the collar and hauled him off Harper. "Oh my God, Harper . . . I am so sorry."

Thank God, she was laughing. She sat up, her legs straight in front of her. "I have never in my life been greeted with such *gusto*. But you failed to mention your dog is actually a Shetland pony."

"An untrainable Shetland pony," Jonah said. Truck was demonstrating just how true this was by still trying to greet Harper with enthusiasm, leaping at her with that goofy look on his face, seemingly unaware that Jonah was holding him back.

Two guys jogging by asked Harper if she needed help. "We've got it," Jonah said. It would be even worse if he didn't help her up. He held out his free hand to her.

"Thanks." She gripped it with some strength. He gave a firm tug, and Harper came up with too much force—she bounced a step and landed very close to him.

They stood like that for a moment.

He thought he could hear her heart beating. She was a little breathless, and her eyes were shining with excitement. And he thought . . . he thought her lips looked plump and perfect and completely kissable and he realized he was staring at them. "I'm sorry," he said. "I should have warned you that my dog is an idiot and a beast. He never does *that* . . . but it's not exactly surprising."

"He's perfect." She put her hand on Truck's head and stroked his snout. "But how do you run with him? One good yank and you're a sled."

"Accurate," he said with a grin. He brushed a bit of the trail's crushed granite from her sleeve. "It's not easy, as you will discover soon enough."

She brushed more of the granite dust from her tights. "I'm ready if you are."

Truck had lost interest in Harper and had pointed himself in the direction everyone else was going, straining the leash, wanting to join the runners and walkers and other dogs. "Tell me if we're too fast?" Jonah asked.

"Sure," she said, and punched her watch to mark the miles.

They started slowly, fitting into the flow of the many other walkers and runners who had come out at the end of a workday. Their pace was leisurely, and they chatted as they jogged along. Harper said she hadn't always been a runner. "But then I gained a little weight a few years ago, and I tried a couple of things . . . but lying about your weight doesn't actually take the weight off. So I decided to run."

He laughed and told her he'd run track and cross-country in high school and had kept up with it all these years. They talked about a football player who had recently run forty yards in just four seconds and agreed that they could not be enticed to run that fast unless there was a pot of gold or, at the very least, something decadent on the other end of the dash.

"How decadent?" Jonah asked. "Does ice cream count?"

"Ice cream!" Harper said between gasps for breath. "I wouldn't run that fast for ice cream. I'm talking something *really* decadent, like free and unlimited spa treatments."

Jonah discovered that she was a fan of the University of Texas Longhorns football team, like he was, and they playfully argued about which young freshman quarterback should lead the team next season.

As they reached the Ann Richards Congress Avenue Bridge, the sky was starting to turn the dusty shades of sunset—pink and orange and blue. They paused along with hundreds of tourists to watch a famed colony of more than a million bats emerge from beneath the bridge. Truck stuck his head through the rail slats, his tail wagging, his attention rapt on the boaters below, completely clueless about the bats flying out. People were crowding the bridge, trying to see, so Jonah put his arm around Harper's shoulders and pulled her a little closer, squeezing Truck between them. She slipped her arm around his waist and leaned her head against his shoulder.

It felt good. It felt like they'd been doing this for a while now, instead of having just met.

With the bats still streaming out in a dark ribbon into the dusk, Harper, Jonah, and Truck continued on the path, turning west at the end of the bridge, running along Auditorium Shores and to the Stevie Ray Vaughan memorial on the banks of Lady Bird Lake. They paused there because Harper said she wanted to pay homage, but then she put her hands on her knees and gasped for breath and didn't look at the statute at all.

"Maybe we should take the pace down a little?" Jonah suggested. He leaned down to look her in the eye. "I thought you were going to tell me if the pace was too fast."

"Not too fast," she gasped. She straightened. "Okay. Maybe a smidge."

When she was ready to go again, they ran at a slower pace to a low point on the trail where dogs could access the river and swim. They sat together on a rock and watched Truck try and play with other dogs. He was so big and clumsy that every time he put a paw on the other dogs, he almost sank them. "It's like taking care of Baby Huey," Jonah said with a sigh. "I better get him out." He called Truck, who came, which was a slight miracle and a huge relief to Jonah—he didn't want to have to go in after him—but when Truck came out of the water, he rushed past Jonah and a few feet up the path to where Harper was still sitting on the rock. This was the place Truck chose to violently shake off his coat.

"Jesus, Truck!" Jonah shouted as the dog sprayed dirty lake water all over Harper. She squealed and hopped up, and when she did, she misstepped on the uneven ground and stumbled backward into the trunk of a tree.

"Ouch," she said. She tried to right herself. "I think my vest is caught."

Jonah reached around her—her vest was caught on a small protuberance in the bark of the live oak. They were on rocky ground, and it was difficult to access. He had to press against her to reach it, was acutely aware of the feel of breast against his chest. Maybe she was, too, if the red splotches on her neck said anything.

He freed the vest, but when she stepped away, he noticed the material had been damaged. "It's snagged. I'm so sorry, Harper. I'm the worst dog trainer ever."

"It's okay! It was my fault, really. It's not like I don't know what dogs do after they swim—I should have been more alert."

What stars had aligned for him to find this woman? But he was going to pay for that vest. He reached up and used his thumb to wipe water from beneath her eye.

"I must look a mess." She smiled.

"Not even close." He wiped another spot of water from her cheek. And then one from her top lip.

Harper's gaze fell to his mouth, and even though it was getting late, he never wanted this date to end, and Truck had obviously wandered up to someone he didn't know because he heard a woman say, "Oh my God, he's *wet*."

"I know a place where they smother everything in cheese and let dogs hang out on the patio."

Harper's brows rose. "Where is this magical place?"

"The Cedar Door."

"Of course. An Austin institution."

"You know the place?"

"Can you call yourself an Austinite if you don't know the place?"

She poked him in the belly. "I would do anything for cheese. I would run forty yards in four seconds for cheese."

"Wanna go?"

"Wanna go."

Jonah's ridiculous dog was exhausted, so it took some work to get him into the truck. Harper was already on the Cedar Door patio by the time Jonah arrived. Truck crawled under the table, moving it about a foot without even realizing it in his quest to settle in. Harper reached down and rubbed his head, and Jonah noticed that her long-sleeved shirt was splattered with muddy lake water. Christ, what a great date he was.

They agreed on beer and tacos and chatted over the plates of food beneath a portable heater that the server had switched on.

Harper asked if he had siblings.

"Not now. I had a sister," he said. "Jolie was her name. Not that I really remember her, to be honest. She died of leukemia when I was four."

Harper looked up from her taco, wide-eyed. "Oh my God, Jonah. I'm so sorry. How awful for your family."

"Thanks. It was tough for all. But I really don't remember much from that time, other than mostly my parents were sad, and that Jolie wasn't there anymore." He didn't like thinking about it still. "What about you?"

"Only child. There's nothing much to say about my family. I was a surprise, I know that much. My parents are older." She told him they were readers and patrons of the arts. And that they'd named her Harper Atticus Thompson. "Harper for Harper Lee, who wrote *To Kill a Mockingbird*, and Atticus for one of the main characters in the novel."

"For real?" Jonah asked, grinning.

"For real." She told him they were currently on a Mediterranean cruise. "They travel a lot," she said, looking at her plate. "Like, all the time."

"Do you travel with them?"

"No." She smiled a little. "Three's a crowd."

Jonah snorted. "Parents don't think three is a crowd."

"Mine do. Don't get me wrong, I'm glad they have a life like they do. They love each other's company and have the means to do what they like. It's just that sometimes, with them gone as much as they are, the family scene feels a little lonely." She smiled and shrugged. "Hey, I've been dying to ask—what's your job like? I mean, do you look at calculations all day long?"

"Something like that. A lot of physics and math involved." He thought about his conversation with his boss, Edgar, just before the holidays. "Actually, I have an offer on the table to lead a big deep space satellite project."

"Well, *that* sounds awesome and exciting and important! What do you mean offer? Are you in competition for it?" She selected a taco.

"Not really. It's mine if I want it. I'm seriously thinking about it. I really want to do it, but I've taken a leave of absence to help my parents out."

"Is everything okay?"

"Yes, everything is fine." He smiled reassuringly. He didn't really want to get into the nitty-gritty of the Star, so he said merely, "My dad is recovering from cancer treatment. They have a mom-and-pop shop that needed attention while he was laid up, and so I took a leave of absence to help them out. And then this really great opportunity comes along. The problem is, they need a start date before the end of my sabbatical. I'm thinking about what I should do. I might not have another chance like this come around again for a very long time."

Harper looked wide-eyed. "Wow . . . that's a tough one. How long do you have to make a decision?"

Edgar hadn't given him a definitive date, but it was imminent. "A couple of weeks or so."

She stared thoughtfully into the distance a moment, absently scratching Truck's head. "It's funny—I have a great opportunity on the horizon, too. All I have to do is knock one project out of the park, and if I do, I'll be moving up the corporate ladder."

"Oh yeah?" Jonah took a bite of his taco. "What's the project?"

Harper winced. "I can't actually talk about it yet. My boss wants to keep it super secret."

"Are you a spy?"

She laughed. "Just an ambitious lackey. Remember I told you that my boss was insane? He's also really superstitious. I promised I wouldn't breathe a word to anyone until he's ready, but in a couple of weeks, everyone will know, and I can—"

A blur of white startled Jonah. Harper cried out as Truck snatched the taco she'd been holding in her hand and inhaled it in one bite. The dog looked at her, tail wagging, as if he expected to be rewarded with another taco.

Jonah and Harper stared at Truck. "Did that just happen?" Harper asked, looking at her empty hand.

"It did, and I'm going to kill him now," Jonah vowed.

"Wow. The fun with Truck just keeps piling up." She laughed, her eyes shining with delight. "That was amazing. I can't wait to tell my best friend about this dog."

Just how amazing could one woman be? Did *anything* ruffle her? "I cannot apologize enough for how terribly behaved my dog is. Or how terrible I am at teaching him. I know I've been saying that all night, but he just looks at me with those eyes and I give in. I'm a putz."

"You are not a putz, and Truck is awesome. I didn't need that taco anyway. I ate so much over the holidays." She patted what looked to him like a pretty trim stomach.

"Nevertheless, this evening has been such a disaster and unfair representation of my dating game that you have to give me another chance. Let me take you to dinner sometime soon. And without him," he added, pointing at Truck. Truck seemed to sense it was all his fault; he put his head on Jonah's leg and looked up at him with puppy eyes. A master manipulator.

"Awww. He loves you. And I still really like him, in spite of everything that happened today. And I really like you, too, Jonah. In spite of everything that happened today." She grinned.

Her words sparked a bit of a tingle in his belly. He really wanted her to like him, in spite of everything. He reached for her hand and laced his fingers with hers. "I really like you, too, Harper Atticus Thompson. What are you doing Saturday?"

"Saturday? Saturday is the day I pay a visit to my old friend Bob. He's got a very short temper, and he doesn't like most people or animals, but he will tolerate some. He's gone deaf, so you have to shout at him. But I wouldn't miss an afternoon with Bob for anything."

"Is he a relative?"

"He's a bulldog. I walk rescue dogs on Saturday afternoons at the Austin Canine Coalition. They are good dogs, and they don't chase dicks or ducks."

"Thanks for bringing *that* up again."

"Would you like to join me in walking grumpy old Bob? Are your feelings hurt easily?"

He stroked the back of her hand with his thumb. "I can handle grumpy Bob. But only if you'll let me take you to dinner afterward."

"That sounds like the best Saturday ever."

Jonah paid the bill and they walked out, holding hands. Jonah put his dumb Truck into the actual truck, then turned to Harper. "I have really enjoyed this time with you."

"Me too." She shoved her hands into her pockets. "I was afraid you'd run circles around me or complain about the pace."

"Same." He tucked a bit of her hair behind her ear. She was so pretty.

Harper tilted her head up. Her eyes had gone soft and shimmery, and he would swim in them if that was possible, but since it wasn't, he decided the next best thing would be to kiss her. And he thought maybe she wanted to be kissed, too, because she didn't move, and there was a pert little smile on her face, and she shifted a little closer. Or maybe he did. Whatever—Jonah lowered his head and kissed her.

Her lips were the perfect amount of soft and plump. She tasted like the chocolate mint she'd popped into her mouth as they left, and her body felt perfect against his, and there was a tide of heat rushing through him and a physical sensation of being swept to sea.

When he lifted his head, Harper's eyes were blazing. She touched the corner of her mouth with her fingertip. "I'll see you Saturday?"

"You will definitely see me Saturday."

She gave him a little salute goodbye and walked to her car.

Jonah got in his truck. The tidal wave was still rolling through him. He watched her car turn onto the street and move away.

This was perfect. *She* was perfect. How much more perfect could it be? It was like Santa had dropped a big gift from the sky on the eve of Christmas Eve, just for him. Was it possible that she was the one? "*What?*" he whispered to himself, shocked he would think it. Obviously, there were miles to go before he knew that . . . but what if?

What if. The thought, surprisingly, put a smile on his face.

In that moment, he could not have imagined how fickle the finger of fate would prove to be.

Eight

That kiss was awesome. One might even say inspiring.

The run, however, was not.

Harper could hardly move—her legs felt like two limp strips of rubber. Jonah had almost killed her with his pace, but her competitive nature wouldn't allow her to ask him to slow down. When she thought her lungs would explode, she'd immediately turned into the Gloria Steinem of the running world—if he could do it, then so could she. Except that she couldn't, and now, every time she took a step, her quadriceps reminded her that she had never run that fast for that long in her life.

She was still limping when Soren and Kendal met her at the Deja Brew on Congress, and Soren frowned with displeasure. "What is the matter with you?"

"I went for a long run yesterday, and I'm a little stiff."

"Ah." Soren nodded. "Exercise is to ratiocination what sleeping is to resuscitation."

Usually, Harper could sort of follow along with Soren, but today, her butt hurt so bad, she was in no mood. "Sorry, but I don't know what that means."

"It means good job," Kendal offered.

Soren laughed. "It would appear that Kendal shares my understanding of the nuance of expression."

Excuse me? Harper was incensed. No one spoke Soren better than she did. But Soren had already turned away, his gaze moving over the interior of the store.

The three of them were watching two workmen hang one of the last few egg basket seats. The iron and wood mirrors had been hung in the bathrooms, the toilets had been installed, and the refrigeration unit for the kitchen had arrived. They were less than two weeks from opening.

Soren bored of the basket installation and walked to the area of the store where they'd installed a false floor that flashed different colors of light with one's footfall. It was something he'd seen in London and had to have. Privately, Harper guessed the upkeep on something like that would outweigh the cool factor, but when Soren made up his mind, there was no talking to him.

He made Kendal walk across the lighted floor, which Kendal did, striding to the end, then turning back and striding to Soren's side once more.

"Good." Soren put his hands together at his heart center. "I approve. One can create a harmonious symphony of pleasure here."

"Absolutely," Harper agreed.

"Tell me again the plans for the grand opening," he said, and perched one hip on top of a puzzle table. It had a ridge around the perimeter so no pieces could fall, and the table itself had been bolted to the floor. Soren seemed to think there was nothing worse than working a jigsaw puzzle and watching it tumble over. "All that work," he'd said wistfully when they'd discussed options.

"We have three local artists who will showcase their work and provide some sort of art experience." Actually, Harper hadn't worked it out yet, but she was thinking of something people could make and take with them.

"State fair caricatures?" Kendal asked.

"I was thinking something more zen than that." The word *zen* meant nothing in this context, but she knew her boss, and Soren did indeed perk up.

"Caricatures, yes. Everyone appreciates the artist's eye trained on their person. An excellent suggestion, Kendal."

Harper stared at him. Then at Kendal. "I was thinking of something immersive. Something people could make themselves and take home. What if we gave away small succulents and have an artist paint a pot for them to plant it in? We could have it set up in the courtyard."

"I like caricatures," Soren said breezily. "What else?"

Harper could feel her face burning with something that felt a little rage-y and embarrassed. She looked at her clipboard. "Our baked goods suppliers, three in all, and all vegan, of course, will be on hand with samples of their food. We have the baristas from our other locations who are transferring in to work here, and they will be making craft coffee drinks. We will have the games set up in the garden. There are still a few things on the punch list left, including stringing the lights in the garden and installing those above the coffee bar." What she did not say was that the lights she'd ordered for the bar—round globes that looked to be spinning on an iron axis—had been delayed. She didn't know if she could get them in time for the grand opening—she hadn't received a reply to her urgent e-mail about them, and none of her calls had been returned.

"About that," Soren said.

She looked up from her clipboard.

"Kendal discovered that the lights have been delayed. He suggested a solution and I agreed."

Harper's heart began to beat like it was marching around in her chest, preparing to launch itself at Kendal's throat. "Oh. Funny . . . I didn't tell him there was a problem with the light shipment." She looked directly at Kendal.

"No," he agreed cheerfully. "But in my review of purchases, I noticed it and followed up. Just trying to help out."

"Kendal got us lights. But not the fixtures you selected. When he brought the requisition to me to sign, I thought the selection was a bit . . . industrial. A symbol of laissez-faire economics that does not enhance my gratification."

She didn't see how bar lights could possibly figure into his gratification one way or the other. "I wish you would have mentioned your lack of gratification when we had the meeting about fixtures."

"If wishes were fishes." Soren chuckled.

Okay, she wasn't going to guess what she was supposed to do with that. So she forced a smile and asked, "What did you get?" and turned her blazing attention to Kendal.

"Lights that look like bursts of dandelions. Soren found them gratifying."

Soren laughed roundly. "Indeed I did!"

"Bursts of dandelions," Harper repeated. That was possibly the most absurd thing she'd ever heard. "And when are these bursts supposed to arrive?"

"Next week. A full month earlier than the manufacturer said he could get your lights to us."

A *month*? She was going to kill that rep.

"Kendal saved the day for us on this one." Soren stood up, bored with the discussion of light fixtures. "I'll have a look at the garden." He started in that direction.

Kendal moved as if he meant to go along, but Harper stepped in front of his path. "What are you doing?" she whispered hotly.

"What do you mean?"

"Why didn't you tell me about the lights? This is *my* project, Kendal."

He blinked. "I was trying to help you out. Sorry." He stepped around her and followed Soren.

A gear inside Harper kicked on, turbocharging her. She had worked so hard for this opportunity. She had worked so hard for *years* for Soren. And then Kendal Malone shows up and suddenly he is the golden child around here? *Game on, Kendal.*

She stalked after the two men and into the back garden. *Go ahead and find something to critique here, Soren.* She'd outdone herself in the garden.

On one side of the space was a giant outdoor checkerboard with chips as big as steering wheels. On the other side of the space, a traditional pit for the game of tossing washers. Because, Soren had said, Deja Brew was for everyone. Harper didn't know what inclusivity had to do with checkers or washers, but she'd had both games installed.

The lights they'd selected for the garden were the best of them all in her humble opinion. They were shaped like small umbrellas, and when they were strung, it would look as if umbrellas were quietly descending from the sky beneath the spread of the old live oaks.

"Outstanding," Soren said, looking around, and Harper shot a look at Kendal. "When will the lights be installed?"

"A couple of days at most."

"And the entertainment? You have that lined up?"

Kendal took his phone from his pocket and looked at it.

"I've got calls into four local bands. Lolita Lynne," she said, holding up a finger.

Kendal typed.

"A lovely quality to that particular style of music," Soren said.

"Nané—"

Kendal typed some more.

"Interesting choice," said Soren.

Harper wondered if he actually knew these bands or if he was just talking. And what was Kendal typing on his phone with such urgency?

"Why Bonnie is the third act."

"Yes, *Why* Bonnie," Soren repeated.

Harper paused. "Are you . . . are you asking?"

"I am saying."

"Right. And the last one is the Suzanna Harper Band."

"Suzanna," Kendal said, and glanced up from his phone. "She goes simply by Suzanna now. I would say she's the most mainstream of the four."

"And an excellent choice. Her music is the sort one should make love to," Soren opined as he walked back into the main room.

"*Eew*," Kendal muttered at the same moment Harper whispered, "*Good God*." They looked at each other as they followed Soren inside. Well, that was at least something they agreed on.

She looked down at her clipboard. "Veronica is helping out and rounding up some waitstaff from the other stores for the opening, and the new staff hires will begin when we fully open the following day. We'll have a frappe station there." She looked up from her clipboard and pointed at a spot near the coffee bar. "Oh, and one last, sort of fun thing, I think." She paused and grinned at them. "I have a tarot card reader coming."

Soren's head swiveled around. He looked her up and down as if she'd mismatched her shoes. "*Why?*"

"It's fun. A novel experience."

"Sure, it's fun if you have a good reading," Kendal said. "It's when you don't get a good reading that everything goes to hell."

Soren looked almost alarmed. "Do you want to chance a bad reading with potential customers?"

"What?" She laughed. "It's a gimmick. The reader knows this is a promotion. She'll probably give them readings about coffee or something. It will be fun."

"I'd rethink that," Soren said, and glanced at Kendal, almost as if seeking approval. Kendal kept his gaze on his phone.

There was a time Soren would have loved something as different as a tarot card reader. He loved all her ideas. What was happening here, exactly?

"Fine. I'll cancel the tarot card reader." Maybe not before she got her tarot cards read.

"If that is all, I have no indubitable queries at this time. This looks quite good, Harper. We may expect to be proud of our achievement, and you in particular." He winked at her. And with that wink, balance was restored. She didn't want to read too much into it, but she felt confident she was getting the promotion.

"Carry on," Soren said grandly. He gestured for Kendal, and the two of them started for the door.

She suddenly remembered something. "Wait!" she called after them. She'd forgotten that the publicist she'd hired, Carly Kennedy, was chomping at the bit to put out invitations. "When are we going to announce this thing? It's going to be just us standing around if we don't get some publicity."

Soren paused, then turned to look at her. "You never announce before you have the musical entertainment lined up. Never."

"Right, but we have to get things printed and Carly needs lead time—"

"Then get the music arranged. Come along, Kendal," Soren said, and continued on his path to the door, his long trench coat billowing out behind him.

"Because it's really hard to keep this a secret!" Harper shouted after him. "Everyone on the block knows we're opening a Deja Brew here!"

Soren didn't respond. He didn't even turn his head to look back at her.

She followed him out onto the street, because sometimes, you had to stalk Soren to get his attention. "I'm going to get the music lined up and tell her to announce it as soon as possible!" she shouted at Soren as he and Kendal walked down the street to his car.

If Soren had heard her, he gave no indication. But Kendal heard her and looked back at her with a thumbs-up before climbing into Soren's car.

"You little . . ." What did you call someone whose ambition clearly matched your own?

"Whatever," she muttered, and stalked back inside to make some calls.

While Harper was making her many calls to the Suzanna Harper Band's—correction, *Suzanna's*—manager, and texting back and forth with the publicist, Jonah and Amy were scowling at fairy lights hanging from the interior beams of the Deja Brew in North Austin. This store had been made to look like a winter cabin, with faux log walls and beamed ceilings. The music was a cross between a ballad and electronic dance music, sort of what Jonah imagined popular music in Norway must sound like.

Amy pointed at the chalkboard that listed the day's fresh items. "It's all vegan. Not one thing on that list has even a *smidge* of butter. Personally, I'm offended. Even the damn ice cream is vegan."

At the bottom of the chalkboard was a note that today's items were supplied by the local Merry Vegan Bakery. Jonah wondered what the margins were on the baked goods in a place like this. His margins were razor-thin. "Ready?" he asked Amy.

"Ready."

They stepped up to the counter to order. Jonah took a vegan cupcake and a regular cup of coffee. Amy ordered a mint matcha tea and a vegan matcha brownie. They took their selections to the floating egg basket chairs. They were prepared to find the chairs intolerably gimmicky, but they were surprisingly sturdy and comfortable. They tried to guess how much the baskets cost. How much it would take if they were to get rid of standard wooden chairs and tables in the Star and replace them with something . . . hip?

Neither of them had a clue on either front.

"When did the vegan, no-dairy, no-sugar craze become a thing?" Amy asked, scowling at the brownie with the bright green top.

"Around the time diabetes became a thing."

She snorted, then took a bite of the brownie. She chewed a moment, and her eyes opened wide inside her large-framed red glasses dotted with turquoise-colored crystals. "It's *good*."

Jonah chuckled. "It has to be good or people wouldn't keep coming back."

"I know, but still. I had no *idea* vegan could be so good. What did they say it was sweetened with? Prune juice or something?"

The cupcake he'd picked up was good, too. And so was the coffee. Straight-up, fair trade coffee.

Jonah looked around at the clientele. Two men were seated at a table playing a game that looked like *3D Battleship*. A woman was perusing the books in the small lending library. Another man wearing headphones was bent over a laptop. The place was aesthetically pleasing, the clientele straight out of Austin central casting. The food and coffee were good, and there were enough attractions such as games and books to attract people in every day of the week.

Jonah put down his cup. "We can't compete with this, Amy. Do you know how much we'd have to invest to come even close to competing with this?"

"You have to stop looking at this place like it's the end-all, Jonah. I think it's kind of uppity."

He looked around them again. "What's uppity? Where? How?"

Amy looked around, too. "I don't know. It just feels elitist."

"Because they're vegan?"

"Because they think they're so woke."

"That's the way Austin is going."

She adjusted her cat-eye frames. "I know. Believe me, I know. But there are still a lot of people like you and me and your parents in this town. There has to be a way the Star can exist alongside places like this."

"If the Star was in the suburbs, I'd agree with you. But we're not. We're right in the middle of town, in the middle of a clientele that likes this sort of thing."

Amy stuffed the rest of the brownie in her mouth and chewed thoughtfully. She swallowed and said, "We are two reasonably smart people. We can think this through. What is the opposite of healthy?"

"Unhealthy?"

Amy swiped a crumb from her lip with the tip of her finger. "Exactly. A lot of people will pull into a Sonic for a Blast. They aren't interested in vegan brownies. We ought to double down and make pies so rich, they make you want to slap your mother."

"Not sure that is a winning campaign slogan."

"But you get my point."

"I do." He looked at the half-eaten vegan cupcake. "For every health-conscious bakery in town, there has to be a bakery known for lethal sugar content."

"Now you're getting it." Amy beamed. "We're going to save the Star yet!"

"Don't get your hopes up too high." Jonah wished he could feel as confident as she did.

Nine

When Harper called Olivia to tell her about her date, Olivia squealed and said she couldn't believe Harper had lucked into a good guy, because they were so hard to find, and why didn't *she* ever find a good one, and it didn't seem fair, really, because she was always looking and Harper wasn't.

Harper said she was protesting too much, that Olivia always had guys around. Olivia acknowledged that she did, but they weren't the *good* ones.

Harper had Olivia on speakerphone. In preparation for her date, she'd busted out the fancy bath bombs and was currently soaking in the tub.

"What are you doing right now?" Olivia asked when she was done being jealous.

"Taking a bath and thinking of new ways to impress Soren."

"Ugh, *Soren*." Olivia said his name as if she knew him. She didn't. She'd never even seen a picture of him as far as Harper knew. "You shouldn't have to think of ways to impress him. It's obvious how awesome you are! Your boss should recognize you based on your performance of the job he hired you to do. You shouldn't have to *perform* for him."

"You just contradicted yourself," Harper pointed out. "And besides, I *do* have to perform for him. That's what he likes."

"I think what he likes is you," Olivia said. "My theory is that he keeps throwing curve balls so he'll have an excuse to talk to you."

Harper laughed, loud and long. "He doesn't like me, trust me. He has a new favorite."

"You're kidding! Who?"

"Remember the guy I thought was the receptionist and he was actually an administrator? Well, apparently, he is also some sort of accountant and advisor. And also, suddenly in the running for my big promotion."

"What? That's not fair."

"No." Harper sighed.

"You're going to get the promotion, Harper. You've done everything for that man. And if you don't get it, I will come over there and personally kick his ass."

Harper smiled. She loved Olivia's belief in her. But she wasn't feeling like it was a slam dunk.

"So forget Soren. I want to talk about your date. He's so hot! How old is he? Does he have any STDs? Arrests?"

"Olivia!" Harper laughed. "It's a date, not an interrogation."

"Call it what you want, but you need to know these things if you're going to sleep with him."

"I'm not going to sleep with him."

"Really? Because it's been a hot minute."

Harper stood up from the bath. "I have obviously confided too much about my sex life to you."

"Or lack thereof."

"Whatever. I *like* him. He's funny and he's got a great dog, and he's an aerospace engineer and there are no red flags. Not a single one."

"Oh my *God*," Olivia said, as if something had just that moment occurred to her. "You're going to fall in love and get married and I'll have to go to your wedding by myself! I'll be the bridesmaid without a date!"

Harper wrapped a towel around her. "Never fear. I'll toss my used bouquet to you on my way out the door."

"Don't tease me," Olivia said tearfully. "You know someone will knock those flowers out of my grasp at the last minute. Hey—did you tell your mom about him?"

"I have not. They are getting ready for their month-long sojourn in China."

"Well then, let me do the motherly thing and advise you to go right now and get some condoms just in case."

Harper laughed. "Bye, Olivia."

"You better call me tomorrow with all the details!"

Harper promised she would and hung up.

Did she have any condoms?

Not that she was going to need them. She didn't fall into bed with guys on the first date. Or the second. Or the third. Actually, she didn't have a rule because she didn't date like that. But she went in her bedroom to search for condoms. In the back of her nightstand, behind the nasal spray she'd used when she'd had a massive cold and a wrapper from a chocolate bar, she found six. She was surprised—that was about five more than she would have guessed. But Harper was always prepared, always so careful to have her p's and q's lined up, every situation diagrammed out, all materials ready to go. She supposed she had her parents to thank for that—she'd been alone so much growing up that she'd had to learn how to get things done on her own.

It wasn't that her parents didn't love her—they did. They just didn't know how to be parents. So Harper had taken over the duty of herself, and had learned that if she planned everything, not only did time go by more quickly, but there were never those embarrassing moments when she showed up to drill team practice without the cookies or water she was supposed to bring.

And there had been Olivia to teach her, too. Life treated Olivia differently than her, and that had been just as an important proving ground as her parents. From Olivia, Harper had learned that she would never have the beauty to attract attention, but she could attract it through hard work. Did the kitchen need cleaning after a holiday meal? Harper was the one everybody wanted on their team. Was there a project that required creativity and leadership? Harper was your gal. Had your parents forgotten you were on the volleyball team? Arrange your own rides to practice and impress them all!

Somewhere along the way, doing things became the thing that drove Harper. Set a goal and meet it. Set the next goal and meet it. Keep setting goals, keep going, look at all the victories she'd racked up. Don't look at anything else, don't look back, don't think about loneliness. Stay in your bubble, think about the next task, and the next one, and you would not suffer from disappointment. She liked to picture each accomplished goal as wrapped in tissue paper and neatly stacked on a shelf somewhere. A stack of her accomplishments.

She moved the condoms to a more readily accessible part of the drawer and closed it, then returned to the bathroom to put on her makeup.

Did condoms expire?

She was surprised by how much she was looking forward to this date. She was generally okay on her own. She didn't feel a void in her life without a boyfriend like Olivia did. In fact, it used to annoy her that her mother couldn't be without her father. Not even for a few hours. Her mother would call her father several times in the course of a workday. Dad never complained. Their closeness was their secret society, and Harper was only a peripheral part of it. She didn't

need to be with a man like that. She didn't need to be with a man at
all, really—she had plenty of friends to go with for drinks and movies. Houston was close enough that she could pop over any weekend
to hang out with Olivia, and Lord knew Olivia showed up at her
door in Austin regularly.

There were times, however, that Harper worried something
might be a little off about her. Was it normal to be okay by herself?
To not *need* a guy? She wasn't sure she really even needed sex. Not
that she'd admit that to her horny friends. She *liked* sex, but she
didn't think about it *all the time*, and didn't measure her happiness
by the number of guys she'd banged. She didn't think about it much
at all, really—she was too busy.

Which was why this thing with Jonah Rogers was so . . . startling. The first time she'd thought about sex—*real* sex, like in-it-to-
win-it sex—was when she'd met him up close and personal.

She would never forget walking up to him outside the Dive Bar.
She couldn't believe that a man who looked like him was waiting for
a woman who looked like her. He was fit, and hard-bodied, and
handsome. He was the type of man who could spur even the dullest
of hearts to imagine sex, and Harper had imagined it, all right, and
her insides had gotten a little fried, so maybe she wasn't sexually
subhuman after all.

She'd find out soon enough, she supposed.

But it wasn't only that. He was fun and good-natured, and for
reasons that totally baffled her, he seemed to really like her, too. No
wonder she was thinking about him all the time.

Harper finished dressing for the first portion of the date. They'd
agreed that they would go and walk Bob, then change for dinner.
Harper had a dress hanging on the back of her closet, but for now,
she pulled on a pair of gray Adidas joggers with the brand's famous
black stripes down the sides, a long-sleeved T-shirt, and a puffy
vest. She had just put her hair in a high pony and, for the first time

since she'd begun walking rescue dogs, a full complement of makeup. As she was dabbing on a little more blush to give her cheeks that rosy, girl-outdoors look that Olivia had once told her she needed, her phone pinged.

Here.

He was here? She walked into the living area and texted, Like HERE? Or in the parking lot?

The three dots appeared, and then a picture popped up of the display window at Mandola's. The Italian eatery and deli was about a half a block from her apartment. In the middle of the frame was an Italian cream cake. "*Nice*," she murmured under her breath. That is the most gorg

Her door buzzed and Harper jumped. And inadvertently sent the half-written text. She went to the door and peeked through the peephole to see Jonah grinning back at her.

She opened the door. He was wearing a ball cap with the bill turned to the back of his head and a black hoodie. He held up a paper bag. "Okay, I don't know how you feel about sugar or cake, but judging by your Insta—"

"Get in here," Harper said, and wrapped her fingers around his wrist and yanked him inside.

He laughed as he bounced across the threshold. He paused to take in her small apartment. Harper reached down to take the bag from his hand, and when she did, she noticed that he was wearing the exact same joggers as her. Gray Adidas, with the signature black stripes down the side, cuffed at the ankle. A giggle of mortification escaped her.

Jonah turned back to her. She pointed to their sweats. "Wow," he said, and took off his cap, ran his hand over the top of his head, and reseated the cap. "This is a first."

"Jonah . . . are we *dorks*?" she asked in faux horror.

"Wait . . . *yes*," he said, feigning horror, too. "You look amazing in yours."

The compliment flustered her, and heat crept up her neck. "Thank you. So do you." Her gaze fell to the bag. "Did you really bring cake?"

"I did."

"That is a *move*." She smiled. "I *love* cake."

"If you didn't, I'd have to end this now."

"You would be totally justified. My best friend Olivia dated an Ironman competitor once, and he didn't let anything that wasn't a whole, natural food pass his lips."

"Hideous bastard."

"The worst." She grinned. "Come in! Let me put this in the fridge and grab my wallet and keys."

He followed her the few steps necessary to put them in the middle of her small apartment. She went into her kitchen and placed the bag into her refrigerator. She had to do a quick reorganization of one shelf to make room for it, and some things went into spaces that she didn't like, because Harper liked to keep her food groups together, categorized by type and meal, such as breakfast, lunch, or dinner . . . but she would fix that later.

Jonah stood in the middle of the living area, his hands in the pockets of his hoodie, looking around. "This is . . ." He seemed to look for the right word.

"Small, I know. But it has the hardwoods and quartz countertops and you can't beat the location."

"I was going to say tidy."

"Oh!" She was a bit of a minimalist, that was true, and firmly believed that there was a place for everything and everything in its place.

"Am I crazy? Or did you measure to make sure there was equidistance between these framed photos?"

Her cheeks flushed. "Guilty."

"And there is not a speck of dust on the shelves. Or a thing out of place."

"That's not true! That vase isn't supposed to be there." She pointed to the blue vase in the middle of her dining table.

Jonah looked at it, nodding. "I admire people who can do tidy. It's definitely not a state of being I can achieve."

"Most people can't achieve this level of tidy. I might have a bit of a problem." She smiled and picked up her wallet and her car fob.

"Any other problems besides excessive tidiness?" He walked to the shelving and her perfectly spaced pictures and leaned forward to look at them. "Any strange phobias? Irrational fears?"

"I don't think so."

He looked at her pictures. She had only a few. When she'd first moved to Austin and rented the apartment, she'd thought the location was temporary until she could decide what part of town she wanted to live in. She hadn't unpacked everything. The boxes were neatly stacked, cataloged, and color-coded in her storage unit in the garage.

"Who is this?" he asked.

"Mom and Dad. My grandmother, Mimi."

He moved on to the next photo, of her and Olivia and some other friends in Jamaica. "That was taken a few years ago." She pointed at Olivia. "My best friend."

She watched how he leaned forward a little. But he didn't *look* at Olivia—his attention went back to her parents. And then he looked at another photo, one a stranger had taken of Harper at the Charles de Gaulle Airport. She was standing at the gate, her backpack strapped to her back, holding her passport. She was beaming, because she was the happiest person in the world that day.

"Where was this taken?"

"Paris. That was part of my college graduation present to me from me."

"What?"

"I decided if I graduated with honors, I would reward myself with a trip around the world. I saved up the money for years. I graduated with honors, and I did it."

"Around the world? By yourself?"

"Yep."

He looked at the picture. Then at her. "That's kind of sad."

"*Sad?* It was a great experience. And I needed that time to myself. You know, to figure out who I was."

"Huh. So did you? Figure out who you were?"

"No." She laughed. "What can I say? I was young and optimistic. But I learned a lot about myself and the world."

"Like?"

"Like, I don't handle situations well if I don't have a solid plan. I'm not spontaneous and I panic if there's too much that's loosey-goosey. But," she said, holding up a finger, "I also learned that I am a creative problem solver. And I learned that you can get a Big Mac in any corner of the world. Any corner. Name a corner, and there is a McDonald's nearby." She glanced at the picture of herself in her Rice hoodie and her hair so long that she'd had to keep it in one thick braid. "That trip is when I discovered I like to have a list and cross things off of it. See the Eiffel Tower, check. Take a boat down the Danube, check. Eat weird stuff in Seoul, check."

"Oh, I can imagine that list," he said. "I got your calendar notices for a week, and ninety-five percent of them were notices about your many lists."

"I feel exposed. You couldn't have seen *that* many."

"Let's see if I can remember. 'Eat healthy,'" he said, holding up a finger. "'Meditate for ten minutes.'" Another finger. "My personal fave, 'Order pizza,' closely followed by a 'Check to see if Lombardi's makes personal-sized pizzas,' followed by the words 'pepperoni,' 'black olive,' and 'onion.'" He held up a third finger. "That is a woman who wants to make sure no pepperoni is left behind."

"Oh my God, I *am* a dork."

He laughed and put his arms around her, hugging her close. "You are an adorable dork, which makes it okay." He kissed her forehead. Then her lips, lingering a moment. "You want to go walk some dogs?"

"I really, really do."

He took her hand, wrapped his long fingers around hers and held firmly. She felt like she was floating—this man had seen her lists and he was still here.

Ten

The Austin Canine Coalition, or the ACC as it was known around town, was a citywide consortium combining the forces of several local dog rescue organizations into one. Austin was a no-kill city, so groups that couldn't find appropriate and permanent placement for their dogs took them to the ACC. The ACC, funded by donations and city grants, then attempted to train those dogs as companions and therapy dogs. The dogs served as comfort buddies to veterans, to kids who had to testify in court, to autistic youth in the classroom. They appeared at medical and senior centers, in children's hospitals and hospice facilities.

The dogs that flunked out of the ACC training program were put up for adoption. While they waited for their forever home, they lived on fifteen shaded acres in the heart of Austin, where they romped under the boughs of some grand old live oak trees and played on preschool play sets and cooled off in kiddie pools shaped like paws and dog bones.

When Jonah and Harper arrived at the facility that chilly afternoon, several dogs were out for group play. Those that weren't lounging on the play sets were chasing one another around the acreage. Even more were sitting at the fence, waiting for the attention of anyone who happened to walk by.

A woman at the volunteer station had bright pink hair tied in two knots on top of her head, and a large cupcake tattooed just above her cleavage.

"Hi, Cinder," Harper said. "How's Bob today?" She handed her driver's license to the woman.

"I haven't seen him yet. But he's always happy to see you, Harper."

Harper snorted. "No, he's not. But thanks for pretending."

"If you come here enough that Bob is happy to see you, why don't you adopt him?" Jonah asked as the woman stepped aside for a moment.

"I've thought about it. He's been here almost three months. He's blind in one eye and has selective hearing and he's super grumpy, so he's not a big winner with kids."

"Old dog, huh?"

"Seven or eight years old, I think. But you saw my apartment. Where would I put a dog? This is the best of both worlds. I get to hang out with Bob, and then I go home to my tiny space with no yard."

The woman handed the license back to Harper, then turned a dazzling smile to Jonah. "Are you a frequent flyer, too?"

"Nope. First time." He handed his license to her.

"We promise to be gentle with you your first time," Cinder said, and she and Jonah laughed.

Jonah signed the usual waivers. Cinder asked them to wait in a gazebo while she fetched the dogs. But Jonah and Harper both started for the fence without hesitation, to where dogs hoped for attention. It was a mistake—dogs were suddenly barking and jumping on the fence, vying for that limited attention, certain something exciting was about to happen. Jonah grabbed Harper's hand, and laughing, they retreated to the gazebo.

A bench had been installed around the entire circumference of the gazebo, and the shutters had been opened to the chill air. In between the open spaces were signs, petitions, and posters tacked to the wall. Dog sitters, guitars for sale, rentals available in the neighborhood, a local theater production. In the middle of one section was the largest poster:

KING MUTT!

A MARDI GRAS TRADITION

VOTE WITH YOUR DOLLARS FOR YOUR FAVORITE MUTT
FROM AUSTIN CANINE COALITION AT ALL
PARTICIPATING LOCATIONS!

ALL PROCEEDS WILL GO TO BENEFIT THE
AUSTIN CANINE COALITION

FOR INFORMATION VISIT WWW.AUSCANINECO.COM

KEEP AUSTIN WEIRD!

"That's interesting," Harper said.

"They do it every year during Mardi Gras," Jonah explained. "Businesses sponsor rescues from the ACC. They keep vote jars and people vote with their dollars for their favorite dog. At the end of the fundraising drive, the dog with the most money wins the title of King Mutt. Look, see?" He pointed to a picture at the bottom of the poster. An Afghan hound sat regally on a stage. What looked like a cardboard crown was tipping off its skinny head. It also wore a sash—KING MUTT.

"Is there ever a Queen Mutt?"

"Don't think so." He glanced at her sidelong. "Branding, you know."

"Here they are!"

They turned around to see Cinder with two dogs. Jonah first noticed the English bulldog. He was missing half of one ear and walked with a slight limp—one leg seemed to jut out at an awkward angle. But he motored along nonetheless, all business.

The other dog was a white Chihuahua with black eyes that bugged out of its head and ears that pointed straight up. The dog couldn't have weighed more than five pounds and was a quivering mess of nerves.

"Hey, Bob!" Harper went down on one knee to greet the bulldog. Bob stopped walking a good foot from her, just out of reach, and sat. He glared past her, to Jonah, with one slightly milky eye, one clear. His lower teeth jutted out from his jaw, and his belly was at least three rolls thick. Bob wasn't missing any meals.

"I know. I'm late," Harper said apologetically. She reached forward and tried to scratch him behind his good ear, but Bob dipped his head, snorted, and looked toward the gate.

"Well . . . here's Bob," Harper said, rising to her feet. She was all smiles for that grumpy bulldog. "He's not the friendliest pup at the ACC."

"That's for sure," Cinder said jovially. "He's very particular. This is Snowball." She held Snowball up as if she was offering her as a gift to Jonah. Snowball was shaking so hard, Jonah worried she would pass out.

Harper took Bob's lead from Cinder. Bob instantly came up to his lopsided all fours and pointed his body toward the gate, ready to proceed.

"I'm afraid you'll have to carry Snowball," Cinder said. "At least in the beginning."

"No walking for her?" Jonah asked uncertainly.

"She'll walk once she gets used to you." Cinder said this with great confidence and held the dog out to him again.

Bob yipped, and Jonah had the impression the old boy was annoyed at being made to wait. As if to confirm it, he yipped again. In the meantime, Jonah had taken Snowball, who looked on the verge of busting into a full-scale panic attack at any moment.

"Thirty minutes," Cinder said. "And please don't cross Anderson Lane. We nearly had a terrible incident the other day."

"Oh no!" Harper said.

Cinder nodded. "There's a popular bar just across Anderson Lane and our walkers lost track of time. It was two-for-one margaritas."

"That's too hard to pass up."

"It's a wonder they didn't lose the dogs, they were there so long! We had volunteers walking up and down Anderson looking for them before they came stumbling back."

"We won't cross Anderson Lane," Harper promised. "We'll go in the direction of the greenbelt." She looked at Jonah. "Ready?"

"I—" Before he could speak, Snowball tried to leap from his arms, her front legs frantically pawing air in the direction of Cinder. Jonah held her firm. "I don't think she wants to go."

"She's always like that. She'll be fine once you get going," Cinder said. She was already walking away. "Have a good walk!"

Bob, on the other hand, was straining against the leash Harper held. The moment she gave Bob a little slack, he shot out, causing Harper to stumble. "He's stronger than he looks," she shouted over her shoulder at Jonah.

They started off at a brisk pace, Bob rumbling along like a little tank at a pace that seemed impossible, given the length and bend of his legs. Harper and Jonah had to walk quickly to keep up. At the street corner, Harper tried to go right, but Bob went left. He clearly had a destination in mind.

"Come on, Bob," Harper pleaded. "You're embarrassing me. Jonah thinks you mind me."

Bob took a seat in protest, looking away from them, refusing to go another step.

Harper looked at Jonah. "What do you think?"

"I think Bob is really determined."

"Fine, Bob. We'll do it your way," she said, and allowed Bob to lead.

He led them a half block up to where an alley met the street. It ran behind a strip mall. There was a distinct odor . . . and not a bad one.

"Is that donuts I smell?" Jonah asked.

Harper gasped. "Yes! There's a donut shop on this corner."

She was a little breathless because Bob was now trying to pull her down the alley and having some luck. "You have to hand it to Bob," she said, straining against his pull. "One, that he could sniff that out with his squashed nose. And two, he's clearly been here before." Bob tugged on the leash. "No way," Harper said. "What kind of volunteer would I be if I let you eat donuts out of the trash? What if they wouldn't let me come see you anymore, then what would you do? *This* way," she insisted, and forced the dog around. He barked at her, but he reluctantly came along.

Jonah put Snowball down, who had finally agreed to walk, and they went back the way they'd come. After a few blocks, they turned onto a path that ran through an urban greenbelt. Bob pulled over at a bench in the shade of an oak tree. He marched right up to it and went underneath it and stretched out on his belly. The only things visible were his hind paws, which peeked out from beneath the bench.

Snowball pawed Jonah's leg. He picked her up as they took a seat on the bench, and he held the small dog in his lap. Bob began to snore. Harper put the lead down and stretched her legs out long in front of her. She stacked her hands behind the back of her head and smiled up at the branches of the tree. "This is a *gorgeous* day. What does your weather app say we have in store for next week?"

"Rain."

"Is that all it said? When I had your phone, it had a lot to say."

"That's all the weather app said. But my NBA app said the All-Star game is this week." He brushed a bit of hair from her cheek. "I'm a huge basketball fan."

"Oh yeah? What's your favorite basketball?"

Jonah laughed. "Remind me again how you are single?"

"I know, right?" she said, pretending to be mystified. "They should be lined up around the block."

"I'm serious," he said. "Why are you single?"

"Why not?" She gave him a sidelong look. "It's okay to be single."

"Sure. But there are all kinds of people in the world looking for love, and you are this amazing woman, and it surprises me."

She smiled sheepishly. "Well, you surprise me, too. Why don't *you* have a girlfriend, handsome dude with a great dog?"

He liked that she thought he was handsome—he liked it a lot. He was also very pleased that she thought Truck was a great dog. Not many people did. "My life has been consumed by responsibilities and work. And I'm too much of a dork to keep women around for long." He gestured to their matching joggers.

Harper laughed. Jonah liked the way the late afternoon light caught her features and made her look luminous. He tried to remember Megan's eyes, but he couldn't, really, other than they were blue. What he could remember was that he'd never been compelled to look into her eyes quite like he wanted to look into Harper's.

"See, when I say I have too many responsibilities, my best friend Olivia always says no one is that busy, and I work too much, and I am avoiding my inner Harper. But when someone like *you* says it, it sounds important and I know everyone thinks, of *course* he's a very busy man."

Jonah was about to ask her what she did that kept her so busy, but Snowball startled him by suddenly lunging at his face. "Whoa!"

He caught the dog as she started to lick him, and he held the dog away from him.

"You weren't paying sufficient attention to her."

"She was on my lap. Should I encourage this?" He tried to calm the squiggling little dog.

"Here, let me," Harper offered, and took the dog from him, putting the pup on her shoulder and stroking her back.

"Snowball is blowing my good-with-dogs reputation." He looked down, brushing dog hair from his clothing. "And for this reputation to be blown on a dog-walking date is the height of humiliation."

"What about Truck?"

Jonah caught the twinkle in her eye. "No fair. I have tried my best with Truck, but he's a linebacker with a strong need to be liked by everyone."

Harper laughed.

"Let me rephrase—my reputation is a guy who is good *for* dogs, because I'm a complete pushover. But in my defense, Snowball is the size of a kitten and is named like one, too. I don't know what I'm supposed to do with her."

"Are you size shaming her right now? Snowball may be tiny and have those weird bug eyes, but she is still a dog. Right, Snowball? Right, Bob?" They both leaned forward and looked down to where the bulldog's hind paws were last seen. Except his hind legs were not there. "Bob?" Harper shoved Snowball back at Jonah, then leaned forward even more.

They realized it at the same moment, both of them shooting up, searching wildly about for Bob. The dog had escaped. "Oh my *God*!" Harper whirled back around and grabbed Jonah's arm in a death grip. "*I lost Bob!*"

"Try not to panic." He was already panicking for the both of them. How could he be this bad with dogs?

"How can I not panic? I lost *Bob*!" she cried. "Bob!" she shouted.

"Bob, come! Wherever you are, Bob, you better get back here right now!" She turned around in a circle, scanning the greenbelt. "He was right *here*. Where could he have gone? I lost a *rescue dog*, Jonah! Do you know how bad that is?"

"Take a breath," he said soothingly. "I have an idea where he might be." He grabbed Harper's hand and began walking briskly. And then he thought of Bob marching into traffic on Anderson Lane and broke into a run.

"You're going too fast!" Harper cried.

Jonah stopped. He handed Snowball to her. "I'm just going to run ahead and have a look." And he started to run.

Jonah found Bob just as Harper caught up to him. He was where Jonah thought he might be, halfway down the alley behind the donut shop, his butt high in the air, bobbed tail wagging, his head in a box. "*No!*" Harper roared. "Leave it!"

Bob ignored her. Harper handed Snowball back to Jonah. "I'll handle this," she said with steel in her voice, and strode down the alley. Just as she reached for Bob's collar, he darted out of reach with what looked like a cruller between his jaws. But Harper closed in on him, and Bob wasn't so clever that he could overcome the length of his legs. He sucked the cruller in a little deeper, making sure he had a hold on it.

Harper caught the end of his leash, and Bob managed to swallow the cruller whole.

"Great! Just great, *Bob*," Harper scolded him. "You'll poop all night and they're going to put me on the blacklist because of you. Is that what you want?" She squatted down beside him and began rubbing his ears. "What were you thinking? You know you can't run off like that. You don't even have both ears and can't hear well." She rubbed his face until Bob growled. She stood up, and she and the dog trotted back to where Jonah was standing with Snowball.

"Crisis averted. Bob has learned an invaluable lesson about running off and he's not going to do it again."

Bob looked over his shoulder at the donuts, and Jonah was certain the dog shrugged indifferently. "Yeah, I can see his resolve."

On the way back to the ACC, they swore each other to secrecy. No one was hurt, they reasoned. They'd *all* learned a valuable lesson. When they handed over the leashes to Cinder, she did not seem to suspect anything was amiss. She didn't seem to notice the bit of cruller stuck on Bob's muzzle. "Thank you so much. We'll see you next week." She headed off toward the kennels, Snowball on her shoulder looking mournfully at Jonah, and Bob leading the way without a single, tiny remorseful look backward.

"We are the worst dog walkers ever," Harper whispered.

"We are. But he's the worst walkee ever," Jonah muttered.

Jonah and Harper took one look at each other. A bit of laughter escaped Harper. Jonah grabbed her hand, and they ran to the parking lot like two kids about to be caught red-handed, laughing.

"How do you lose a rescue dog on a thirty-minute dog walk?" Harper asked as they collapsed against the side of her car.

She was glorious when she was laughing. Everything about her made it impossible for Jonah to look away. He caught her, cupping her face in his hands and kissing her with exhilaration. And then he kissed her slower. Deeper. But more urgently. Harper's hand landed lightly on his arm, and she sort of sighed, and Jonah sort of melted. He lifted his head. "Okay."

"Okay."

"We can't stay here like this. I haven't even impressed you with dinner yet."

"You don't have to—"

"Oh, yes I do. So far we've had one dog mishap after the other. I need you to know that a date with me can be good and trouble free."

"I can see this is very important to you. Lucky for you, I am often and easily impressed."

He leaned down and kissed her again. "Prepare yourself, Miss

Thompson." He opened the driver door for her. "You might get swept off your feet."

"Way ahead of you." She smiled pertly and dipped under his arm to get behind the wheel.

Jonah grinned like a loon all the way around the back of her car to the passenger seat.

Eleven

They parted at Harper's apartment. Jonah said he'd be back in a couple of hours to pick her up and take her to dinner. Harper felt like a human magnet, everything in her pointed and pulling her toward Jonah . . . and it felt amazing.

She changed into the gold-and-green dress with a full skirt that floated just above her knees. She'd bought it on sale before Christmas for a special occasion. In Harper's world, this was as special as it got. She put her hair up in an artful twist that Olivia had shown her how to do, with the requisite few tendrils framing her face. Heels as high as her kitchen counter.

Later, when she opened her door to Jonah's knock, he surprised her with flowers.

"Wow." She meant that sincerely—*wow*. How in heaven was she about to go on a date with this drool-worthy man? He was dressed in a blue-checked shirt, a dark blue blazer, and jeans. He was clean-shaven and he smelled liked the woods and oranges and something else that spiraled straight into her groin. He looked exactly like the kind of self-assured, handsome man she and Olivia would spot in a bar and swoon over. They would play a game where they would try to guess what sort of girlfriend he would whisk away to Saint-Tropez, because that's what happened in the movies. Jonah looked like the perfect strong romantic lead.

She wanted to squeal. She wanted to snap a picture of him standing there with those flowers at her door, then text it immediately to Olivia with a proper emoji.

Jonah tilted his head to one side. "I'm not exactly sure what we're doing right now, but I'm starting to feel a little conspicuous."

"Oh!" Damn, she really was drooling over him. "Come in."

He walked into her apartment and handed her the flowers. "For your single blue vase."

"You remembered! This is really . . ." She tried to find the perfect word. Charming. Chivalrous. Sexy.

"Impressive?"

"At the very least." She could feel the wide, cheek-stretching grin she could not rein in. This giddiness was so unlike her, and she didn't know what to do with herself. The vase. Yes, she needed the blue vase. She grabbed it off the dining table and turned to the kitchen.

"You look amazing, Harper."

He was eying her the way she took in a plate of nachos. Invested. Ready to dive in. "Thank you." She felt like a fucking supermodel right now. She went into the kitchen, brushing past him, intentionally making contact with his shoulder in a manner she had never in her life employed. She filled the vase with water and arranged the gorgeous bouquet of dahlias, tulips, and peonies in it. "These are beautiful, Jonah."

"So are you." He smiled and held out his arm. "Ready?"

She was ready. She was so ready, she was thinking about sex. Quite fervently, she guessed, because she really didn't know what happened next. She looped her hand through his arm, and he put his hand on top of hers, and she meant to grab her beaded evening bag, but she grabbed him instead.

Something amazing happened between them. Some switch was thrown, an electric charge melding them together. There were a thousand things she wanted to say, and yet she could not summon a single word.

Jonah's gaze moved over her hair, her eyes. They dropped to her lips and her fingers. She felt sparkly and alert.

"Harper?"

"Jonah?"

"I really like you. And by 'like you,' I mean that I am actually crazy about you."

No one had ever said those exact words to her before, and she was astounded by how they seemed to spark an explosion of rainbows inside, bits of colorful confetti falling into her bloodstream. "I'm crazy about you, too, Jonah Rogers."

There was a beat or two, and then she launched at him, or maybe he launched at her, but her arms were tight around his neck, and his hands were around her waist, and they were standing, and they were kissing. Madly, frantically kissing.

With a gasp, she pulled herself free. She stared at him, wondered if he was making the same calculations she was making. She slipped her hand into his and pulled him down the short hall to her bedroom.

"Dinner reservation," he said, but the words sounded thick, like he was speaking another language.

"Skip it?"

"Erg," he said, which she thought was a yes. His gaze was on her face and he was grinning, and they had clearly reached a consensus.

In her room, she watched him look around as she kicked off her heels. Her bed was covered with a soft, plain gray cover, and white fluffy pillows were propped up against the black headboard. There wasn't much on the walls, or other furnishings other than a dresser and a small chair covered in clothes. Very tidy. Orderly.

Jonah looked at her, and she thought he was going to say something about it, but he grabbed her up, his hand on her back, sliding up to her neck. There was fire between them, a mix of reverence and desire. *Blistering* desire like she couldn't recall ever feeling in quite such an electric way. Their tongues tangled, their hands moved over each other's bodies.

They kissed like two people who had just gotten engaged, who had fallen hard in love with each other and didn't think they could live another moment outside the other's presence. If felt almost theatrical, like two lost lovers finding each other at long last, a scene from a Nicholas Sparks movie.

They somehow managed to maneuver to her bed, and it was here that Jonah pressed his hand to her cheek and said solemnly, "I ruined your hair."

"Ruin it some more."

"Now I really like you."

"*Same*," she said emphatically. She grabbed his head and pushed her leg in between his, pressing against his erection. Jonah lifted her off her feet, then fell backward with her onto her bed. She scrambled on top of him and pressed her lips to his cheek, his forehead, and his mouth again before she began to undress him. She was determined, her focus on the small buttons of his shirt. She pulled the tails from the waist of his pants.

He rose up to discard the unbuttoned shirt. "This is just . . . I am totally into you, Harper. I want this to be right. I want it to be perfect."

More words that had never been spoken to her. Harper cupped his face and pressed her forehead to his in an effort to savor this moment in spite of the desire raging through her. "I'm totally into you, too, Jonah. It's already perfect."

He put his hand on her back, found the top of her zipper, and pulled it down. "One more thing."

"Yes?" She removed her arms from the dress.

"I don't think I have ever been so turned on."

Harper's libido soared. "Then this should go *great*." She fumbled around her bedside table and produced a string of six condom packages. "Do condoms expire?"

"Not for a very long time." He ripped one off the bottom of the string, and she tossed the rest aside.

A wave of prurience crashed through her when he rolled her onto her back and pulled her dress down as he went. He moved down to her breasts encased in black lace while one hand traveled lower, over the curve of her hip. He knew exactly how to explore her body and drive her to madness. She was crazy ravenous for him, hyperaware of his scent, of how hard his muscles were, tensing and flexing beneath her touch. Heat radiated between them, especially when Jonah kept pausing to look into her eyes and ratcheted the lust in her. It felt as if the connection between them was much more than physical.

She kept her gaze locked on his, except when a touch of his lips or a swirl of his finger transported her.

Piece by inconvenient piece, the rest of their clothing came off. Jonah shifted onto his back, pulling Harper to straddle him. She moved above him without true conscious thought, by instinct alone. Her hands were on his skin, her body just above his, and she met his gaze. He remained completely focused on her, which made every bit of her frantic to have him inside her. Every tendon, every muscle, was on fire with want.

These feelings spilling out of her were new and intoxicating— she'd never really yearned for sex. She always participated, happy to be brought along to a successful conclusion. But this was so different than that—she wanted to be the one to bring it to a successful conclusion. She wanted him to feel all the lust and desire and regard he was showing her. She wanted to be the one he would always remember.

A thought nudged in between all the sensory experiences she was having—it was remarkable how everything in her had tilted in his direction—her heart, her thoughts, her gaze. He looked at her like he knew what she was thinking and feeling, gave her a soft smile, took hold of her hips, and guided her down onto his erection.

Oh. *Oh.* She braced herself against his chest and began to move. Her breathing was uneven, her hair tangled, her fingernails in desperate need of a manicure digging into his pecs.

He didn't seem to mind. He was unabashedly moving into her, his lips pressed together, his expression filled with desire and lust and tenderness.

Harper's heart fluttered and skipped around in her chest.

He moved again, flipping them once more, and hooking her leg over his arm, so that he could slide deeper into her. His gaze traveled her body again, every curve, every exposed patch of skin. He cupped her cheek and kissed her as he moved. She gave in completely then, holding nothing back, allowing him to sweep her along the tide to a climax. She finally fell away, cracking open to the sensations and all the new possibilities and feelings and heart murmurs that came with this experience. Jonah was seeping into her pores, his heat mixing with hers. He was so hard, so hot, moving with delicious force, carrying them both along for the ride. And Harper kept pressing back, kept digging her fingers into his hips, pushing him deeper inside her, wanting all of this, everything he had, until she couldn't take it anymore.

She fell to pieces, arching into the sensation of it, the shift in her seismic.

Jonah followed, then collapsed on her when it was done, his breathing as ragged as hers. A few moments passed as she twined her fingers in his hair and traced his spine down his back.

He eventually rolled onto his back. "Harper?"

"Jonah."

He laced his fingers with hers. "I have no words."

She smiled to the ceiling. "Me either. Not a single one."

He lifted himself up on to his elbow and smiled down at her. The room was dark but for the light of a streetlamp, and she imagined his shining eyes a night canvas filled with tiny stars. She would like to explore those stars forever.

"I did not expect anything like this—like you—to happen."

She wasn't sure what he meant by it, but she never had expected anything even close to this happening to her. She stroked his face. "What did you expect?"

"Not the extraordinary person who dripped all over me in the Lyft. I don't know . . . a regular, run-of-the-mill phone swap. A woman with three kids at home, unfolded laundry, a grocery list, and late to work. That's usually about my luck. But not this."

"I try never to expect anything. Then I am always pleasantly surprised. In this case, I was more than pleasantly surprised."

He smiled.

"I mean it. I'm very good about not getting my hopes up. Hope exists to be dashed." She did not say aloud that she was also very good at compartmentalizing her feelings, wrapping them in pretty red bows and sticking them in dark corners, next to her tissue-wrapped achievements. She turned on her side and propped her head on her hand, too, so that they were facing each other. "I didn't expect to feel so . . . intensely hopeful about you."

"Intensely, huh?" He stroked her arm.

"This has been amazing so far, Jonah. I have to pinch myself because I . . . I can't believe how well this has worked out between us. It's like I already know everything about you. It's like we've been dating for months instead of a couple of weeks."

Jonah caressed her arm. "I agree—it's been really surprising and fantastic. It's not like I've had time for squads of girlfriends. My family is a full-time job, and the truth is, my dating life had been pretty damn boring until now."

Harper was pleased that he considered them to be dating. She did, too, especially now, but it was nice to know they were on the same page. "Impossible," she said. "You can't tell me women aren't finding ways to put themselves in front of you all the time."

"I can and I will. And on the few occasions they have, it's been . . ." He shrugged.

"When was your last relationship?"

"A couple of years ago. And before you ask, I will tell you it was fine, perfectly fine, until it came down to who was and who wasn't ready to take the plunge into matrimonial bliss."

"Aha. The age-old 'Will you marry me?' question. Let me guess—you weren't ready for a major commitment?"

Jonah looked offended. "I *knew* you'd say it was me."

"I'm sorry," she said, backpedaling. "I—"

"It was *totally* me." He laughed at her expression. "She wanted to get married. And I . . . didn't. Now you probably think I'm a commitment-phobe."

"I don't."

He grinned. "You do."

"Okay, maybe just a little. Aren't all guys a little bit commitment shy?"

"No," he said, clearly appalled by it. "I'm not a commitment-phobe, Miss Thompson. I liked Megan and we had some great times together. But I never felt that way about her, the 'let's do this the rest of our lives' way."

"No one should be made to declare yes or no before they are absolutely ready."

"Or maybe, if it's not a yes early on, it's never going to be a yes."

"Or maybe, sometimes, you just know."

Jonah held her gaze a moment. "Yeah," he said. "Sometimes, you just do."

Her gut began to swirl with emotions. Desire. Curiosity. Fondness. *True* fondness. If she had to make a list of all the things a person feels as a precursor to falling in love, she would add all these emotions to it—and an inability to draw a full breath. A tingling in her scalp. A rush of something warm and gooey in her chest. If she had to say yes or no right this minute, she would say yes. If someone asked her if she knew, she would say she did.

"What about you? When was your last relationship?"

Harper thought about her last boyfriend. Douglas. Perfectly nice guy. They'd lasted six months, which was actually pretty good for Harper. She didn't like to be too attached. She liked to be able to go at a moment's notice for the right opportunity. "It's been a while," she admitted.

He stroked her arm. "Tough breakup?"

Harper smiled wryly. "Not for me."

"*Oof.* That had to hurt the poor guy." Jonah winced sympathetically. "What went wrong?"

"Nothing really. He didn't like how much I worked and wanted me to scale back to spend more time with him. He thought that after six months of dating, I owed him a reduced work schedule. In fairness, I *was* working some long hours, but it couldn't be helped. Or maybe it could have been helped . . . but he wasn't the one I was going to cut back on the work schedule for. It sounds pretty cold, but I was more interested in my job than I was in him."

"Ah. The age-old dilemma—which came first, the job? Or the boyfriend?"

"Exactly." That probably sounded cold to Jonah, and she didn't like that it did. She changed the subject. "What did you mean, your family takes up too much of your time?"

Jonah bent his arm behind his head and idly scratched his chest. "I'm not complaining," he said. "But they aren't good with technology. We have a small store, and they need to upgrade and change with the world, you know?"

"Boy, do I."

"We were sort of getting there, but my mom had a scare, a lump in her breast."

Harper gasped.

"She's okay—it was benign. But then my parents went on vacation, and while they were gone, Dad started feeling bad. When they came back, he found out he had cancer. All that time we were worried about Mom having it, and it was him all along." He turned his head away from her.

"I'm so sorry, Jonah," Harper murmured. "How awful for your family. How stressful."

"Yes," Jonah agreed. "Dad is the business guy, but he couldn't go into the office while he was doing chemo—he just felt so sick all the time. He wouldn't even talk about it for the longest time. Every time I tried to bring it up, he shut me down. So I started going in around my work schedule to help out, and it became too much of a job to do part-time. I took a leave of absence from my engineering job, but I really waited too long—things were falling through the cracks and the business was losing money."

"How is your dad now? Is he okay?"

"He's still recovering from treatment." He turned back to her. "He's better. But he's not the same. He's really quiet now, like he's rethinking everything."

She had so many questions—what sort of business was it, what was falling through the cracks, what was his dad rethinking? But she remembered that he had said he had a big opportunity at his engineering job. "Wait . . . what about the satellite project?"

"Right." Jonah rolled on his side again, facing her. There was a different look in his eyes. Excitement. "They want me to lead it. It's a once-in-a-lifetime opportunity, but it would require time out of the country. NASA has a deep space communications facility outside of Madrid and I would be training and researching there for about six months."

"Jonah!" Harper sat up and pressed both hands against his chest. "That's amazing! Oh, I am so envious right now. Spain? Are you kidding? For *work*? How can you not take that job?"

"Because my family needs me. They have always needed me. Ever since my sister died, it feels like they are afraid of losing me, too. I don't know, I'm not trying to imply that Dad's illness and me helping out were because of my sister, but honestly, they've always felt a little helpless to me. Like they need me to approve of what they are doing. I don't know what to do. I mean, what would you do if your dad had cancer and they needed you at home?"

"For starters, my parents have never needed me. If anything, I was kind of in the way."

"I'm sure that's not true."

"Oh, it's true," she insisted. "Don't you worry that if you don't take this opportunity, you will regret it? That you won't have this chance again? Do you want to be on your death bed and think about the fantastic opportunity you had, that you let go to help with your mom-and-pop shop? Don't you believe you have to make your own way in the world, because in the end, you only have yourself?"

Jonah's brow rose. "Well, *that's* cynical. I hope I will be proud of myself for being there for my parents."

"You're right, it probably is cynical, and you should be proud of the man you are. But maybe it's also a little practical? Or maybe I'm just . . . I don't know, like I said, my parents have never needed me."

Jonah pushed himself up and put his back to the headboard. He touched his fingers to her cheek. "I don't know what is up with your parents, but that sounds really sad to me."

"It's not like that. I know they love me. But . . ." She didn't know how to explain how distant their relationship was. "I've always been a loner—I just pour myself into work and get gratification from that. I would love a new challenge and to see a new part of the world. To live there and really immerse myself."

"Still sounds lonely."

"People from close families always say that," she said, smiling. "But I find it fulfilling. Accomplishments are my jam."

He stroked her cheek again. "So what do you do anyway?"

Her job was not easy to explain, but it was easy to show. "Can I take you there? I have to swear you to secrecy, but I think it's pretty special." She laughed at herself. She was feeling so carefree. "I don't want to say too much because I really want to see your reaction. What do you say we go check it out, and then we can get pizza?"

Jonah leaned forward to kiss her. "That's not quite the dinner I had planned, but I would love to see this super-secret job of yours."

Twelve

Harper wouldn't give up any details as they headed south on Lamar. "You'll just have to wait and see," she said coyly, and laughed when he complained that two people who were obviously an item should not keep secrets from each other.

"We're an item!" she shouted out her car window.

"I'm crazy about this woman!" Jonah shouted out of his.

He held her hand between the seats, and it was all fun and games until she turned onto Congress Avenue and headed south. The Lucky Star was on South Congress Avenue. Call it intuition, but a hard knot formed in the pit of his belly. At first, Jonah thought it was some kind of joke. "Where are we going?"

"Hold your horses, cowboy. We're almost there." She pulled up to the light at Riverside and grinned at him. "*So* close."

Jonah tried to laugh, but it came out in a cough. The knot got harder. He tried to shake it off. "This is a really big buildup to your job. Why is it such a secret anyway?"

"Because my boss wants to make a big splash. We have a press release going out tomorrow. If I'd had my way, it would have gone out a week ago. I've told you a little about Soren. He's a bit out there with his beliefs."

Jonah shook his head. He had a bad feeling about this. But Harper seemed perfectly at ease.

She told him about Soren Wilder, and his weird habit of speaking with words that were completely made up or didn't fit the context. After that, he lost the thread. They were getting closer to the Lucky Star.

"Jonah?" She laughed. "You seem like you're a million miles away right now. What's wrong?"

"I'm just trying to guess where we're headed."

"Almost there." At Mary Street, she turned left. The barriers that Deja Brew had erected on the avenue yesterday to finish the signage had been moved back to the sidewalk. There was no doubt now what the new building would house—big, shiny gold letters with a steaming coffee cup separating the words DEJA BREW.

Harper pulled to the curb and turned a beaming smile to Jonah. "Are you surprised?"

Surprised and a little nauseous. He was fool enough to hope that he was just a bit carsick and not actually heartsick. "I am," he said.

"Hey." Her smile began to fade. "Are you okay?"

Jonah shifted his gaze to the building. "I'm fine. I'm just . . . confused."

"Be confused no more! What do you think?"

He didn't mean to be obtuse. "About what exactly?" He suddenly had the idea that she could be a sales rep of some sort. That she wasn't actually Deja Brew.

"The new Deja Brew Coffeehouse! I built it! I mean, *I* didn't build it, but I oversaw the building and outfitting of it. Wanna see?"

"Should we?" he asked faintly.

Harper poked him in the shoulder. "What's the matter? Nothing is going to jump out of the bushes and grab you, I promise. I built this place and can come and go as I please. Look, here is the key. Let's go see." She hopped out of the car.

Jonah got out, too. His legs felt wooden. He couldn't put it all together because he was buckling under his disappointment. It wasn't as if she'd done it on purpose. She hadn't picked up his phone then decided to quickly build Deja Brew to mess with him.

Harper slipped her hand into his and pulled him around to the glass door entrance. She unlocked the door, and held it open for Jonah. "You first."

He stepped hesitantly into the building, then walked to the middle of the room. He turned one full circle, taking in the shiny fixtures and high-end finishes before facing her again. "Harper, I—"

"Wait!" She was bubbly, excited. "Don't say anything until I show you everything. You're going to love it." She grabbed his hand and pulled him along. "So this is it! My super-secret project. Not *that* secret, really, since anyone driving by can figure it out. Anyway, I've been tasked with building and opening this store. And now I'm working on the grand opening. And if it goes well—and I know it will, because I have worked my butt off—and the store performs well at this site—which it absolutely should, because we did a lot of market research, and even though Starbucks is a few blocks away, there isn't another coffeehouse like this around here. Anyway, if it performs as we expect, I will be promoted to a new position." She was beaming as she looked around the room. "I'll be opening coffeehouses all over the country."

"Okay," Jonah said uncertainly. "Wow."

She gave him a funny look, obviously not understanding why he wasn't more enthusiastic. "I bet you've never seen a coffeehouse like this, right? What do you think?"

Jonah had to think of how to say this delicately. He put his hand on one of the suspended basket seats and pushed. It swung slowly, almost as if a breeze had rustled it. He looked up to see how it was anchored. "I think this place is very cool. Very hip. Exactly the sort of place that does well in Austin."

"Right?" She beamed with pleasure. "This is going to blow every other coffeehouse within five miles out of the water. At least, I hope it does. I feel confident that we have a decent chance of drawing the Starbucks clientele."

That wasn't the only clientele she had a decent chance of drawing.

She walked behind the counter and pointed at a machine. "Check this out. It's a Sanremo Opera volumetrics espresso machine. Dual pump. That probably means nothing to you, but it's a top-line coffee maker. Soren saw this coffee machine in Switzerland and had to have it. They don't get any better than this."

"Dual pump, huh?" He stared at the machine. He didn't even know what that meant exactly.

"Yep. I've become a bit of a coffee machine geek. Oh, and look over here." She showed him the small bar for evening alcoholic drinks, and the compact kitchen area. She took him back into the main seating area to the egg baskets. "Try it!"

Jonah sat. They swung silently for a moment, twisting a little that way, then this way.

"I haven't shown you the library!" She popped out of her egg basket and walked to the library shelves. She gestured to them like Vanna White.

Jonah stood up, too, and came to have a look. "So people just find a book they like and walk off with it?"

"If they walk off with one or don't come back with it, we'll replace them."

"Is that cost-effective?" he asked curiously.

"Not entirely," she admitted. "But the books are very popular and our philosophy is that the benefit of drawing customers outweighs the loss of a few books purchased at wholesale. Surprisingly, most people bring them back. Want to see the garden? Oh look! The lights in the courtyard were hung yesterday."

She hurried to the glass doors and flipped a switch. Suddenly, a dozen little white umbrellas appeared to be floating gently to earth. The effect was really nice. It was a cozy outdoor space that could be used year-round, which would be a big draw.

Harper was talking about the menu. The locally sourced ingredients from farms such as JB Gardens, the vegan options, the keto options, the Tiny Pies.

He nodded dumbly. "What about your coffee beans?" he asked, his gaze on the coffee machine.

"Fair trade, of course. Mostly sourced from Brazil and Colombia." Her smile was waning—she kept looking at him with a worried expression. He was trying, he really was, but his thoughts were spinning like so many tops. He wanted to be over the moon for her, but he kept thinking of what this meant for the Star.

She finished the tour at the front windows, where they had installed cushioned window seats, six of them, separated by hanging panels of etched glass.

Jonah traced the peace sign that had been carefully etched into one panel. "It seems like you thought of everything."

Harper beamed. "I really hope so. I've worked hard to make this place a unique experience."

"It really shows."

"Okay," Harper said, throwing up her hands. "You're being really weird about this, Jonah, and I don't understand why."

"I'm sorry." He *was* sorry. He didn't have much of a poker face. "I don't mean to be a jerk. It's obvious you've put in a lot of hard work, and it's a very cool place. I'm just trying to absorb it."

Harper frowned. "Okay."

Jonah put his hands on her arms and tried again. "I'm really impressed, Harper. I am. I'm happy for you, too. But . . . do you see that?" He pointed out the window. She followed his gaze to the squat building across the street. The blue-and-white neon sign read, THE LUCKY STAR COFFEE SHOP, and beneath that, PREMIUM QUALITY

BEANS. The sign was bordered with little coffee cups, and curlicues rose out of each one to indicate steam. The door was weathered, and the windows too small to let much natural light in. There was the stack of small Christmas trees piled next to the door and a rusted bike rack on the curb that was sitting lopsided.

"What about it?"

"You said there weren't any coffeehouses around here."

"But that's an old-timey diner. It's not a coffeehouse. That's the kind of place where the coffee sits on the burner all day and gets that weird taste."

"What? That's not true. Have you been in there?"

"No." She looked at him. "But you can just tell. Are you worried about that place? It won't be any competition for us, if that's what you're thinking."

He couldn't fault her for saying so—that was his assumption, too. "You're right, it probably won't. But it doesn't help when this ginormous coffeehouse"—he put finger quotes around *coffeehouse*—"blocks the street on a Saturday to hang its sign and no one can get into the parking lot of that little place."

Harper's brows knit. "I am so confused. Why are you making a big thing out of that diner? Do you go there or something?"

"It's not a diner, it's a coffee shop. A dated coffee shop, I will grant you, but it is a *coffee* shop."

"Okay," she said defensively, throwing up her hands in surrender. "It's a coffee shop."

Jonah suddenly sighed to the ceiling and shoved his hands in the pockets of his jeans. He was going about this all wrong. "I am worried that the old coffee shop will be no competition for you—but you will be great competition for it."

She looked across the street at the Lucky Star Coffee Shop again, and the windows that still bore painted Christmas scenes. A snowy hill dotted with Christmas trees in one window. A reindeer leaping in another, and of course, Santa with his bag of toys slung over his shoulder in the last. She shrugged helplessly. "I don't know. Not necessarily. I guess it depends on what type of business they have, doesn't it?" She turned away from the window. "When we opened our store in North Austin, Summer Moon had to move its location to Burnet Road."

Jonah's brows dipped. "And that's okay with you?"

"Is it *okay* with me?" She dragged her fingers through her hair. "It's not *okay* with me. I mean, I feel bad for them if that's what you're asking. But we live in a capitalist society, and people vote with their dollars."

"Vote with their . . ." His voice trailed away. "What about the people who work there?"

"Jonah . . . this is starting to feel like some weird morality test. I don't know what you want me to say. It's always been survival of the fittest when it comes to business. Particularly this kind of business. It's supply and demand, and I'm not saying it won't survive, I'm saying it depends on a lot of things. But *this* coffeehouse," she said, gesturing grandly to the store they were standing in, "is the one that concerns me."

He looked across the street. "You know what's so funny? I've been saying the very same thing."

"To who? About what? Will you please tell me what is happening right now?"

"I'm sorry." He touched her cheek. "I'm being a jerk."

"Yeah, you kind of are."

His gaze moved over her gorgeous face, her hair falling around her shoulders. He thought of the magic of tonight and still couldn't believe this had happened to them. That he would meet the first woman to excite him in such a unique way and she would be his competition. It was unfathomable. "Okay, here goes. I'm helping my parents out, right?"

She nodded.

"A family business that we've had for generations. My grandparents, and then my parents, and my aunt and uncle, and my cousins. All of us have a stake in it."

"Okay."

He pointed to the Lucky Star. "That's the business."

It seemed almost as if Harper was on some sort of time delay. It took a few moments of blinking and gaping at him, as if the words had landed in her brain and were struggling to arrange themselves in some meaningful order. She slowly turned her head to look at the Lucky Star with its cheerful holiday window displays. She didn't seem to be breathing. "Harper?"

"*That* is your parents' business? When you said mom-and-pop, I thought you meant a bodega!"

"Yeah, well, I thought you were a financial advisor. When I said mom-and-pop, I meant a small, family-owned business. A mom-and-pop coffee shop."

She gaped at him, wide-eyed. "You thought I was a *financial advisor*? How did you get that idea? I work for StreetSweets!"

"*Who?*"

"StreetSweets! It's a company that specializes in upscale food trailers and coffeehouses. Your *parents* own the Lucky Star?"

He nodded. "My life has been spent in that coffee shop."

"Oh my *God*." She stacked her hands on top of her head and turned away from the window. "How could this have happened?"

"I'm asking myself the same thing," Jonah muttered. "How in the hell."

"This is bad," Harper said.

Jonah pulled one of her hands off her head and held it. "Listen, Harper. Deja Brew is a great place. You've done an amazing job—it's innovative and it's going to be a huge hit. You should be proud."

"Thank you. I *am* proud. But . . . but I don't know what to say. What can I possibly say? No wonder you were acting so weird. I would be, too, if I were in your shoes. This is a disaster, Jonah!"

"It's not the greatest thing. I feel pretty certain you will put us out of business."

"No," she said, and looked to the window again. "Don't say that.

There has to be a solution." She looked at him, as if she was hoping he would suddenly have one and present it to her. "Right? We have to figure this out. I mean, everything is going so great."

"I know. And I hope there is a solution."

His answer deflated her. She faced the window. Jonah did, too, and they stood shoulder to shoulder, silently staring at the Lucky Star.

His disappointment was nauseating him. This was so unfair. He didn't know where to go from here, what that meant for either of them. But he didn't want to lose her over this. She glanced uncertainly at him. "Is this going to be a problem? I mean, it's a problem, obviously. But is it going to be a problem for us?"

He slid his arm around her shoulders, pulling her into his side, squeezing affectionately. "I'm crazy about you, remember? That hasn't changed one bit. This is just a weird coincidence."

"It's mind-blowing. But . . . can't there be room on this street for both of us?"

Jonah really wanted to believe that, but his head wasn't allowing it.

"Maybe?" Harper amended.

"Maybe."

One of the Christmas trees near the door of the Lucky Star rolled off the pile and onto the sidewalk.

She put her arm around his waist and leaned against him. "I'm so sorry, Jonah."

"Don't say that. We'll be fine. This will all be fine."

And then Jonah set about trying as hard as he could to believe those words.

Thirteen

How. *How?* How was it possible that the beautiful, unique woman he'd clicked with right away after a couple of years of not clicking with anyone could be behind Deja Brew? How was it that the woman he'd casually thought might be the one for him would also be the woman to put his family out of business?

"Un-freaking-believable," he muttered. He opened the door to his house, waved at Harper one last time. They'd decided to skip the pizza and call it a night, as the discovery had put a damper on the day. Personally, he needed to absorb the body blow of finding out he was in competition with her, with so much riding on the outcome for both.

He watched her pull away, then walked into his house.

He was so stupefied by the day that he forgot his huge, clumsy dog was waiting for him, and was assaulted by Truck's attempt to hug him and lick him at the same moment when he stepped through the door. When he managed to thwart the attempt to lick his face, Truck instead leaped in a big circle of glee, and sent all of this week's mail flying from the console, where Jonah had put it earlier. "Come on," he said, and grabbed a leash and strapped it onto Truck's collar.

He walked Truck down the street (or rather, they meandered along, as every bush and every crack in the sidewalk required serious investigation and a lifting of the leg) while Jonah tried to wrestle with the notion that Harper was Deja Brew.

On the one hand, he was still experiencing the glittery, bone-deep elation from having found someone with whom he'd connected right away, and of having some pretty amazing sex. On the other hand, he felt incredibly sad, as if he'd been robbed of it all. As if Deja Brew were a battle-ax that had crashed through the bubble he and Harper were living in.

He kept thinking about what she'd told him—how work always came first, how she lived her life, achieving a goal and moving on to the next. Her goal in making Deja Brew a success included the demise of the Lucky Star.

But that was irrational thinking, wasn't it? This thing with Harper wasn't *over*; there was no reason for it be *over*. She wasn't intentionally trying to put him out of business. No one could expect any relationship to be free of obstacles and some hardships. Things happened, worlds collided, paths intersected.

Maybe he was looking at this all wrong. He ought to think of this as a great proving ground for the two of them—if they could weather this, they could weather anything.

And then again, maybe not. Because this was one gigantic roadblock and he didn't have any idea how to hurdle it. Just continue seeing her all the while knowing that her store would probably hammer the last nail into the Star's coffin? Stop seeing her because of it? Was he being too pessimistic? Was there really no way to see this as a glass half full?

"Jesus, I'm making myself crazy," he said to Truck.

But even as he and Truck made their way around the block, he knew that there was one thing he was probably ninety percent certain about, and that was the financial impact of Deja Brew on the Lucky Star. Numbers didn't lie. The trend in daily receipts didn't lie. Deja Brew was going to end them if he didn't figure out how to turn things around and get more people in the door. Which meant he was going to have to root for the home team and hope his girlfriend lost.

She was his girlfriend, wasn't she?

Yes. She was. He didn't need to slap a label on them, but he was going to anyway. Harper Thompson was his girlfriend, the Lucky Star be damned.

Jonah spent a restless night that made him late to work the next morning. When he came in, Amy was behind the counter in blue-and-white-checked cat-eye frames and a purple pinafore. Her dark red hair was wound into two knots at the top of her head, which had the effect of making her look a little like Minnie Mouse.

"Well, well, well, look what the cat dragged in," she sang at him as he walked into the main dining room. She poured a cup of coffee and slid it across the counter to him.

Jonah gratefully took it. "Thank you and hello, Amy. How was your weekend?" He lifted his hand to Robert and Lloyd. They nodded. "Coffee good and hot today," Lloyd said, holding up his cup.

"My Saturday was fine. I had to work, but who cares," Amy said. "What we all want to know is how was *yours*?"

He sipped his coffee. It needed a little cream for his tastes. "Who is 'we all' and why do you ask?"

"Why do I ask?" she scoffed. "*You* had a date. *I* cleaned out the old fridge in the back room here."

He sipped again. "Do you have any cream back there?"

She picked up a pot of cream and set it on the counter. "You're being awfully coy."

"I'm not being coy."

"Jonah!" She reached across the counter and tried to swat him, but he dodged her. "You're *impossible*."

"Fine, all right, I had a great day." He smiled.

"You had a great day?" Jonah's mother entered the room from the kitchen. She had anchored her hair in a top bun and used it to hold her reading glasses. She was wearing a dark blue apron that was covered with what looked like flour. "Good morning, my beautiful, wonderful son."

"Hi, Mom."

"Jonah is dating someone," Amy said.

"Amy, for Chrissakes."

His mother's eyes lit up like they did when she'd had a bit of wine "with dinner." She stuck a pencil behind her ear, propped her elbows on the counter beside Amy, and fixed her son with a look. "You mean the person you dated once is now someone you are dating? Do tell, Joe."

"Okay. This?" Jonah said, gesturing between the two of them. "Is not going to happen. My life is not open to your casual perusal."

"When are we going to meet her?" Amy asked, as if he hadn't spoken. "Do we know her?"

"I have the very same question," his mother chimed in. "When and who and may I say how happy this makes me? I was about to give up my dream of grandchildren."

"Mom!" Jonah protested.

"I'm allowed to dream of them! So when are we going to meet her?"

"Oh, let's see," Jonah said, pretending to think about it. "Can't do it today, and Wednesday's no good. How about never?" He picked up his coffee cup and started for the office.

"Jo-Jo, don't go away mad," his mother called after him in a singsong voice. "We love you! We want to be part of your life! And we always love your girlfriends."

"Well," he heard Amy say behind him. "We didn't exactly love Megan."

Jonah stopped walking. He turned back and looked at his mother and Amy, still standing side by side. "What does *that* mean?"

"Nothing," his mother reassured him, and put her hand on Amy's arm. "It's just that Megan had a way about her."

This was the first he was hearing that Megan had any kind of "way" about her, and it confused him. "What way?"

His mother looked at Amy, who nodded encouragingly. Clearly, these two had discussed it. His mother said, "Just that there were times that she seemed to think her cotton was a little taller than it actually was."

Jonah had no idea what that meant and decided he wasn't going to ask. Megan was the last person he had to time to think about this morning. "And that, ladies, is why I'm not bringing anyone around here." He continued on to his office.

"You're so sensitive!" Amy called after him. "I thought you'd be in a better mood after your recreational Saturday!"

"Go to work, Amy!" he shouted back at her, and to Robert and Lloyd, he rolled his eyes. "Family."

"Got that right," Robert said.

In his office, Jonah locked the door in case Amy thought she might pop in to grill him. He tried to focus on work and the many problems he had to tackle. The price of coffee had skyrocketed, and either they were going to have to switch to an inferior brand or find a different supplier. Burt had chased off the last of the kitchen help. Burt was a good guy, and no one could throw together sandwiches and salads like he could. But he didn't like chitchat and he didn't like people who used their phones too much, which to a guy like Burt, was anytime other than an emergency phone call.

The truth was that Burt had done Jonah a favor. It was hard to keep staff in the kitchen under the best circumstances, as the jobs tended to be labor-intensive and paid only $10 an hour to start. Jonah would love to pay more, but until they started generating more business, they couldn't afford it. His mom was helping out in the kitchen for now, which was great. But his mother was not afraid of Burt, and chitchatted the day away, ignoring Burt's glower and not caring if he responded to her at all. Burt complained often to Jonah that his mother didn't listen, and thought she knew how to run a kitchen, and had Jonah hired him to cook, or what?

The situation had only gotten worse yesterday, apparently, when his mother and Aunt Belinda had proceeded with their idea of pie day. Which was par for the course—they never seemed terribly compelled to ever take his advice. They had made a bunch of pies to offer a free slice to anyone who came in for coffee. Jonah knew this because Amy had already posted it on the Facebook and Instagram accounts. Now Burt had two women in the kitchen with him and had sent Jonah a text this morning: We need to talk.

Jonah had called him on the way into work and had assured him they wanted and *needed* him to make the food. Jonah promised he would talk to his mother about her chattiness but warned Burt it wouldn't do any good. "She doesn't think she's chatty."

"Then she must be deaf," Burt had said crossly.

Jonah would talk to her, and his mother would try very hard to keep her comments to a minimum for a day or two, but she always slipped back into being her chatty self, and Burt slipped back into being his grumpy self, and Jonah was desperate to find someone to replace Mom before Burt quit.

There was also the issue of what they were going to do to get customers in the door. He couldn't imagine that the pie idea was sustainable for long, but he guessed they were going to give it a shot. He'd also thought about what Amy had suggested. There was no way he could compete with Deja Brew on the cool factor. So maybe they did need to cater to the other side of the coin. He'd toyed with the idea of putting a new burger on their limited menu that would rival any burger around. He made a note to talk to Burt about it.

His phone pinged and Jonah picked it up—a photo of his Christmas trees was on his screen. They had been scattered up and down Mary Street.

Another text popped up from Harper. Hey over there at the Lucky Star! I don't know if you are aware, but someone trashed your Christmas tree pile. I have a guy here who is carting some things off for me and he can drop them off at the city recycling program if you like. Lemme know.

"What?" Jonah tried to stride out of his office (he was hampered by forgetting he'd locked himself in, and he slammed into the door when it didn't open with a yank), and went into the dining room. Robert and Lloyd had gone, so he leaned across their usual table, craning his neck to see down the street. "Jesus," he mumbled. Someone really had scattered the trees.

"What are you looking at?"

Uncle Marty had wandered into the dining room and leaned over the table, too, spotting the Christmas trees. "Well, now, that's unfortunate." He squinted at the mess. "We better get that cleaned up before the city code inspector drives by and dings us. I'd say it's going to cost us. Remind me again, what did these trees run us? Two fifty?"

Jonah snorted. He wished. "Three twenty-five." He was never going to live down those trees.

"Ooh boy. Well, we better go and round them up," Marty said.

On the sidewalk they could see that the culprit had spread the trees much farther than they'd been able to see out the window, covering about three blocks. "Great," Jonah spat. "Just *great*."

"Hey!"

Jonah and Marty turned at the same time to see Harper jogging across the street from Deja Brew. She hopped up onto the curb and waved as if maybe they hadn't seen her. As if nothing had happened yesterday. Jonah wished she didn't look so delectable in her slim black pants, her boxy pink sweater, and her hair in a high ponytail.

"Who's that?" Marty asked as she strode toward them.

"A friend," Jonah said.

Harper was beaming at Jonah when she reached them. "I caught you!" She shifted her green-eyed gaze to Marty. "Harper Thompson."

"Marty Rogers."

She shook his hand. "A pleasure."

His uncle didn't let go of her hand right away, and Jonah thought he was going to have to reach over and push his eyes back into their sockets.

"Looks like you've got yourself a tree problem," she said.

"Yep. It's number one on today's list of problems."

"It's not my nephew's fault," Marty said. "He was trying to be creative and get people to stop in. He had the idea to sell them to apartment dwellers." He gestured loosely in the direction of some of the newer apartment complexes that had popped up along the avenue.

"That's okay, Uncle Marty—"

"We all thought for sure they'd stop in for a coffee and a tree on their way home from work, but the truth is, we didn't get many takers." Marty gave a shake of his head. "Can't figure it out."

"You'd think people would like the convenience," Harper said.

"Wouldn't you? I've got a theory—"

"I think she gets the picture, Uncle Marty," Jonah said before his uncle outlined the book he apparently intended to write about the debacle. He had a *theory*?

"I sure do," Harper said. "It was an interesting idea."

She was being kind, but he felt a little like a moron. She probably had a list as long as his arm of great promotional ideas, and nowhere on that list was *sell Christmas trees*.

She looked up the street. "Wow, whoever did this must have been determined to cause some mayhem. Just untying the bundle of them must have been a job, right?"

"They weren't tied," Uncle Marty announced. He looked at Jonah. "I guess we didn't have enough rope?"

Okay, so Jonah hadn't tied them together. It had not occurred to him that someone would want to come along and scatter them up and down the street, and he did not care to stand on the sidewalk and rehash all his bad decisions that involved Christmas trees, so he said, "You said you have someone who can haul them to Zilker Park to the tree recycling?"

"Yep. He's one of our guys, and he's picking up a few things today. We were looking at your trees and he mentioned that he had plenty of room. Shall I send him over?"

Jonah just imagined the conversation across the street. Were they sitting in the egg basket seats, swinging back and forth while they discussed what a pity his trees were? Did they laugh while they drank their fancy coffee? "Thank you, Harper. That would be great."

"There's a stroke of luck," Marty said. "We didn't know what we were going to do with all these damn trees. Been fretting over it for days."

Jonah tried to shoot the universal *shut up* look to his uncle, but like all the septuagenarians he knew, Marty didn't notice.

"I'll tell him right now." Harper slipped her hand into her pocket, but then quickly snapped her fingers. "I forgot my phone across the street. I'll send him in, what, a half hour? Does that give you enough time to pick them up?"

"I don't know," Marty said, peering around Jonah. "Might want to give us forty-five. They look to be spread *way* on down the street."

Could the crack in the sidewalk just open up now and allow Jonah to drop into the earth's fiery center?

"I'll let him know. Oh, hey—I wanted to let you guys know about an event." She reached in her pocket and withdrew a rolled-up sheet of green paper. She handed it to Uncle Marty.

Jonah didn't ask what sort of event. He was feeling completely conspicuous right now. In way over his head. She was a professional in this game and he was merely playing like he was. "Thank you," he said again. "I really am grateful for the offer." He would have had to rent a truck to haul these things off, just adding to the cost of his failed experiment.

"Very nice to meet you, Mr. Rogers," Harper said.

"You just call me Marty," he said with a wave of his big hand. "Nice to meet you, too, little lady. Come on over anytime. We're one big happy family over here at the Lucky Star."

Jonah didn't want to look too closely, but he thought his uncle, who was suddenly talking like John Wayne, was blushing a little.

"I'll do that." She turned to check the traffic, then darted across the street again.

"*Well*," Marty said. "She's a looker." His gaze was still on Harper as she disappeared inside Deja Brew. He slowly turned toward Jonah. "Just when was it you got the chance to meet the girl from a business that's not even open?"

"Ran into her," Jonah said vaguely. He would eventually need to explain him and Harper of Deja Brew, but at the moment, they had some trees to pick up. "Let's do this."

It was with Lloyd's help, who had come back for a free piece of pie—his second, because they had not established rules about people who stopped by several times in a day—that they managed to get the trees stacked just when a Penske truck pulled up at the curb. A thin, dark-haired young man hopped out and strode around to the back to lift the cargo door. "You Jonah?"

"Yep."

"Marco. Harper sent me."

"Really appreciate this, man."

Marco shrugged like it was no sweat off his back to haul a dozen unsold Christmas trees. And then he had to add insult to injury by picking up four trees at a go while Jonah could only manage two.

Marco worked quickly around him. Jonah was seriously considering telling him that he was an aerospace engineer, that everyone had their strengths. But the trees were loaded, and Marco pulled the cargo door down. "Anything else you need me to haul away?"

Just his damn pride, but he'd need a bigger truck for that. "No. Thanks again."

"No problem," Marco said. He gave Jonah a peace-out sign, hopped in the truck, and drove away.

Jonah went back into the store. It was just after noon, and there was a sum total of four customers. The crossword game he'd been so proud of was empty—no one had attempted to fill a single letter in. With a grim shake of his head, he started back to the office, but he noticed his family gathered at one end of the counter. They were all bent over something. In spite of his foul mood, his curiosity got the best of him, and Jonah walked up to the group. "What's going on?"

Jonah's mom held up the sheet of green paper Harper had handed Uncle Marty. "They're having a grand opening."

"Who?"

"Deja Brew."

"We were just talking to that gal," Marty said.

"What gal?" Belinda asked.

"The Deja Brew gal."

"Let me see?" Jonah asked, reaching for the paper. His mother handed it to him, and he read the announcement:

Please Join Us!

Grand Opening of South Congress Deja Brew!

*Sample local vendors with options presented
for vegan, keto, and Paleo.*

*Featured vendors include delectables from
Tiff's Treats and Tiny Pies!*

Complimentary frappes!

With Special Musical Appearance by
Suzanna in our dog-friendly garden!

Amy suddenly shoved him. "*Suzanna!*" she shout-whispered. "I *love* her."

"Is that good?" Belinda asked.

"It's *great*. For them," Amy said.

The six of them turned as one toward the shop windows, staring out at the emblazoned DEJA BREW sign across the street.

"Amy?" One of the patrons seated at a plain wooden two-top table raised his hand.

"Be right there!" Amy called back.

"What are we going to do?" Jonah's mother whispered.

"We're going to go, that's what," his father said.

They all looked with surprise at Roy. Jonah's dad was a steady presence, but rarely spoke up unless the situation involved finances. Jonah's personal theory was that he'd learned over the years that his wife was going to say everything that needed saying. And since he'd been sick, he said even less. That he had an opinion about the grand opening was unexpected.

"We *are*?" Jonah's mom asked, sounding suspicious.

"Yes. All of us."

"You're going to have to explain yourself, Roy. Why do we want to go to the grand opening of our competition?"

"Excuse me, Amy?" the customer tried again.

"Hold on," Amy said to him, holding up a finger. "I don't want to miss this."

"Really?" Jonah asked her with a withering look.

Amy waved him off. "That's Arnie Messer. He'll wait." She turned back to Jonah's dad. "Yeah, why are we going?"

"The Lucky Star has survived in this town for seventy years. If that is the thing that's going to do us in, let's see what it is. Always know your executioner."

Belinda wrinkled her nose. "*That's* some disturbing advice."

Jonah's father pointed at the paper Jonah still held. "It says dog friendly. Why don't we bring Truck?"

Amy gasped. "You wouldn't!"

"*Roy,*" his mother said . . . but she was giggling. So were Belinda and Marty.

"Oh my God. Are we in kindergarten?" Jonah asked them all.

Apparently, they were, because all of them were giggling at the idea of Truck rambling around that fancy new coffeehouse. "Show of hands," his dad said, and five hands instantly shot up.

"Amy, come on," the customer said.

"I'm coming, Arnie, I'm coming," Amy called back. But she didn't move. They were all looking at Jonah. He looked back across the street. He didn't want to ruin Harper's night, but at the same time . . . she was going to ruin his, wasn't she? He slowly raised his hand.

"That's my boy," his father said, grinning. "That's the Rogers spirit in you, you know. We get it from our distant cousin, Roy Rogers."

"We are not related," Jonah's mother said wearily, as if she'd said it a thousand times.

"You don't know that," his dad shot back.

Jonah looked across the street. He thought he saw Harper inside, staring back at him.

Fourteen

Jonah seemed a little . . . distant. He had since they had discovered they were running shops across the street from each other.

He wasn't doing anything obvious, but Harper felt like he wasn't completely present when they were together. Obviously, he'd been thrown for a loop, just as she had been.

Or maybe she was just seeing his work face. Everyone had a work face, as Harper had once explained to Olivia. "People adopt a persona and go to work, and they may not have that same persona in real life."

"Ridiculous," Olivia had declared. "My face is always my face."

"Your face is always a work face. You have a beautiful face and you use it to get interviews."

Olivia smiled with delight. "You're right! I do."

Anyway, Harper wanted to put her and Jonah back on track. She wanted that more than she wanted to breathe. What surprised her was just how badly she wanted it. It had been a while since she'd been in a relationship, obviously, but still, this was the point in their dating life she was certain he would find out she had a prettier friend, or she was too driven, or she color-coded too many things, and she would have to detach before he dumped her. Olivia had once opined that her parents had convinced her no one wanted her around. Harper had said that wasn't true, but she privately wondered if maybe there was some truth to it. She was always the first to pack up and go.

She desperately did not want to do that here. This thing with Jonah felt very different, and very real, and she'd never felt so urgent about someone in her life.

But what to do about it? She stewed about it a lot, and today, she stewed about it all the way to her office in the Domain.

When she walked into the offices, she immediately noticed that Kendal had rearranged the reception area. The two waiting chairs— leather and chrome and not very inviting—had been placed at angles to each other so that anyone sitting in them could carry on a chat. The chairs were separated by a round end table that sported a large vase of fresh-cut flowers. On the ottoman between the chairs was a decorative tray that was filled with magazines. Kendal had also installed a blue rug over the industrial blue carpet in the seating area. It looked like someone's idea of a reading nook.

She glanced at Kendal sidelong. He was doing his best not to look at her. "This looks pretty cozy. Is it for your coffee klatch?"

"If I had a coffee klatch, I'd be happy to meet there. But I don't. Sounds like that's more your speed."

"If your goal is to create an inviting seating area, you need different chairs. You know what? We should put some egg baskets in here. It's kind of our thing."

Kendal raised his head. "Interesting you should mention that. I've already ordered them. These chairs are placeholders," he said crisply. "Soren wants to talk to you."

Harper suddenly realized why the idea of Kendal bothered her so much: he was her in male form. He was taking on things no one had asked him to do, striving for recognition. *Damn.* It was like competing with herself.

Harper walked on to Soren's office, the scent of incense growing stronger and stronger the closer she came to his door. It was a pity StreetSweets was too small to have a bona fide HR department, because she would have made an anonymous complaint. She knocked on the door.

"Namaste. Enter," Soren called from inside.

Harper opened the door and was hit with the scent of patchouli so strong that she coughed. Her eyes began to water. Soren was on the floor, stretched out on one side, propped up by a pillow. He was leafing through glossy photos.

He glanced up at her and pushed his scraggly hair from his face. "Come, Harper, and observe the lavish affluence of our opportunity."

"Come again?"

He gestured lazily for her to take a seat on the cushion beside him. With a grimace, she lowered herself to the ground. More than once, she'd suggested to Soren that having people sit on cushions in professional settings was maybe not the most professional thing to do, and he told her that she exhibited an overly controlled line of thought about pillows.

"I have before me the aesthetic presentation of our destiny." He spread the eleven-by-fifteen photos across the carpet so that she could see them. They appeared to be the interior of a restaurant. The chairs were wing-backed and upholstered in leather. The tables, none of them bigger than seating for two, were made of highly polished wood. The fixtures, all brass, reminded her of a fancy steak house.

"What place is this?"

"This place is not a place, but a prototype."

"A prototype of . . . ?"

"The coffee bistro I have designed."

The coffee bistro? When Harper thought of bistros, she thought of something a little more relaxed in feel. "This looks like a steak house. You've designed a steak house bistro."

Soren laughed. He pushed himself up and sat cross-legged before her and spread his hands wide in a *see-what-I've-done* manner.

"I'm serious. I thought the plan was to open upscale coffee bistros."

"This *is* a bistro. But it's a new way of looking at a bistro. Why should we expect tablecloths and sharp knives and rich interiors from a steak house, but not a bistro? We have to be on the cutting edge, Harper. The arbitrary forces that affect our lives could be consumed by serendipity if we don't."

"Soren, that makes no sense." She did not have the patience to pick her way through his strange vocabulary to understand what was happening now.

But Soren smiled as if she were a precocious child who was asking who ate the moon. "Allow me to present you with something that makes sense. The young shall lead us, and you may be the person to lead us to the promised land."

She almost gasped. This was it! She was getting the promotion. Of *course* she was getting it. Look at what she'd set up at the South Congress store! Look at the grand opening she had planned! Who *wouldn't* give her the job? "Really?" she asked, delighted. "What will my title be?"

"Executive vice president."

"Oh wow!" She clapped her hands. "I can't believe it!" She stacked her hands over her heart. "I've worked so hard for this!"

"You have indeed. And you are most certainly one of the top contenders for the post."

Harper's smile faded. "Not *the* top contender?" she asked, and for one tiny breath of a moment, she believed Soren was going to say that of course she was the top contender, that she'd misunderstood him.

But he did not say that. He moved his head side to side, as if mull-ing it over. "I have not as yet felt the right energy in a decision about you. Therefore, I am considering many things. I plan to open two bistros at once. The properties have been purchased. The architect will arrive in Austin at the end of the month."

"You bought *two* properties? But I thought we were going to scout a property together."

Soren shrugged.

Harper smelled a rat. When exactly had he scouted these properties? "Where are these two places?"

"Rochester, Minnesota. And Cary, North Carolina."

Neither were cities that Harper would have chosen off the top of her head, and certainly were not cities Soren had ever mentioned. Her eyes narrowed. "When did you say you visited these cities?"

Soren sighed. "During the season of pagan ritual and religious pageantry."

"You mean the week I was in Houston."

Soren put his hands together in prayer pose and bowed.

Kendal, that weasel. No wonder he'd been so vague about his holiday. He'd gone in Harper's place. "May I ask why you chose that week to go visit two cities we never discussed?"

"Are they not interesting prospects? Are they not inventive convention? The cities are perfect for testing the bistros, and if successful, we will roll out four more to larger markets."

"That's going to take a *lot* of cash up front, Soren. Where are we going to get that kind of money?"

"Ah, you've struck on the challenge of inventive innovation."

"It's the challenge of finding investors. Do you have any lined up?"

Soren hopped nimbly to his feet. "I have ideas, Harper. The garden of my mind is verdant and lush. But the task of bringing investors will be another aspect of the work you may perform."

Wait a minute—Harper had envisioned running things, not funding them.

She had to roll on her hands and knees to get up off the floor and hated Soren even more because of it. "Just one thing," she said before Soren could flit off to another topic.

"Life is never one *thing*, Harper. Life is a series of spiritual journeys."

Whatever, Soren. "This job, this . . . new vision looks like there is a lot of advance work involved. What is keeping you from promoting me now? Deja Brew on Congress is about to open. You like what you've seen so far. What more are you waiting to see? I've worked for you for four years now—surely you know whether or not I'm capable."

"It is true I like what I've seen, my fair girl, but the *operation* is where the tropical plant latex may come into contact with the path to prosperity."

Could he not just once say *where the rubber meets the road* like normal people?

"And to reiterate, you're not the only candidate."

"But I should be," she said boldly. "Veronica is very clearly where she wants to be. I know, because I asked her. And Kendal is . . . an administrator?"

Soren looked as if her confusion about Kendal's exact title confused him. "Harper . . . what sort of custodian of creativity would I be if I didn't encourage all of the gifted to join us? My job is not to lead, but to encourage growth."

"*Oh my God*," she muttered in frustration.

"Now." Soren picked up his phone and typed into it. "Kendal will provide the prospectus I've been inspired to create for your review and input. You'll need to have read it by the time the architect comes to town. I'll be critiquing the breadth and depth of your imagination."

"Had I known that—"

She didn't finish her thought, because the door opened, and Kendal bustled inside. Harper looked at him and he looked at Harper. "*Hello*, Kendal. I hear you had a great holiday."

Kendal smiled faintly. "It was not my idea."

She didn't know if she believed that or not. "Where is the prospectus? I look forward to reading it."

"Perhaps you ought to look forward to viewing it instead," Soren suggested, and chuckled, clearly pleased with himself. "Kendal?"

Kendal whipped his phone from his pocket and began tapping. "I am forwarding it to your e-mail now."

"*Great*. That's just *great*." Harper stepped around Kendal and went out, her heart thudding with each step she took. It was plainly obvious to her that if she was going to win this promotion, she was going to have to pull out all the stops. She did not intend to lose to Kendal. She could do this! She was an overachiever, she excelled at everything she did, and this wasn't going to be the time she didn't, damn it.

By all rights, this job should be hers to lose. How was she losing it? Was this happening because she was a woman? She considered it, but shook her head. Soren was many things, but he'd never given her the sexist vibe. He tended to think they were all equal creatures of the universe, right down to the nasty crickets that appeared all over town in the fall.

It was far more likely that this was some philosophical exercise that had to do with the development of the executive's mindset or some such nonsense.

In her office, she angrily tried to wave off the scent the incense had left on her clothes, which smelled like wet soil. She sat heavily behind her desk and pulled out her phone. She opened the file Kendal had sent her. The picture on the video icon was of Soren seated on his blasted cushion, his hands in prayer pose, his head bowed. Harper stopped the video and turned her phone facedown on her desk. She shifted her gaze to the window and stared out at the familiar WHOLE FOODS sign just below their offices. *Minnesota? North Carolina?* She wondered what her parents would think if she moved across the country. They wouldn't care, she already knew that. They would say, "Oh, wonderful! What a great opportunity," and plan another trip. The only person who would care would be Olivia.

She tried to picture losing her promotion to Kendal. What would she do if Soren passed her up? Would she stay with StreetSweets? She couldn't imagine that she would. She then tried to picture herself in another job. She'd invested so much into this one. What would her goals be? She had to have goals. If she didn't have goals, who was she?

And then she tried to imagine herself without Jonah.

Nope. Not to be borne. She couldn't think about it, not for a second. She wouldn't allow herself to think about his opportunity in Spain. She just wanted things to go back to the way they had been before he found out about Deja Brew. She could really use something happy right now. She wanted to see Jonah, to figure out how to turn this situation between them around.

She picked up her phone and pulled up the text box. Hey! I'm thinking of running later. Would you be interested?

A couple of moments passed, and her phone pinged. Please choose one:

-I'm thinking of running a few miles later.

-I'm thinking of running out of money later.

-I'm thinking of running a fever later.

She smiled. I'll take running a few miles for $500, Alex.

The three dots appeared, and then, $500? Then I've been running with the wrong crowd. Nyuk. Nyuk. I will have to bring my very bad dog.

Great. We can watch him chase dicks.

They arranged a time to meet after work. But Harper couldn't sit here with Kendal and Soren just outside her door for another two hours. She knew what she needed to do to cheer herself up.

At the ACC, Cinder was surprised to see her. "Hey, you're here during the week! Bob will be so happy to see you. No one walked him today."

"What? No way!" Harper couldn't imagine coming to the ACC and not choosing Bob to walk.

"Let me get him for you," Cinder said after she'd checked Harper in. She disappeared into the back and returned a few minutes later with the bulldog. He marched out as if he'd been waiting for her all day and was mad she was late. When she leaned down to pet him, he growled and turned his head. Harper reached again, and Cinder gasped. "Be careful!"

"It's fine. He's just mad," Harper said, and petted the stubborn dog. After a few seconds, Bob glanced up at her. His bottom teeth were jutting out. He would never admit it, but he liked a good scritch of the ears. "I'm sorry no one walked you today," she murmured. Bob licked her hand. Not once, but twice.

They had an understanding.

She and Bob set out in the opposite direction of the alley behind the donut shop. Bob didn't seem to mind today. As they walked, she told Bob about her day. "I know you don't care," she said, "but this has been a very shitty day. Until now." Bob grunted once or twice as she talked, but mostly he was interested only in the path before him.

Harper stopped at the greenbelt like they always did. But this time, Bob didn't crawl under the bench. This time he sat and leaned against her leg. It was a first. "Wow," Harper said. She bent down and caressed his head. "Don't think I didn't notice. I guess you were listening after all."

Bob slid down onto his belly and sighed loudly. They sat together for fifteen or twenty minutes, together and silent, each lost in their own thoughts.

Eventually, they made their way back to the ACC, and Harper told Cinder about Bob leaning against her.

"Really?" Cinder sounded amazed. "I don't know why you don't adopt him. You obviously adore him."

"I can't," Harper said. "I work really long hours and I live in a tiny apartment. Bob wouldn't be happy."

"Hmm," Cinder said. "People always think that, but it's funny how these things work themselves out."

Not for her. If things went her way, she'd be moving soon anyway.

Harper said goodbye to Bob, who was already pointed away from her, straining at the leash, wanting to return to his crate. "See you Saturday!" she called after him. She turned and walked out of the gate, passing the gazebo, where people waited for their dog walking assignments. The King Mutt poster caught her eye and Harper paused. What if . . .

The idea floated into her head. "Nah," she said to herself. "How much trouble would that be while opening a new store?"

Olivia called her as she drove to meet Jonah at the trail entrance under the Loop 1 Bridge. "Hi, Olivia."

"Don't sound so excited. Where are you and what are you doing?"

"I'm . . . actually I'm about to go for a run. Can I call you back?" She pulled into street parking and glanced around for Jonah's truck. She didn't see it.

"No. You can talk to me while you run because you didn't call me back like you promised the other day."

"Did I promise? No matter, I promise now I will call you back, but I can't talk and run because, a, I am not that coordinated and, b, I need to breathe."

Olivia was silent for a minute. "Is something going on with you?"

"What?" Harper laughed too loud. "No!"

"Really? Because you sound super weird, like you're hiding something."

"Nothing is *weird*, Livvie." She saw Jonah's truck coast into a spot under the bridge.

"I know what it is. You think I don't, but I do. You hooked up with that totally random phone guy, didn't you?"

Harper barked a laugh of surprise as she got out of her car. Truck was straining on his leash, and it looked like Jonah was having to use all his strength to hold him. "Olivia! He's not random, he's Jonah. And I really can't talk right now—"

"Just yes or no, Harper. Let me know that much."

"I promise I'll call but I—"

"Yes or no!" Olivia shouted.

"Yes!" Harper shouted back, and with a laugh, she ended the call and slid the phone into her pocket. It began to vibrate against her leg, but she let it go, because Truck had reached her, leaving a swath of slobber across her running tights as he sniffed out the phone. "Truck!" she cried, and bent down to hug the dog's neck.

"I am so sorry," Jonah said, and kissed her. "He's so bad."

"He's perfect." She smiled as she reached up to knock some of Jonah's dark hair from his brow. "It's so great to see you."

"You too."

With her hand, she shaded her face from the late afternoon sun, assessing him. "Are you still crazy about me?"

He smiled. "I'm still crazy about you." He pulled her in for a deeper kiss. But Truck was straining again, his nose moving over Harper's legs like she was made of mutton, whimpering like a baby, and Jonah let her go.

"What is the matter with him?" Jonah asked.

"Oh . . . I went to see Bob today."

Jonah pulled Truck off her leg. "And how is good ol' Bob?"

"Grouchy."

"This one will be, too, if we don't get started. Ready?"

They began to jog, but were soon running to keep up with that enormous, exuberant dog. Harper was grateful that Truck stopped to mark his territory every so often, because that was the only way she could keep up with Jonah. In spite of the pace, they managed to talk, and Harper's job woes melted away from her. They talked about their favorite episode of *The Office*, how hungry they were for good, greasy burgers, and how they couldn't wait to take a dip in Barton Springs when the weather was a little warmer.

They talked about sports, and the new smoothie place by campus, the homeless camping ban the city had just passed, and the lineup of music at South by Southwest, which would be happening in a few weeks. Everything they discussed was easy and fun and they thought the same way and they laughed at the same things, and Harper still couldn't believe that she'd lucked into this man. That they were in competition seemed like a distant dream.

When they'd finished their run, Jonah said he had to go. "I have to finish some paperwork tonight and I know I won't be good company. But this has been fun. I needed it." He wrapped his arms around her waist and drew her in.

"Me too," she agreed, and as he bent his head to kiss her, she decided that there was nothing wrong, that everything was as perfect with Jonah as it had been before she ever took him to Deja Brew. That and all the foreboding she'd been feeling the last couple of days were silly. Everything was awesome. Or as Soren might say, everything was formidably sublime.

She just wished she could ignore that tiny seed of doubt.

Fifteen

Everything was *not* awesome, at least not on the Lucky Star side of the street.

Jonah had spent the last couple of days going over their expenses, squeezing the proverbial blood from the turnip. But there was only so much squeezing he could do and he made the painful determination they were going to have to let go of Paula, their part-time morning server. He didn't think she'd be surprised—the Star simply didn't have enough business to justify paying her, especially when there were five members of the Rogers family milling about every day. They could easily cover her work.

Also, it looked like he was going to have to break his promise to Burt. They couldn't afford a part-time kitchen assistant. Burt was going to have to keep working with Mom. Burt was not going to like it. Neither was his mother.

Mixed in with his anxiety of how to make the Lucky Star work, they all kept an eye on Deja Brew. Amy reported seeing the coffee delivery come, and how she could smell the roast across the street.

Uncle Marty had been cleaning off the painted Christmas pictures and had noticed the Tiny Pies van pull up and unload its wares. Artwork arrived, and so did books. The Little Stacy Book Club had peeked in the windows of Deja Brew and reported that the titles were recent bestsellers. They were excited about that little library.

This business was maddening as hell. Jonah wondered what Grandpa and Grandma had seen in a coffee shop. Maybe things had been vastly different back then, but from where Jonah sat, it seemed like his family had been riding along on the Lucky Star's make-or-break teeter-totter his entire life. One year was good, the next one depressing. Up and down, up and down—give him aerospace engineering any damn day. Jonah would much prefer to think about velocity and astrodynamics and propulsions than how to pay staff and where to cut corners. Here, there were too many people to consider, too many feelings to be hurt, too many sleepless nights agonizing about the bottom line.

But on the other hand, the Lucky Star was teaching him a few things. It presented a puzzle he was compelled to work through.

Business had dropped off since the first of the year. Every January saw a drop-off—after celebrating a long holiday season, people tended to stick close to home in the opening month of the year. This January was worse than usual, which Jonah reported to Allen one evening when his cousin called to check in. Jonah gave him a litany of the Star's woes, to which Allen had said, "Just get to spring, Jonah. That's what Dad always says—you just have to get to spring when people are out more, and things will bounce back."

"Do things really bounce back in the spring? Like, what's so magical about spring? The Star is not bouncing, Allen. We are landing with a thud every day. Other places are bouncing back, but not us."

"You sound like you want to throw in the towel. Just get to spring."

Jonah had taken offense. "I'm not throwing in any towel. I am telling you what we are up against."

"You know what I mean."

It annoyed him that Andy and Allen did not understand what he was trying to convey.

Spring was on his mind for another reason. Jonah's boss had called to check in. "How's it going?" Edgar asked jovially. He was a big man with a military crew cut and hands like baseball mitts. He was always joking around, but the man was brilliant when it came to aerospace dynamics.

"Good, Edgar. How about you?"

"Doing good, Jonah, doing good. Hey, I got one for you—how do astronauts throw a party?"

This was classic Edgar—he loved bad jokes as much as he loved engineering. His office was filled with engineering jokes and quips taped to the walls. *How do you tell the difference between a mechanical and civil engineer? Mechanical engineers build weapons. Civil engineers build targets.* Or another one—*I can explain aerospace engineering to you. But I can't understand it for you.* "I don't know, Edgar. How do astronauts throw a party?"

"They planet. Ha! Get it? They *plan-et*."

"I get it." Jonah chuckled.

"Had to share that gem with you," Edgar said jovially. "So hey, buddy, have you given any thought to our offer to head up the deep space satellite project?"

"I have given it a *lot* of thought," Jonah said. "I want it, Edgar, I do. But I'm still trying to work through these family issues. I can't bail on them yet. My dad is better, but he's still not recovered from the chemo."

"And you're the only man for that job?"

He wasn't the only man for the job, but he was the only man who was willing to stop what he was doing and help. "For the time being. This place has been my family's livelihood for decades, Edgar. I'd never forgive myself if I didn't try and help figure it out while my dad is recovering."

He could hear Edgar drumming his thick fingers on a desk. "I hear you, Jonah. How much longer do you need?"

"A month. Six weeks, tops," Jonah said, and winced, waiting for Edgar to say that wouldn't work.

But Edgar didn't say that. He was unusually silent on the other end. Jonah couldn't hear anything but the squeak of his office chair. He imagined Edgar twirling himself around to face the windows and the traffic on Highway 183.

He expected this to be the end, and he felt a hot rush of sorrow— a deep space project like this would set him up in his career for life. But he wasn't sorry—some things were more important. A family legacy was worth more than a spectacular work assignment.

But oh, God, how he wanted that work assignment. He wanted it so bad that he could taste it.

"Tell you what," Edgar said. "The partners and I really want you, Jonah. No one understands in situ particles and CME transients as well as you. Or attitude orbit control systems, for that matter."

Jonah closed his eyes for a moment. He opened them again. "Edgar . . . thank you. If you can give me a little time, I would really appreciate it."

"Let me see what I can do. I'll see if we've got someone who can do preliminary work until you're ready. I'll check with the partners, but I think we can work around it. This is a big project for us. We need you on it."

The effect on Jonah's mood was instantaneous—he could have cried with both relief and joy at once. "Thank you, Edgar. I owe you, man. I appreciate this more than I can say. I really want that project."

"Well, do what you need to do there, but make it fast. We'll work with you to the extent that we can. In the meantime, your folks are lucky to have a kid like you. Hey, by the way, have you ever heard of Den City?"

Jonah suppressed a sigh. "You mean mass over volume?"

Edgar laughed loudly. "Density! I've told that joke before?"

"At least a thousand times," Jonah assured him.

"It's a good one."

"It is," Jonah agreed. He thanked his boss again and promised to keep in touch.

Jonah and Harper were both so busy the rest of the week that he saw her only twice. He was taken aback by how much he missed her—he wasn't usually the type to pine. When the two of them finally caught up for burgers near the end of the week, he made some excuse about needing to feed Truck and enticed Harper home with him.

Truck was so excited to see Harper that he lifted his leg as if he intended to mark her, but Jonah stopped that in the nick of time. So Truck tossed his massive body onto the ground and presented his undercarriage to Harper. She obliged him with a two-hand belly rub, and that was it—Truck would be devoted to her for the rest of his dog life.

Jonah gave her a quick tour of his house. It was definitely a bachelor pad, but he'd hired an interior decorator when he'd bought the place. He'd always thought the furnishings and window treatments were too color coordinated. He wasn't a great housekeeper, but he didn't like clutter, so there wasn't much of a mess, save his running shoes, his basketball, and a skateboard he hadn't used in ages propped up against the entry wall. He had a few books on the shelves, mostly science fiction and engineering books. But what he had in abundance were pictures. Framed pictures of his family through the years, of his friends. There he was in a baseball uniform standing next to a birthday cake at the Lucky Star. There he and Allen and Andy were handing out cups to runners in the Austin marathon. There were his parents, their arms around each other, dancing in front of the fireplace in his childhood home. There was Amy with her glasses shaped like old-fashioned television sets, making an espresso behind the counter.

"Wow," Harper said as she slowly examined the shelves, her fingers trailing along the edges as she took in all the pictures. "It's your whole life."

"Yeah, I guess it is."

"How lucky you are."

He showed her his lovely brown houndstooth upholstered couch, and how one of the cushions was missing its stuffing. "I need to get that fixed."

"Truck?"

"I didn't actually see him do it. And he claimed no knowledge. But I found him lying in the middle of the chewed pieces of foam. And he pooped foam for two days."

"Hmm," Harper said, and smiled at the dog, who was standing next to her. "Sounds pretty circumstantial to me. You can't convict on circumstance. Isn't that right, Truck? Isn't that right, big boy," she cooed to the dog.

Truck lapped it up, leaning against her leg and looking up at her with big brown cow eyes.

Truck had left the two armchairs alone, Jonah said, because he was too big to fit in them. There was a dark brown wooden coffee table, one leg gnawed.

Jonah showed Harper down the hall, past a spare bedroom and into the master bedroom. He thought this room was well done by the decorator. Not too froufrou.

He pointed out the large picture window and the wooden blinds that were destroyed about a foot up from the bottom.

"Separation anxiety?" Harper asked.

Jonah snorted. "I was asleep right there when he did it. He just likes to chew."

They returned to the main living area. He went into the kitchen and picked up a bucket, filled it with water, and poured it into an enormous water bowl on a rubber mat. The floor around the rubber mat was perpetually wet. Truck couldn't drink without slinging it around.

Jonah opened the pantry door, and Truck began to scramble away from Harper's side, knocking into a barstool and jumping up and down to show his excitement. Jonah caught him and braced his giant head in his hands. The dog looked up at him adoringly, his long pink tongue hanging out the side of his mouth. "Listen, buddy," Jonah said, and Truck's tail began to *thwap thwap thwap* against the door. "Take it down a notch. I really like Harper and I don't want you chasing her off with your slobber and your drool and your bad manners."

Truck panted louder. The velocity of his tail ratcheted.

It was hopeless.

They fed Truck, and then tried to find something on TV to watch. But they were more interested in each other. "This is boring," Jonah announced, and traced a line from Harper's chin to the top of her shirt. "I've got a couple of ideas for something else we could do."

"What?"

"I have to show you. It's in the bedroom."

A slow smile lit her face. "Sounds pretty interesting. But what about Truck? Because I get the sense he thinks he should be included in everything."

"Your senses are accurate. Truck is about to get a very large bone," he whispered.

Truck's hearing was amazing—they heard him start panting as he jumped up from his dog bed, and they listened to the click of his nails as he hurried to see about said bone.

Jonah kissed Harper's ear and whispered, "Here's what we do. I'm going to get up and slowly advance to the kitchen." He kissed her neck.

"Okay."

"You very *carefully* and *quietly* tiptoe to the bedroom." He kissed her cheek.

"Okay."

"Shut the door, but don't lock it. And no matter what you

hear . . ." He slipped two fingers under her chin and made her look him in the eye. "No matter *what*, Harper—do not open that door."

She giggled. He kissed her, but Truck tried to climb in his lap, as the promise of a bone had been given and he would not rest until he had it.

"Ready?" Jonah asked as he pushed Truck's body from between them.

"Ready."

"Go!" He sprang up and over the back of the couch and raced for the kitchen. With a squeal of glee, Harper ran toward the bedroom. And Truck? Truck barked and tried to go both ways at once. But the moment he saw the bone, he forgot everything else, and was happy to settle down on his dog bed with it. Jonah took his cue—he walked briskly away from his dog, slipped into his room, and shut the door behind him.

"Did he fall for it?" Harper asked.

"Works every time." Jonah grabbed her up, and the two of them fell onto his bed, laughing about Truck in between kissing and hands roaming.

Sixteen

If Harper had known sex could be this fantastic, she would have engaged in it more frequently, starting a long time ago. Jonah kissed her into that sizzling space of oblivion, but they slowed down from there, taking their time, exploring and fondling and enjoying the ride, their damp skin pressing together, their breathing shallow.

She wondered, as his mouth moved around her body, if she ought to say something, if she ought to remark that absence made the heart grow fonder, or maybe, *I really missed you. I am shocked by how much I missed you this week. How did we get here, how did we become so completely enthralled with each other?*

But she didn't, because he had turned her to jelly, and she was incapable of speech. All of her libido had revved into overdrive and was pulsing at the surface of her body—every place he touched her, she expected to explode with pleasure. He pressed his hardness against her, caressed her with one hand. The heat between them escalated quickly—they were on his bed, and her clothes were coming off, and all Harper could think about was how she wanted his mouth on every bit of her naked body. She felt out of control, unwilling and unable to contain herself, caught up in the whirl of a physically elec- trifying blender, and they were only getting started.

His hands slid up under her shirt to her breasts and then down, sliding into the waist of her skirt, his fingers digging into the flesh of her hips. Her nose was filled with his scent—an aphrodisiac of coffee and cardamom.

Jonah pressed against her and Harper pressed back. She forgot about their competition, she forgot how she'd had that single mo- ment of wondering if she ought to end this because of it. She forgot about everything but Jonah Rogers, and how sexy and *virile* he was, and how she was probably ruined for anyone else.

His hands swept up to her breasts again, squeezing, and Harper wrapped her arms around his neck, holding on in the storm they'd created in this bed.

He reached behind her and unhooked her bra and, with two fin- gers, slid that undergarment down her arms. He drew a shallow breath as he looked at her bare breasts, and with the palm of his hand, he pushed her back as he skimmed her abdomen, and down. They stared at each other for one highly charged moment, each of them taking in the other, and then at last their eyes meeting. It was an unspoken check-in, and maybe he was asking if they were going to give this relationship a go, or maybe he was just asking if he could proceed, but either way, the answer was yes, *yes yes*.

He began a gentle descent over her body with his mouth and hands. Harper closed her eyes and sank into the sensations that washed over her, riding the wave as his mouth and tongue dipped and slipped on her and in her until she was pulling his hair and cry- ing out.

Jonah rose up, reached across her to a bedside table to get a con- dom. A moment later, he was inside her. He began to move, and so did she, meeting him, pleasure reverberating in her body with each stroke. The end came for both of them with such an explosion of light and color in her head that Harper was momentarily discombobulated. But then Jonah was kissing her neck, and her shoulder, and her mouth.

So this was what people meant when they talked about great sex. Her adoration for this man fizzed in her veins. She caressed his cheek, rough with new beard growth. She wrapped her arms around him. She'd given it her all, had let him know how she truly felt about him, had left it all on the field for him.

They were frivolous and light at first, talking about childhood heroes and favorite shows—her hero had been Sabrina the Teenage Witch. His favorite show was *Breaking Bad*. "With Walter White? The guy who started making meth?"

"What can I say? He turned a bad situation into a . . . okay, a worse situation. But he learned a lot about himself along the way."

They took turns recalling commercial jingles from their youth and making the other one guess. Harper sang, *"It's a lollipop, without a stick! A ring of flavor you can lick—"*

"Ring Pop!" Jonah shouted so loud that Truck barked. He'd apparently moved to the other side of the closed door. "Go to bed, Truck!" Jonah called.

Sometime later, they let Truck into the room when the whimpering got too loud. As usual, the dog acted as if he'd been stranded on an island by himself for a year and rewarded their generosity by leaping onto the bed and draping his huge body across both of them. There he remained until Harper said she couldn't breathe and Jonah made him get down.

They did not speak about the coffee business. They didn't mention the reality of their lives. It was as if both of them wanted to pretend it hadn't happened at all, as if they were just continuing on as they had from the moment their phones had gotten mixed up— happy, laughing, the world at bay.

∾

They spent the weekend together. Harper ignored texts from Soren and Olivia, responding with a Busy, call you later. They walked Bob and a new dog, a dachshund missing a leg. Her name was Lulu and she had attended the same Eager Beaver School of Bad Dog Behavior that Truck had attended. The only difference was that little Lulu with only three legs was manageable. She kept trying to engage Bob, but Bob growled at her and motored ahead with his lopsided gait and ears. He had things to smell, places to mark, and had no time for a dog half his size.

Harper made caprese chicken for Jonah on Saturday night. He made pancakes for her on Sunday morning. It rained most of Sunday, so they stayed in, each of them on the opposite end of his couch, sharing a blanket, reading books and talking.

She told him about her solitary childhood. "You make it sound like your parents were never around," he remarked.

"They were around. But they were usually reading. Or taking off for a show or afternoon at the museum."

"But what about school activities, or having friends over, or all the things kids do?"

Harper shrugged. "Olivia lived next door. I did things with her family."

Jonah was frowning.

"Hey," she said, nudging him with her toe. "They were good parents in their own way. I learned how to fend for myself."

"Yeah, I'm beginning to understand where you get your drive."

"Okay, so I was a lonely kid. But I meant it when I said you were lucky. I've known people who don't get along with anyone in their families. You do. You have a great family," she said, and waved a hand in the direction of his framed photos.

"I *was* lucky. We are a tight-knit group. But it could be a little stifling, to be honest."

Harper laughed. "Too many sleepovers?"

Jonah nodded. "Definitely that. But what I mean is, they needed me too much."

Harper looked up from her book. "How so?"

"It's hard to explain. I just . . . I always had this feeling growing up that I was making up for Jolie dying. Like I had to stay close and help them in any way that I could because her death had left them so vulnerable. I remember my grandfather telling me once that my dad had never been the same after Jolie died, and how glad he was that I was there for my parents. And then I felt like my grandfather needed me to be the son he'd had before Jolie died."

"That's heavy. I can't imagine."

"No one could. You can't imagine how the death of a child can echo for years. But you're right, Harper. I am very lucky—we've stuck together and I think we all genuinely like each other. That's why I'm reluctant to take the new job. They need me."

"And I guess, over the years, you've made yourself indispensable to them."

"Exactly. Sometimes I wonder if they realize just how much they rely on me."

Harper felt for Jonah's dilemma. At the same time, she was mildly envious. She would love to know what it felt like to be needed the way he was.

On Monday morning, Harper was showered and dressed by the time Jonah woke. She was strapping her watch to her wrist when he groaned and rolled over. "I have to jet. You would not believe my day." Or rather, he would not believe how guilty she was feeling for having turned a blind eye to her job for a full weekend.

"I can believe it." He yawned.

She figured he had the same sort of day ahead of him. Deliveries, invoices, personnel. But she didn't say it out loud because she believed they had tacitly agreed not to talk about their jobs. Or their business rivalry. And how that rivalry might impact their situation.

They'd left it blissfully untouched, a living breathing thing in the background, next to Truck. They had not mentioned it once the entire weekend.

Was it the right thing to do? Were they being smart and letting their relationship flourish . . . or were they hiding from it?

She didn't have time to figure it out that week—she had too much to do.

Because they both had busy weeks, and she was at the company offices more than she was at Deja Brew, they texted for the next couple of days to keep in touch.

From her: Newsflash—no matter the size of the bowl you choose to make your salad, it will be too small, guaranteed.

From him: Late start this morning. Spent a little longer staring at the wall and pondering the meaning of life than I normally do.

From her: I HAVE to start eating healthier. But in the meantime, here is a picture of the cake I'm about to destroy.

From him: Behold the "extremely durable" dog toy, made for the "extreme chewer." He sent a picture of the carnage Truck had heaped on a toy. It was a pig.

Your dog is so cool.

It was funny, Harper mused, how quickly someone could slip into the fabric of your life and weave themselves in. Just like that, he was a thread, a seam, and without him, she feared things could unravel. Maybe she was romanticizing it, which was very unlike her, but she felt like Jonah was supposed to be there, that he was the thread that was sewing up her loose ends.

Of course, that was easy to think while Deja Brew still wasn't open and therefore, the conflict between them only theoretical.

Seventeen

Harper was at Deja Brew meeting with Carly Kennedy, the publicist she'd hired to help with the grand opening, when she got the text from Soren. She was to be at the Domain by three.

"What? There's no way," she said aloud.

Carly looked up from her notes.

"*Shit,*" Harper said, looking at her phone. "It's Soren. The architect he said would be in Austin in a few weeks is here, today, and obviously he doesn't care what is on my agenda, because I am suddenly expected for a meeting at the Domain."

"But we still have so much to discuss," Carly said, gesturing to the clipboard holding her to-do list.

"I know, I'm so sorry, but I have to go," Harper said with a sigh. This could not have happened at a worse time. She was also expecting the bar lights to arrive this afternoon.

"Maybe we can circle back." Carly glanced at her watch.

Carly was friendly, she was funny, and she loved what she did. Who could resist that? But the thing Harper liked best about her was that she was driven. It felt almost as if Carly had a job promotion that hinged on the success of Deja Brew's opening, too. "Honestly, if I didn't think my job was riding on it, I'd tell Soren I can't make it. But I don't think I can risk missing it."

"What?" Carly laughed, as if she thought Harper was joking.

"Remember Kendal?"

"The admin guy? Good-looking? Sort of a clothes horse?"

"Bingo," Harper confirmed. "Turns out, he's in the running for my big promotion."

Carly leaned forward in her egg basket and put her hand on Harper's knee. "You're kidding, right?"

"Oh, believe me, I wish I was kidding."

"But how? You're a vice president! You're in development and he's in administration."

"That's Soren for you." Harper felt a swell of resentment. "He takes a liking to someone, and regardless of their qualifications, he'll bring them into the inner circle. He said his job was not to lead but to encourage creativity."

"Really?"

"I don't know, maybe it's all in my head. But I keep looking for reasons that Kendal is suddenly the man for the job."

"You can't let that noise distract you. On the other hand, a woman's instinct is rarely wrong," Carly opined. "Unless you're me, of course, and you think that you are totally getting that publicity gig for the Pecan Street Festival, and then find out another publicity firm got the job when you receive a promotional e-mail about the festival designed by that publicity firm. *That's* bad gut instinct. But generally speaking, I trust my gut and you should trust yours. *My* gut says you should sign up for the King Mutt competition. No one can resist a puppy in the window, you know."

Harper smiled. "I've seriously thought about it. But you have to foster the dog you sponsor."

"What's wrong with that? Dogs are *great*."

"I work long hours and I have a small apartment. No yard."

"Then don't foster a Great Dane. And the dog is going to be here, bringing in the bucks, baby."

Harper thought about Bob. She doubted he had the type of personality to get many votes, but she wouldn't mind having him around. "Maybe?" she said tentatively.

"Maybe is good enough for now. I can work with maybe," Carly assured her. "Just one thing, though—if you really want to do this, I need to know ASAP. I have connections at the ACC and can get them to fast-track you. They could maybe even be here at the grand opening. But I'll need to know today."

"Jesus, Carly. No pressure." Harper laughed.

"Just saying," Carly said. "It would be awesome and you'd be raising money for a worthy cause. How can you even hesitate?"

Harper tried to picture Bob stomping around here with his leg at that odd angle and growling at everyone. It made her want to laugh, but she wondered if most people would think Bob was mean and wouldn't vote for him. Harper totally got Bob because they were so alike. Just like Bob the Bulldog, she was a unit unto herself in this world. She didn't growl, but like him, she didn't need anyone. Still, maybe sponsoring him would give him the shot he needed for finding a forever family.

Wait. What the hell was she thinking?

"Think about it," Carly said, and stood up, gathering her things. "Text me later and let me know, will you?"

Harper said she would and saw Carly out. She glanced at her watch. That damn bar light delivery. What was she going to do about that? Harper looked up, her gaze landing on the Lucky Star.

Jonah was in the storeroom doing a coffee inventory when he heard Harper's voice. She was asking what coffee drinks they served. He was surprised she was here—they'd both complained about how much work they had this week.

"Listed right here," he heard Amy say, and imagined her pointing to the chalkboard. "Coffee, café au lait, and Mexican coffee. Choose your poison."

Jonah stepped out of the storeroom. "Hey!"

"Hey!" Harper smiled at him, and Jonah instantly felt like he was riding a sunbeam. He also felt conspicuous because Amy was staring at him, clearly wanting to know who Harper was.

"I'm thinking of ordering a Mexican coffee," Harper said to him. "Do you like them? What *is* a Mexican coffee anyway?"

She was speaking as if they all knew one another, like they'd all come together for a coffee.

"What's a Mexican coffee?" Amy repeated the question as if she was stunned that someone could possibly not know. "You know . . . Mexican roast, milk, chocolate, and cinnamon?"

Harper's eyes lit with delight. "That sounds *delicious*. I'll take one, please." She shifted her gaze to Jonah. He was still standing in the door of the storeroom. "Care to join me? My treat."

"No thanks. I'm coffee'd out. How about we make it our treat?"

"Who is 'we'?" Amy asked sharply, giving him a look.

He returned her look with one of his own. Amy frowned, which was even more noticeable when one was wearing purple frames with sunflowers in the corners. But she turned to the coffee machine. With her back to Harper, Amy glanced at Jonah and mouthed the words *Care to join me?*

Jonah ignored her and walked out from behind the counter to where Harper was standing. "What brings you in today?"

"Not much," Harper said. She was looking at the pie display case.

"You two know each other, huh?" Amy asked over her shoulder, clearly unable to let any facet of Jonah's life go unexamined.

"We sure do," Harper confirmed.

"Is that coffee almost ready?" Jonah asked.

Amy muttered something under her breath.

"These pies look delicious," Harper said. "Who makes them?"

"My mom. So are you taking a break? I thought you were at the Domain mostly this week."

"Me? No. I'm just checking out the competition." Harper laughed at her joke.

Jonah gave her a small smirk.

"Not funny?" She picked up a laminated menu. "Ooh, cobb salad. I love cobb salad."

"Do you want one?" Amy asked.

"No thanks. I'm watching my waistline."

"Oh, that's too bad. Because we are giving away a slice of pie every day this week."

"*Every* day?" Jonah asked, not having heard this news.

"You are?" Harper echoed.

"Want a piece of pie?" Amy asked.

"Are you kidding? They don't call it a piehole for nothing. Forget watching my waistline. Is that blackberry? I *love* blackberry pie."

"I will take that as a firm yes," Amy said. She turned back to the counter with the Mexican coffee. "So how do you two know each other? And is anyone going to introduce me?" She slid the door of the pie case open.

"I'm sorry. I'm Harper Thompson." Harper reached her hand over the counter.

"Amy Mercer," Amy said, taking her hand. "How do you know Jonah?"

"Funny story—"

"Harper is opening Deja Brew across the street," Jonah said, cutting Harper off before Amy began to grill her.

The news clearly caught Amy off guard. She looked at Harper. "*Oh.*"

Harper gave a self-conscious little laugh. "That's me!"

"Amy, you don't mind warming up that pie, do you?" Jonah asked.

"Of *course* not."

Amy's voice was dripping with . . . ire? Fury? Jonah wasn't sure what. But he knew how Amy could get when she had something stuck in her craw. "Come, have a seat," he suggested to Harper, and steered Harper and her coffee to the booth in the window—the only booth with an unobstructed view of Deja Brew. It was better than having her sit at a wobbly table and on a rickety chair.

"Hi, Jonah!" A woman with an empty stroller went by the booth on her way to join the other moms for their weekly Mother's Day Out. "Please tell your mom how good the chess pie was."

"I will," he said, and lifted a hand to the other women in the back.

Harper glanced at the group of women. "Regulars?"

"Yep."

She sipped her coffee. "So good. Who is the artist?" she asked, pointing to a speaker where music was drifting out.

"Patty Griffin."

"Oh," Harper said. "I love her." She put the cup down and smiled at him. "I really like this place, Jonah. It's cozy." She was looking around at the dated fixtures. The cheap pictures of Texas bluebonnets on one wall. The autographed Roy Rogers and Dale Evans head shots on another. "And eclectic. I ask you, where in all of Austin can you find a cutout of Roy Rogers?"

He smiled. "No place but the Lucky Star." He didn't need her to try and make the place sound cool somehow. It was the nineteen sixties in here. "What are you up to? What brings you in?"

"Well, for one thing, I miss you."

"An excellent reason to drop by."

"And two . . . because I sort of need a favor." She winced, as if the favor might be distasteful.

"What do you need?"

Amy appeared with the pie and placed it before Harper. She also had a can of whipped cream. "Want some?" she asked, pointing at her pie.

"Yes, please!" Harper watched as Amy delivered a tower of

whipped cream to her blackberry pie. She laid down a set of utensils wrapped in a paper napkin. "Thank you."

"Mmm." Amy walked away.

"What's the favor?" Jonah asked as Harper forked a big bite of pie and stuffed it into her mouth.

Her eyes closed. "My God, this is wonderful." She opened her eyes. "Who is making these again?"

"My mom. The favor?"

"Mmm." She washed down the bit of pie with her coffee. "I have to run back to the office for an important meeting. Like, I'm afraid to miss it. Because if I miss it, I might get maneuvered right out of the promotion I want."

"What?"

"But," she said with an airy wave of her hand, "that is neither here nor there. The thing is, I'm stuck, and I am expecting the special bar lights we ordered." She paused to look up from her pie. "They are supposed to look like starbursts. Or dandelions—I don't remember what Kendal said now, to be honest. Anyway, they are supposed to be very cool, and those lights are the last thing we need to install before our grand opening this weekend. So I can't really reschedule the delivery and I can't miss the meeting."

"Okay."

She looked at him with her green eyes. "Could you please accept the delivery for me?"

"What? Harper, I—"

"I know, you're working, and it's a huge imposition, but I'm really in a bind."

He was working, but he was sure she'd noticed there was no one in the shop this afternoon except the mom group. And it was really hard to look in her lovely eyes and say no.

"It would be super easy. Just let them drop it and sign for it, and voilà, my problem is solved."

Jonah was always willing to help—ask anyone who needed help

moving. Ask Burt. Ask his family. So why was he hesitating now with the person he was developing such intense feelings for? Was it the competition? He stared over her head at the empty crossword puzzle on the wall. He was being ridiculous.

The little bell attached to the door behind him announced the arrival of a customer. A barista from the Starbucks down the block entered the store. Jonah had seen her a couple of times before, had noticed the ubiquitous green apron slung over her arm. Amy, with all the aplomb of a bank robber, said, "What are you doing here?"

"You mean because I came from Starbucks? Or because you're closed?"

"We're not closed," Amy said, sounding offended. "It's just slow. There's an entire group of women sitting right there."

That entire group of women—three of them—were getting up to go.

"I'm here because I would like a real sweet tea. You know, the kind that rots your teeth."

"You're in luck, because that's the only kind we serve. None of that syrup crap they put in the drinks at Starbucks."

Jonah's dad, having heard the siren call of sweet tea—he had a terrible sweet tooth—wandered in from the little private dining room they had for that very rare, really nonexistent special event reservation, and where his parents and aunt and uncle set up camp every day. His dad stood with his hands on his bony hips.

Amy was pouring the tea into a to-go cup. "Starbucks, man. Gotta say, I never liked the coffee. Too strong."

"I don't like it, either," the barista said. "But you didn't hear that from me."

Amy laughed.

Jonah's dad glanced over and spotted him.

"What do you guys think about that?" Amy asked. "The Deja Brew monstrosity?"

"Oh boy," Jonah muttered.

"Wait. What?" Harper looked up from her pie.

The barista turned to look out the window, and so did Jonah's dad. "I know the general manager is pretty pissed about it," she said, and turned back to the counter to accept her tea.

"They've got no business being on this end of Congress," Jonah's dad said gruffly. "That's not the kind of clientele we have around here."

Harper blinked. She leaned forward, squinting a little. "Is that your *dad*?" she whispered.

Jonah nodded. "How'd you know?"

"Because you look just like him."

"Well, I don't think anyone around here is going to pay that much for a cup of coffee, that's for sure," the barista said. "We get complaints all the time, you know. Four bucks for a cup of coffee?" She spoke in a way that Jonah assumed was meant to mimic an uppity customer.

"It's two dollars here," Amy said. "'Cause not everyone needs a handcrafted cup of coffee." She smiled sheepishly at the barista. "No offense."

"None taken. I just work there." The barista picked up her tea and put down her money. "Y'all have a great day." She went out.

Jonah's dad walked to where Jonah and Harper were sitting.

"Dad, this is Harper Thompson. Harper, this is my dad, Roy Rogers."

"Roy Rogers!" Harper grinned. "Suddenly, this place makes sense. My grandpa loved Roy Rogers."

"I'm named for him," Jonah's dad said. "So was the Lucky Star."

Harper gestured to her plate. "I'd shake your hand, sir, but my fingers are sticky with excellent pie."

"We make a good pie. We aren't fancy like that outfit going up across the street, but you won't find a better pie in town." His dad hooked his thumbs into his belt loops like an old cowboy bragging about a bull ride.

"It is the best. I'll definitely be back for more."

"We'd love it if you did. Bring your friends—"

"Harper works at Deja Brew!" Amy shouted, much like Jonah imagined Paul Revere must have shouted to warn that the British were coming. It worked—Jonah's dad stared at Harper. He could almost hear his dad's thoughts—how could a woman love their blackberry pie and then stab them in the back with Deja Brew? It was a legitimate question.

"That's right." Harper stood up. "It's a pleasure to meet you, Roy Rogers. But speaking of Deja Brew, I have to run. Thank you all for that outstanding piece of pie." She turned her lovely green-eyed gaze to Jonah as Burt wandered into the now empty dining room. He was wearing an American flag bandanna and a muscle shirt. "Did you say if you could help me out?"

"Someone moving?" Burt asked as he wiped his hands on a dish-cloth.

"Hope so," Amy muttered.

Jonah could feel the eyes of Amy and his dad on him, and probably Burt, too, although Burt was rarely interested in what was going on in the restaurant. He was already at the soda machine, refilling his cup.

Still, Jonah could feel eyes boring through him, curious. "Sure," he said. "Happy to help."

"*Thank* you, Jonah! I owe you one." Harper fished a key out of her bag and slid it across the table to him. "Fits the front door. I'll leave a note for them to contact you when they arrive." She picked up her bag, waved at Amy. "Great to meet everyone," she said with a smile. "We're going to be neighbors! I hope you can all come to our grand opening on Saturday. I'll return the favor of your pie with the Tiny Pies. They are spectacular. It's going to be *great*."

Amy and Jonah's father exchanged a look. "Supposed to rain this weekend. This time of year, you might get ice," Jonah's father said.

Harper laughed. "Your weather app didn't tell me, Jonah!"

Jonah smiled a little. It was the evergreen fantasy of Austinites every winter that there might be a freak snow to make winter feel like winter.

"Anyway, I'm not worried about ice. It's seventy-five degrees outside," she said. "They say it's one of the warmest winters we've ever had."

"I hope for your sake it's not too bad," Jonah's dad said. "Would be awful to have to cancel."

"Canceling would be a disaster. I've got several vendors lined up and a musical act, lots of fun things planned. But not a tarot card reader, unfortunately, which would have been great."

"A what?" Jonah's dad asked.

"Oh! I'm sorry, I just noticed the time. I'm going to be late. That's what I get for stopping in the middle of the day for pie. Okay, again, nice meeting you all! Thanks so much, Jonah. You're a lifesaver." Harper gave them a cheery wave and hurried out.

Jonah, his dad, and Amy watched Harper dart across the street and disappear into Deja Brew. Even Burt hung around to watch her go.

"I hope it ices over," Amy said. "Everything. Just a solid sheet of ice."

"That's not going to happen," Jonah said. "All the wishing in the world won't make it happen. And even if it did, it wouldn't matter, because canceling the grand opening will not stop them. You guys know that, right?"

"Hey," Amy said, turning to face him, her arms folded. "How does she know that you get notices about the weather on your phone? How come you didn't tell anyone here that you're friends with the Deja Brew staff?"

"The whole world knows I get weather notices on my phone," Jonah said. "And I didn't know she was with the Deja Brew staff until very recently."

Amy's eyes narrowed. "I feel like there is something you're not telling us."

"I kind of get that feeling, too," his dad agreed.

"I'm out," Burt said, and went back to the kitchen.

But Amy and his father kept staring at him. "What?" Jonah asked. "Okay, Harper and I have gone out a few times."

"*Traitor!*" Amy hissed.

"Now just a minute, Amy." His dad put his hands on Amy's shoulders. "Maybe Jonah has a plan." He and Amy stared at Jonah, waiting for him to announce his grand plan to do God knew what.

"Are you kidding?" he asked with all sincerity. "I don't have a *plan*. I'm dating her. That's all, that's the plan."

"Oh. My God," Amy said, her eyes widening. "You're sleeping with the enemy, Jonah!"

"You're crazy," he said and, with a shake of his head, picked up the enemy's key. "Don't you have something to do?" he asked the both of them.

"Belinda finished the jigsaw puzzle we were working on," his dad said. "I was just going to check the news."

He turned and went back to the private dining room. Jonah could see his aunt's knitting basket at the end of the dining table. Nothing said success like TV and jigsaws and knitting.

Amy gave him one last glare and started back to the counter. Just then, a cable news network blasted into the dining room. "Roy! Turn it down, please!" Amy shouted.

Jonah sighed and returned to the office to await Harper's delivery.

Eighteen

When Harper burst into the StreetSweets conference room, fifteen minutes late and panting slightly from her jog up the stairs, the door just missed hitting the back of Kendal's chair. He was sitting with Soren, Veronica, and the architect around the Japanese-style dining table. And he wasn't there to take notes, quite obviously.

"I am so sorry I'm late," she said. "Traffic is *horrible*." Always a good excuse and avoided the airing of the family laundry—namely, that no one had told her about this. She strode around the table to an open cushion.

"Ah, Harper. We are all cock-a-hoop that you are able to join us at all," Soren said. "Please—affiliate and dovetail into the discussion."

The architect looked curiously at Soren. Veronica rolled her eyes and looked at her phone. And Harper? She was focused on putting herself on that stupid cushion without looking like a clown getting into a clown car in her short dress.

When she had settled, she happened to glance at Kendal. He gave her a smile so cool that she could almost believe someone had opened a window and an icy blast had come into the room.

"Harper, it is my great pleasure to acquaint you with Pradeep Luthra, the principal architect at Anderson, Luthra and Pearson."

Harper turned her attention to Mr. Luthra and smiled. "It's such a pleasure to meet you. I'm Harper Thompson, Vice President of Development. I'm so sorry I'm late."

"Think nothing of it," Mr. Luthra said. He was a handsome man with manicured hands. He wore a diamond pinky ring that kept catching the light of the candles Soren had lit, because of course he had lit candles. Mr. Luthra leaned across the table to shake her hand. "I've heard you're planning a grand opening of your latest store. I'm looking forward to seeing it."

"If you're in town over the weekend, I would love to have you at the grand opening."

"It's supposed to rain this weekend. But we've already taken him to the north location, so . . ." Kendal said.

So what? "Then he can compare and contrast," Harper said, and smiled at Mr. Luthra.

"I'm just saying that if he can't make it, Mr. Luthra has seen the concept of the Deja Brew Coffeehouses, albeit it on a smaller scale, so he will have an idea of it."

"Excellent thinking on your part, Kendal," Soren said.

Harper couldn't argue. But the other stores didn't have two stories and Suzanna in their courtyard.

Mr. Luthra, probably sensing a squabble brewing, said, "It's a very inventive use of space. Kendal was very good about showing me all the design features."

That tour should have been left to Harper or Veronica, as either vice president of development or vice president of assets, respectively. But if Veronica was bothered by Kendal's usurpation, she didn't show it. She was probably very happy to have someone do the tour for her.

"Pradeep has drawn up some conceptual renderings of the bistro," Soren said, and gestured grandly to the blueprints spread across the table.

Harper leaned over to look at the blueprints. They were quite detailed. How long had Mr. Luthra been working on this? She looked at Soren, but his attention was on the plans. She wondered if he felt any remorse at all for having misled her.

"Here," Soren said, pointing. "The quiet room. Headphones required. No phone conversations, no videos. This is where our customers will go for contemplation. We'll have bookshelves along one wall, no?"

"Yes," Mr. Luthra said, and pointed to where the bookshelves would go.

"Harper? Have you any input for Mr. Luthra on the quiet room?"

Input? She hadn't even seen the plans yet. "Well, based on the very little bit I've seen here . . . for the first time"—she glanced pointedly at Soren—"I would say it looks good at first blush." Not to mention she was having to contort her body from the damn floor cushion just to see it.

"Interesting," Soren said. "Kendal?"

Kendal looked at Harper. He seemed almost . . . apologetic. "This room is too big, in my opinion," he said, pointing to the quiet room. "Soren and I have a difference of opinion about it. I think customers will come to our establishment with friends and families. There should not be significant demand for single space, which is essentially what this is. And I think," Kendal continued, leaning across the table to have a better look, "that there needs to be more space in the foyer. Perhaps with some bench seating."

"Hmm," Mr. Luthra said. "We'd have to shorten the counter a bit to make that change."

Harper was being trounced. *Get it together!* "But this isn't a restaurant," she quickly pointed out. "People won't need to wait for a table. They'll come in, walk up to the counter and order, then take a seat or go on about their day."

The three men in the room looked at her. Even Veronica looked up from her phone.

"What?" Harper asked.

"Ideas can be revised, reformed, and recast," Soren said.

"Meaning," Kendal said, looking directly at Harper, "that may be true in our current configurations, but in the new bistro, they'll be waiting for a table."

"Excuse me?"

"It will be hostess seating," Soren said.

Since when? Why was this all news to her? Harper looked at Kendal, but he studiously avoided her gaze. She looked at Soren, who was studying the plans. Oh, but she hated him right now with the force of a thousand suns.

And so it went—every time Harper spoke, trying to reiterate the vision that she thought they'd agreed to, the three men looked at her, talked over her, or just outright ignored her. Veronica seemed bored with the whole thing. Harper couldn't figure out what was happening, and that left her feeling a little panicky and a lot furious. When had the plans been revised and reformed and recast behind her back? This concept was not a coffee bistro—it was a fucking steak house, and when she had asked Soren about that very thing, he had said it was a different take on a coffee bistro.

Why hadn't Soren told her? What was with all the gamesmanship? Could Kendal be taking advantage of him? Soren had a tendency to get lost in his imagination, so Harper could see how it could happen. But Kendal was new to the company and had moved straight from some mystery administration job into restaurant design, and it seemed outrageous that he'd go straight for the jugular.

No. She was beginning to realize this was all Soren's doing. After all her work for him. She'd started with a food truck and worked her way up through all the facets of Soren's company, had put up with his weird communication style, and his sudden decisions that left everyone scrambling. She'd listened to his stupid advice and had jumped when he said jump, and worked her ass off, and this was the thanks she would get? She had to compete for what was rightfully hers with Kendal because he was the new shiny hire?

By the time the meeting concluded, Harper was looking for a brick wall to put her fist through.

Soren and Mr. Luthra went out together, talking about some show on Broadway. Veronica was still on her phone, almost as if she hadn't noticed the meeting had broken up.

Kendal slowly came to his feet and glanced at Harper. "I know you think I'm after your job, but I swear that's not the case. I'm just trying to do my job as best I can. That's it."

"Okay," she said slowly. She couldn't think of a retort—she was too furious.

Kendal shrugged and went out. Harper glared at his back and his perfect haircut, then shifted her gaze to Veronica. "What the hell is going on around here?"

Veronica looked up from her phone. "What are you talking about?"

"What is Soren trying to do?"

"How should I know?"

"Come on, Veronica. You know this is my promotion. Why is Soren trying to give it to Kendal?"

Veronica slid her phone into her bag and stood up. "That one is easy. You know Kendal came from Starbucks corporate, right?"

"*What?* No, I didn't know that."

"I think Soren offered him a pretty good deal to come here and do the same thing for us he was doing for them."

"Wait a minute—he brought Kendal from Starbucks to be an administrator?"

Veronica laughed. "That's just the title Soren gave him. He's here to do pretty much what we all do—whatever Soren dreams up. But he has experience in design and opening stores."

Harper gaped at her. "I didn't know that."

Veronica laughed and started toward the door. "You know what your problem is, Harper? You are so used to looking down your nose from your solitary mountaintop that you forgot to watch your back."

"That's not true. I have worked for my mountaintop. I deserve this shot."

"Maybe. Maybe Kendal does, too. Not for me to say." She went out . . . and left Harper reeling.

What had happened here? She had not seen this coming. She was out of the office most days, running around to see after all the stores they had, and building a new one, and what, she was supposed to have pulled up a chair to the receptionist's desk in the middle of a chaotic day and ask what his background was?

Something dark moved across her thoughts, and Harper quickly shook it off. Once, a long time ago, she and Olivia had had a fight about yet another breakup Olivia had suffered. *You're so busy with your made-up to-do list that you don't even see what's happening with me!*

Olivia had not been wrong. Harper was a master at building tasks around her so that she was never without a moment to think about how alone she was. She'd learned it early on and not to question it.

Whatever—she didn't have time for Soren's games right now. She had to pull off the best grand opening this company had ever seen. She would show him, remind him why he'd hired her in the first place.

She walked into her office and shut the door. She stared out the window a long time before she finally pulled her phone from her purse and texted Carly. Pulling out all the stops. On board for the King Mutt competition. I even know the mutt. I'd like Bob the Bulldog. Also, I'm going to need a list of things to buy for said dog.

Nineteen

The day of the grand opening was cold and gray, and two hours before the event, rain came in on a strong north wind. No snow, but it was going to be a cold and wet night.

Very few people had come into the Star today. Just Old Man Harris, who came every Saturday morning for breakfast, and Robert and Lloyd, who had both put on puffy jackets and come for their afternoon cup of two-dollar coffee and free pie.

Word about the free pie had traveled through their regulars— some that they hadn't seen in a couple of years. They were starting to come around again.

"Good pie," Robert said. "Hope Mrs. Rogers doesn't get a job across the street." He and Lloyd chuckled.

"If she does, you can expect to pay a premium for that slice," Jonah said.

The veterans chuckled again.

Jonah had watched deliveries coming and going to Deja Brew all day, and even now, with the lights on, he could see people moving around the interior. The doors were supposed to open at five.

Amy stepped up beside him and peered at the windows of Deja Brew, too. "Who is going to come out in this weather to the opening of a coffeehouse?" She was dressed in her party best: a full skirt with a petticoat, a black bolero jacket, and rhinestone glasses. Her red hair was in a messy knot at her nape.

"Well, we're going."

"We don't count. We're doing reconnaissance. And we only have to cross the street."

Jonah was suddenly struck with such force that he had to catch himself on a chair to keep from falling on his ass. He didn't even have to look around to know it was Truck. The dog was rarely invited to the Star for this very reason, but today was a special occasion. He was even wearing a black bow tie Belinda had put on him and had managed to twist it around so the bow was standing at a weird angle and was partially covered by one of his floppy ears.

Amy scratched the top of Truck's head. "Okay, Jonah, I have to ask. I don't want to ask, but I can't stand it another minute. What did the receipts look like this week?"

"Guess," he said.

"Five hundred?" she asked hopefully, even though five hundred dollars in sales for a week was what they used to do on a slow Monday.

Jonah shook his head. "Four thirty-six."

Amy's mouth dropped open. "Oh my *God*, how are you going to pay me?"

"I'm going to pay you, don't worry about that," Jonah assured her. It would have to come out of the Star's rainy day fund, but he would pay Amy and Burt.

"This is really getting bad," Amy said softly. "I've been working here so long, I can't imagine working anywhere else. Like, where am

I going to get a Darlene and Roy and Marty and Belinda and Burt? Or even someone as annoying as you?"

Jonah put his arm around her. "I've always known you were in love with me."

"*Ugh*," Amy said, and shoved him away from her.

"I think we have to stop the pie giveaway," Jonah said. "It's been great getting people in this week, but we can't do business selling a two-buck cup of coffee and a free slice of pie. Hardly anyone ordered off the menu." Jonah paused and glanced over his shoulder. "And Burt is in some kind of mood because of it. Thinks it's his fault."

"Okay, we stop the free pies. I mean, if your mom will agree, and don't be so sure about that. And then what?"

Jonah thought the "then what" was obvious. Hadn't he said this to them? Sometimes, you just had to call it. Admit defeat. But he didn't want to broach it now—he needed them all together and they needed to be focused when they discussed it. "I'm working on that. But right now, we've got a party to go to. Let me leash this guy up and we'll close shop."

Jonah turned to get Truck, and when he did, his gaze landed on his giant crossword. Someone had written the words *suckit* as one answer.

That thing was coming down tomorrow.

Fifteen minutes later, the family was assembled in the dining room. His dad shrugged into his coat. "Operation Takedown begins," he said.

"We don't have an operation name, Dad."

"I like it," Jonah's mother said. "It's a great day for coffee and sabotage."

"Oh yeah? If it was such a great day for coffee, why did no one come in here for some?" Marty asked.

Jonah's phone pinged in his pocket. He withdrew it and looked at the screen—it was a text from Harper.

Can't wait to see you. I've missed your face! I've got a big surprise for you.

He'd missed her face, too. She'd been so busy this week, getting ready for this event. What surprise?

Can't tell you. Have to make sure you come. Party is starting!

"Well? Shall we go see what all the fuss is about and engage in a little subterfuge?" Belinda suggested.

"This really isn't a spy operation," Jonah tried, but no one was listening to him.

They huddled together as they crossed the street, all of them crowding under the only two umbrellas they could find, Truck barreling ahead and straining at his leash.

The moment they stepped into Deja Brew's vestibule, they were hit with a scent so pleasant that Jonah was instantly reminded of his grandmother's house, where the smell of baking cookies had hung permanently over her kitchen. The music drifting toward them was a harp and strings, and it brought to mind the mists of Ireland.

"Is that an air freshener?" Amy asked, mystified. "A fresh-baked cookie air freshener? How did they do that?"

"It's the subliminal manipulation all the big stores are doing now," his mother said, her eyes narrowing.

Jonah looked at her curiously as he opened the interior door and held Truck so that they could all walk in.

He and Truck had hardly squeezed inside when a woman wearing red pants and polka dot heels, a white-collared shirt, and an apron made to look like clouds floating across a blue sky appeared before them. "Welcome!" She was holding a tray. "Would you care to sample a Tiny Pie?"

"A Tiny Pie!" Belinda echoed. She and Jonah's mother reached for one at the same moment. His aunt instantly took one and bit into it. Her eyes widened and she looked at her sister-in-law. "It's so *good*."

So much for the sabotage and subterfuge.

"We have blueberry, apple, and peach," the woman said cheerfully, pointing them out on her tray.

All of them but Jonah crowded in for a Tiny Pie, proclaiming them excellent. He looked around the main room as Truck examined something beneath a large table in the entry, moving it two feet to the right.

It was warm in here. The music wafted overhead, coming from speakers he finally realized were cleverly disguised in the paneled walls. The lights were drifting with color, changing pink, green, blue, and gold. A man was moving across the floor near the coffee bar, watching the floor light up with the same colors. Somehow, the lights overhead caught the colors and sent them into the room. What the hell? There were light setups like that?

People were starting to filter in, shaking off their umbrellas and glancing around. People who seemed almost foreign on this part of Congress Avenue, chicly dressed, the men lean and toned, the women in high-end coats. Definitely not the sort of customer they got at the Lucky Star.

"Will you look at that?" Uncle Marty said, his voice full of wonder as he nodded at the egg baskets. He and Jonah's dad each took a seat in one of them.

"Welcome to Deja Brew!" a young man said. "We have some vegan pastries for you to try. And please, help yourself to a sample of our delicious frappes at the frappe bar." The young man leaned down to pet Truck.

Amy punched Jonah in the arm. "They have a *frappe bar*," she whispered. She shrugged out of her patchwork coat, draped it over her arm, and turned her gaze to the second floor. "Look!"

Jonah looked up to the second floor. It was about half the size of the room below, and an iron railing allowed people to look down. A man with a wild patch of hair was seated at an easel and canvas. He was painting the scene below.

"Why is he up there by himself?" Amy asked.

"Because there is no—"

Truck yanked on his leash so hard that Jonah's arm was almost wrenched from its socket. The only thing that saved him from sprawling was the concrete floor—Truck couldn't find purchase, couldn't get his grip. But it had startled Jonah, and Truck seized the opportunity to take off, slipping and sliding across the floor, banging into a basket. That's when Jonah noticed what had caught his dog's attention. He couldn't believe his eyes. "That's *Bob*," he said.

"Who?" Amy asked.

Truck was causing such a commotion that people were turning to look. Jonah strode over to get his dog.

Bob glared at them both, clearly annoyed to have been bothered in this way. He was sitting on a dog bed that had been made to look like a throne. He sniffed at Truck as Truck barked at him, and Truck took that to mean Bob approved. But Bob did not approve, and when Truck put his paw on Bob's head, Bob bared his teeth and let out a terrifying growl. It did the trick—Truck's tail went between his legs, his ears flattened, and he tried to retreat by shoving in between Jonah's legs.

"Truck!" Jonah tried to step over his dog, but he was so big, Jonah didn't have room to maneuver.

A dark-haired woman suddenly swooped in and picked up Bob—no easy feat, as that dog was as thick as they came—her eyes wide with fright. "What happened? Is everyone okay?"

"What is—oh *hey*, Truck!"

Truck vaulted for Harper.

Jonah was momentarily made mute—Harper looked amazing. She had on slender black crepe pants, and a red silk blouse that tied at the side of her waist in a very festive bow, the tails of which hung to her knees. Her hair was in a messy bun to one side of her head. "I'm so glad you came," she said to his dog, and squatted down to scratch his chest. Truck greeted her as usual, with a violent wag of his tail and an attempt to lick her lips. And then he would not leave her side. But he kept one eye on Bob in case that door opened.

The woman had put Bob down, and he'd curled up on his throne and put his back to them all. That's when Jonah noticed he was wearing a tux.

"Hey!" Harper said, beaming at him.

"You look great," he said.

"Thank you! So do *you*, Mr. Rogers. Surprise!" she said, casting her arm in the direction of the bulldog.

"I didn't know Bob was invited."

"I know, right? Meet the newest member of our team. We are sponsoring Bob in the King Mutt competition. Maybe you could vote for him tonight." She pointed to a bone-shaped jar Jonah hadn't noticed. It was on a shelf above the dog throne. Someone had Sharpied across it *Vote for Bob! King Mutt sponsored by the ACC.* A crisp one-hundred-dollar bill was plainly visible with a few other smaller denominations.

"What?"

"The ACC was supposed to be here tonight to talk about their fabulous program," the other woman said. "Unfortunately, the weather has prevented them from coming. They are having some sort of flooding problem at the kennels."

"Oh! I'm so sorry," Harper said. "This is Carly Kennedy, our publicist. And this is Jonah. He runs the Lucky Star across the street." She looked back at Jonah. "Carly helped me put together the grand opening."

"Hello, Jonah," Carly said, and offered her hand to shake. "We're so glad you could come tonight! If you ever need some publicity, give me a call."

Like they could ever scrounge up the money to pay for a publicist.

"That's my competitor, Carly," Harper said, and then laughed. "Just kidding."

And yet, something sour sluiced through Jonah. He did not find that amusing.

In the meantime, Truck had inched closer to Bob. The bulldog, with his back still to Truck, growled. Truck instantly sat on Jonah's foot. Jonah had to admire that old, half-blind bulldog—it wasn't easy to stare down a bigger dog. "So, King Mutt, huh?" Jonah said. "I thought you didn't have the time or space for a dog."

"I know, right? It was actually Carly's idea. She convinced me and said he'd be here most of the time. So I made room," Harper said, and leaned over to pet Bob, but he growled at her and burrowed deeper into his throne. "And this is such a worthy cause! Look, he's already getting votes! Isn't it a great idea? Bob is going to bring people flocking to our door, aren't you, Bob, aren't you, *bobbybobbybobo*?" She leaned over Bob again, trying to rub his belly. Bob gave in with a heavy sigh, lazily lifting one front leg to give her a bit of space to rub his chest.

"You should think about doing it," Harper said. "It's great for foot traffic. You can put a picture of the dog in the windows, and people will definitely notice you."

Jonah felt out of sorts. He didn't like her giving him advice—it didn't feel exactly good. Truck wasn't a rescue dog, at least not anymore. He wasn't eligible to compete for King Mutt.

Bob liked the attention and rolled completely on his back, his paws flopping in the air. But then Truck stepped forward and tried to sniff Bob, and Bob got so flustered, he rolled right off the throne. Truck went into down dog, his tail wagging, certain that Bob wanted to play. Bob took one look at him and climbed back on his throne.

"Can I show you around?" Harper asked. "Everything is all finished now."

Jonah looked at Truck.

"I'll dog-sit," Carly offered. "I love dogs."

Jonah thanked her, then gestured for Amy to join them.

They went to the doors that led to the garden and stared out, shivering from the cold that seeped in. Rain was dripping from the tips of the little umbrella lights. Since he'd last been here, cushioned seating and plenty of heat lamps had been installed. A pergola was strung with glittering gold lights over the small stage. He could imagine how nice it would have been to hear Suzanna had the weather cooperated.

"What about the live music tonight?" Amy asked.

"She's going to set up upstairs."

They returned to the main room, and Harper pointed out the artist from Imagine Gallery above, painting them all below as if they were clay figures. Another artist had arrived and had set up on the ground floor, doing caricatures of the guests who wanted one. "We'll be featuring artists from that gallery. You can purchase their artwork here."

"Cool," Amy said.

"Harper."

They all turned to see a man in a sheepskin coat that made him look like a polar bear, a leather pageboy hat, and blue turquoise earrings. He was in the company of a slender young Black man dressed in tailored clothing and a nice wool trench coat that Jonah wished he owned. Behind them, Truck had found the lighted floor and was jumping, slamming his front paws into the floor and watching it change colors. Several people had gathered around to watch him as if he were part of the entertainment.

"Soren, I'd like for you to meet the owners of the Lucky Star," Harper said. "It's a coffee shop just across the street from here."

Amy helpfully pointed at the window. The man in the sheepskin squinted. "Aha. The delectability of kaveh is widespread."

Jonah and Amy stared at him.

"This is my boss, Soren Wilder." Harper caught Jonah's eye. "And my associate, Kendal Malone."

"Vice president of administrative operations," Kendal said, extending his hand to Amy to shake.

"Amy and Jonah," Harper continued. "Jonah is an aerospace engineer. He builds satellites."

"The cosmic essence of embodiment," Soren remarked.

Jonah had no idea what to say to that. "Umm . . . yes," he said, opting for the path of least resistance. "Harper was just showing us—"

"Jo-Jo, look at this!"

Jonah's mother sailed into their midst. She was carrying a tray lined with small paper cups. "These are the frappe samples. They are *delicious*," she said, and held the tray up to him.

Great—was this her brilliant sabotage plan? To work for the enemy? "Are you handing out samples, Mom?"

"Just helping out," she said cheerfully. "Take one!"

Jonah reluctantly took one. "My mother, Darlene," he said to Soren. "We're a family-operated business." He introduced her to the Deja Brew people.

"Roy and I own the Lucky Star with Marty and Belinda." She pointed at her partners with the tray. The three of them waved from their post at the frappe station.

"And that's Burt. He's our cook."

Jonah hadn't seen Burt come in. In a way, he resembled Bob—he was standing off to one side in a light denim jacket with a dark scowl on his face. The sample cup of frappe in his hand looked tiny.

Soren looked around at them all, nodding. He looked as if he'd just worked something out.

"You know what would really amp up these frappes?" his mother was saying. "A shot of vodka."

"Darlene!" Amy exclaimed.

"It's just a suggestion."

Soren stared at her. But Kendal laughed. "I like the way you think. It's great for you all to have come."

"We do have some adult libations, Mrs. Rogers," Harper said, and pointed them out.

In the meantime, the dude in the sheepskin coat looked all around them. "Well then," he said. "I think we've seen what we have wanted to see. Kendal, send for a car."

Kendal pulled out his phone. "We might have a bit of a wait in this rain."

"You're going?" Harper said, turning back to them. "You just got here."

"I find the evening shrouded in the cloak of unfortunate meteorological conditions. I prefer my hearth."

"We should probably go, too," Amy said.

"No, no, don't go," Harper said to Amy. "We've just gotten started. Our vegan vendor should be here any minute. Suzanna is going to perform." She glanced at her watch.

"I don't know," Amy said. "I have to drive all the way to William Cannon. What about Truck?"

Jonah and Harper glanced across the room, where Truck had tired of the changing floor lights and was sprawled like a rug on the floor by the dog throne, his adoring gaze on Bob. Bob was facing away from Truck. "I've got him," Jonah said.

"Nice place," Amy said to Harper. "You've got that on us, for sure. But what we lack in aesthetics, we make up in family." She gave a thumbs-up and walked away. Just beyond her, a couple entered the store. They removed their hoods and looked around.

"I'm going to give them a frappe!" Jonah's mother said brightly.

Soren had turned around to study the bar lighting, so Jonah leaned into Harper. "Come over to my house when you're through here. I miss you like crazy."

"Me too," she said, her gaze on the couple. "But I don't know how late I'll be." The couple sat in the swinging baskets and twirled around.

"It's fine. Text me when you leave."

"Wait . . . I'm sponsoring Bob now."

"Bring him."

"Are you sure that's okay?"

Jonah glanced at Truck again. He was in love. "I'm sure."

Jonah's mother returned, all bright-eyed. "Amy says we are going." She looped her arm through Jonah's and smiled at Harper. "This place is fantastic, sweetie. You're going to put us out of business!"

"Oh no. No, no, that won't happen." Harper laughed, but it sounded a little high and a little forced.

Jonah wanted to laugh, but he feared his mother was right. He tried to give Harper a reassuring smile, but he couldn't quite fake it.

"Sorry to interrupt, Harper," a young man said, "but Suzanna's manager is on the phone."

Harper excused herself to take the call.

Jonah forced Truck to come away from Bob. The family gathered in the vestibule, the parents taking time getting their coats on and fastened. While he waited, Jonah spotted a sign he hadn't noticed before—it was a hastily assembled poster of the King Mutt competition that looked as if it might have been put together by a middle school art class. It featured five pictures of Bob. He sat exactly the same in all of them, and it was clear that the camera had moved around him.

KING MUTT CHARITY FUNDRAISER!

MEET BOB THE BULLDOG

FAVORITE ACTIVITY: LONG WALKS IN THE RAIN WHILE
YOU HOLD THE UMBRELLA OVER HIM.

FAVORITE FOODS: HOT DOGS AND PEANUT BUTTER COOKIES,
NEITHER OF WHICH HE IS ALLOWED TO HAVE.

FAVORITE TOY: THE REMNANTS OF WHAT WE THINK
MIGHT HAVE BEEN A STUFFED SHARK.

FAVORITE SNOOZLE SPOT: ON A COUCH WHERE HE
CAN SEE YOU AND IGNORE YOU.

FUN FACT ABOUT BOB: HE LIKES TO WEAR SUNGLASSES.

WORST FACT ABOUT BOB WITH SILVER LINING: HE WAS
RESCUED FROM A DOG FIGHT RING AND REHABILITATED BY
AUSTIN CANINE COALITION.

(VOTES TO BE TALLIED BY ACC AND ANNOUNCED DURING
CITY MARDI GRAS CELEBRATIONS.)

Jonah looked over his shoulder at Bob. The dog was staring at him, like he knew what Jonah was thinking, like he knew Jonah believed there was no way Bob would win King Mutt, but it didn't matter, because he would bring a lot of people into Deja Brew.

At last, Jonah's family was ready to go, and they trooped back across the street to the Lucky Star. Once inside, his family began to dissect Deja Brew. "*I don't know about those baskets. I could hardly fit my hips into them.*" And "*Those Tiny Pies were so* TINY."

Jonah wanted to laugh, but he was still trying to swallow the idea that Deja Brew was going to work circles around them. He didn't know how to compete with that. He didn't have artists or vegan options, or a separate frappe station. He didn't like this. He walked to the front of the store and peered across the street. Bob was in one of the window seats, and from here, it looked as if he was glaring at Jonah.

"We should do that," Amy said. She had crept up beside him, clad in her puff coat and wearing thick mittens. "We should enter the King Mutt contest. She's right—people will flock in to pet a dog."

"Truck isn't a rescue."

"God, not Truck. He'd send people screaming into the streets. I'm talking about a rescue dog, like that one."

"What's that?" Belinda had joined them.

"I was saying, we should enter the King Mutt contest," Amy explained. "Get an ACC rescue and beat Deja Brew."

"But Truck is the Lucky Star dog," Marty said. Truck, having heard his name, squeezed in between them all, his nose going to each hand, looking for someone to pet him.

"He will always be the Lucky Star dog," Amy said, scratching his head. "But Truck loves other dogs. I think he'd love to have someone to play with."

"She's right," Belinda said.

Jonah looked at his aunt. "You can't seriously think getting another dog is the thing that's going to save us."

"No, but I think it can help. Why not? They have cat cafés in Japan, you know. Why not a dog café?"

"I don't know, for all the reasons we don't let Truck in here very often? Food snatched from plates, horrible licking sounds when people are trying to eat, hair everywhere?"

Jonah's dad joined them and slid into a chair. He looked exhausted, as if the trip across the street had depleted him. "We've got bigger problems that a dog isn't going to solve."

"But entering the contest isn't going to hurt anything and could help," Belinda pointed out.

"We're already a burden on Jonah as it is. Let's not add that to the list."

"We're not a burden!" his mother protested, and looked hopefully at Jonah.

Jonah didn't answer. He loved his family. But they were a burden at this time in his life.

As the rest of them argued about it, Jonah caught his dad's eye. Maybe he should have been happy that at least one of his parents was listening to him about the true state of the Lucky Star . . . but Jonah didn't feel happy. He felt confused. He had a strong urge to assure his father they could do this. They could save it.

There was something else, too, that he didn't want to admit. He really liked Harper. He thought he might be falling in love with her. Or maybe he'd already fallen.

But that didn't mean he wanted to lose his business to her.

Twenty

Harper was disappointed in the grand opening. It had gone okay by anyone else's standards, but she'd envisioned streams of people coming into the store. She and Carly had papered the surrounding neighborhood with flyers. They'd placed ads on local television stations and radios until the costs began to get out of hand. Harper had spent more of her budget on advertising than she probably should have, all because she was so determined to prove to Kendal and Soren that she was the best at what she did and, therefore, deserved the promotion.

All it took was a heavy winter rain to ruin what would have otherwise been a spectacular debut.

She closed up shop at about nine, after Suzanna had finished playing the hour she'd squeezed in after being late. Most of the people who had come to hear her left when she did, leaving little frappe cups littered across the floor.

Harper sent the staff home when most of it was picked up, and finished cleaning behind the coffee bar while Bob snoozed on his throne.

She was alone, like she often was, the last person to leave a job, the one who stayed behind and made sure all was in order and ready for business the next day. She did one last pass through the store, then leashed Bob and picked up his throne bed. He'd taken a definite liking to it and had remained there most of the evening, unconcerned with the people who'd tried to befriend him. The only time he'd come off it was to get in Truck's face. "You better be nice to Truck," she warned Bob.

He grunted and licked her hand when she bent down to boop his nose.

So the grand opening hadn't been all that she'd hoped, but at least Harper had Jonah to look forward to. They hadn't seen each other much this week, all because of what she was trying to do last minute to prepare for this event. She'd had to make the thirty-minute drive to San Marcos late one afternoon to pick up some glassware, but the drive back had taken twice as long because of snarled traffic on the interstate. By the time she'd dropped off the glassware, she'd been summoned to the Domain, where some invoices for the grand opening had to be signed. She'd been too exhausted to see Jonah that night.

The next day was an even bigger blur. Every day, she waited for Jonah to complain about her work hours. When he didn't, when he appeared to understand her life, she felt . . . grateful. Respected. She felt all the things she'd been taught by romance novels and rom-com movies that you were supposed to feel when you were in love and he loved you back.

Was she in love? All signs were pointing in that direction. Big neon green arrows, pulsing in the direction of Jonah.

Headed your way, she texted him.

She loaded Bob into her car and fastened his ride harness, which

Carly had insisted she buy. She bounced into her front seat, squealing at how wet she was. Her phone pinged.

Excellent. Don't suppose there were any Tiny Pies left? Our master pie baker said they were excellent.

No, Harper texted, with a sad emoji.

A GIF of a crying Will Ferrell popped up.

But lucky for you, I stole four of them before the evening ever began and they are in my tote bag.

The three dots popped up, and then, I think I love you.

Harper stared at those words. Warmth gushed through her. Had he really just typed that out? Did he mean it? Because she loved him, too.

See you in a few.

Jonah answered the door after just one knock. "Thank God," he said, taking her by the elbow and pulling her inside. "Truck is driving me crazy." He kissed her hard on the mouth, pushed back the hood of her coat, and said, "I think I'm suffering from a bad case of separation anxiety."

Bob, who was standing next to Harper in the open doorway, gave a short yip. Truck realized Bob was there and began to bark. "I've missed you, too!" Harper shouted over Truck's barking. "Are you sure this is okay?"

"No," he said loudly. "But it was the best idea I could come up with on short notice. *Truck!* Stop barking!"

Truck stopped. For a minute. And then he started back again with gusto. But Bob wasn't having it—he suddenly charged Truck, even though he was a fraction of his size, his bark louder and somehow more ferocious. "*Bob!*" Harper cried.

But Truck's tail began to wag. He raced around the living room like a loon, sliding and skidding on the wood floor, and then galumphed back with a toy clenched in his jaw. He went down on his belly and presented the toy to Bob. Bob sniffed it, then trotted past Truck and into Jonah's kitchen. They could hear him drinking from Truck's water bowl.

"That's it?" Harper asked. "That's the end of the fight?"

"I guess so," Jonah said.

Truck heard Bob, too, and he got up and hurried into the kitchen, going around one end of the kitchen bar as Bob exited the other. He marched right up to Jonah's couch and crawled up, settling in. When Truck tracked him down, he was so flustered that he started barking to the ceiling, trying to convince Bob that they should play. Bob closed his eyes.

"It's going well, right?" Jonah asked hopefully.

"I think so?" Harper said.

"Truck!"

Truck stopped barking and laid his head on the ground and looked wistfully at Bob, his tail doing a slow sweep of the floor behind him.

"Want a drink?" Jonah asked.

"Oh my God, *yes*."

He led her into the kitchen and opened a bottle of wine. He put some chips and salsa into bowls, too. "Thank you," she said, dipping a chip. "I was so busy today that I didn't have time to eat, and then I worried all day I would starve, and look, here I am, starving." She took the wrapped pies from her tote bag and put them on the kitchen bar.

"You are one perfect woman," Jonah said. He lifted his glass and touched hers. "Congratulations on your opening."

Harper snorted and sipped the wine. "Thank you. I wish it hadn't been raining. We would have packed the place."

Jonah shrugged. "Maybe. Opening is tomorrow?"

"Nine o'clock sharp."

"*Nine?*" Jonah laughed.

"Why is that funny? I want to make sure everything is ready."

"I don't know. People who drink coffee are often early risers."

Jonah's explanation struck her as something Kendal would say. Jonah was running a diner, which wasn't the same thing as an upscale, artisan coffeehouse. "I know the habits of people who drink coffee," she said pertly. "We need to get new staff in and comfortable with everything. After this week, we'll be opening earlier."

Jonah said nothing.

In an attempt to change the tone, she asked, "How about you? How was business today?"

"Not great." He slid his palm over the top of his head. He seemed a little . . . what, unhappy? Not exactly. Anxious? "Our receipts have been awful this year. I'm not sure what's going on."

"I'm sorry to hear that. Maybe it's the time of year?"

"Maybe," he said with a shrug.

What was with all the maybes?

Jonah sipped his wine. "Tiny Pies, huh?" He picked one up.

"Have you thought about doing frozen coffee drinks? They are so popular," she suggested. "And the margins are fantastic."

He looked up from his study of the pies. "We're not going to do frappes."

He said it as if frappes were some unsavory, possibly unethical thing. "Okay," she said. "I was just trying to think of ways to help you."

A bitter laugh escaped him. "You know how you can help? Don't open Deja Brew."

Harper tried to laugh, but she wasn't sure that was actually a joke. "I know it seems like we are going to ruin you, but honestly, I think there is room for both of us on South Congress Avenue." The minute those words left her mouth, she realized how they must sound to Jonah. Like she was patronizing him. And sure enough, he looked up with a frown.

"What?"

"I'm just trying to say that it's not really a competition." Nope.

Still wrong. She waved a hand, trying to erase that. She was just tired, that was all. "Sorry, this isn't coming out right."

"Nope," he agreed. "You don't have to make it sound like the Star is on life support."

Well, wasn't it? He'd just told her sales were awful. She didn't like his accusatory tone. She took a big slug of her wine. Was she supposed to pretend she didn't see the issue with his family's dated business? Was she supposed to behave as if she didn't get what it meant when he'd taken a sabbatical from his job to help save the family business? "That is not what I meant, but . . . I had the impression from the things you've said that you're struggling. And . . . you know, I've been in your store."

Jonah blinked. He put his glass down. "What's *that* supposed to mean?"

Harper put her glass down, too. "I'm sorry, Jonah, but your diner is a little dated."

His eyes narrowed. "It's not a diner, it's a coffee shop. And you just offered an opinion that I didn't ask for. I know you think you've got the market cornered, Harper, but there is more than one way to skin the coffee cat."

She stood up off her stool and walked to the end of the bar, where he was standing, and squared off with him. "First, *gross*, and two, Deja Brew is a coffee*house*. And I don't think I have the market cornered, I'm only trying to say that we have two different types of stores, and I don't know why you are assuming I am trying to put you down. I thought we weren't going to let this be a problem between us."

"It's *not* a problem," he said curtly. "Why should it be a problem that your coffee*house* could put our coffee *shop* out of business? We'll just have to go on the offensive."

Harper's mouth gaped. "On the *offensive*? Are you kidding me right now? What does that even mean?"

"I don't know what it means—I just know that I am not going to let my family's livelihood die because a new place is selling over-priced coffee and *frappes*."

Harper blinked. She folded her arms across her body, suddenly defensive. She was annoyed, but she didn't know how to have this fight. It had come out of nowhere, and it felt lopsided, and it made her mad. "I hope you take this in the constructive way I intend it, but your coffee shop is going to fail with or without Deja Brew if you don't bring it into the twenty-first century."

Jonah's face darkened. "So let me see if I have this right. You are an expert on the Lucky Star after, what, four years in the coffeehouse business?"

"No. But I'm very good at what I do, and you need some expert help to turn it around."

He shifted closer, his gaze boring through hers. "You know what, Harper? You've done me a great favor because I suddenly feel *enlightened*. No more of this fatalistic bullshit I've been walking around with since Christmas. The Lucky Star is an Austin institution, and not some artsy-fartsy shop of egg baskets."

Harper gasped. "I feel bad for you and your family. But your institution is as old as the dawn of time and, for reasons I cannot comprehend, is anti-frappe and dresses Roy Rogers for the holidays."

"You leave Roy Rogers out of this. You can be really arrogant, you know that?"

Her skin felt inflamed. Her head was spinning with anger, but her heart was pounding with hurt. "I'm arrogant? What about you? You seem to think I should just lock the doors and go home because it's going to make things hard for you. Well, I'm not closing any doors, Jonah, *obviously*. Even if I did, Soren would hire someone to open it back up again. Why are we fighting about this?"

"Because I don't like the way you look down at my family's business. And for all I know, you're going to achieve your goal," he said, mimicking her and the things she'd told him, "and leave the Lucky Star wreckage in your wake."

She was stunned. She stared at him, and he stared back.

"At least I'm not going to be a martyr and let my dreams and aspirations pass me by."

Jonah's face darkened. "That's unfair."

"Oh, and what you've said is fair?" She grabbed her purse. "I think I'm going to go now."

"Not a bad idea," he snapped.

She couldn't believe this was happening. She couldn't believe that she'd driven over here, realizing she was in love, and was now feeling the sting of rejection or whatever it was sliding through her on a wave of hot molten lava. "Come on, Bob," she said, and dug his leash out of her purse.

Bob slid off the couch and trotted over, as if he sensed this was urgent. She expected Jonah to stop her. She expected him to at least follow her out to her car and apologize for letting his emotions get the best of him.

He didn't try to stop her. He didn't follow her. He didn't say anything at all and quietly shut the door behind her.

Harper was almost hyperventilating by the time she reached home. The rain had let up, and she took Bob to sniff around the dog areas in the complex, and when he'd finished what he had to do, she took him to her apartment.

She called her parents, needing to hear a familiar voice. Her mother answered after several rings, but Harper could hardly hear her over the crackling noise.

"Harper, honey, is that you?"

"Mom, I need to talk!" Harper said.

"Honey, I can't hear you! We're in China! Is this an emergency? Are you in the hospital?"

"The hospital? No, Mom, I'm—"

"Let me call you back when we get to Beijing! The reception is *terrible*!" The line went dead.

Harper tried Olivia's number, but it immediately rolled to voice mail. Of course it did. It was a Saturday night and she was probably on a date.

Harper could not sit here and ruminate about Jonah, or else she would go crazy or fall to pieces. So she moved into task mode, which had always served her—busy hands, quiet thoughts. She was like a robot, setting up Bob's bed and putting out a water bowl, and laying out the striped shirt she intended to dress him in tomorrow. And then there were no more tasks, but none were enough. The weight of their argument began to sink her.

God help her, but she didn't want to lose him.

She didn't realize she was on the floor in her living room until she pressed her face into the couch so that Bob wouldn't see her tears.

It was too late. Bob had finished his inspection of her small apartment. He fit his body half on her legs and half on the floor, licked her arm, then with a snort, lay his head against her belly.

He stayed there, allowing Harper to stroke his half-ear, until Harper had cried all the tears she needed to expend.

That night, she and Bob ignored his throne dog bed. He slept with her, his body pressed reassuringly against her side.

Twenty-One

It was a bad day when you woke up still in love with someone but so mad you couldn't think clearly. And Jonah couldn't think clearly because he couldn't figure out why he was so mad at Harper.

Yes, she was confident in what she was doing. But he'd called her arrogant. Yes, she'd been a little insensitive about the differences between her shop and his. But that didn't mean she was wrong. Hadn't he told his family the same thing? They needed to update? To stay in touch with what was popular right now?

He was mad in general, at a life that was not his, that seemed to belong to his family when he wanted it to belong to his career and to Harper, and none of those things—*none* of them—were compatible. They were a Venn diagram, and in that tiny part in the middle, the only intersection between his career, the Lucky Star, and Harper was him.

So what was he going to do about it? Mope? Remain angry for reasons he couldn't even state?

He hoped not, but this morning he was moving in something of a fog. He wandered into the kitchen for coffee, feeling a little like he'd been mowed down. He hated fighting, hated being at odds with Harper. He wanted to laugh with her and talk about their lives. He wanted to hypothesize with her as to why Bob was grumpy and Truck such a goof. He wanted to come home to her and wake up to her and solve work problems with her and share what they'd been like as seventh graders and college students and how they envisioned themselves when they grew old.

She was the first woman about whom he'd ever actively imagined those mundane things in a life spent together. He wanted that . . . but the reality was she was trying to get a promotion that would take her to another city. And he was hoping to turn the Lucky Star around so he could be in Spain for six months. Their souls were compatible, but their lives were not. Could they survive this weird competition between them, and then live separate lives?

Not knowing the answer made him angrier.

He felt uncharacteristically angry at everything this morning. Angry that his parents needed him like they did. Angry that Harper didn't need him. Angry that he was having to make choices about his life because of all that oppressive need juxtaposed against the desire to be needed but then resenting the need, and *dammit*, what was the matter with him? He leaned his head against a cabinet and closed his eyes.

What was the matter with him was that he had fallen in love and there wasn't room for that in his life right now. He could design a satellite to launch into space for years, but he couldn't figure out how to maneuver through his personal life.

One thing was certain—he was not going to let the Lucky Star go down without more of a fight. That was at the center of all his troubles. If he could just turn it around, half his problems would be solved. One circle removed from that fucking Venn diagram.

He looked at Truck. "Listen, buddy. We're going to make a couple of changes around here." And he told Truck what they were.

Truck listened with rapt attention, and if the wag of his tail was any indication, he was very excited about the changes.

The rain was gone, but north winds made it bitterly cold when Truck and Jonah drove to the Star for the standing Sunday afternoon weekly meeting with the family.

As usual, his family was gathered in the private dining room, bundled up in the thick, cable-knit sweaters that came out once or twice a year.

"Joe, my wonderful son," his mother called in greeting as Truck raced around the table, looking for fallen morsels, moving furniture with his tail and his unwieldy frame. "Come and sit. Belinda made King Ranch chicken for us today."

Jonah took a seat at the head of the table, shrugged out of his coat, and tossed aside his knit hat. He ran his fingers through hair that badly needed a trim.

Amy was seated to his left, her feet propped up on the chair beside her, her nose in a book. His dad was at the end of the table with a cup of tea and his phone. He looked a little gray. "How are you today, Dad?"

His dad grimaced. "I wish everyone would stop asking me how I am. I'm fine." Roy Rogers never liked anyone to fuss over him. He yanked up the Sunday edition of the *Austin American-Statesman* so he didn't have to look at anyone.

Uncle Marty looked up from the new jigsaw puzzle they had working on the table and nodded at Jonah.

"Where's Burt?" Jonah asked.

"He said he was going to Wheatsville Co-op to pick up a few things." Amy turned a page in her book. "Italian tomatoes or something."

He would have to proceed without Burt, then, but he'd catch him up. "We need to talk about last night."

"That sounds like we had a fight. Did we have a fight?" his mother asked, looking up from her needlework. From where Jonah sat, it looked like a leprechaun.

Before he could answer, his aunt swirled in with a casserole dish. "There's my favorite nephew! Ooh, sweetie, did you just roll out of bed? You need a shave." She put the casserole dish in the middle of the table. "Hey, everyone, I thought, given how cold it is, I would make some hot toddies. Anyone interested?"

"I am!" Amy's arm shot straight up.

"Me," Marty said.

"Well, don't leave out me and Roy," Jonah's mother said. "Joe?"

"No thanks. Belinda, can it wait a minute?"

"Why?"

"I would like to discuss last night with everyone."

"We all know what you're going to say, Joe," Marty said, and fit a piece of the puzzle into place. "You're going to tell us there is no way we can compete with Tiny Pies and we need to sell more coffee. It's not rocket science. That's your other job."

"I wasn't going—"

"I don't think we have to compete with Tiny Pies," his aunt interrupted. "Darlene has cornered the pie market on this street. I think it's more about those silly foo-foo drinks. We aren't a foo-foo drinks place, especially if there isn't a shot of vodka in them. We're more meat and potatoes here."

"There is not one item on our menu that is meat and potatoes," Marty countered.

"Burger and fries," Amy said.

"Besides that."

"And there was the time we did the roast beef and potato special—"

"Okay, Amy, sometimes we are meat and potatoes," Marty said impatiently. "I'm trying to say that we are a cross between a coffee shop and a diner."

"Call it what you want, Marty, but we don't do the foo-foo thing, and that seems to be what all these young people want," Jonah's mother said. "I like it. Those frappes were delicious. But I agree with Belinda, a little bit of vodka would have gone a long way."

"What are you saying, Darlene? You think we ought to sell?" Marty asked. "Or we ought to sell frappes?"

"That's not what I am saying at all, but I'll be honest, I'm beginning to wonder if Jonah wasn't right to begin with."

"Wait," Jonah said, putting up both hands. This had gotten away from him fast. "That's not what I am going to say. I've been thinking about this a lot, and I was wrong."

"*What?*" Amy's feet came down from the chair where she'd stacked them with a bang. "You've been telling us to get ready to sell for months!"

He suddenly had everyone's attention. Belinda slid into a seat beside him, her eyes wide with alarm.

"I know," Jonah said. "Trust me, if you spent fifteen minutes with our books, you'd recommend the same thing. But last night, I had an epiphany." He looked around at them. "*We* are the home team here," he said, jabbing his finger into the table. "*We* are the ones who have been up and operating in Austin since before Austin was cool. Are we going to let a bunch of newcomers chase us out? Are we going to allow people who move to Austin in droves tell us this isn't Austin anymore? That we have to look like that?" he asked, swinging his arm out and pointing in the direction of Deja Brew.

"No?" Amy answered uncertainly. She looked around at the other four. "Are you all hearing what I am hearing? Or is this a dream?"

"It's not a dream. I've been looking at this wrong. *We* are the legacy," Jonah said. "And we need to act like it. If Deja Brew thinks they can sweep in here and take all the coffee business, we should show them what we're made of. *We're* Austin. Not them."

His proclamation was met with silence. Once again, Amy was the only one to speak up. "No offense, Jonah, but does this change of heart have anything to do with you dating the chick from Deja Brew?"

"The chick's name is Harper Thompson, and no, it does not."

Amy's eyes narrowed.

"Not directly," he said, giving in. "Okay, yes—but hear me out. We know we haven't been doing so well for a year, and we've tried things . . . but we haven't gone full-out attack on the problem. We haven't really changed things up, or tried advertising, or challenged our business model. I'm starting to think we've been looking at this all wrong. I was trying to think of ways to get people in the door, but I wasn't really thinking big picture. I look at what they've done, and I think we can do that and then some."

"Well." Belinda leaned back and folded her hands on her stomach. "I'm not going vegan, I'll tell you that right now."

"I'm not suggesting we go vegan. That is definitely not us."

"It certainly isn't," his mother scoffed. "My grandmother taught me how to make pie and I'm not about to change now."

Marty leaned forward, folding his arms on top of the puzzle. "So what *are* we talking about here?"

"Just off the top of my head, better signage," Jonah suggested. "Maybe instead of snowmen in the window, we put up something that says what we have with some excellent prices. I think a two-dollar cup of coffee might look pretty good compared to the prices across the street. We get some new signs made, something like, *Our pies aren't tiny and they're free*."

"They're free?" his father asked. "I thought you said it wasn't cost-effective."

"It's not. Not yet anyway. But Mom was right—it gets people in the door. The only reason we had any sales this week to speak of is because of that offer of a free slice of pie. So maybe it's costing us a little more right now, but in the long run, if it gets people in the door, they'll come back for food and coffee. And I think it one-ups the frappe station across the street. I say we run with it, see if we can build on it. If it doesn't work out after a month, fine, we go another route. If it does work out, great."

"Fine with me," Aunt Belinda said. "If it will help us save the Star, I'm all for it."

Jonah could feel Truck's hip against his foot. "And I think we get a dog."

Truck's tail thumped against the floor.

"We have a dog," his mother said.

Truck's tail wapped louder.

"I'm talking about the King Mutt competition. Listen, I know that bulldog across the street, and he doesn't have the personality to win this contest. But he's going to be a draw. For every person that goes to see that bulldog, we ought to have a cuter, friendlier dog over here."

"But Truck—"

"Definitely not Truck. I'm talking about sponsoring a rescue from the ACC in the actual King Mutt competition. We refresh our menu, we invest in better signage, we take the crossword down, we study the situation, get a dog, and plan our attack."

Again, no one spoke. He wondered if he'd made his case too well for selling the Star, because he could feel the reluctance around the table. "Come on, guys," Jonah said. "You want to save the Lucky Star, don't you?"

"Yes." That *yes* was uttered by Jonah's dad and earned everyone's attention.

"I thought you of all people would be against it," Marty said.

"I'm all for it, since I'm the reason we're in this mess."

"That's not true, Roy," Jonah's mother said.

"Look, back when I was getting chemo, I thought we ought to sell and take our money and go. But I don't like that upstart pushing us out. So I say we listen to Jonah and try again."

"Well, I agree, and for purely selfish reasons," Amy said. "Who else is going to hire me full time and then make me an honorary member of the family?"

"No one," Jonah said with a wink.

"Exactly. And what other option do I have? Get a job at Deja Brew and make frappes all day?" She visibly shuddered. "No thank you."

"I'm in," Jonah's mother said. "But we need to talk about the menu. Burt doesn't like change, but you know what's popular right now? *Tapas.* They're all over this town! Even the food trucks are selling tapas. We should tapas the hell out of our dessert menu."

Jonah didn't know how one could "tapas the hell" out of anything, but he would give anything a try. "You mean like a dessert sampler."

"Yes, except that we call them tapas," his mother said. "We don't need Tiny Pies! We need tiny cakes and brownies and cinnamon rolls to go with our pies."

"You know what else?" Marty asked, sitting up. "Those frozen coffee drinks are good, but they take forever to make. What if we had an express line over here? Guaranteed coffee in two minutes, including lattes and cappuccinos. You want to wait in line, go across the street."

"I have an idea," Amy said. "We don't have swinging baskets, but we could do some rocking chairs. You can get them cheap from Wayfair. And I think they are more comfortable than those baskets."

"What about a giveaway?" Belinda asked. "Our book club has been taking a ceramics class and they have been bringing in their own coffee cups. We could get them to make some for giveaways and pay them for the materials. They would be thrilled to be asked. And they're very creative."

Jonah got out his phone and started to make a list. "These are all great ideas. Why didn't we think of this before?"

"Because now it's a competition," his dad said. "Sometimes you have to feel the fire to get inspired."

"One more thing," Amy said. She sat up, setting her book on the table. "I listen to the radio on my way into work. Deja Brew is advertising on the air. How do we get the word out?"

Jonah rubbed his chin. "I had an idea about that. I think we need to take something from savings and put it toward a publicity plan. We're going to have to compete on a level playing field."

"Our savings?" His dad snorted. "What savings? We're surviving on fumes as it is."

"Then the five of us pitch in," Jonah's mom said, gesturing to everyone but Amy.

"Point at me, too!" Amy insisted. "I'm in. Plus, my brother works as a printer and makes big signs. He can get us signs at cost."

"Wait just a minute. Our *personal* savings?" Marty looked around at them with an expression of horror. "We need our personal savings to live. Belinda, we're retiring in a couple of months."

"No gain without risk," Belinda said. "We're up against Goliath here. It's going to hurt to tighten our belts, but what choice do we have? I think we should ask the boys to chip in. They have a stake in this, too."

"What has gotten into all of you?" Marty demanded.

"Marty." Roy drew his brother's attention back to him. "You said just last week you didn't want to lose this place."

"Well, I don't. I don't want to lose what Belinda and I have saved, either." He scratched the top of his semibald head.

"Marty, we have to be all in," Belinda said. She put her hand on her husband's knee and squeezed. "We've got enough money."

"You always said the Rogers family is made up of winners," Jonah's mom pointed out.

"I never said that," Marty scoffed.

"Well, maybe someone else said it, but the point is, we are," his mother sniffed.

"Darlene is right," Jonah's father said. "Haven't we always been in it to win it?"

"What about your health?" Marty asked. "You haven't been feeling up to snuff."

"Maybe this will get me there." He grinned. "I'm not going without a fight, either."

Marty sighed. "Okay."

"Okay what?" Jonah's dad pressed.

"Okay, I'm in it to win it," Marty muttered.

"But not you, Joe."

Jonah laughed. "What?"

"We try these things, but then you go back to work. I want your word that you will step down as soon as we get these things underway."

"Dad, I—"

"No argument." His father had mustered the voice that he'd used when Jonah was a kid and wasn't listening.

"Okay," Jonah said, for the sake of argument.

There was a beat or two as everyone looked around at one another, and then all of them burst out into cheers. In the years that would follow, the Rogers family would point to this day as the reason a black three-legged dachshund named Lulu came into their lives.

Twenty-Two

Harper's brain felt like someone had poured molasses into it. She couldn't seem to form a coherent thought or follow a conversation like she should.

For three days, she'd loitered near the front windows of Deja Brew, pretending to pet Bob, who always made it clear he did not want to be petted, just so that she could watch what was going on at the Lucky Star and look for any sign of Jonah.

It had been radio silence between them since the night they'd argued.

The Lucky Star seemed to be a busy little beehive of activity. The weird crossword puzzle had come down. Tables and chairs had been rearranged. Big boxes of something had been unloaded and wheeled around to the back entrance.

She spotted Jonah a couple of times, usually behind the counter, usually speaking with Amy or the cook. One day, a group of women she'd recognized as regulars walked out, each of them holding a stack of brightly colored paper. *Flyers.*

Harper knew a flyer when she saw one.

She couldn't stop obsessing about Jonah and what was going on across the street. She had enough to keep her occupied—Deja Brew business was picking up, and of course she was thrilled about it. But so was business at the Lucky Star. Maybe it was the unusually warm temperatures they were experiencing. People were wandering up and down the avenue, and both stores were benefiting from the foot traffic.

There was only one way to find out what was going on. Every hour she debated if she should text or call. Break the ice. Send up a flare. But she didn't, uncertain if she should make the first move.

One day, Amy came into their shop. She'd put her flaming red hair in two pigtails and was wearing rainbow frame glasses. She walked around when she first came in, handing colorful slips of paper to customers in the egg baskets. She stopped at the window seat and tried to engage Bob. He sniffed her hand, which was as much interest as he'd shown in anyone.

Amy made her way to the bar and placed the slips in front of Tyler, the barista. Harper walked over to have a look. The slips were coupons for new dessert tapas at the Lucky Star. "*That's* ballsy," she said.

"We don't play," Amy said cheerfully, and Harper couldn't help but respect that.

Amy was carrying one of the complimentary insulated copper YETI cups Harper had given to the first fifty customers on the opening day at Deja Brew. "Hey, you," she said to Tyler. "You know where you can get the best burger in town?"

"Uh . . . P. Terry's?"

"No! The Lucky Star." She pointed across the street. "Grass-fed beef," she said, glancing at Harper. "We've changed our menu."

"Yeah? I'll stop in."

"Hey," Amy said. "Just curious . . . how many of those frappes can you make on a shift with that blender?"

"Don't answer that, Tyler," Harper warned.

"Why?" Tyler looked confused.

Amy wasn't confused. She gave Harper a slow, knowing smile. "That's okay. You can look it up online, you know."

"So look it up." It was a dumb thing not to reveal, but Harper's competitive spirit had kicked in, and she could tell Amy liked it.

"Hey, how's Jonah today?" She tried to sound super casual, but she had already ripped one of Amy's slips to little pink shreds.

"He's fine. Why?"

"No reason." Harper smiled again.

"Y'all have a good day." And Amy left, bopping across the store with her sock-hop-era skirt swinging around her knees.

When she'd gone out, Tyler looked Harper up and down as if she'd just said something offensive. "What was *that* about?"

"That . . . was an overreaction on my part," Harper admitted.

"Like, for real."

Okay. All right. So she'd been discombobulated since their fight. Why hadn't Jonah texted her? Why hadn't she texted him? What *was* this standoff, and how was it supposed to end? She was so . . . inept when it came to relationships. She was probably overthinking it. Maybe she should just text him and tell him what she was thinking. Maybe not. But they couldn't go on like this.

She looked at Tyler. "Hey, let me ask you something. Do you ever fight with your boyfriend?"

Tyler, a six-foot-two tanned, blond hunk in a very tight T-shirt, snorted. "All the time."

"How does it end?" she asked. "Like, after you fight . . . how do you end it?"

"*How?*" Tyler seemed befuddled by her question. "You just get over it."

Ah. So you just get over it.

That was no help at all.

She wondered if she should just call Jonah and hash this out. She'd obsessed about their argument, and the things he'd said. And the things he hadn't said. And how she had implied things that she shouldn't have implied. She couldn't deny that she'd thought the Lucky Star was inferior to Deja Brew. But it wasn't inferior, she'd realized. It was a completely different type of establishment. The only thing they had in common was that they sold coffee.

That had prompted her to pore over some of the old market data they'd gathered when deciding to place Deja Brew on South Congress. It was as she remembered—there really was room on the avenue for more than one coffee shop. She knew that, theoretically, but her desire to win, to be the best, had gotten in her way.

It was habit.

It was how she justified her existence.

But this didn't have to be a competition between her and Jonah. It could actually be a partnership. They could work together to bring business to the street. Harper had even called Carly and asked her if her theory was completely bonkers or maybe a real one.

"Of course it's real," Carly had said. "Anything is possible with the right publicity."

Harper just had to convince Jonah of that. If he ever spoke to her again.

When Harper could stand it no longer, she headed for the offices in the Domain to take care of paperwork.

She leashed Bob and straightened his Hawaiian shirt. Harper was still experimenting with Bob's look. As with everything, Bob couldn't care less if he wore a shirt or not, as long as he got the promised treat for putting up with it.

Funny thing, though . . . in spite of how much Bob didn't seem to care about anyone (which went against everything she ever thought she understood about dogs—*cats* treated you with indifference while *dogs* were slavishly devoted to you), Harper was surprised by how much she loved having him around. It wasn't as difficult as she'd made herself believe. She'd been so convinced that her tiny apartment and lack of a yard were deal breakers, but in reality, Bob seemed content merely to exist in the same space as her. His require-ments were few. He followed her around the apartment, as if he ex-pected something fun to happen. When it didn't, he was content to climb up on furniture and snooze. He wasn't like Truck, and his greetings were never enthusiastic. But he always lifted his head for a scratch and licked her hand.

She wished everything were so easy.

She found herself talking to him quite a lot, giving voice to the stream of thoughts in her head. When she muttered about sales, Bob looked up with an expression of *That again?* When she announced, apropos of nothing, that she was sick of strawberry Pop-Tarts, he rolled onto his back, his stumpy legs in the air. When she said it was time to go to bed, he didn't even look at her but trotted into the bed-room, always ready for sleep. She wasn't certain Bob would throw her a life ring if she was drowning, but he was sitting by her bed ev-ery morning, breathing hard because he was hungry. He never com-plained about a car ride, and sat behind her, harnessed in, his entire body pointed at the window, watching the world whiz by.

And in the evenings, he liked to climb on the couch and snuggle in next to her, his head always pointed away, but his body warm and a little stinky and comforting. Sometimes, she thought this old dog needed the reassurance as much as she did.

In spite of being gruff and disinterested, Bob's cute tilt of the head was filling his vote jar at Deja Brew. He was a truly great dog, and it made her sad that no one had seen that yet.

She and Bob arrived at the office bearing gifts—day-old Tiny Pies. Harper set them down on the receptionist's desk. That's when she noticed that Kendal was not at the reception desk. It was com-pletely empty, cleared of coffee cups and pictures and even a com-puter. Her first thought was that he'd been fired. But that couldn't be—Kendal was too smart to get himself fired. Maybe he'd leveraged this job into a better opportunity. At last, now she could get back to the business of being the shining star in this office and—

"Good afternoon."

Aaand no such luck. Harper swallowed down a sigh and turned to see Kendal standing in the door of the office next to hers. It had previously been used as storage, but she could see a desk and lamp behind him. He was holding a sky blue folder in one hand, a Deja Brew coffee in the other.

"Hi, Kendal. New office?"

"Yes." He put his things aside, then squatted down and held out his hand to Bob. To her amazement, Bob sauntered forward and allowed Kendal to pet him.

"Wow," Harper said. "He doesn't like people."

"Neither do I. Can I speak to you a moment?" Kendal asked, rising to his feet.

She was instantly on guard. "Sure."

He glanced at Soren's office, then motioned for her to come to him.

She looked at Soren's closed door, too, then walked over.

Kendal chuckled a little and looked down at Bob. "Why is he wearing that?"

Harper looked down at Bob, too. He was sniffing a potted plant just outside the office door. "Do you mean why is he wearing a Hawaiian shirt in the dead of winter? Or why is he wearing a Hawaiian shirt in general?"

"It's weird when dogs wear clothes."

"You work in this office, and *that* is what you think is weird? Anyway, Bob likes it." Bob liked the potted plant, too, because he turned slightly and lifted his leg. "Bob, no!"

Bob put his leg down and trotted toward Kendal's highly polished dress shoes.

"No thank you," Kendal said primly.

"What do you want to talk about?" Harper asked. *How about I'm sorry, you win, I was mistaken about everything, you are the bomb, Harper, who was I even kidding?*

He glanced at Soren's door again and said quietly, "Soren canceled your order of the copper YETIs with our logo."

Harper gasped. "He did *what*?"

"You said you had fifty to start—"

"And I want to do another fifty. They are very popular giveaways!"

"I agree. But the engraved cups are expensive and he's on a rampage. The grand opening was more expensive than he thought." He winced. "He also cut your operating budget."

"*What?*" Harper was stunned. "Wait—is this a joke? I was within budget for the opening. He never said he was concerned about it."

"Yeah, well, he is now." Kendal bent forward to look out his door, and said quietly, "Just giving you a heads-up. I didn't want you to be blindsided."

"Why is he doing this?"

"My personal opinion?"

She nodded.

"He's overextended himself with the architect and the land purchases and needs to make it up somewhere. I gather he's not great at admitting mistakes, and buying two pieces of property was a mistake. The utilities alone in Cary are enough to open another store."

Harper studied Kendal. "How do you know this?"

Kendal scratched his ear. "I'm the new administrative director. That includes budget. So he talked to me about it."

"We have an administrative division now?"

Kendal shrugged. "Something like that."

It was not surprising—Soren was great at making up titles for people. He'd made hers up, after all. "How much did he cut?"

Kendal winced. "Twenty grand."

Harper's stomach sank. Her thoughts began to swirl around the very many things that would have to be reevaluated in light of such a large cut. "What, is Mr. Luthra made of gold or something?"

Kendal smiled.

"Where is Soren?"

"In his office."

"Come on, Bob." She stepped out of Kendal's new office. But before she left, she looked back at him. "Thanks, Kendal—I really appreciate it. And by the way . . . your bar lights were better."

Kendal's smile was a little lopsided. He gave her a two-finger salute and turned back into his office.

Harper and Bob walked across the reception area, and she knocked on Soren's door.

"Enter."

She opened the door and was hit with the sickly-sweet smell of incense. Soren was standing by the window. He was wearing a caftan-looking thing, and her first thought was that he looked like a Bedouin. "Hello, Harper. Come in. I want to talk to you about a few things."

"Same," she said, as she and Bob entered. "You canceled my promotional YETI cups without telling me."

"I beg your pardon?"

"My YETI cups. They keep coffee hot and iced drinks cold? They have the Deja Brew logo on them, and they are my giveaway for new customers. To get people in the door."

"Oh, right." He looked at a piece of paper on the table beside him. "They seemed extravagant."

They were hardly extravagant. "You should have told me. I brought the grand opening in within budget. I had the money."

Soren squatted down and whistled at Bob. But Bob remained by her side, even taking a seat on her foot.

"Soren . . . you're hamstringing me. I have to ask—are you doing it on purpose?"

"Purpose." He appeared to mull the word over. "Purpose is the reason we exist. The thought behind creation."

Great. Normally, she would endure his philosophical bullshit, but not today—she was on edge. Because she didn't know what was happening with Jonah, or her job, or anything else. "Is that your answer?"

Soren sank down onto one of the pillows. Bob took that as an invitation and climbed onto one nearby, curling into a ball. "Enlighten me, Harper. What purpose would inspire you if you were in my shoes? What intention would set your course?"

"Could you, just this once, give me a straight answer?"

"An answer is neither straight nor crooked. It is an answer."

"Oh my . . ." Her voice trailed away. She braced her hands against her knees and took a few deep breaths. "Is this some sort of test?"

He laughed. "*Life* is some sort of test."

"Why did you cut my operating budget? You gave me three months to develop the clientele at the South Congress store and I need that money."

"And now we come to the source of your disapprobation."

"No, we come to the source of my frustration. You don't play fair, Soren." She gave a couple of yanks to the end of Bob's leash to get him off the cushion. "So no YETI cups, no explanation of why you cut my operating budget."

"Harper!" He laughed gently. "Don't leave in a state of ambiguation. Let us disambiguate your—"

It was too late. Harper had already walked out with Bob in tow. She had never in her life wanted to kung fu kick someone like she did right then.

Kendal was still standing in the doorway of his new office again. "Well?"

"He was giving me the runaround and I'm in no mood today."

He nodded. "Look . . . I'll see if I can find some money in another pot for you."

She felt a flicker of fondness for Kendal—she'd been arrogant about him, too. "Thank you. Thank you so much. I owe you an apology. I've been so suspicious—"

"Don't worry about it. I wasn't exactly forthright with you."

She smiled. "May the best man win?"

He smiled back. "Depends on what the prize is."

The rush-hour traffic was just beginning to pick up when Harper returned to Deja Brew. She parked, and she and Bob were walking up to the entrance when she noticed Jonah and his uncle outside the Lucky Star. They were hanging a sign.

She paused, watching as they unfurled the sign and stretched it above and across the entrance door, then tacked it up.

She blinked when she read it: OUR PIES AREN'T TINY AND THE FIRST SLICE IS FREE.

"Huh," she murmured. "Well played." Her gaze fell to Jonah.

He was standing in the middle of the sidewalk, staring back at her. Even across the street she could see the hollow around his eyes.

Neither of them moved. Marty picked up the ladder and went off, and still, Harper and Jonah stood staring at each other across the street.

She didn't know which of them moved first, but they were suddenly jogging across the street to each other, Bob trotting along. Jonah caught her elbow and pulled her and Bob out of the street and onto the nearest sidewalk.

Neither of them spoke at first—they stared at each other as if they couldn't believe they'd fought. "I'm sorry," she blurted. "I am so *sorry*—"

"No," he said, shaking his head. "It was my fault. I can be a dick sometimes."

"You weren't. It's not your fault, it's—"

"Listen." He cupped her face and kissed her. "There is something I have to go do. Come over tonight? Let's talk."

She was nodding before he finished. She was nodding so hard that he smiled. "I have so much to tell you, so much to talk about, and I was so scared that—"

"Me too, Harper." He stroked her hair. "Me too. Eight?"

She nodded again. Eight, ten, one in the morning—she didn't care, she was so relieved that he wanted to see her.

He kissed her lips, bent down to say hello to Bob, who growled at him, and then went back into the Lucky Star.

Harper grinned at Bob's upturned snout. "See? I told you everything would work out."

Bob barked at her, calling her out on that little white lie.

Twenty-Three

When Jonah applied to the ACC to sponsor a King Mutt candidate, he had in mind something from the regal canine catalog, like a German shepherd, or a Siberian husky. A dog that would stand in stark contrast to the crooked-legged, surly English bulldog across the street.

It took a couple of days to be approved as an official sponsor, and during that time, Jonah would glance across the street every day and see Bob in one of the window seats of Deja Brew, stretched out like he was on a lounger, dressed in some festive shirt, his head lolling toward the window. One afternoon, Jonah watched as two kids stopped and tapped on the glass, trying to get a reaction from him. Bob refused to indulge them. He pretended they weren't even there. And when he tired of them, he slowly rolled over and off the window seat, disappearing from view.

Jonah was determined to have a more welcoming dog than Bob. A dog who would adopt the family's new in-it-to-win-it motto, and eagerly greet people at the door. Like Truck, only gentler and much smaller.

What he got was one of the last rescues approved for the fundraising campaign—a female dachshund who was missing a back leg. Her name was Lulu. Jonah knew Lulu. He had carried Lulu on a walk with Harper and Bob. "She's perfect," he said, instantly smitten.

The missing leg didn't seem to bother Lulu much. She hopped around like she was on a pogo stick and wasn't the least bit fearful of Truck. She spent the better part of a minute trying to leap up to put her snout to his. In Truck's eagerness to make a friend, he kept knocking Lulu onto her side. She finally rolled onto her back and let Truck have the full sniff of her. When he was satisfied, she managed to scramble up onto her three legs and hobble off to explore.

"Wow. She's super friendly," Amy said, watching her wander around the Star this afternoon. It was Lulu's first day on the job. They already had twenty bucks in her jar. "But aren't you a little worried someone will step on her?"

He was, a little. "Let's hope not."

Amy's brother—the metal band guitarist—was an artist in more ways than one. For a nominal fee, he'd made the pie sign and two additional signs. One for the window, announcing their participation in the King Mutt contest. Another, larger sign for inside, announcing Lulu. He'd Photoshopped Lulu's mug into a big circle of bone-shaped dog biscuits. Beneath the picture was VOTE FOR LULU in bold letters.

Next to it, they hung another large sign with Lulu's platform.

VOTE LULU FOR KING MUTT*

(*SPONSORED BY THE AUSTIN CANINE COALITION)

LULU VOWS TO:

SLASH TAXES!

PROVIDE FREE HEALTH CARE FOR ALL!

REACH ACROSS THE AISLE TO WORK WITH CATS!

PUT A DOG BONE IN EVERY DOG BED!

VOTE FOR LULU!

SHE IS THAT BITCH.

"So you've got this, right?" Jonah asked Amy as he shrugged into a denim jacket.

"Of course I've *got this*," Amy said, her eyes flashing with irritation through her tie-dyed frames that matched her shirt. "First of all, your mother and Belinda are here to help. Second, she's a dachshund with three legs. It's not like she can outrun me. What time are you picking her up?"

"Seven. Seven thirty."

"So get out of here! We've got this, Jonah—go be an astronaut."

"Aerospace engineer, but you've only had ten years to remember that."

"Whatever. Astronaut, engineer, they all spell geek," Amy said, and gave him a friendly shove toward the door.

He was on his way to his real job. Earlier that morning, Edgar had called. "*Dude*," he'd said, as jovial as ever. "What did Mars say to Saturn?"

"You got me, Edgar." Edgar didn't have him. Jonah knew exactly what Mars had said to Saturn because Edgar recycled his puns on a regular basis, and this one he'd told no less than five thousand times—a conservative estimate.

"Give me a ring sometime!" Edgar shouted, then laughed long and loud. "Van down in Materials reminded me of that one. I'd forgotten how much I like it. So hey, Jonah, do you think you could swing in for a meeting this afternoon and maybe stick around for a drink afterward? Some of the NASA folks are here and we'd really love for you to listen to what they have to say. And they want to hear from you."

Of course Jonah could swing by. He was eager to hear what NASA had to say. At first, he'd looked at the desk calendar where they all jotted down notes about everything to do with the Star. He was supposed to meet with Burt to talk about the new menu. "Grass-fed beef for the burgers," Jonah had told him recently, and Burt had looked at him like Jonah had grown two horns before his very eyes. It was going to take some cajoling, so he'd rescheduled Burt.

He arrived a little early at Neptune Industries and stopped into say hello to his office mates. They were happy to see him, all of them clapping him on the back, reaching out to shake his hand. He caught up on the office gossip and laughed hard at the tale of a propulsion design gone all wrong that had come very close to blowing up the building.

Edgar came in from another meeting and actually gave Jonah a bro-hug, including the obligatory chest bump. From there, they met the team from NASA.

It was fascinating.

Jonah learned about the deep space exploration project in detail, the goals NASA had for it, the desire to push current technology into a new realm.

The conversation continued into drinks. When Jonah stood up to go, one of the guys on the NASA team told Jonah he hoped he would come on board. "We need bright young minds like yours," one said. "Space is the next frontier, you know."

Of course Jonah knew that. Anyone raised on a steady diet of science fiction and *Star Trek* reruns knew that.

Edgar walked with him to his truck. "Enjoy yourself?"

"I did," Jonah said. "Thanks for inviting me along."

"Should I remind you of what the job pays? Or that your housing in Spain is paid for?"

"No need to remind me. I haven't forgotten a single detail."

"Good," Edgar said, and clamped both of his mitt-sized hands on Jonah's shoulders. He peered intently into his eyes. "I really hope to hear from you soon, Jonah. Understand?"

"Understood," he said. He needed to give his answer sooner rather than later.

As he drove away, he realized that the afternoon and evening spent with his colleagues had dredged up his feelings for the aerospace industry. He loved this work. He *missed* this work. It was easy to get caught up in the day-to-day of the Lucky Star and to forget the fire in his belly for his real calling. That fire was glowing red-hot this evening. This work excited him and he wanted to do it. He did not want to order coffee beans or grass-fed beef.

He wanted this job in the worst way.

He wanted Harper, too. And his dad to be healthy.

He wanted more than he could have.

Jonah had chicken in the oven by the time Harper arrived. When she knocked, Truck darted in front of him in his rush to be first. Bob barely glanced at Truck when Jonah opened the door, even with all the barking. He trotted straight for the couch, almost as if he'd been waiting for it all day.

"Hey!" Jonah kissed Harper, then glanced at the dog. "Looking good, Bob."

Bob sneezed.

They heard a small yap from somewhere near the end of the couch.

Harper stared in the direction of Bob. "What was that?"

Jonah grinned. "Stay right here and I'll show you." He went into the living room and fetched Lulu, carrying her under his arm.

Harper gasped. "You have Lulu?"

Lulu was wagging her tail so hard that it was a miracle she didn't launch from Jonah's arm and propel herself right into Harper's chest. "Lulu!" Harper scratched the dog beneath her chin. "You're so *cute*. But what are you doing here?"

"Lulu has entered the King Mutt competition, and the Lucky Star is sponsoring her."

"No way!" Harper cried with delight.

Jonah put Lulu down so she could say hello to her old friend Bob. Truck knocked Lulu over so that he could be first. But Lulu bounced right up and pogoed to the couch, leaping to see Bob, her tail going in full whirl.

Bob watched the two dogs dispassionately.

Jonah glanced at Harper. Were her eyes welling? "Hey," he said, and put his arm around her. "Are you okay?"

"Yes," Harper said tearfully. "Sort of. I just love dogs, that's all."

Jonah pulled her into his arms. He kissed her neck, then whispered, "Do you concede the title of King Mutt?"

"No," she murmured into his shoulder. "*Never.*"

"That's my girl." He slipped a hand beneath her chin and lifted her face. He kissed her, smoothed her hair back. "Come in. I'm making dinner."

"Oh my God, thank you," she said weakly, and allowed him to lead her into the kitchen. "It smells delicious."

"Lemon chicken and new potatoes. I hope you like it."

"Oh. Disappointing fare, seeing as how my plan was to motor through a box of Cheez-Its tonight. I didn't know you were a gourmet cook. Why have you not confessed this skill?"

"I guess I learned a few things growing up. I like cooking."

"Did you learn to bake pies?"

"Not really. I could probably throw one together if I had to, but it is not my forte."

"Damn," Harper muttered. "I thought I'd hit the jackpot." Lulu suddenly raced through the kitchen with Truck behind her. She crashed into the cabinets because of her inability to turn a corner properly. Jonah looked over the top of Harper's head, in search of the third dog. He could just see the top of Bob's head. He was sitting on the couch, facing a TV that was not on.

Lulu took off again. Truck was delayed by something interesting on the kitchen floor.

Harper watched Lulu try for Bob's attention again. "So you *copied* me."

Jonah scoffed. "You can't call it copying when it's something that the whole town is doing. I saw a black Lab at The Tavern this week. Maybe I copied them."

Her eyes narrowed. "Sorry, but Labs are a dime a dozen. You saw how awesome Bob is and tried to one-up him with a tripod."

"That is a crazy conspiracy theory," Jonah said. "I can't one-up a bulldog in a Hawaiian shirt. Which, let's be honest, you put him in because you think you've already won. Well, I'm here to tell you, people are stuffing bills into Lulu's vote jar left and right. They like her platform."

"Bob doesn't even have to do anything and they are showering his vote jar with greenbacks. He's that magnetic."

"Yeah, he's a real magnet, all right."

Harper smiled. "It's so good to see you, Jonah. I was afraid you'd never talk to me again."

"I know. I'm sorry about that. I needed a couple of days to get my head together."

"I did, too, I guess." She leaned across the bar as he stirred the sauce. "I've been thinking a lot about what you said."

He winced. "Don't remind me." He glanced up from the pan. "But . . . what, exactly?"

"About our two shops."

"Mmm-hmm." He wasn't certain he wanted to hear this right now. He turned off the burner and poured the sauce over the chicken, then left it on the counter to cool. He leaned back, his hands in his pockets. "I shouldn't have gotten upset, Harper. I was jealous and frustrated with the Star, and that's it. But it wasn't fair to take it out on you, and it's not really like me to do that. I think it was just a culmination of everything."

"Everything like . . . ?"

"Like . . . having to save the family business. It's not easy, and it feels imperative, and it's not something I am either skilled at or interested in."

"But I am."

Jonah laughed. "Yes, you are. You want a drink? I could use a drink. How about a gin and tonic?"

"I would love one. It's been a day."

"Yeah," he agreed.

"I shouldn't have been so arrogant, Jonah. I didn't mean to be— I get caught up sometimes and forget the rest of the world doesn't view life through my eyes. You were right, and it got me thinking."

Jonah walked to the far end of the bar to get the gin out of a cabinet. "About what?"

"About how we—okay, me—are making a competition where there doesn't need to be one. Look." She reached into her purse and pulled out a sheaf of papers as he placed two highball glasses on the bar between them.

"What is that?"

"It's dated, but it's the market research we did for Deja Brew before we built. The reason we picked that location is because it is growing fast, and there really aren't that many coffee places in the area. There is enough business to support us both. We have different clientele. We could make this work, especially if we worked together."

He snorted as he opened the gin. "Together?"

"Yes, together. I know it sounds crazy, but we could cross-promote. We could help build each other while we build our own business. Like . . . you could put discount burger coupons in our store. We could put discount frappe coupons in your store. Those are just examples of ideas we could come up with, but see what I mean?"

Jonah poured the drinks. "I think so." He didn't see. She was right, it sounded crazy.

Her phone rang from deep inside her purse. She dug around until she found it and looked at the screen. "It's Carly. I asked her to call, but I'm not ready."

"Who?"

"Carly Kennedy, my publicist. I've got some money left on her retainer, and I called her and asked her what she thought, and she agreed, and she said she'd think through some ideas."

"Wait, wait, wait," Jonah said, holding up one hand. "You're suggesting we publicize our places together?"

"I am. I think it makes sense."

"It makes *no* sense," he said with a laugh. "First of all, my family isn't going to want to pay for a publicist."

"You don't need to. Not yet. Just wait and see what happens."

"And second, I'm pretty sure I'd put in a lot of effort only to watch you get all the business because you're trendier."

"But that's just it—the more I think about it, the more I am convinced we have completely different audiences. Do you know how many people we've already had walk out and go across the street for pie that is not tiny and is also free? But we've had a few come from your shop wanting a frozen coffee drink."

Jonah slid one of the drinks across the bar to her. He had to be losing it, because it was beginning to make a little sense.

"Respectfully, you know the Lucky Star needs decent publicity. And Carly is the best."

"Isn't it a conflict of interest for her?"

"Nope. I asked her. She said she did things like this all the time, represent two clients who did the same sort of work. And then she reminded me that it's not a competition between us. She said we've made it into one, but it's not a real one. She says it's just good, healthy capitalism. And she is going to be over the moon that you've already signed on for King Mutt."

He sipped his drink.

"Will you talk to her?"

Jonah pondered this question. "You think the publicity you've generated has worked to get people in?"

"It's hard to say for sure, but I think so. Especially the radio."

If Harper's idea worked, and they actually saw some benefit from it, he could take the job and go to Spain. "I'll think about it," he said, and tapped his glass to hers. "I mean, since it's not a competition. Who knows, maybe we can get Suzanna to play at the Star."

Harper's eyes took on a gleam and locked on his. "I see how this is going to go."

"It's just capitalism. Because we're a team, right?"

She walked around the end of the kitchen island to where he stood. "What next? Is Lulu going to show up in a Hawaiian shirt?"

"Maybe."

"That's not fair—you'll get the cute pup *and* the tripod vote."

"Ha!" He pointed a finger at her. "I *knew* it was a competition."

She slapped his finger away from her face. He grabbed her hand and yanked her into his chest. "You turn me on, Thompson, especially when I've been missing you."

"Not as much as you turn me on when you are *copying* me."

"Wanna bet?"

"Nope. I wanna prove it."

He grabbed her head between his hands and kissed her hard. "May the best man win."

"*Person*," she hissed.

He twisted her around and started maneuvering her in the direction of his office, just off the kitchen. Once inside, he kicked the door shut to all the curious canines, and he and Harper fell onto a wide leather chair. Papers he'd left on the arm fell to the floor; one of them kicked over a water bottle. They came together in a blistering swirl of hands and mouths and bodies, whispering how they planned to undo each other, and challenging each other to try and stop it from happening.

Neither of them could stop it. To Jonah, this part of their dating life was the most intoxicating. He'd never had a relationship where he felt so completely in sync with his partner's desires as he was with Harper. They felt made for each other in so many ways, but in this way in particular. The chemistry was sizzling.

When they were spent, Harper was half dressed and draped across the chair, her legs hanging over the arm of it.

Jonah was on his back on the floor, still trying to catch his breath. "Hey," Harper said. She dropped her arm, and her hand dangled over his chest. He took her hand, lacing his fingers through hers. "Is the sex going to be this hot when I get my promotion and leave you in my dust?"

"When you're executive vice president? I think it's going to be even better. You'll be so cocky, you'll probably grow a rooster tail."

"Do you think it's possible?"

"That you can be cockier?"

She giggled and leaned over him. "Is it possible that this thing between us could be better?"

Jonah grabbed her arm and slowly pulled her down on top of him. He wrapped his arms around her and kissed her. "Not only is it possible, it is guaranteed." He closed his eyes, savoring this moment. He liked this. It was nice to lie on the floor of his office with her. It was nice to be anywhere with her.

"What if I'm in Rochester?"

He opened one eye. "Where?"

"Rochester, Minnesota."

"Why?"

"That's where the job will be. Or in Cary, North Carolina."

North Carolina? He kissed the back of her hand. "What if I'm in Madrid?"

She lifted her head and met his gaze. "Does that mean you're going?"

He didn't say yes or no. Not yet. "I really want to."

Her lips parted slightly, as if she meant to speak . . . but she closed them again and propped her chin on his chest.

Neither of them spoke. Neither of them tried to answer the question *what if?* But he could feel it hanging over them, a dark cloud over this makeup and this near perfect relationship, formed on a serendipitous meeting in a dark car and built on a mutual love of dogs and horror movies.

Jonah brushed her hair over her shoulder with his fingers. It felt as if they both had something to say but needed the other to say it first. The big *what if* would remain a mere question for the moment—any discussion mercifully cut short by whining on the other side of the door.

They got up and arranged themselves, then opened the door.

Lulu, the dog who was doing the whimpering, raced ahead of them back into the main part of the house, curling up next to a snoozing Bob, who had helped himself to Truck's dog bed. Bob didn't seem to notice Lulu at all, and Lulu, apparently content now that they were all together again, circled three times, settled with her back pressed to Bob's side, and with a heavy sigh, closed her eyes.

They'd left no room for Truck. That dog wandered in from the kitchen, stared at the two of them on his bed for a moment, then slid down onto his belly, his head between his paws, and licked his chops.

His chops. "Shit!" Jonah suddenly bolted for the kitchen.

Just as he'd feared—Truck had eaten the chicken.

Twenty-Four

Heavy panting and the distinct smell of dog breath woke Harper the next morning. Groggily, she slowly recalled everything that had happened the previous evening. She and Jonah had ordered a pizza after Truck had polished off the chicken. They had sat on his bed with three dog sentries, talking about how they could work in concert to build business at both stores. She gave him suggestions that she could think of right off the top of her head—how a loss leader would work to sell more products (that free slice of pie had to be used properly to sell more). The sort of advertising that worked successfully for diners and coffee shops (pictures, and lots of them). How he should look into merchandise with consistent branding.

Jonah was clearly not a marketing guy—he seemed impressed and amazed by all of her suggestions, even jotted them down on his phone. "So we're doing this," he'd said to her at one point. "We're going to work together."

"We're going to help each other. But Deja Brew is still going to kick your butt."

Jonah laughed and rolled on top of her. He slid his thumb slowly across her bottom lip. "Here's a little secret about me . . . I like making my girlfriend eat crow."

"Oh, so *now* I'm your girlfriend." She nipped at his thumb, and he slid it into her mouth.

"Obviously. I wouldn't put up with this crap from anyone else."

She bit his thumb. "Ouch," he said, and withdrew it, then slipped his hand under her T-shirt, sliding up to her breast.

"Guess what?" she said. "I like taking *any* opportunity to tell my boyfriend he's wrong."

"Then I hope one day you have that opportunity. But you won't have it this time." He kissed her neck, then the hollow of her throat.

She angled her head to one side. "I'll have so many opportunities, I'll be hoarse from saying I told you so. It's going to be embarrassing for us both."

"Dream on." He nibbled on the lobe.

"Keep living in your fantasy world," she said breathlessly, and grabbed a handful of his hip.

"I'd be seriously concerned with your smack talk right now if you weren't so damn hot." He kissed her, his tongue tangling with hers.

Harper had decided then and there that they would end every fight his way. All her anxiety had melted away and she'd tumbled down the rabbit hole. She had tried to get her T-shirt off, but Jonah had to help her. "How are you going to outsell me?" he'd asked as he pulled the shirt free. "You can't even get out of your T-shirt."

"Student, meet teacher," she'd said breathlessly, pulling him back to her.

Sex with Jonah was delicious. It was a fizzy cocktail of touch and desire in one intoxicating romp. It was uninhibited and satisfying and real. Harper's sexual experiences before him had felt anxious and stilted in comparison. With Jonah, it was all amazingly uncomplicated and she loved sex. Her! They swam along in their little stream, reaching and stroking, kissing and sliding, her emotions mixing with the physical sensations he was creating in her and around her until it all erupted in a tsunami of gratification.

When it was done, he'd looked at her with an unfathomable expression in his eyes. Whatever he'd been feeling, she was convinced she was feeling the very same thing: bewitched and confused and sober and in love.

She turned her head—Jonah was there, his back to her, sleeping on his side.

It had happened. It was real.

Harper fell back against the bed and yawned. This was so *nice*. Everything felt comfortable and natural.

Ten hours ago, she wasn't so sure if it would ever feel this way again. There had been the fight, which had thrown her for a loop. And then Soren raiding her budget. And then her reconciliation with Jonah, for which she was so grateful. But something was niggling her this morning.

He wanted to go to Madrid.

Of course he did. Who wouldn't want that gig? The only thing holding him back was the Lucky Star.

If she was holding him back—and she didn't think she was, not really—she didn't want to be. She would never stand in the way of an opportunity like that.

Harper really did believe she could help him achieve his goal. That's what she did, after all. She set goals. She achieved them. And then she wrapped them neatly in tissue paper and put them in her mental closet and went on to the next one.

But something else was pricking at her, something she couldn't quite put her finger on. She dropped her arm over the side of the bed and scratched Bob's head. He licked her fingers.

She really did want to help Jonah, in any way that she could. She'd never gotten to do that before, never gotten to be the someone to help a loved one, because she flew solo. So for the first time in her life, she could be that person, could help someone achieve something they wanted, just like she'd always wanted someone to help her.

She pushed up, pressed her lips to Jonah's shoulder.

One of his eyes fluttered open. He turned his head and looked at her. "So it wasn't a dream."

She giggled at discovering he had the same thought. "Nope." She smiled. "It wasn't a dream twice."

"Twice and an attempt at a third," he reminded her. "Which we agreed would have happened had we not eaten so many damn carbs."

Harper laughed at the memory. She nibbled his shoulder. "I have to go."

"Don't go."

"I have to. Soren raided my operating budget and I have to regroup."

"He what?" Jonah came up on his elbows. "Why?"

"Because he overextended himself, and he needs money to pay the architect for the new bistros. Or steak houses. Whatever they are."

Jonah frowned. "That doesn't sound good. But listen, if you need to know how to run a shop with no money, I'm your guy."

Harper laughed. "I'm not *that* poor." She crawled over him to get her things and managed to step on Lulu's tail, since the little dog was sleeping under the bed. The dachshund let out a high-pitched shriek, which caused the other two dogs to hop up to investigate.

"There are too many dogs in here," Harper complained. She grabbed up her clothes and headed for the bathroom, Truck on her tail, his snout on her skin.

"Call your dog!" she exclaimed.

But Jonah was laughing too hard to get his name out.

Twenty-Five

The new "partnership" between Deja Brew and the Lucky Star didn't feel or seem like much at first—they carried on as usual, Jonah with his free pies, Harper with her egg baskets. She figured out how to trim some money out of her budget. Nowhere near twenty thousand, but she had at least covered the next month.

Jonah did talk to Carly and proclaimed it a productive conversation one night as he and Harper had dinner. "She suggested a happy hour event with some radio advertising. But the rates are really expensive."

"Are you going to do it?"

Jonah dragged his fingers through his hair. "We would have to figure out some logistics, and I don't know how the guys are going to feel about it. But I'm thinking about it."

On the day Deja Brew introduced their new birthday cake batter latte, a sign went up across the street—NEVER WAIT BEHIND A FRAPPE AGAIN. COME IN AND TEST OUR EXPRESS COFFEE LANE AND GET A FREE SLICE OF PIE WHILE YOU'RE AT IT. ALWAYS FASTER AT THE LUCKY STAR.

Harper snorted and said to Elizabeth, one of the new baristas, "Like that's going to do anything for them."

"I don't know," Elizabeth said. "I've been watching a pretty steady stream of customers go in over there. We had three standing at our door, and one of them pointed to the Lucky Star and off they went. It's probably the radio ads, too."

Harper turned her head to Elizabeth. "What radio ads?"

"Haven't you heard them? Do you listen to KGSR? *Visit us at the Lucky Star on South Congress! An Austin original coffee shop with free pie*," she said, mimicking the announcement with jazz hands.

Jonah had complained about the expense, but he must have ponied up after all. "So that's what they're calling themselves now? An Austin original?"

"I guess." Elizabeth returned to her work.

Harper should have done the same, but she lingered so that she could glare at Jonah's shop across the street. Just then, the door to the Star opened, and Jonah's mother stepped out. She had Lulu on a leash, and the dachshund was wearing a weenie-dog vest in spite of temperatures near seventy degrees. There was writing on the vest. Harper squinted and leaned forward. She could just make out the words, VOTE FOR ME. She gasped softly—they'd put a King Mutt billboard on Lulu!

Harper slid down onto the window seat next to Bob, her back to the Lucky Star. Bob snorted, but he put his head on her lap. "It's supposed to be a partnership," Harper muttered.

She looked around her shop. A couple was in the egg baskets. One of them had a frappe. "Hey! Glad you came in today. Did you try the birthday cake batter latte?"

The woman, a blonde with the longest false lashes Harper thought she'd ever seen, nodded. "It's delish," she said. "It's like drinking a milkshake."

Harper beamed. "Right? I think it's one of our best. Did you know it's sweetened with monkfruit? It's amazing how good drinks and food can be when you remove the processed ingredients and replace them with natural ones, right?"

The woman blinked up at her. "Umm . . . I guess?"

"Enjoy!" Harper walked away from the table and texted Jonah: People would rather experience a birthday cake batter drink sweetened with monkfruit than get a quick cup of black coffee, FYI.

A half hour later, his response came through. It was a picture of him holding a stopwatch, and Amy smiling devilishly at the camera as she steamed a latte.

Harper smiled in spite of herself. She texted: Nerds.

Jealous.

Nothing to be jealous about, she shot back.

But okay, maybe she was a little jealous. Especially when Kendal called her later to tell her what money he'd been able to scrape together. "It's not enough to cover your shortfall," he said. "If we could cut down on utilities, that would help."

"How?" she asked, looking around her. "We need lights. And refrigeration."

"It's just a suggestion."

"Thanks, Kendal." She sighed. "I'm trying to find places to cut, too. But I have to go. Our publicity person is due any minute."

"I hate to say it, Harper, but that's a big chunk of change you're paying her."

"I know, I know," she said wearily. She'd already thought of that.

The first thing Carly did when she came in was squat down to Bob's throne. He actually sat up and turned his face to hers.

"Hey!" Carly said when she'd finished cooing over Bob. She walked across the shop to Harper. "Girl, I've got a great gig for your garden. You know Marla Sadler, right?"

Harper had to think a minute. "The woman running for mayor?"

"The very one. She's surging in the polls, according to her campaign manager, and she wants to have a very exclusive fundraiser. You need some action in your beautiful garden. And voilà, just like that, a great idea is born."

"Really?" Harper perked up. "When?"

"Week after next. And get this—she comes with her own music. Her husband is Derek, as in Derek Sadler and the All-Star Texas Band. We'll need to serve wine and beer, but you have a license, and they'll pay for it, plus some light catering, and then the space rental. *And* you can hand out all the swag and treats you want. I have some ideas for that, too."

This could make up the difference in the budget shortfall. Harper brightened. "That's fantastic, Carly!"

"I made sure to schedule it on a different weekend than when Suzanna is playing."

"Suzanna is coming back?"

Carly laughed. "Not here. To the Lucky Star. We just confirmed it this morning."

Harper blinked. Jonah hadn't been kidding when he said he'd try and get her. "*That's* who is coming to play at their happy hour? I thought we were doing a partnership!"

"We are!" Carly assured her. "His signage will advertise the Sadler event. And we'll pop a sign in your window about Suzanna."

"That doesn't feel like much of a partnership," Harper complained. "A political event versus Suzanna? And did you see Lulu? She's a walking billboard now."

Carly's face lit up with her smile. "Isn't she *adorable*? And the little vest! What a great way to advertise the charity fundraiser and the coffee shop. I thought it was brilliant."

"You thought of it?"

"Nope. But I approve one hundo p. And listen, that political fundraiser will be *lit*. These people are movers and shakers, and you have no idea how much they can drink."

The next day, Harper put a sign in the window, courtesy of the

Sadler campaign, to announce the upcoming fundraiser and the performance by Derek Sadler and the All-Star Texas Band. She and Bob
went outside to examine the sign placement from all angles, and
while she was standing there, she received a text.

It was, of course, from Jonah. My various weather apps say rain on
that date. In the next few seconds, she received a picture of a big red
bucket. You're going to need this. Again. She looked up. He waved at
her from the window.

She flipped her hair and said, "Come on, Bob," and went back
inside.

Later that afternoon, she decided to do a little reconnaissance.
She and Elizabeth made up slips of paper offering one dollar off their
keto-friendly bakery options. When she entered the Lucky Star, Lyle
Lovett was crooning from the speakers, and the place smelled like
pie. There was something about it that was charmingly nostalgic.

Lulu was the first to greet her, the wiggling brown swirl of dog
and helicopter tail. She was wearing her billboard, and Harper
couldn't help noticing that Lulu's vote jar was at least as full as Bob's.
"Don't let that snoot of yours get too high in the air," she said,
scratching Lulu under the chin. "Bob hasn't even begun to work it."

She stood up and that's when she noticed rocking chairs had replaced the old wooden chairs that had been there before. She walked
around to the tables, handing out her slips of paper. The two gentle-
men in Marine Corps caps were skeptical. "What's keto?" one of
them asked.

She thought maybe the technical explanation was neither wished
for nor did she want to give it. "It means it was made with almond
flour, basically."

The two men looked at each other.

"You should check it out sometime."

"Don't think so," the other one said, and the two of them chuckled as they pushed the slips of paper back across the table to her.

"Gonna have to be a good sight better than Darlene's pie to impress us."

"Well. We happen to have some wonderful bakers at Deja Brew, too."

One of the men smiled at her. "We like it just fine here at the Star."

All right. Every store had their loyal followers.

She moved on, to a group of six women seated around a round table. Three of them were rocking along in the new rocking chairs. And all six of them had coffee cups that looked handmade. But upon closer inspection, she could see that all the cups featured the Lucky Star in some fashion. The one closest to her had been painted with the words *An Austin Original*. A couple of them appeared to have the old sign out front. One ambitious artist had tried to capture Roy Rogers.

The women all had the same book in front of them in either a physical copy or on an e-reader—*The Secrets of a Suburban Mom*.

"Hello! I don't mean to interrupt, but would you like a coupon for some of Deja Brew's bakery items? They are keto and Paleo friendly." She handed the slips around.

All six of them seemed delighted and each of them reached for one. "My sister is doing keto," said a woman with long dark hair streaked with gray. She'd piled it on top of her head. "She's lost twenty pounds."

The women all looked at the slips with renewed interest.

"We have a test kitchen at our north store where we are constantly trying new things," Harper said. "Have you checked out Deja Brew yet? It's an artisan coffeehouse across the street. Most of our products are low-carb, full of antioxidants, and naturally sweetened with monkfruit."

One of the ladies, with a short bob of gray, looked at the window and shook her head. "That's not my style. I like this kind of coffee shop—you can't miss with free pie. And of course, we go way back with the Rogers family."

All six of them loudly voiced their agreement about the Rogers family.

Harper's teeth clenched behind her smile.

"What's this?"

Amy appeared wearing green overalls and a bright yellow blouse with a Peter Pan collar, and yellow-and-green-striped glasses.

"Coupons to try a keto bakery item across the street."

Amy took two. "Keto. I tried a keto cookie once. Thought it had a metallic taste."

As if. "Not these," Harper said, her smile getting thinner.

"I'll try them," Amy said, and stuffed the two slips into a pocket. "Hey, did you see our coffee cups?" She pointed to more of the hand-made coffee cups on the counter. "The ladies here made them. We're giving one away to each new customer."

"Well, that's original," Harper said with a side-eye to Amy. "Do you have new customers?"

The women laughed. So did Amy. All was fair in love and part-nerships. "We do now," she said proudly.

"You ladies made them?" Harper asked.

The one with the long hair streaked with gray gave an easy flick of her wrist. "Oh, it's just something we do to keep out of trouble. We enjoy it."

"Would you like one?" Amy asked with a sly smile. "You're sort of a new customer."

Harper *did* want one. "*Yes*, thank you. Now which one of you is stuffing Lulu's vote jar?"

"We all are!" one of the women gleefully announced. "Isn't she just the *cutest puppy?*" she crooned as Lulu wobbled over for attention. The woman bent over to pet her. "Just the *cutest puppy*," she squeaked.

"You should come across the street and say hello to Bob the Bull-dog," Harper suggested.

"Oh, I did," said another woman. "His little University of Texas T-shirt was adorable."

"His vote jar is pretty full, too," Harper said, and looked at Amy.

"It's not a contest," Amy said sweetly.

"King Mutt is *literally* a contest," Harper countered.

"I mean that all dogs are winners."

"Truth!" one of the women said heartily.

"We've had three different people stop in to inquire about adopting Lulu. What about Bob? Any interest in adopting him?" Amy asked.

There was an acute interest on Harper's part. One woman had seemed interested until Bob growled at her. "Everyone is—"

"What's going on?"

Marty Rogers had joined them. He, too, was holding one of the ladies' cups. How many had they made?

"Harper brought some coupons for her Paleo bakery items."

"Keto," Harper corrected.

"What?" Marty took a slip of paper from her hand and read it. "Belinda!" he suddenly bellowed. "Belinda, come out here and remind me why we don't like this keto business!"

"Okay," Harper said with a sigh.

"Hey, ladies, what did you think of our express lane?" Marty asked the book club.

"Marty, that was without a doubt the fastest and best cappuccino I've ever had. I don't know why you didn't do that a long time ago," the woman with the short bob said. "I miss Paula, but I sure like that express lane."

"She got another job," another of the ladies piped up. "She's working at Trudy's."

"I *love* Trudy's," one of them said. "They have the best enchiladas in town."

"Disagree," said the tiniest of the six women. "The Eldorado Café. Those enchiladas are authentic Mexican."

"How would you know if they were authentic Mexican enchiladas, Karen?" one of them asked, and they all laughed.

"Hey! My great-aunt was from Juarez."

"But she wasn't Mexican."

"She wasn't Mexican, she was Cuban," Karen said, and launched into a description of an ancestral line that grew increasingly hard to follow. She'd gotten pretty far up the family tree when the bell above the door sounded, and they all turned as one as a woman entered the Star. Harper recognized her as the Starbucks barista who had come in the day Harper sampled the pie.

"Oh, hey, Everly, come get a coupon for a keto bakery item at Deja Brew," Amy said.

The woman walked across the dining room and took a slip from Harper. "Hmmm," she said.

"It's sweetened with monkfruit," Harper offered.

Everly shrugged and tucked the slip into her shirt pocket.

"Sweet tea?" Amy asked the barista.

"Yes, please."

Amy started toward the counter. "Harper, you still want a Lucky Star cup?"

"I do. Thank you." They had plenty of mugs at Deja Brew, but she liked it here. She liked that everyone knew one another. That they had regulars and they liked to sit around and talk. That they all had homemade coffee cups and were loyal and kind and liked pie. She had a crazy urge to pull up a chair with the book club and ask about the book and sign up for pottery classes.

When Amy went to get the cup, Everly looked down at Lulu, who was begging for attention. "She's so cute." She looked at Harper. "How's the new place?" she asked, indicating Deja Brew with her head.

"Good! Building every day."

Amy came out from behind the counter with a handmade coffee cup and the sweet tea for Everly.

"We have an adorable bulldog in the King Mutt competition," Harper added.

"You mean a stuck-up bulldog," Amy said with a laugh. "How's it at Starbucks?"

"Oh, you know. It's going along." Everly shrugged again. She shrugged a lot. "We've had a lot of traffic lately. Probably because of Duke."

"Duke? Who is Duke?" Amy asked.

"The Saint Bernard puppy we are sponsoring for King Mutt."

It took a moment for that to sink in, but Amy and Harper exchanged a look of shock and horror, then looked at Everly the Barista. "You have a puppy in the King Mutt competition?"

Everly nodded. "Cutest thing. He's got a little barrel collar. You know . . . like he's going to save someone." She giggled. "He's *so popular*. Like, who knew? We had to get a bucket for all the votes. Needless to say, we had to bring on an extra person just to keep up with orders. Everyone's coming to see Duke." She cast a meaningful look at Lulu's vote jar.

Amy handed Everly the tea. "You've been coming in here every afternoon for tea and never mentioned you had a dog?"

"Didn't come up," Everly said. "Thanks for the tea—see you later." She smiled, clearly enjoying the surprise, and went out, that green apron draped over her arm.

"What the hell?" Amy muttered.

"A Saint Bernard puppy?" Harper muttered back. "No one can beat a Saint Bernard puppy. Where were the Saint Bernard puppies when I went to the ACC?"

"Has she been coming in here all this time just to spy?" Amy asked, clearly hurt by the turn of events. "Because if she has, this means war."

"It damn sure does," Harper agreed. She looked at Amy. "Thanks for the cup." She dipped down to give Lulu some love. "You're as cute as any puppy, Lulu, and don't let anyone tell you differently." She stood up, waved to the women in the book club. They all waved back. One of them wished her luck with her keto bakery products. Even Marty shouted at her from the private dining room and his jigsaw puzzle to have a good day.

Harper walked back across the street, to her swinging baskets, to her artisan coffee, her keto-friendly foods, and her stuck-up bulldog. She went back to all the latest trends, and the sort of customers who followed the latest trends, who liked Tiny Pies and locally sourced products and no GMOs.

She sat beside Bob in the window seat and stroked his back. He pressed against her and propped his head on a pillow, gazing out at the Lucky Star.

Harper felt a weariness seep into her bones. A weary loneliness, if she was going to be precise. This feeling . . . this wasn't like her at all. She had always been capable of finding the bright side of any situation. But there was something about the Lucky Star that felt so warm. And familiar on some level.

Was it because the people who tended to gravitate to Deja Brew were young professionals rushing off to work, and they really weren't building any sort of community? Harper had envisioned writers and musicians filling her egg baskets. Locals who wanted to make this a little home away from home. So far the clientele seemed to be touristy and transient, in a hurry to be somewhere else. But the vibe at the Lucky Star was so different—everyone seemed to belong there. To be an actual part of the place.

She looked around at the iron and chrome and trendy baskets. She watched Elizabeth hand an oversized cup with a tower of whipped cream to a woman who was wearing high-heeled thigh boots. She glanced at four young men around a table, all of them drinking green smoothies, all of them muscle-bound. Gym rats, she guessed. Men with disposable income who probably didn't think twice about the cost of a green matcha smoothie.

Deja Brew was obviously not the same sort of place as the Lucky

Star. And it really shouldn't be—it catered to people in high-heeled thigh boots and green smoothie drinkers. But Harper? *She* wanted to be in a place like the Lucky Star. Looking across the street now, she felt a little like she used to feel when she was a kid, looking at Olivia's house. She'd wanted to belong in their world, too.

It was even more than that. The thing she hadn't quite been able to grasp the morning after she and Jonah made up, that thing that was teasing her from the far reaches of her mind, had finally crystallized in her thoughts. She realized now that in partnering with Jonah to help bring business to the Lucky Star, she was helping him leave Austin for Spain.

She was helping him achieve a goal that didn't include her.

Twenty-Six

Jonah had agreed to go for a morning run with Harper.

The night before, they'd eaten from a pan of macaroni and cheese, both of them too tired to make it a proper meal. Harper had fallen asleep on the couch, the dogs had piled up on Truck's bed together, and Jonah had flipped through a silent round of basketball games, nursing a beer.

He'd had a lot on his mind. Earlier that day, he'd come into the Lucky Star and found an actual lunch crowd. He'd counted twelve tables, enough that Aunt Belinda and Amy were stressed. Burt was complaining about needing help, his mother had flour all through her hair and seemed to have trouble keeping up with the pie baking.

He couldn't believe it . . . but they were really starting to turn things around. And it wasn't just the fine weather, either—it had turned cold again. Somehow, through dumb luck and some ideas they never would have had if Harper hadn't come into his life, they were infusing new life into the Star.

He'd stood there, staring at the store that looked exactly as it had when he was growing up. How could it be that nothing was the same but *looked* the same? Robert and Lloyd were in their usual spot at the booth in the middle of the window with their slices of pie, but there were new faces in the store. Younger customers, and all of them with slices of pie. A few of them had the coffee cups the book club had made. More than one had ordered a grass-fed beef burger and truffle oil fries.

Was it really this simple? All they had to do was give away some free stuff and people started coming in again?

"It's the advertising," Harper had informed him later that night when they had shared the pan of macaroni. "With good advertising, people think nothing of paying five bucks for a rainforest muffin. It's truly amazing what the right ad can get people to buy."

Jonah was wondering why it had taken them so long even to *consider* the possibility of a gentle marketing campaign.

He was patting himself on the back when his dad had come into the office after the lunch rush. Jonah had assumed it was to fret about the money they were spending on advertising and was prepared to show him the receipts from the last week.

His dad had eased himself down onto the chair with a grimace.

"Are you all right, Dad?"

"Stop asking, I'm fine. It's pretty busy out there. We might need to think about bringing Paula back."

Jonah grinned. "Right? At long last, something is clicking."

"Pie always clicks. Your mother is a great baker. I wanted her to go on one of those baking shows she likes, but she doesn't want to take time from the family or the Lucky Star."

Jonah had nodded. "Sounds like Mom."

His dad had drummed his fingers on the arm of the chair, studying his son. "I think it's time I took back the helm, Joe."

Jonah wasn't expecting that. It sounded vaguely like he was being fired. "Why? Is something wrong?"

"Course not. But the Lucky Star is not your life. It's ours. I can take it from here."

It was funny how you could want so badly to be released from something, but the minute you were released, you felt bad about it. Jonah had gotten used to steering the ship. "Are you sure, Dad? It's pretty stressful, and your oncologist said to avoid stress with your immune—"

The chair had squeaked loudly when his dad suddenly surged forward. "Jonah? I know what he said. I feel fine. We don't need you here."

Maybe Jonah had had too much on his mind, or it was the way his dad had said it—but that had sounded pretty dismissive and Jonah had snorted and said, "Since when?"

His father's pale face had taken on a definite hue. He had stared hard at his son, and then said quietly, "You're right. You've been a help to me and your mother all your life. From the moment Jolie died, you were our bright spot. But this time, we went too far. You're in the prime of your life, and you need to live it the way you see fit. Not for us. Now, I appreciate everything you've done, Joe, and God knows we owe you a debt for pulling us back from the brink. This is not your place. It's not what I want for you, and if you're honest, it's not what you want for you, either."

Jonah said nothing. All of that was true.

His father had eased back in his chair. "And the truth is, I feel useless around here. I need to be running this place like I did before. That's *my* place, and I'm not helpless and I don't need you to save me."

It took several moments for Jonah to respond. "Okay," he said at last.

Jonah really did understand his dad's point of view. It had stung at first, after all Jonah had sacrificed and done to help. But there was something liberating in how forcefully his father had said it. His father didn't need him, but Jonah realized he needed his father's tacit approval to take the job of a lifetime.

Still, he hadn't slept well, his warring thoughts mixing into uncomfortable dreams.

This morning, Harper woke him up at the ridiculous hour of 6 A.M. "We've got to work the kinks out."

With a groan, Jonah got up and fed the dogs. When they left, Lulu and Truck were stacked against the wall, pretending not to look at the bowl of food Bob was taking his own sweet time about eating.

They set off at a leisurely pace, talking about their busy schedules for the rest of the week. Harper told him she'd figured out a way to fix the budget shortfalls Soren had left her with. She was going to delay delivery of something until the next month, although he didn't hear what exactly. His thoughts were still racing. He was going to call Edgar before he went to work at the Star.

"So let me ask you something," Harper said as they came to a red light at the corner. "What is the worst thing that ever happened to you at work?"

The light turned green. They started running. "Hmm . . . once, I mistakenly sent an e-mail to my boss intended for my cousin. I said he'd acted like a douche the day before and he was lucky I didn't kick his ass."

Harper gasped. And then laughed. "Oh my God! What happened? Did you get fired? Is that the real reason you're back at the Lucky Star?"

"It was a long time ago, so no. Fortunately, my boss thought it was funny and sent back an e-mail confirming he's a douche. Why do you ask? What's the worst thing that ever happened to you?"

"Well, there was the time I brought some coupons for keto baked goods to the Lucky Star and no one knew what keto was."

"I could have told you that. People on my side of the street are very particular about their processed carbs and sugar overload."

"There was another time, too, also at the Lucky Star, when I found out that barista wench from Starbucks has been hiding something from us. They have an entry in the King Mutt contest."

"That crappy Starbucks down the street?" He snorted. "What do they have?"

"A Saint Bernard puppy!"

Jonah stopped running. "No way. Nothing is cuter than that."

"This is what I am saying!" Harper grabbed his arm so she could dig her sock out of the back of her shoe. "Then you agree this is an emergency. That a cute puppy could ruin Bob's turn at the crown, and then Bob would ruin Lulu's respectable second place finish. I think we need to go look at this dog."

"I agree about everything except your delusion as to who wins and who is a respectable second. But we have some serious reconnaissance to do, my friend."

Harper bounced up on her toes and kissed him. Then she started running again. "I knew you'd see it my way!"

"This afternoon?" Jonah asked. "We're meeting with Carly. We can go after that. Then I'll take you to dinner if you're up for it—a place where you can get a chicken-fried steak as big as your first car."

"Oh, *Jonah*. Don't sweet-talk me like that—I'll have to drag you into the bushes and have my way with you."

Jonah laughed—Harper always made him laugh.

"So what else is up with you this week?" she asked as they rounded a corner.

"Well . . . I'm taking the job." Jonah hadn't meant to blurt it out quite like that.

Harper stopped running. He did, too. He turned around, a few feet ahead of her.

"You *are*?"

He couldn't tell if she was excited or mad. He put his hands on his waist and sucked in some air. "I think so. Our business is . . . it's doing pretty good, thanks to you."

"Me?"

"Yes, *you*, Harper Thompson. You've taught me a lot about marketing, and upgrading our . . . what do you call it?"

"Aesthetic."

"Right. That."

"But I didn't do that." She ran a hand over her head, her expression one of confusion.

"Yeah, you did. It started with a dog named Bob. When I saw that vote jar and realized how many people would come into your shop to see that grump, things started to click. They clicked slow, I admit, but the more I listened to you, and saw what you were doing . . . and then, Jesus, your idea to *partner* together to bring in business was maybe the craziest thing I'd ever heard. But it worked! Do you know this week alone we have had twelve people come in from Deja Brew?"

She dropped her hand. "I didn't want it to work *that* well."

"So thank you, Harper."

She smiled. "I'm so happy, Jonah. I'm so happy you're going to take this job, because you would never forgive yourself if you didn't."

She did indeed seem happy. But she also seemed a tiny bit off. "But . . . ?" he prompted her.

"But six months is a long time. And if I get my job, I'll be in Rochester or Cary. It's just . . ." Her voice trailed off, and she dropped her gaze to the sidewalk.

Jonah walked back to her and wrapped his arms around her, resting his chin on top of her head. "I haven't worked through everything yet," he said. "We'll figure something out."

"Sure we will," Harper said into his shoulder. She didn't sound very convinced of it.

He didn't know if he was convinced of it, either.

Twenty-Seven

Jonah and Lulu bounced into work later, saying hello to the regulars, welcoming the newcomers, Lulu charming them almost right out of their pants. He asked Amy if she could man the shop while he met with his parents and aunt and uncle. He said he'd find her and Burt afterward and fill them in.

The first thing he'd done when Harper had left for the day was call Edgar. His boss had hooted with delight that Jonah was taking the job.

On the way in, Jonah had called Carly to discuss plans for going forward. She was coming in today in case the rest of the Rogers crew had questions about the next steps.

As he was explaining it to Amy, Carly arrived for their meeting.

"Hi, Amy!" she said, going in for a one-armed hug. "Thanks for setting me up with your brother. I have a client downtown who was looking for some banners, and your brother got them out in record time."

"He's the best! Hey, want to go with me to Deja Brew after the meeting? I'm taking some pictures of our new dessert tapas plate to hand out to their customers."

"You are?" Jonah asked.

"Yep. Harper said I should. We're getting flyers of their frappes tomorrow."

"Sure!" Carly said. She grinned at Jonah. "Are you ready? Let's do this."

His parents and aunt and uncle were already inside the private dining room. It looked a little different than it had before. They hadn't made any progress on the jigsaw puzzle, for one. And instead of the usual scattering of papers and magazines, there was a calculator, some recipe books, and empty coffee cups. Jonah's dad was at the far end of the table, propped against the wall. He gave Carly a curt nod. He looked tired, which Jonah didn't like. He feared his dad was taking on too much too soon . . . but he was not going to worry about that today. He had his marching orders from his father.

Carly started talking before Jonah had even taken a seat. "Well, hello, everyone! I've got some great news to share." She put her tote bag on the floor beside a chair. "I've got Jonah and Darlene booked on *Good Day Austin* next week. Isn't that fantastic? They'll be on during the cooking portion. You can make a pie on the air, can't you, Darlene?"

"What? Me? I . . . guess?"

"The producer thought it would be great to have a mother-son baking team."

"I don't bake," Jonah said at the very moment Belinda said, "How fun!"

"You'll need to demonstrate how to make one of your excellent pies," Carly continued as if Jonah hadn't spoken. "If you can give me a list of ingredients, they'll have them ready to go. Oh, I should warn you, we're going to need a finished pie before we begin. You know, to show what the final product looks like."

"They do that on all the cooking shows," Belinda said excitedly.

"While you're mixing things, Jonah is going to give a little background on the Lucky Star and talk about the free pie program."

"I wouldn't call it a *program*," Uncle Marty said gruffly. "It's not like we're feeding the homeless. And I thought we were going to do this free pie thing only for a little while longer."

"You have to admit it's working for us, Marty," Belinda said. "Our receipts are way up. This morning we had a line for our apple."

Uncle Marty frowned. "A line for *free* apple. This is getting out of hand. We can't just give pie to all of Austin."

"If it gets out of hand, you could change the program," Carly said. "Make it like a once-a-week thing. Friday Pieday! Or do it four times a year—this week, pies are free. There are no limits to what you could do, if you think about it. Darlene, you'll only have about five minutes," Carly said.

"Five minutes! You can't create a beautiful pie in five minutes."

"Sure, you can, Darlene," Belinda said. "This is so exciting! I bet we get a rush of customers from this. I watch *Good Day Austin* every morning. You know, I've been wanting to make rhubarb forever. This will be a great time to do it."

"Fabulous. We can mention that during the segment," Carly said. "Okay, we have the *Good Day Austin* spot," she said, holding up one finger. "We have the happy hour on Saturday, which I think is going to be a huge hit. We have another month's worth of radio advertising already booked, and I got that for you for a song." She paused. "Ha! I just made a radio joke. Oh, and you've got the King Mutt competition going, which is mentioned in the radio advertising."

"It is?" Jonah's dad asked.

"Yes sir. The ad says come in for a free slice of pie and to meet Lulu. People cannot resist dogs." She beamed at them. "All in all, I think it's been a great campaign on a shoestring budget."

"I wouldn't call it *shoestring*," Jonah's father said, sounding slightly offended.

"A smaller budget?" Carly cheerfully amended. "I'm going to of-fer a word of professional advice here, and that is, if at all possible, you should continue with the radio advertising after you're done with me. That will continue to get mileage for you. And I'm happy to step in on an as-needed basis to shore up the advertising message and get you some good rates."

That was the same advice Harper had given Jonah—keep up with the advertising.

"We really appreciate your help and all you've done," Marty said. "But the cost to advertise looks pretty high to me." He looked to Jonah. "Do you think it's worth it?"

All eyes turned to him. "I do," he said without hesitation. "The results speak for themselves. Nothing we've tried on our own has been this successful. Our receipts are improving every day. Who knew that with a little advertising, we could spur sales like this?"

"Well, I did," Carly said. "Also, I think you can more than cover the costs of whatever you put into monthly advertising. Once people start discovering the Lucky Star again, they will love it. This place is really kitschy, and people love that."

All of them but Jonah stared at Carly with confusion. "Kitschy?" Jonah's mother repeated.

"You know. Campy."

"I think what Carly is trying to say is that we're dated," Jonah translated.

"But in a good way!" Carly insisted. "Who has a shrine to Roy Rogers? Only the Lucky Star, that's who. It's unique, and people in Austin are *dying* for the old hippie days."

"Who is dying for them?" Belinda asked suspiciously. "And who said we're hippies?"

"Well, I don't know any personally, but I hear about them all the time." Carly glanced at her watch, then picked up her tote bag and stood. "I'm going to have to run. I'll e-mail you with the details for the *Good Day Austin* show. Anyone have any questions?"

They all shook their heads, and Carly cheerfully wished them all a good day and exited the room.

When the door had closed behind her, Jonah looked around the room. "Well? What do we think?"

"I think we're doing great!" Belinda said. "This has been an eye opener for me. Just think how a few changes could bring our business back. Harper gave me the name of a place that does branded shirts for a really good price. We can start selling those! Oh, and we could rehire Paula! And you know, it doesn't cost much to make those pies. Even if you hire a little kitchen help to bake them every day, it's not bad, and that's the beauty of it. I don't know why we didn't think about it a long time ago."

"We've come a long way," Jonah agreed.

"I have to make a pie on TV!" his mother said. "I better practice." She started to rise, but Jonah held up his hand. "Mom, there is something else—I have some pretty big news."

His mother's expression turned to one of concern. She sat. "What is it?"

"You know that my boss wants me to come back to work."

They all nodded.

"Because there is an important project my company wants me to head. It's developing deep space satellites with NASA. We are on the forefront of new technology, which is really cool, and this is a once-in-a-lifetime kind of thing. And if I take the job, it's a pretty substantial raise, plus six months of training and research in a facility outside of Madrid."

"Jonah!" His aunt beamed at him. "That's fantastic! I'm so proud of you."

"Thank you." He was grinning, because he was pretty proud of himself. "I'm really stoked about it. I've known about it, but I wasn't sure what to do here. But now that we have turned the Star around and Dad is feeling better, well . . . I'm thinking of going back to work earlier than I had planned. I need to know what you think. If there is anyone who is leaning towards selling, we should probably put it on the table and talk about it, because Dad is ready to take this on again. And spring would be a good time to hit the market if we go that route. However, if we're not selling it, I think we should hire Carly to help us get back up to where we used to be."

Once he started, the words had rushed out of him. He didn't know what he expected from them, but other than Aunt Belinda, no one looked happy. No one was offering an opinion or congratulations. "What is it?" He laughed self-consciously. "What did I say?"

His mother looked at his dad, then looked back at him. Her expression had turned sour. "I'll tell you what no one else will, Joe. Your dad—"

"Don't, Darlene," his father said sternly.

"What?" Jonah asked, looking at his dad.

"I'm sorry, Roy," his mother said. "But I'm telling him. You're his father and he deserves to know."

There was something in his mother's tone and the set of her jaw that told Jonah what she was going to say before she actually did. But she said it anyway, said the words as clear as anyone could. "Your father has cancer again. Lymphoma."

Jonah felt a swell of nausea, like he'd been spun around too fast. He couldn't speak. Could only stare at his father, who avoided his gaze.

But the doctor had given him the all clear!

Jonah could feel the wind leave him, the buoyancy of a dream job and a chance to build a satellite and Madrid leak out of him. In its place rose the fear of losing his father, of watching him suffer again. "Why did no one tell me? When? How—why didn't you *tell* me, Dad?"

"I'm okay," his father said, and put up a hand as if to stop an argument. "I have a treatment plan, and it's going to be fine. Don't look at me like I've got one foot in the grave."

"But you—"

"And now this meeting is over," his father said stiffly. He cast a dark look at his wife and stood. "Look, all of you. We're right where we wanted to be. We aren't out of the woods yet, but it's a good start. I don't think we need to make any life-altering decisions right now. As for you, Jonah—you pulled us up from the bottom of the barrel and you're leaving us afloat. That's all we've ever needed of you, and your work here is done. Now, I'm about as proud of you as I could ever be. Go build that stinking satellite. Go to Spain. Stare at the stars and the moon. We'll be *fine*." He moved around the table but paused as he passed Jonah. He put his hand on his shoulder and squeezed on his way out.

Jonah stared at the rest of them. "Why did no one tell me?"

"I'm sorry, Jo-Jo," his mother said. "He wouldn't let me tell you. And now he probably won't talk to me for a week, but I had to get that out in the open. I don't like the four of us knowing and not you. But we can't talk about it now, because we have too much to do to get ready for our happy hour and we're going to be on TV!" She stood up, too, picked up her things, and started for the door. Belinda and Marty exchanged a look and then followed.

But Jonah couldn't talk about it later. He'd told Edgar he was taking the job, barring any sudden changes at home. Well, this was a sudden change.

He couldn't believe his dad hadn't told him. All that talk yesterday, the "I don't need you." If his dad was going to have to endure chemo and radiation again . . . how could Jonah leave him?

He covered his face with his hands, seeking a solution somewhere in his engineer brain. Lulu came in through the open door and sat, her little body resting against his leg. Jonah unthinkingly dropped his hand to her head to stroke her long snout until his phone sounded, bringing him back to the present.

Twenty-Eight

Harper's day had begun with a phone call with Soren, who told her that Kendal had saved the day with some order that had gone awry at the Westlake store. "His mental agility is inexhaustible," Soren said. "Eruditely sagacious, that one."

Harper turned her gaze to the ceiling and privately prayed for deliverance. She wondered what Soren said about her to Kendal. She was exceptionally unexceptional, probably. The small hope she held on to for the promotion was shrinking.

When he had finished praising Kendal, Harper asked, "When are you going to decide on the promotion?"

"Soon," Soren said. "When inspiration has reached its zenith and doubt has tumbled into its nadir."

"A week? Two?"

"A week," Soren said, giving in.

Thank God for it. She couldn't bear his constant provocation. She was starting to wonder if he was a closet sadist.

Olivia called as Harper had gathered her things to go to work.

"I'm coming to town this weekend. It's too hard to get you on the phone, and besides, I need to see this place and this guy."

"Great," Harper said. "Bring something to wear to a happy hour," she added as she'd leashed Bob up.

"Oooh, where?"

"The Lucky Star. Jonah's place."

Olivia shrieked so loud that Harper had to hold the phone away from her ear. "Yes, please!"

Harper didn't hear what else she said—she was locking her door, and at that moment a door in her hallway opened and a woman emerged with a white terrier. It startled Bob, and he tried to lunge for the little dog, his teeth bared.

The woman cried out and grabbed her dog.

"I'm so sorry!" Harper said. "He's old and he's easily rattled."

The woman glared at her, as if Harper had taught him to lunge at little dogs, and hurried on ahead, grabbing the elevator before Harper. She glanced at her watch. She was running late and decided to take the stairs. But halfway down, Bob refused to go any farther, and had to be carried, and as he was not a small thing, she reached the ground floor already wearing a fine sheen of perspiration.

That wasn't even the worst of her day. Her brilliant ideas for how to make up her budget shortfall had backfired (Kendal had already made the adjustments), the new T-shirts had arrived with some mysterious bleach splashed across half of them, and Tyler hadn't shown up for work.

She'd wished she could go to the Lucky Star. She'd wanted to sit at the table with the book club, or try and get the cook to smile, or talk about signage with Marty. He was very interested in signs, she'd discovered one day this week. He'd walked across the street and engaged her in a very long discussion about one of theirs. Hell, she would have even had a piece of pie with the two old guys who came in every day.

At least she had Jonah to look forward to today. Seeing him always brightened her mood, no matter what. So much that when he told her this morning he was taking the job, her scalp had tingled and it felt as if a vise were closing in around her chest for a moment. Her very first thought was that she couldn't do without him.

It was an uncharacteristic thought for her to have. She was so good at being alone, at packaging up and packing away her feelings. She was *so good* at not being attached to anyone like boyfriends or parents. But now she was worried that maybe she couldn't do without him? What did that even mean? Did she think she wouldn't get out of bed?

She didn't know what to do with that feeling, but it was strong and refused to be banished.

When the clock at last struck the magic hour, Harper leashed Bob up, straightened his new bow tie collar, picked up his vote jar, and went across the street.

Bob growled when they entered the Lucky Star, wary of everyone and everything inside. There was a lot to be wary about—there was quite a lot of business at this time of day. There were more than a few tables filled and empty pie plates everywhere.

Lulu, having spotted Bob, came hopping and surfing across the floor, taking a shortcut underneath a couple of tables. Bob sat and grunted when she reached him but allowed the dachshund to sniff him out. Harper dropped his leash and strode through the dining room with his vote jar. "Vote for Bob," she said to each table as she passed, showing them the jar with Bob's picture on it. "He's a bulldog."

A few people cheerfully ponied up, and when she was done, she set Bob's jar next to Lulu's on the counter.

"What's this?" Amy asked, gesturing to Bob's jar.

"Jonah and I are going to go and check out the enemy," Harper said low.

"You mean Duke?"

"Yep. Bob needs to hang out for an hour or so."

"Sure."

"Don't try and persuade Bob's voters to move to Lulu."

"I don't need to," Amy scoffed. "No one is going to vote for Bob while Lulu is here. Trust me."

Just behind her, Jonah emerged from the office. He wore a black leather jacket and a knit cap, and he had a shadow of a beard. He looked so damn good, and Harper was struck by that viselike grip in her chest again. It felt a little like a burn, and she thought she would probably incinerate from the inside out when he moved to Spain and she moved to Rochester or wherever she ended up.

But the dark clouds that had begun to gather were puffed away when he smiled at her, a dimple in his right cheek. "Hey, gorgeous."

Was it possible to feel true love after only a few weeks?

He leaned in to kiss her cheek. "I am so glad to see you," she said, and she meant it. Glad and grateful and happy and all those words that tried in vain to summarize the feelings of love.

"Same here. Amy, you got this?"

"Do I got this," she repeated. "I've always *got* this, Jonah."

He squatted down to say hello to Bob and comment on his bow tie, then he linked Harper's arm through his and out they went. They ambled down the street together, two lovers, two best friends, chatting about the day, and the number of people in the Lucky Star this afternoon, and what a dick Soren could be. Jonah announced Burt had developed a new chili. "He's using grass-fed, grass-*finished* beef. Are you impressed?"

"Extremely," she said. "Did you even know that was a thing before you met me?"

"I'd heard rumors."

Harper suddenly gasped. She grabbed Jonah's arm with both hands. "*Look*," she whispered.

Jonah's head jerked around, obviously thinking they were about to be hit by a car, but then he saw what Harper saw. "Oh my *God*."

Across the street, in the Starbucks display window, Duke had managed to get his enormous front paws onto the sill to look out at the world. He was looking right at them, his nose moving, his tail wagging, as he tried to smell the outside from within. He had fluffy black ears, a brown-and-white face, and a round, boopable black nose. That creature was adorable. "It is so much worse than I feared," Harper whispered.

"Okay," Jonah said, taking her hand in his. "Let's not panic. He's cute, but puppies can be a pain. Let's go in and see how obnoxious he is. Try and get him to bite you."

"Roger that. You see if you can get him to piss on something."

They jogged across the street and entered the store. Everly the barista was behind the counter. She smiled wickedly when Harper and Jonah walked up. "Well, *hello* there, and welcome to Starbucks. Never thought I'd see any of you in here. What would you like?"

"Where's the bucket?" Harper asked smartly, harkening back to Everly's boast.

She pointed behind Jonah and Harper, and when they turned, there was indeed a big red bucket on its own table, with Duke's picture and King Mutt scrawled across it. Jonah immediately leaned forward to see how much was in the bucket. When he turned back, Harper didn't even have to ask. His expression said it all—it was stuffed.

He picked up a clipboard. "What's this?"

"Oh, that. It's the list of all the people in line to adopt Duke. Sorry, we don't have any free pie or dollar Frappucinos, but then again, we don't need gimmicks. We're Starbucks and people come in all day long to get a look at Duke. So do you want anything to drink besides your steady stream of tears?"

"Yes," Jonah said confidently. "The cheapest thing you have on the drink menu. What's that going to be? Coffee dregs?"

"It's going to be boring, that's for sure. Two blonde roasts coming up." Everly the barista turned away, but did indeed come back with two ubiquitous Starbucks paper cups. "It's on me," she said. "I'm going to enjoy watching you bawl like a baby when the winner is crowned."

Jonah picked up the cups. "Don't count your chickens before they hatch," he said smartly.

"Is that all you've got?" Harper whispered as they found a couch.

"Sorry. I don't think that fast on my feet."

They sat side by side and watched Duke play tug-of-war with some random customer.

"We're doomed," Harper said.

"We're not going down without a fight," Jonah said. He gave a soft whistle—the dog instantly dropped its end of a soggy piece of rope and raced to where Jonah and Harper sat, his paws like curling disks on the wood floor. He was unable to stop himself from sliding into a table, but he cheerfully righted himself and continued on, running as fast as an ungainly puppy with no traction would. When he reached them, he hoisted his front paws onto Harper's knees, and she caught him. "I can't," she whimpered. "He's too adorable. Look at the brown eyes, that pink tongue, and the sweet, sweet puppy fur."

"Yep. This is a straight-up disaster." Jonah leaned into her so that he could pet Duke. "It's the timing. One year from now, this little guy will be a monster wearing a drool bib. But right now, he's perfect. Harper, we have to keep this puppy a secret."

"How? You saw his vote bucket—word has already spread."

Duke tried to bite Jonah's hand, and then, captivated by something new, he suddenly yanked his paws away from Harper, but with too much energy, and he tumbled onto his back. Jonah and Harper laughed. Duke got up and trotted away, tail high.

Harper sipped the coffee Everly had given them . . . and nearly spit it out, it was so hot. She lifted the cup to see if the label gave any information about the offensively hot brew. It said HOME OF THE KING MUTT WINNER on the label, and then someone with a Sharpie had written *Loser I* on her cup. She looked at Jonah's. Sure enough, *Loser II* was on that label. "Oh, she is *evil*."

Duke had picked up the rope toy and was slinging it around, growling, as if it were prey he was trying to kill.

Harper sighed. "I love Bob, but he's such a curmudgeon, always mad about something. And he won't give anyone the time of day. He could never beat this dog."

"I love Lulu, too," Jonah agreed. He leaned back, stretching out his legs and crossing them at the ankles. "But she keeps peeing in the hallway by the bathrooms."

"Can't imagine the health department will be down with that."

"Not for a minute," he agreed. "If you had to vote for King Mutt, right this minute, and your vote is the winner, who would you pick?"

"Who would *you* pick?"

"We'll say it together on the count of three."

Harper nodded.

"One . . . two . . ."

"Duke!" they said in unison. And then laughed at themselves so hard that Jonah nearly spilled his coffee.

Jonah put his arm around her shoulders and pulled her closer. Harper's leg was pressed against his. "What are you thinking about now?" he asked.

"I don't know . . . well, I *do* know." She sighed. "I don't think I'm getting the promotion."

"What? Why?"

She shook her head. "It's just a feeling I have. Soren is playing some kind of game with me, but I don't think it's the winning game. I think Kendal is going to win." She twisted around and smiled at him. "Dude. You really pulled out all the stops at the Lucky Star. I think you're actually going to win this thing."

"There's not a competition, remember? We're working as partners."

"If I had opened the Lucky Star, I would have won," she said. "That's the kind of place I could have really kicked ass with, and that's exactly the kind of thing Soren would like. He loves out-of-the-box stuff."

Jonah blinked in surprise. "I thought Deja Brew was out of the box."

"Really?" Harper asked. "I think Deja Brew types are all over Austin. But the Lucky Star, places like that don't exist anymore. It's special."

He gave her a funny smile. "You really think that? Because there was a time you didn't think so."

Harper thought about that a moment. She hadn't really considered the Lucky Star at all until she'd met Jonah. It was a lesson learned—you never knew what sort of experience was behind some weathered doors in plain red brick buildings. "I see it in a different light now. I mean, is there any other place themed around Roy Rogers? And your regulars—all those old Austinites. You don't see them at Deja Brew—you see all the trends. And a thousand yoga mats a day, strapped on to the backs of hip people. Plus, your pies are so much better."

"Wow." He brushed a lock of her hair back that was stuck in her collar. "This is high praise coming from Miss Deja Brew. I never thought of the Star as being outside the box. Just . . . old."

"It's vintage. I'm glad I'll be around to see what you do with it from here on out." She meant that—she couldn't wait to see where the Rogers family took it next.

"I can't believe what I'm hearing," Jonah said with a laugh. "You're so cocky about your artisan coffeehouse."

She smiled sheepishly. "You have to believe your smack talk. But you also have to be able to see things clearly."

"Don't sell yourself short, and don't throw in the towel. You've done an amazing job with Deja Brew. Soren would be an absolute idiot to go with the other guy. You've earned this job, Harper."

His support meant the world to her. It seemed like such a simple thing, to have her back in this. But all her life, her goals had been her own burden. She'd never really had anyone to cheer her on, and it felt pretty amazing. Her chest felt full of . . . well, joy.

Duke found a napkin on the floor and pranced through the tables with it, trying to eat it while showing it off. A woman caught him and grabbed the napkin from his mouth, and it was almost as if she'd taken the windup key out of him. Duke sank down onto his belly, his head between his paws, and closed his eyes.

"*Aaawwww,*" said absolutely everyone in the store.

"Maybe I'll put my name on Duke's list. Bob needs a friend, and Truck probably won't be available while you're in Madrid." She laughed, thinking about Duke and Bob.

"Yeah . . . I don't know about Madrid," he said soberly.

Harper jerked her gaze to him. "What do you mean? You said—"

"I know." He picked up her hand. "But I don't know if I can go now. Not for six months." He swallowed. "My dad's cancer is back."

Harper felt a thickening in her throat. "Oh my," she said softly. She twisted around to face him. "Isn't there someone else who can cover for you? What about Amy?"

"Amy is perfect as the front face. But she doesn't have the business side of it. Allen and Andy have their practices in Chicago, and Marty and Belinda are moving there. Mom is in the kitchen. There is no one but me." He glanced away, as if having to absorb the news all over again.

"But this job . . ."

He shook his head.

Harper didn't know what to say. She couldn't imagine what she'd do if she were in his shoes. She leaned her head against his shoulder. "You're such a good man, Jonah."

He snorted. "I'm a putz. I set myself up to be this guy. It didn't happen by accident."

"You're fortunate to have a family who needs you."

He smiled a little, but the comment sailed right past him. Because, she suspected, for someone like Jonah, it went without saying that family relied on family. That's what families did—they were there for one another.

It would be nice to be needed. It would be nice to be someone other than an afterthought.

"This coffee is too strong," Jonah said, putting it aside. "Where are you taking me to dinner anyway?"

"Kura."

Jonah smiled with delight. "The sushi place with the revolving sushi bar?"

"Yes!" Harper sat up and clapped her hands. "It's so much fun!"

"This is going to be the best dinner date ever." Jonah kissed her temple. "*You're* the best date ever," he murmured into her ear, then kissed her cheek. And when he lifted his head, he looked at her as if he was trying to work something out, or maybe she was, she didn't know . . . but something felt different. She felt attached and detached at the same moment, like part of her couldn't live without him, and part of her was preparing for the day she would. It was uncomfortable.

They each stuffed a couple of dollar bills into Duke's bucket on their way out and promised not to tell anyone. They stepped out to a warm afternoon breeze. Things were changing. One season was winding down and every now and again you'd catch a glimpse of the next one, and you'd feel both nostalgic and excited.

She felt a little nostalgic and a little excited.

Twenty-Nine

Preparing for the Suzanna happy hour was more work than Jonah could have imagined when he'd agreed to it. Her popularity had grown exponentially over the last year, and there was far more demand for tickets than Jonah thought they could accommodate. Marty had been working on removing the doors to the private dining area to provide overflow to the main dining room, but still, it was going to be impossible to pack everyone inside. Jonah complained loudly to anyone who would listen that they were going to have to hire some security to help.

"My brother and his band can do it," Amy offered.

In addition to being a heavy metal music enthusiast, and a printer by trade, Amy's brother was the size of a tractor. "Deal," Jonah said.

He and Harper kept in touch through texts. She sent him a picture of Bob wearing a crown of shamrocks for no apparent reason. And every day, Jonah checked Deja Brew's window, where Bob could be found ignoring more and more people who tried to get his attention. Someone had hung a sign crookedly over his spot:

VOTE FOR BOB THE BULLDOG FOR KING MUTT AND
HELP US TURN HIS FROWN UPSIDE DOWN

Jonah thought Bob was actually smiling, because he seemed to really enjoy ignoring people.

Harper also texted him about Kendal, the guy he thought was her archnemesis, but was maybe beginning to look like a friend. Big news. Today a client got a little irate and Kendal actually saved the day. I was almost impressed.

Jonah's brow rose. You're not going to start dating him now, are you?

Harper responded with the green going-to-be-sick emoji. I told him he was really brave and he told me not to get my panties in a wad, it was nothing. So no, not dating him. How is it going over there? Walked over to watch Marty unfurl the big signs. We agreed that they look pretty spectacular.

The signs were pretty spectacular. Jonah glanced around—things were starting to shape up. The happy hour might be more fun than I originally believed was possible. You're still coming, right?

Are you kidding? You are my competition. I have to come and make snide remarks about everything. Also, bringing my bestie Olivia. She's a flirt, so brace yourself.

He didn't need to brace himself. He was wound up like a clock, and the only things that could get through that tight coil were Harper and a few dogs.

By Saturday, the Lucky Star was starting to look like a newer, younger version of itself. Jonah didn't know how they had managed to pull it off, how it could look the same and yet . . . cool. *Hip.* Little star lights hung from the ceiling and wrapped around the fixtures (Harper's idea). Roy Rogers had gotten spiffed up, a new set of clothes that included a leather vest with fringe, and a speech bubble attached to his head that said, VOTE LULU FOR KING MUTT, complete with the blowup picture of her little face (Amy's idea). There were plenty of pies, a portable bar, and the small plywood stage he and Marty had constructed near the hallway leading to the bathrooms. His dad worried that removing three four-tops to make room for the stage was not a good idea. But the stage looked good, and after tonight, they could return the tables to the stage.

Jonah was proud of what they'd done, how they'd all worked together to make this happy hour happen. Even though his dad looked grayer every time he saw him, and tired quickly, he'd hung in there as best he could. But it was the gray of his father's face that had convinced Jonah—he couldn't leave the Star. Not now. He needed to be around to help his parents in spite of their very clear wishes that he not be around.

It wasn't just a feeling—his mother said it very directly to him early Saturday. They were in the kitchen working alongside Burt, who had embraced the grass-fed beef idea and was making sliders. His mother's exact words were: "Jonah, I don't want you at the Star anymore."

Jonah just happened to be looking at Burt when she said it and watched one of his thick brows rise up to the bandanna tied around his head before he silently turned around and walked into the cold storage locker.

"Excuse me?"

"I don't want you at the Star. We didn't raise you to run a coffee shop, we raised you to be someone important."

"No, you didn't, Mom—you once told me I could be a gravedigger as long as I was happy with my career choices."

"I say a lot of things I don't mean. We did not send you to school to be a gravedigger or to run the Lucky Star. We sent you to school to pursue your dreams. And now we don't need you here, and you're not happy with this choice."

"That's not true. I love the Star."

"You are not staying here!" she said loudly.

"Mom? Now is not a good time for this discussion," Jonah said, and gestured to the work they had ahead of them.

"I'm just saying. It's been on your father's and my mind a lot lately."

It had been on his mind, too. "Let's get through tonight, okay?"

"Get through whatever you want. I've said my piece." She turned away from him and stalked out of the kitchen. Burt walked out of the locker. Jonah wondered if he, too, wanted to say his piece.

"Don't look at me, man. I've got enough on my hands with this grass-fed business."

Jonah didn't have time to think about this right now, and honestly, he didn't need to think about it. He'd made up his mind.

An hour before doors opened, he did one final check of preparations. People were already lined up down the street. Four of the book club ladies had come in, volunteering to help hand out samples to the crowd. Amy had dressed up for the evening—she was wearing a sequined tank top under lime green overalls and black Clark Kent glasses. The only real staff expense for the event was the bartenders, which Carly had arranged through her seemingly bottomless list of contacts who were willing to give her cut rates.

It was time. Jonah went into the office and shrugged into the sport coat he'd brought to wear over his collared shirt. He washed his face, combed his hair, and sat down and texted Harper.

Crazy line outside. Not sure LS is ready for this.

She instantly texted back. You're nuts. The LS can handle anything. Guess who's coming?

Jonah groaned. They were already looking at being over capacity. Who?

Soren. He loves Suzanna. Also, I think something must have happened between him and Kendal, because he has been clinging to me the last few days, calling and texting ideas and questions.

So Soren is into you now?

Harper responded with laughing emojis. Then: I think Soren's idea of being into someone is finding the person who will actually listen to him relate the theory of relativity in a relative way.

Jonah laughed. He couldn't wait to see Harper. And then he couldn't wait for the night to be over. Hosting big events like this was definitely not his thing, and while it was a boon for the Lucky Star, he found it exhausting in a way nothing else could exhaust him. He was not an extrovert. What he wanted after this was a quiet weekend with Harper, with no thoughts about Madrid, or his dad's health, or any other major life decisions.

His gaze happened to land on a picture of him and Allen and Andy when they were boys. Allen had a skateboard. Andy was looking at someone or something to the side, and Jonah was seated on top of a table, laughing. He loved those two like brothers, but sometimes he wished he had a sibling, someone who could help him with the Lucky Star now. He wondered what Jolie would have thought about the Star.

He wondered what this job would be like after Harper was gone, too. She'd made this part of his life bearable—how motivated would he be when she was gone?

How sad would he be when she was gone?

But she would be gone, he was certain of it. He might not know the business quite like Soren, but he knew Harper, and he knew that Soren would be a fool to pass her over. He figured Soren knew this. She would be in Rochester, and he would be here, hosting happy hours.

Well. He couldn't think of any of that right now. But he could acknowledge that the idea of her leaving Deja Brew, and him, and Truck and Lulu for that matter, stung. It stung even though he'd planned to leave her. He was selfish to the core—he wanted the deep space project and Harper by his side.

But it never seemed to come down to what he wanted.

Olivia took forever to get ready for the Lucky Star happy hour. Harper and Bob sat on the floor, watching her. Well, Harper watched her, but Bob faced away, having lost interest in the many outfit changes Olivia had made, all in and out of Harper's clothes. "How many hours of my life have I watched you try on clothes?" Harper asked idly. "Can't you wear what you have on? It's just a happy hour."

"*Just* a happy hour is an opportunity to meet the man of my dreams, hello." Olivia turned one way, and then the other.

Harper thought about everyone she'd ever seen frequent the Lucky Star. "I don't think it's that kind of happy hour."

"You never know. You have to be open to kismet." Olivia turned back to the mirror to check herself out once more. She was wearing Harper's slim black pants, a gold shimmering blouse Harper had bought at the Houston Galleria last summer, and her own high heels. With her long dark hair, Olivia looked gorgeous, as always. Harper felt a surge of . . . interesting, she felt a surge of something new. Usually it was envy, but for the first time in their very long friendship, she had the guy and Olivia didn't. It was a rip in the universe they'd never experienced. She felt sorry for Olivia.

Wow. Her life had definitely changed.

Harper stood up and checked herself in the mirror. She was wearing a black dress with a white Peter Pan collar and cuffs. It fit her perfectly through the bodice and waist, and flared at the knees. Olivia said it was gorgeous. She'd put Harper's hair in a chic up-do that Harper could never re-create on her own.

"You look like Audrey Hepburn," Olivia said.

Harper snorted. "Except that I'm probably forty pounds heavier."

"Still, you look like her. You're gorgeous in that dress, Harper. Okay, let's do this."

"I hope you're not disappointed." Harper picked up her evening bag and checked the contents. "This could be a huge bust. You can't blame me if it is—it's not my event."

"Why are you being so pessimistic?"

"I'm being practical."

"There is a time for practical, and there is a time for optimistic. I would like to suggest that this is a time for optimism."

Harper laughed. "Whatever. Let's go."

They said good night to Bob, who, honestly, looked like he wanted some time alone with his bone anyway. They parked in Harper's spot at Deja Brew. But when they stepped onto the sidewalk, Harper stopped dead in her tracks and put her hand on Olivia's arm.

"What?"

"It's *packed*," Harper said.

"Great!" Olivia grabbed Harper's hand and pulled her across the street and into the throng of people trying to squeeze into the Lucky Star.

It was a truly amazing transformation from the Lucky Star she'd dismissed so quickly a few weeks ago. Carly was brilliant, but all the work Jonah and his family had put into the Lucky Star had clearly paid off. The diner had been transformed. Harper looked at the star-shaped lights hanging from the ceiling, interspersed between little potted cactus plants, also suspended, and those scattered around on tables and windowsills. There was a new stage at one end of the room. Some of the women from the book club, all of them wearing matching aprons emblazoned with a picture of a woman dressed in fifties clothing and holding up a pie, moved through the crowd carrying trays of pie samples and burger sliders. Two more book clubbers moved through with drinks.

One of them stopped in front of Harper and Olivia. Harper recognized her as the one they had called Karen. "Oh, hey! It's great to see you!" Karen said. "Care for a cactus martini? The little ones are on the house. If you want a bigger one—" She leaned in and whispered conspiratorially, "and who doesn't?" She leaned back. "You'll have to buy it at the bar."

"The bar?" Harper asked.

Karen indicated with her chin a portable bar in the corner opposite the stage.

"Wow," Harper murmured.

"Thank you, we'll have one," Olivia said, taking two of the plastic cups and handing one to Harper. "Cactus!" she said excitedly. She sampled the drink as Karen moved on. "It's delicious."

Harper looked at hers. "What *is* a cactus martini?" She craned her neck to see the bar. She could see a sign draped across its front and recognized the name of a new bar two blocks down. "Clever," she said. Carly had apparently taken the idea of partnering and brought in the new guys down the street.

Speaking of Carly, Harper caught sight of her in a sparkly gold dress in the company of a very handsome man wearing glasses. She left Olivia chatting up some random man and made her way over to say hello.

"Harper!" Carly said as Harper neared her. "I'm so glad you're here. This is Max, my fiancé." She beamed up at him. "This is Harper from Deja Brew."

"You're the one with Bob the Bulldog." Max smiled charmingly. "Love that guy. We have a couple of bassets. Did Carly tell you?"

"She did!"

Max pulled his phone from his pocket. "Let me show you—"

"Max!" Carly caught his hand. "She doesn't want to see pictures of our dogs." She grinned at Harper. "Don't mind him. He's kind of a nerd."

"Not kind of," Max protested. "Fully realized." He slid the phone into his pocket. "Very nice to meet you, Harper. And may the best dog win. My vote is on Bob."

"Really? Thank you! But have you met Lulu, the three-legged dachshund yet? You might change your mind."

"Actually, I heard the Starbucks dog is pretty darn cute."

"Max, you're not supposed to say that," Carly said, laughing.

"I am not offended," said Harper. "It was totally unfair of Starbucks to bring in a giant furball to the competition. And speaking of Lulu, the tripod dachshund . . ." Harper shifted her gaze to Carly. "Have you seen Jonah?"

"Last I saw him, he was behind the counter, loading pie samples onto trays. Great turnout, isn't it? I'm so proud of us."

"I am so proud of the Lucky Star. They really are an Austin institution. Nice to meet you, Max. I'm going to say hi to Jonah."

She heard Olivia call her name and turned around to see her friend trying to make her way through the crowd. Behind Olivia, she saw Soren and Kendal enter. "Wow," Harper said as Olivia reached her. "He dressed up."

"Who dressed up?" Olivia turned to see.

Harper nodded in Soren's direction. "The man in the strangely shiny blue suit is none other than Soren Wilder in the flesh." The suit was so shiny, in fact, it was almost reflective. But it was tailored, outlining a masculine figure that Harper was not accustomed to seeing. He'd also combed his hair and tied it at his nape. And it looked as if he'd found some turquoise suede shoes to complete the outfit.

"Wait . . . who is that with him?"

"Kendal."

Olivia's eyes bugged out of her head. She looked at Harper, then at Kendal.

He'd dressed simply—a white shirt, a black wool zip-up vest, and jeans that fit him like a glove. Harper was so used to seeing him in a suit and tie, she had never noticed how fit he was.

"Why did you never tell me Kendal was so *hot*?" Olivia asked accusingly as Kendal and Soren made their way to them. "He's *gorgeous*."

"Gross," Harper said. "He's like my cousin. Hi, Soren!" she said in the next breath. "You look great!"

"I look as I feel," he said, and bowed his head, she supposed, to accept her compliment.

"This is my best friend, Olivia. She came in from Houston."

Soren turned his gaze to Olivia, and it swept all the way down

Olivia and back up. "It is with happy satisfaction that I make your acquaintance. Namaste."

Olivia blinked. She looked at Kendal.

"I'm Kendal," he said, reaching around Soren to offer his hand. "Very nice to meet you. I didn't know Harper had any friends."

"Funny," Harper said.

"*Very* good to meet you," Olivia said, and shifted her weight onto one hip, which put her minutely closer to Kendal.

Harper knew that look in her eye. After all the stories she'd told Olivia about Kendal, Olivia said she despised him. She didn't despise him now—she was practically batting her lashes at him.

"So hey! I thought you were out of town for the weekend," Harper said to Kendal.

"He has just arrived from Rochester," Soren said.

Rochester! Harper glanced at Kendal. He looked abashed. "I didn't know I was going until last minute."

"Was it important that Harper know?" Soren asked with feigned innocence.

How many ways could Soren annoy her? "Well, *I* think it was," she said. "I'm in the running for that job, too."

Soren laughed. "You see with your eyes but not your heart, Harper. To see fully, you must see with both eyes and heart."

"That's what I always say," Olivia said.

Harper shot her a look, but Olivia didn't see it because she was smiling at Kendal. Harper couldn't bear to watch whatever was about to unfold here between them. She said to Soren, "Would you care for a cactus martini? Because I can hook you up."

"Absolutely."

"I'll get them." She walked away from Soren and Kendal and Olivia, pushing through the crowd until she collided with a big man in a Hawaiian shirt, holding a tray of burger sliders. It was Burt. He held up the tray. "*Grass*-fed," he said crossly, as if he was annoyed about that.

"Thank you!" She took a slider and pushed on to the bar. She spotted Jonah at the counter, dressed in jeans and a navy sport coat, a crisp white shirt underneath. He was standing with his father, who looked a little like he'd eaten something bad. His mother was there, too, wearing a flowy caftan dress. She was entirely animated, carrying on about some tale to a couple who listened with rapt attention.

Harper lifted a hand and caught Jonah's eye. He smiled. Harper did, too, but then someone walked between them.

She took her phone from her bag and texted him. The place looks great. You really knocked it out of the park.

It took him a minute, but he responded. Does it? Thought it looked a little like Roy came to life one day and decorated the dining room in the style of his barn. And what is with the hanging cactus?

It will be all the rage now. Want to get away for a little bit? She glanced up. So did Jonah. He met her gaze, and a smile curved his lips. He dropped his gaze to his phone again. Harper Atticus Thompson. What are you suggesting? And getting away for a "little bit" means the janitorial closet.

Harper looked at him across the room and made a theatrical gagging motion. I was thinking across the street. At least we know no one is there.

Oh, I'm sorry, is the Lucky Star burying Deja Brew in the dust?

She smiled. He smiled. She texted, No one is there because it is closed, Mr. Smartypants. She watched Jonah glance at his dad, at the people crowded into the dining room and gathered around as Suzanna took the stage. He glanced down.

Fifteen minutes.

Harper looked for Olivia. But she needn't have bothered—Olivia was practically hanging off Kendal, who looked like he wanted to be hanging off her. "Oh my God, not today, Satan," Harper muttered, and started for the bar to get the cactus martinis for them.

Thirty

Blissful quiet at Deja Brew was the first thing Jonah noticed when he stepped inside the darkened interior. He'd come with martinis in to-go cups, thanks to his quick thinking. Burt was the only person to see him go. "I'll be back in half an hour," Jonah had said.

"I ain't your mother." Burt had turned back to his grass-fed sliders. They were a huge hit.

Harper was standing in the middle of Deja Brew waiting for him, her legs about fifteen miles long in that dress. Did she really get better looking every time he saw her? Was he really that smitten?

Yes, he was really that smitten.

They took seats in the egg baskets, turned to face each other. She proclaimed the martinis groundbreaking.

"I didn't know you were a martini connoisseur."

"I'm not. I honestly don't know the difference between this and gasoline. But the name alone makes me want one." She laughed. She sounded a wee bit tipsy. She was twisting in her basket, an act that Jonah feared would loosen it from its bolt above.

Harper lifted her glass and held it out for a toast. "Congratulations, Jonah," she said when she twisted back. "You really did turn the Lucky Star around."

"Are you admitting defeat?"

"I am admitting defeat," she said cheerfully.

"Don't. I told you before the only reason any of this happened at all was because of you. You showed me how to do it. If it hadn't been for your smack talk, we never would have come up with half the things we did." He definitely would not have hired Carly, and that, he realized, would have been a tragic mistake.

"That's very nice of you to say, but this was all you and the gang." She touched his glass with hers in a toast and sipped. She turned her gaze to the Lucky Star. They could see the silhouettes of the many people packed inside to hear Suzanna. "It's going to be so much easier to hand the management off to your dad again, don't you think? Your business is so steady, he can probably kick back and let it roll in."

"No business is ever that good," Jonah said. He couldn't help himself—he sighed heavily. "About that."

"About what?"

He put his drink down and leaned forward so he could better see her. "I've made up my mind. I'm not going to Madrid."

She froze for a moment. Then put her drink aside, too. "Jonah . . . after you've done all this work? That's your dream."

"I know. I've thought about it, and . . . you know, my dad. My parents need me, Harper . . . now that my dad's cancer has returned. And family is more important than a cool job."

"But what about *you*, Jonah? What about all the hours you've put into getting that job? How can you let this go?"

"I'm not letting it go. It's just that the timing is all wrong." She opened her mouth as if she meant to argue. He said quickly, "There will be another project. I can't get too worked up about it. You never know where life is going to take you, right? Look at us, for example."

She was already shaking her head. "There may be another project, but you've also put in the work for this goal, and now it's within your reach, and how can you not reach for it?" She glanced down at her drink. "This will probably come out all wrong, but . . ." She looked him directly in the eye. "Is it possible you are subconsciously putting barriers in your way that don't have to exist?"

He chuckled. "Like I don't have enough? What do you mean?"

"I don't know . . . I've just never seen someone work so hard not to achieve something he's worked so hard to achieve." She blinked. "Good Lord, I sound like Soren. But do you get my point? Why are you making this so hard?"

He frowned. "I'm not making this hard. *Life* is making this hard. I can't help it that my dad has cancer again."

"No. And I'm so sorry about that, Jonah, I am so sorry. But did your dad ask you to take over?"

"No, but—"

"Or your mom? Or your aunt or uncle?"

He didn't say out loud that they'd all specifically expressed they did not *want* him to take over. He shook his head.

"Well, maybe they didn't ask because they can handle it."

He didn't like this conversation. She didn't know if that was true, if they could handle it without him.

"I mean, people do all the time. They suffer hardships, but they keep going, one foot in front of the other. You don't have to be the savior every time."

"I'm not." But he was. He knew, deep down, that it was the role that he'd carved out for himself as a little boy before he even knew what he was doing. He didn't want to believe he was putting obstacles in front of himself. He was *helping*. That's what he did—he helped his family, he helped others. That's what they needed him to do.

But maybe there was some truth to what she said. He had to admit that in moments of quiet contemplation, he had wondered if he could even lead something as big and as important as this project. *NASA* was involved, for God's sake.

Still, he wasn't one to run from a challenge. He thought again of how gray and weak his father had seemed this last week. And he couldn't see himself packing a bag and walking out the door when his father was sick. He shook his head.

Harper said nothing for the longest time. He hoped she wasn't disappointed that he wasn't as ambitious as her. But she suddenly leaned forward and cupped his face with her hand. "How are you such a great guy?"

He gave a rueful laugh. "That is not what you were thinking."

"I've never known anyone like you, Jonah. I thank my lucky stars every day that I was in your Lyft. You are the best kind of guy, and you're so hot, and I love you."

Those words shimmied up his spine. "I love you, too, Harper," he said quietly.

She stood up from her basket and came to his. She fit one knee beside him.

"Oh—"

She straddled him.

"Wait . . . I'm not sure these baskets are rated for this load—"

"They are." She cupped his face. "Did you hear what I said? I seriously *love* you, and this is the first time I've ever said it, and I don't know if I should go first but I need you to know it."

"That's . . . amazing." His heart was suddenly thundering in his chest. He could feel it, could feel her love for him. "So just so we are all perfectly clear, I seriously love you, too." His hands found her thighs. "Since about day one. Since the day I saw you walking down the street to me, I knew that this was different. *You* were different."

"So did I." Harper put her arms around his neck as his hands slid up her rib cage. She began to rock back and forth on him.

"Stop it—do you know what you're doing to me? We can't do this in the middle of Deja Brew with windows everywhere."

"Sure we can," she murmured, and kissed his neck. And that was it—he couldn't stop himself and he wouldn't stop her. He was inflamed by her boldness, and her hands were on him, and he was completely under her spell. She somehow maneuvered out of her panties, and then her bare skin was against him, and she smelled like sex and she tasted like love, and he was so hard for her.

Their unions were generally furious and sexy, but this was reverent, and perhaps a tiny bit sad. There was nothing else in existence in those moments except the two of them. Jonah wasn't sure why he felt so emotional with her—he was having sex in a hanging egg basket, for God's sake—but all he could think was that he really did love this woman, and he wished things were always as easy as they were with her, easy in the way soul mates had of being on the same page about everything. He loved aerospace engineering and he loved his family, but those things were on different pages. He and Harper were always on the same page. The flow between them was as natural as breathing.

And when they'd finished, Jonah pressed his forehead to her chest. She stroked his hair. "Is everything okay?"

He laughed softly. "Nothing and everything."

She didn't ask him to explain. She bent over him and held him so that she could feel nothing and everything, too.

Eventually, they cleaned up, and went back across the street, their arms around each other. They slipped into the door practically unnoticed and stayed there. Suzanna was nearing the end of her set, and the crowd was moving to her music. Harper stood with her back pressed against Jonah, his arms around her waist. His mother was dancing with one of the regulars, who was a head shorter than she was. She was laughing, enjoying herself. Aunt Belinda and Uncle Marty were slow dancing behind the counter, kissing every now and again in the way septuagenarians kissed with fondness rather than passion.

And there was Jonah's father, sitting on a stool, looking like he was about to fall off.

"Oh God, oh no," Harper said, and twisted around, her eyes wide. "What am I going to do?"

"About what?"

"Olivia is with Kendal. Like *with* him." She leaned into Jonah and pointed.

Jonah saw Kendal and, with him, an attractive woman. At least judging by what he could see. But she had her tongue so far down Kendal's throat, he couldn't be entirely sure.

"We have to stop this," Harper said, and before Jonah could react, she'd grabbed his hand and had pulled him forward to break up a lust match.

"Hey!" Olivia jerked around when Harper tapped her on the shoulder. Her gaze landed on Jonah, and she gasped with surprise. "I know you! You're Jonah! I would recognize you anywhere."

"From when I had your phone," Harper quickly explained. "She's not stalking you."

"Not unless Harper needs me to. This is perfect! Kendal and I are going to Péché on Fourth Street. Join us."

"But we—"

"You must pass into this state of being, Harper," Kendal said. "It is freeing." He laughed. "That's my Soren impression." Apparently, Kendal had had a couple of the cactus martinis.

"Thanks, but I feel pretty free in my state of being. Where is Soren anyway?"

Kendal shrugged. "I think he took off."

"Please?" Olivia begged. "I came all this way, and I'm only just meeting your man. You have to come."

"You came from Houston, Olivia. Not exactly a long haul. And speaking of which, I thought you had to go back tonight."

"I can go in the morning," she said, and smiled saucily at Kendal before turning her sultry smile to Jonah. "Please, Jonah?"

Jonah probably would have gone along for the entertainment

value alone, but he shook his head. "Sorry, but I'm needed here. It will take some time to close down."

"Then join us later!" Olivia tossed her long brown hair over her shoulder in a way that seemed entirely designed and practiced to entice.

"I'll try." He smiled at Harper. Her eyes narrowed suspiciously.

"Yay!"

When Olivia turned back to say something to Kendal, Harper grabbed Jonah's lapel. "I can't believe you are going to leave me with them. This is the very definition of hell, Jonah, trust me."

"You have to be quicker on the draw, baby." He kissed the top of her head. "I'm really glad you came. Call me later?"

"Are you kidding? I'm going to call you every five minutes so you don't miss a thing."

"Hope I remember to take my phone off silent." He grinned at her, then leaned forward to offer his hand to Olivia and Kendal, thanked them for coming, and turned back into the crowd at the Lucky Star.

He didn't see them leave—he was cleaning up spilled martinis, certain if he didn't, someone would slip and break a leg and the ensuing lawsuits would sink them. He was cleaning long after Suzanna had gone, long after Carly and Max had gone, even long after Amy and her brother and his band had gone. She'd had a few too many cactus martinis and was no help anyway.

It had been a long day—he didn't mind working solo, alone with his thoughts. But as Jonah finished putting the tables and chairs back in their usual places, his father appeared in the doorway of the private dining room.

"You still here, Dad?" Jonah asked as he walked toward him. "You look tired."

"I am tired, but I'm fine. Got a minute?"

"Sure, but—"

"I want you to take the job, son," his father said before Jonah could utter a word. "It's an amazing opportunity."

Jonah was too exhausted to have this conversation now. "Dad . . . don't worry about that, please. There will be other opportunities."

"That's not the point. Look, I gave everything I had so that you could have the best life. So you could have all the opportunities. It's like I told you before, we've leaned on you too much. After Jolie, well . . . we put all our hopes into you. *All* of them. You were right—we have needed you, but we didn't think about how that affected you. We sent you to school, we gave you the tools you need to sail through this life, we put our hopes and dreams for all the other kids we didn't have into you. But we never told you it was okay to go and live that life. I'm telling you now. It is *okay* for you to go and live your life. You need to take that job."

"Okay," Jonah said. "That's a pretty healthy guilt trip. You also taught me to have compassion, Dad. To help. To think of others and to be there when others are in need. And that means you."

"Don't you think you've helped enough?" His dad moved into the dining room and sat heavily in a chair. "Don't you think you've done as much as anyone could ask of their son? Now maybe you can put yourself in my shoes. Imagine watching your son pass up the very thing you dreamed for him because you got sick."

Jonah swallowed. "I'm sure it must be hard. But Dad . . . if I take this opportunity and go to Madrid for six months, who will be here for you? Marty and Belinda are moving. Mom and Amy will be here, but you know how they are."

"I'll manage. I'm not dead, Jonah. I'm just sick."

"But what if . . ." He had to clear his throat. It felt like it was closing up on him. "What if I don't see you again?"

His dad smiled a little. "Listen. Lymphoma is treatable. My oncologist is very hopeful. If something happens, we won't hide it from you, I promise. You'll come home then. But what if it doesn't? But what if you stayed home and I got better? Are you going to reach the end of six months when I'm feeling great and resent me?"

"No—"

"You might. Son, anything could happen. Your mother or I could die in a car accident tomorrow. But I'm not going to allow my only child, my son, to spend his life watching and waiting for the worst to happen." He extended his hand and Jonah took it. His skin was thin, and blotched red from places they'd inserted IVs. He squeezed Jonah's hand with surprising strength. "Go. Explore your life and this world. The Lucky Star is not your burden. That belongs to me and I can still carry it."

Jonah took a seat beside his father and bowed his head. "You're not thinking clearly," he said softly. "You have to admit that it's a toll on you. And there is no one here to do what you or I do."

"I'm thinking very clearly," his father said. "We'll be all right. You've set some great things in motion here, and I feel confident we can keep it up."

Jonah covered his face with his hands for a moment. If he had a kid, he'd be saying the same thing. But that didn't erase the fact that his father was sick and his parents needed the help, whether they wanted to admit it or not. He leaned back against the bar and settled in to argue about what was best for him, his father, and the Lucky Star.

Thirty-One

Monday morning arrived like a sledgehammer.

After two hours of watching Olivia flirt with Kendal, and Kendal flirt with Olivia, Harper had had enough. She slipped out of Péché with the real excuse of needing to see about Bob. She'd hated every minute of being the third wheel, especially to that dynamic duo. It had been nice, these last few weeks, not to be the third wheel.

It had been more than nice. It had been amazing.

She'd slept fitfully, having had too many cactus martinis and trying to understand all the many emotions she was feeling about Jonah, and Madrid, and her own career. It was as if all her neatly wrapped goals and achievements and feelings had come tumbling out of the imaginary closet and were lying in a mess at the bottom of the stairs.

Things didn't feel right. The universe didn't feel right.

She'd just finished dressing Bob in the dog kilt she'd ordered when Olivia came falling into the apartment, looking like she had fallen off the back of a pickup truck.

"Oh no," Harper said, realizing what this terribly disheveled look meant.

Olivia tried to drag her fingers through her long hair, but it was tangled. "He happens to be a very good lover, Harper. He's into tantric sex."

Bob barked at Olivia at the very same moment Harper groaned. "No! Don't say another word! That's my colleague, Olivia." She attached Bob's leash.

"I really like him, Harper. I mean, I'm *excited* about him. He's so smart, and he's funny, and he makes a wicked smoothie."

It occurred to Harper that this was so typically Olivia—she fell for every guy she came into contact with. All these years, Harper had believed she was doing something wrong, that she should have wanted the same sort of attention Olivia received. But now she realized that what Olivia sought was cheap—it was for the moment. For the gratification of being wanted. It was not for the long haul. That's what Harper had with Jonah—something enduring. "Great, Olivia. Like him all you want. But don't talk to me about it. I have to work with him. Speaking of which, I have to go."

"Fine," Olivia said, clearly wounded by Harper's lack of enthusiasm. "I'm telling you, it's different this time." She kept her gaze on her phone, although Harper could plainly see it was the lock screen. "I'll call you when I get to Houston."

"Great." Harper thought maybe she ought to apologize, but she was too at odds with herself. She and Bob left.

On her way to work, Harper got a call from Carly.

"Hey!" Carly said. "Great event last night, wasn't it?"

Harper agreed that it was.

"Just wait until you see the fundraiser we're doing at Deja Brew. It's going to blow your socks off."

"Oh, I'm sure," Harper said half-heartedly. She was not in the right frame of mind to be excited about a political fundraiser at her store. She actually thought she might not have been able to care any less. That in and of itself was a strange feeling—she couldn't remember if she'd ever felt so blasé about a task.

"Listen, the ACC is coming around tomorrow to collect the vote jars so they can start tallying votes."

Harper glanced at Bob in the seat behind her. He was staring straight ahead. At what, she wondered, as he couldn't see very well. "Okay."

"And . . . they are going to want Bob back for any potential adoption interest he might have generated."

The words *want Bob back* hit Harper in the chest like a wrecking ball.

"Harper?"

"I'm adopting him," she blurted out.

"What? Really? But I thought you were getting a big promotion and moving out of town."

"Yes! I am. But maybe I won't. I don't know what I'm doing anymore, but I'm not giving Bob up, Carly. I'm not." She looked at Bob again. "We have a thing."

"Harper, we—"

"Oh! I'm at work. I'll call you later, I promise." And she hung up before Carly could say another word to talk her out of it.

When she entered the offices—sprinting into them, really, her speed born of her sheer fear that someone would come and take Bob—she nearly collided with the reception desk and the young woman seated behind it.

"Hi!" The pretty blonde stood up and extended her hand. "I'm Andrea. I'm the new receptionist."

"Are you, like, actually a receptionist?" Harper asked, wanting to be perfectly clear this time.

Andrea laughed. "I am actually a receptionist. Ooh, look at your dog! What's its name?" She made the mistake of leaning over and putting out her hand for Bob to smell. Bob growled, and Andrea jerked her hand back, looking at Bob with alarm.

"Don't mind him. He growls but he doesn't bite. His name is Bob. I'm Harper Thompson."

"Oh! So *you're* Harper. Soren called and said he wants to meet at ten this morning." She handed Harper a piece of paper with the note about the meeting.

"Thanks." Harper walked across the reception area to her office. She could see Kendal in his office, bent over some papers on his desk. He didn't look so perfectly put together this morning. His tie was crooked and his suit jacket looked wrinkled.

Veronica was here, too, standing at the coffee machine, yawning as she waited for it to brew.

Harper tried to catch up with some work while Bob snoozed by the window. But she couldn't concentrate—she was distracted by her thoughts racing around Olivia and Jonah and Bob and life in general. When her phone buzzed—Andrea announcing that Soren would see her now—Harper stood up. "Come on, Bob. Let's see what our fate is."

Kendal and Veronica were already in Soren's office, on cushions. Harper lowered herself onto one, too. Bob was having none of that nonsense. He walked to the fern in the corner of Soren's office and sniffed it, then trotted back to lie next to Harper, facing away from them all, his rump pressed against her knee. Whatever was going on in her head, that press of dog calmed her.

Bob began to snore.

She glanced at Kendal. He gave her a sheepish smile.

Soren was seated cross-legged, dressed in a caftan and knit cap. "Excellent, we are gathered." He smiled. "Fate finds a way into our hearts, does it not? The destination is reached by chance."

"And that means?" Harper asked impatiently.

"Always the most direct, aren't you, Harper," Soren said, clearly unamused that she would not allow him this moment. "It means that I have come to considered conclusions."

She thought Kendal sat a little higher on his cushion.

"Accountable independence," he said. "With responsibility comes—"

"For God's sake, just say it," Veronica whined.

Soren looked completely deflated. "Very well. Harper, you are promoted to executive vice president in charge of development. Pack your bags for Rochester."

The news was so unexpected, so the opposite of what she thought would happen, that Harper couldn't speak at first. "What?"

"Kendal, you are now the vice president of administration *and* operations. You will be heading our Austin stores, including the underperforming flagship on South Congress."

"Wait, what?" Harper looked at Kendal, then at Soren. "I think you have to give it more than a month to call it underperforming. We're doing well!"

"Thank you, Soren," Kendal said.

"What about me?" Veronica asked.

"Veronica, you will continue to be Veronica."

She shrugged. "Cool."

"What . . . but Soren . . ." Harper's heart was racing along with her mind. Soren had teased this thing out for so long that she wasn't ready for the decision. "I thought . . . I guess I thought—"

"Thoughts are merely opinions based on something occurring suddenly in your head."

The actual definition of a thought, Harper mused.

"Take the largesse that is offered and congratulate the universe for a job well done." He lifted his hands. "Go. Go, my tutees, and *carpe diem*."

Kendal was the first one out the door, walking swiftly to his office. He picked up his phone. Veronica stood, then gave Harper a look. "Guess you got what you wanted."

Yes. Harper had achieved her goal. She looked at Soren. "Thank you."

"Yes, yes, of course," he said, waving her off.

Harper and Bob returned to her office. She felt stunned. She had been so sure it would be Kendal that she had begun to envision another reality. But this was the reality she had prepared and worked for. She didn't know what to do, exactly, so she picked up her phone and called her parents with the good news. No one answered. She began to text Jonah with the news, but something, like her heart beating a million miles an hour, stopped her. She turned, and through the glass wall, she saw Soren out of his office now, speaking to Andrea, leaning over the desk in that ridiculous caftan. That man literally drove her crazy.

But why was it her? Kendal was better at the development ideas than she was. She could see that. She knew Soren saw it. So why did he choose her? Did he want to get rid of her?

She thought of the Lucky Star, of all the people there. The family, the regulars. She would be leaving Deja Brew and the Lucky Star behind to build and open a bistro that made no sense to her. Harper had always assumed she didn't want a community, she wanted victories. She wanted opportunities. Was that really true? Or had she just been looking for something, anything, to belong to? Whatever she'd been doing, it didn't feel right anymore. She didn't want just any opportunity. She wanted the right opportunity.

She looked at Bob, at his kilt, already twisted around. "What do you think about cold weather?"

Bob sighed and closed his eyes.

Harper glanced at the reception area again. Kendal had come out, too, and she imagined he was relaying his disappointment to Soren at not being chosen.

An internal clock, deep in her heart, began to tick down. Things were rumbling around, rearranging themselves. Harper slowly stood up. "Oh God, Bob," she said softly, "I'm about to do something that is wildly out of my comfort zone."

Bob lifted his head. She put down her phone. "Don't do this, Harper," she muttered to herself. "You've worked really hard for this. You set your goal, you achieved your goal, and now you're going to just throw it out the window? And then what?" She looked at Bob. He wiggled his bob of a tail.

She was in the grip of pure gut instinct. Something was screaming at her not to walk away. She opened the door and entered the reception area. She braced her legs apart and folded her arms. "May I say something?"

Soren shot her a look. "We're in the middle of something here."

"Yeah, and I think it might be pertinent. Soren, thank you so much for the opportunity, but I can't accept this promotion."

Soren slowly turned from Kendal and stared at her. Kendal looked wildly flustered and kept looking to Soren, then Harper, then back again. Even Veronica came out of her office to hear it.

Harper said it again, only louder. "I don't want the promotion." A small laugh escaped her at the sheer absurdity of it all. "I don't want it! Why did I ever think I did? I honestly don't know, I think it's some big character flaw, and I'll work on it, but anyway, I'm just going to keep my job here if you don't mind."

"But . . ." Kendal looked confused. "That's *my* job now."

"Yeah, but you want this job. You can have it, Kendal! You're obviously the best person for it."

"No," he said, shaking his head. "I don't want to go to Rochester. I want *this* job. *Your* job. I want the job I got."

Well, this was news. She'd never actually asked Kendal what he wanted. She looked at Soren. He shrugged apologetically. How strange it all was—one minute, she'd been promoted, and the next minute, after suffering under Soren for nearly five years, she was out of a job. And the strangest thing of all was, she wasn't terribly upset.

Something was changing. It was that feeling of nostalgia and excitement all over again, but this time, surrounded by the hope of something new. Something inside her was about to break, and a new season was coming in. "Well," she said. "This is a turn of events we didn't anticipate, am I right?"

❧

At about the same time, across town, Jonah came out of Edgar's office feeling a little sick. He still couldn't believe what he'd just done. He'd gone in to tell Edgar that he couldn't do it. But he left with a start date in Madrid in one month.

After his conversation with his dad, Jonah had tossed and turned all night, thinking. Thinking about Harper being in Rochester, Minnesota. Thinking about his parents. About the Lucky Star. About his degree and his dreams. And then he'd awakened to the light of a pale blue winter sky.

Edgar was thrilled and so were the other partners. He agreed to be back at work in two weeks before heading for Madrid.

He headed for the Lucky Star to tell them the news. But first, he drove by his house to let Truck out for a few minutes.

He didn't know how he'd break the news to Harper. It seemed almost too simple—after an amazing meeting and a fantastic relationship, they were going to either figure out how to keep up their relationship thousands of miles apart or . . . or go their own ways? But wasn't that life? You met people along the way, some stayed forever, and some passed through.

He'd believed she would stay forever. He had hoped she would stay forever. And in the end, it was he who wouldn't stay.

Truck was bouncing off the walls when Jonah came in, running from one end of the room to the other, then trying to bounce off Jonah. Jonah leashed him, pulled on a knit cap, and went outside. They didn't make it to the sidewalk before a car screeched to a halt at the curb. In the passenger window he saw Bob, staring straight ahead.

Jonah walked over to Harper's car, alarmed. He bent down to the window. "Are you okay? Is something wrong?"

"I got the job!" she shouted.

He smiled as she threw open the door and got out. Truck immediately jumped on her, his front paws on her shoulders. She laughed and pushed him down.

"Congratulations."

"Thanks! But wait, there's more," she said. She darted around to the passenger side to get Bob out of the car. Jonah and Truck joined them on his lawn.

"I knew you'd get it, Harper. He'd be an idiot to do otherwise."

"You were right," she said breathlessly. "And he's still an idiot." She beamed at him, excited. "But I turned it down!" And then she laughed. She laughed loud and hard, to the point where she seemed a little maniacal.

And for Jonah, the world stopped spinning for a moment. Everything in him went still as he tried to process her news. "You did what?"

"I didn't take it! I mean, I took it at first, because, duh, that's what I'd been working toward, but it didn't feel right, and I thought about it, and I came back and said I didn't want it, but he'd already given my job to Kendal, and get *this*," she said, leaning forward, "Kendal didn't want it, either! He wanted my job! Which he's keeping, so in a way, he still wins, but I'm totally okay with that. He's very good at what he does."

"*What?*" Jonah nearly shouted.

"I know, I was so reluctant to admit it, but it's true, he's really good, and now I don't have a job!" She started laughing again.

Jonah caught her arm. "Harper—you didn't take the job?"

"I didn't take it. I'm not leaving! I mean, I have to find another job, but that's okay, I'll get something else, maybe even at the Lucky Star!" She laughed. "Why is your face so ghostly white, Jonah?"

Jonah took his hat off, pushed his fingers through his hair, and tried to think of how to tell her.

"I thought you'd be happy," she said. She was brilliant right now, all smiles and happiness and hope. "Because I meant what I said. I love you. I love you so much and this is where I want to be. With you, Jonah."

"I love you, too, Harper. But I . . . I *did* take the job. I'm going to Madrid."

She looked as if she was waiting for the punchline. And when one didn't come, the light began to leave her face. "Oh. But I thought—"

"I know. My dad . . . he convinced me."

"Ah." She pressed the back of her hand to her mouth, and he thought maybe she was biting it. "So when would you leave?"

"In a month."

"Mmm." She nodded, taking it all in. She looked away. She *walked* away. But then she turned and came back. "Oh, but hey, congratulations!" She was trying, he could see, to sound cheerful. But her eyes said something different. The light in those green eyes had been completely doused.

Jonah shoved his hands in his pockets. Truck was dancing around him, wanting off his leash to say hello to Bob. Jonah dropped the leash, and Truck leaped for Bob. But Bob had an itch on his backside and was twisting around in a circle trying to get to it.

"I just thought that . . ." Harper cleared her throat. "You know, I thought maybe you and I . . ." She gestured between the two of them.

"Me too," he said. "But then you were going to Rochester."

"And you were staying here," she mumbled. She slowly squatted down, then sat in the grass.

Jonah sat beside her.

"I thought this was my fairy tale."

"I thought it was mine, too. But listen, it's six months. It's not like I am moving away for good."

She glanced at him from the corner of her eye. "A lot can happen in six months. What if you meet some amazing astronaut?"

"I don't think there will be any astronauts. But what if you get an amazing job or start dating someone new?"

She covered her face with her hands.

Jonah put his arm around her. "It's not the end, Harper. You can come and see me."

"I would love that. But if I get a new job, I don't know if I could."

Jonah sighed and pulled her into his side. "We'll figure something out." He seemed to say that a lot, and never with any confidence. Six months seemed like a lifetime in a new relationship.

Six months seemed like a lifetime without Harper. And he could tell by looking at her, she thought the same thing.

Thirty-Two

The day before the formal crowning of King Mutt, Harper officially adopted Bob. For the actual crowning, she dressed him in a tuxedo shirt. He growled the whole time and tried to nip her fingers when the neck hole of the shirt wouldn't fit over his head. She snipped it, then put it on him again. He allowed it. "I know you're having second thoughts," Harper said to him. "You've made that perfectly clear. But until you can get a job and support yourself, you are stuck with me."

Lulu was also adopted on that day. Not by Jonah, but by Amy. "She wouldn't be happy with anyone but me," Amy said. "And living with Truck? Please."

Harper couldn't disagree. Good old Truck loved the smaller dogs a little too roughly. Lulu did indeed look very happy when they went to sign the adoption papers.

Duke had not been present at the ACC when Amy and Harper were there, but everyone assured them that Duke was on the verge of being adopted. "We had a list four miles long," one of the men said cheerfully. Amy and Harper held their misfit dogs a little tighter.

Today, they were all meeting at the Lucky Star and walking to the Mardi Gras crowning of King Mutt. Truck was coming, too, and Harper had warned Jonah he better be in the festive bow tie that she'd bought him for the occasion.

Jonah's cousins were in town, too, having come to show off the baby and make the final arrangements for Belinda and Marty to move to Chicago.

As for Harper? Yesterday, she'd handed over the keys to Deja Brew to Kendal. He'd seemed almost contrite and then said something remarkable. "I regret we didn't always see eye to eye. I really like you, Harper."

They were sitting in swinging baskets, and there was a draft somewhere, and the coffee machine was making a weird noise, and the customers were all tourists—she could tell by the shopping bags from up and down Congress where tourists did their shopping in trendy little stores. It was remarkable how glad Harper would be to be free of this place. "I really like you, too, Kendal. You're good for Olivia." She smiled. "And you didn't like me because I was an ass to you. I don't like to lose."

He laughed. "Me either. So what are you going to do?"

"Me? I'm going to look for a new job and house-sit for my parents while they go on a long European river cruise. Who is taking the Rochester job?" she asked curiously.

Kendal gave her a look. "I think maybe Andrea," he said. "Soren keeps hinting at it." He glanced around them, then leaned forward. "I think Soren and Andrea might be sleeping together."

"*Eeew*," they said simultaneously.

Harper didn't know what her plans were, really. She'd agreed to cat-sit for her parents in Houston for a couple of weeks, but the invitation did not extend beyond it because of Mr. Snuggles. They didn't think he would take kindly to a crusty old bulldog. Harper was going to use the occasion to think about what was next.

She and Jonah had continued on as if nothing had happened, falling in love more every day, pretending Jonah wasn't leaving in two weeks for six months. As if Harper had a job. They talked about everything but never the thing that sat between them—it wasn't a question of "What now?" as much as it was "What next?"

Harper had kept her thoughts to herself because it seemed ridiculous and presumptuous of her to ask Jonah to commit to any sort of relationship right now. He was embarking on something so new and different that he might never make his way back to Austin. So she just kept on as if everything was fine, drawing on years of disappointments suffered in living with her parents. She knew how to go through the motions and keep her disappointment hidden from view. She knew how to wrap it up in the end and store it away.

Olivia was talking about moving to Austin now, because she and Kendal were a real thing. Harper meant what she'd said—Kendal *was* good for Olivia. And she was crazy about him.

Olivia didn't want to hear that Harper wasn't going to ask Jonah for a commitment. But she said that if Harper didn't, she needed to get right back out there. Her theory was that the last thing she needed to do was sit and pine. "You have to find someone new. That's how you get over the last guy."

But Harper didn't want to get over Jonah. Or replace him with someone new. She could never replace him. She was destined to pine for him forever and was okay with that.

The entire Rogers family was gathered when Harper arrived at the Lucky Star with Bob in his tuxedo. Everyone complimented him, and Bob barked or growled and refused to make eye contact. Lulu had on a new bright pink collar with a bow, and was hopping around, her tail whirling like a propeller. Jonah's parents were in the store but had opted to stay behind with the book club and Robert and Lloyd so that the rest of them could go to the King Mutt crowning. "Someone better bring home a crown!" Jonah's mother insisted.

Last night, Harper had dinner with Jonah's family, including Jonah's cousins, Allen and Andy, and Allen's wife, Naomi, and their new baby girl. Burt had unveiled his new lasagna, which came with an explanation for why it was so good for you. He'd really taken to improving the menu. "He's been attending some classes at Central Market," Jonah confided. "That's just how crazy things have gotten around here."

Harper sampled the lasagna. Burt stood nervously, waiting for everyone's opinion. "Ohmigod," Harper said through a mouthful. "This is wonderful, Burt! You know what you should do? Get Amy's brother to make a sign that says something like, *Burt's lasagna, voted best in town by the people we have tied up in the basement.* You know, something fun."

And Burt, who never so much as cracked a smile, actually laughed.

"Excuse me?" Jonah's mother put down her fork and looked at Burt. "Did I just hear you laugh?"

"I can laugh if something's funny," Burt said. "Not that you'd know that."

"Whoa!" Jonah exclaimed with glee. "*And* he's got a sense of humor!"

After Burt had gone out, Harper nudged Jonah. "Seriously, this is so good, Jonah. You're going to have more business than you know what to do with."

"Yeah," Jonah said, and looked wistfully at his plate.

They put on their sun hats and gathered the dogs, then walked up Congress Avenue to the site of the King Mutt crowning. They had three strollers, one for baby Lena, one for Lulu, and one for Bob, who had a tendency to lie down and refuse to go farther when he was tired.

They were a little late to the festivities—the parade of King Mutt's court had already begun. Bob had raised slightly more money than Lulu, which Amy insisted was because Lulu had entered a week later. Nevertheless, neither of them had earned enough votes to make the court. The voting public were assholes, Amy and Harper decided. Who could pass up a three-legged dachshund and a mean old bulldog?

In third place was the black Lab from The Tavern, who Harper had proclaimed was a dime a dozen. Apparently, there was a reason for that—Labs were very popular. A Great Dane was the first runner-up, loping down the street as if he'd just woken from a nap and was still a little sleep drunk.

And then came the winner. Of course it was Duke, because he was still an adorable puppy. But he didn't like the look of the walk down the street. He dug his heels in and wouldn't budge. He lay on his side and refused to get up. Someone had the idea of loaning a kid's wagon to the handlers, and two people lifted the Saint Bernard puppy into the wagon. Duke sat up and took notice then and allowed them to wheel him the length of the street to the stage.

The handlers brought Duke up on the stage and set him on the pedestal. He immediately jumped down and ran to the Great Dane, trying to get the bigger dog's attention. The Great Dane looked up, gave Duke a once-over, and then went back to chewing the bone someone had given him.

"Amateurs," Harper said. "This is not how you stage a King Mutt coronation."

A woman with a bright yellow ACC T-shirt and two long braids walked to the mic. "Thank you, Austin! We have raised over eighty-five thousand dollars this season for the ACC!"

The crowd began to cheer.

"Please put your hands together and join us in welcoming this year's King Mutt! Duke!" She whirled around as one of the handlers tried to get Duke to face the crowd. But Duke was busy trying to dig through the synthetic turf on the stage. The crowd began to chant Duke's name. Someone tried to put a crown on his head. Duke thought it was a chew toy.

Amy was still furious about the results. "I can't even watch this. Lulu and I are going to get some beer. Anyone want some?"

"I'll help," Andy said, and went off with Amy to get the beer.

Allen and Naomi were showing their baby the dogs that surrounded them. And Belinda and Marty had stopped at a vendor's booth to look at some vintage prints of Austin.

"Hey," Jonah said. He took Harper's hand. "Can we go somewhere and talk?"

Harper's heart seized. She'd been expecting the official breakup for days now. She'd be a fool not to know it was coming—Jonah was leaving Saturday. She was heading for Houston on Sunday. Her apartment was already neatly packed, and the new dog bed she'd bought Bob carefully tucked into a basket . . . because Bob refused to use it. "Sure!"

She watched as Jonah handed off Truck to Allen, who had to pull the dog back from licking the baby's face.

With his hand on the small of her back, Jonah indicated an empty bench under a stand of trees.

They sat on the bench and Bob crawled under it. "So . . . is this what I think it is?" Harper asked. She tried to smile. "Has the end come, Mr. Rogers? Are you breaking up with me now?"

He frowned. "That's not exactly what I wanted to say."

So he was going to ease into it. *Okay. This is it.* Harper swallowed down the sudden lump in her throat. There was not enough preparation in the world to make her ready for it. She had tried, and couldn't manage to imagine life without Jonah. She looked down at Bob, and for once, he was looking up at her, as if he, too, was concerned that this was the end of the road.

Jonah didn't speak right away. He seemed to be gathering his thoughts.

"Say it," Harper said. "I can't stand the sitting and waiting for the inevitable."

"I know. I'm trying to get my thoughts together—it's not easy."

"Oh *God*," she groaned.

Jonah laughed and brought her hand to his lips. "Will you relax? I've been doing a lot of thinking about us."

"Here we go," she muttered beneath her breath.

"I don't want this to end," he said quietly.

Did he think she did? "So you're inviting me to go to Spain with you." She rolled her eyes.

"Maybe to visit?"

"Right."

"What would you think about running the Lucky Star while I'm gone?"

That was *definitely* not what Harper was expecting. This was not a breakup—this was a job offer? "Excuse me?"

"I know this comes as a surprise, but we were talking about it, my family, I mean, and we need someone like you to run the place. Dad is too sick, and no one else understands or wants to understand the business end quite like he does. Or I do. And you . . . you know everything, Harper. You're perfect for the job."

"Wait . . . are you trying to *hire* me? Like make me your employee?" She almost felt insulted. It seemed impossible to believe that Jonah, the Most Perfect Guy Ever, would ruin that illusion by thinking it was okay to offer his soon-to-be-ex a job.

"No!" he said, as if the very idea were horrifying.

"You just offered me a job!"

"What? No! Wait, wait, wait. Let me start over. Harper, I know this sounds spur of the moment, but it's not, I swear it's not. You are the only thing I have felt one hundred percent right about in . . . in *ever*. I love you so much, and you love me, and the sex between us is so freaking hot, and—"

"And you think for all that I should jump at a chance for a job?"

"Not a job!" he said, as if she was willfully misunderstanding. "As a partner. *My* partner."

She was still confused. "So you're inviting me to buy in, or—"

"Good God, this could not possibly go any worse." He suddenly stood up from the bench, then went down on one knee. Bob thought he'd come to play and crawled out, rising up on his back legs to put his face near Jonah's. "What I am trying to do," Jonah said, dodging Bob's tongue, "and very badly, is ask you to marry me."

A woman walking by gasped.

"What? *What?*" Harper shouted.

"I know! I blew it," Jonah said. "And I don't have a ring. But I am getting one," he hastened to assure her.

Harper stared at him. Bob lost interest and crawled back under the bench. Jonah's smile was a little anxious. "You haven't answered."

"This is like the *worst* proposal ever."

"It really is," he agreed.

"If I were doing it, I would plan something super romantic. With candles and flowers and something really delicious to eat."

"Good feedback," he said. "I had a different plan, but I was looking at you while we were watching Duke, and I didn't think I could wait one more minute. Not one more."

"Oh," she said wistfully. Her heart began to melt in her chest. *He couldn't wait.*

"That is so sweet," a woman somewhere said. "You have to say yes."

"No, she doesn't have to," Jonah said, glancing over his shoulder. "It's totally up to—"

The woman had walked on.

"Yeah, okay," Jonah said, and turned back to Harper. "It's totally up to you. I want to marry you because I love you. Not because I want you to run the Lucky Star. That came out all wrong. Because I want a life with you, and the Lucky Star is all about family, and anyway, it got twisted, but I want you to *be* my family, and I . . . God, Harper, I can't do this without you. I don't want to do anything without you. And it's selfish, but I want you to wait for me, I want you to be here, I want to plan a life with you. So will you marry me?"

He looked so tortured, the poor thing.

"Dude."

Harper hadn't noticed Amy, Allen and Andy, Naomi and the baby, and Jonah's aunt and uncle until that moment.

"This is *not* what we talked about," Andy said.

"Oh my God," Amy said. "This is, like, the worst place to do it, Jonah! What were you thinking?"

"Yes, thank you all, I am getting lots of great feedback here! And there is something digging into my knee, so I'm probably crippled, too, but Harper hasn't answered."

Harper laughed. "Oh my God, of *course* I will marry you, Jonah!"

He looked as if he didn't believe her. "Really? Even when it's this bad?"

"*Especially* when it's this bad. You obviously need me."

"Oh my God, she said yes!" Jonah shouted, and leapt to his feet. Truck lunged at his master with excitement, and Bob began to bark and Lulu whimpered, and people around them began to applaud when Jonah grabbed Harper up and kissed her hard . . . until they got tangled in the leashes and fell onto the bench.

Epilogue

Seven months later

The flight home from Madrid was the worst. The couple seated behind Jonah spent the full ten hours fighting in rounds of sobbing and bitter sparring. His seat's power outlet didn't work, so he spent most of the flight playing his own special game of Befriend, Bury, Eat in case they crashed and he was forced to make some hard decisions.

Mostly, he just counted the minutes until he was home again.

He missed it. He missed them all. He mostly missed Harper. He hadn't thought he could miss her more, but then she'd come to visit him in Madrid, and when she left to go home, he discovered he could miss her even more.

Harper was not picking him up. "We're a little shorthanded," she said. "Can you take a cab or a Lyft?"

He was a little disappointed that she wouldn't be there to pick him up, wouldn't be the first face he saw when he came down the elevator. But he understood.

He walked outside to torrential rain. He saw the Lyft sign on the dash of a van and, after shoving his things in back, hopped into the back seat.

The driver said, "South Congress, right? We'll be there in twenty minutes."

"Seems optimistic," Jonah said, looking out the window.

"Oh no. If my app says twenty minutes, I will be there in twenty minutes. I have a five-star rating."

Jonah's head came up. "Amal?"

The driver looked at him in the rearview mirror. "Yes! Have I driven you before? I work the airport a lot. People are very happy to be in Austin."

Unbelievable. He couldn't wait to tell Harper.

Amal kept a running commentary of how happy visitors were to arrive in Austin all the way to the Lucky Star. Jonah was surprised to see the building had been painted. It was now white, the windows and doors trimmed in green. Where had the money for that come from? No one had told him they were going to do this. Harper had expressly told him he was not to worry about anything, that she and his dad had it under control. If he asked, she reported receipts and staff news, but mostly, he kept his head in his work and trusted that she and Dad were doing whatever needed to be done.

Including painting, apparently. It looked good.

He got out, pulled out his bags, and walked to the front doors. They'd been replaced, too. They were iron now. Where were they getting this money?

He pulled one open and stepped inside—and came to a dead stop. The stage was still where he and Marty had built it—more of a riser, really—and a band was setting up. But that wasn't what surprised him. What surprised him was that the dining room was packed. Standing room only. And not one familiar face. No Mom or Dad, no Harper, no Amy. He could see the top of Burt's bandanna'd head through the kitchen window, which gave him some measure of confidence he wasn't dreaming. There seemed to be another bandanna'd head running around back there, too.

"Hello! Welcome to Saturday Nights at the Star," a young woman said.

She looked familiar, but he couldn't place her. He happened to glance down and noticed the cupcake tattoo on her chest. "Hey, ACC, right?"

"Yes! I'm Cinder. Did you . . . ?"

"I walked a couple of dogs there. I'm Jonah, Harper Thompson's fiancé."

"Oh, of course! Harper talks about you all the time. She's not here . . . did you have a reservation for tonight?"

"A *reservation*?" He nearly choked on the word.

"Only on Saturdays at the Star," Cinder said.

He was amazed by this. They had so much demand now that customers needed a reservation? "I don't, but my family owns this place."

"Oh!" She pressed her fingertips to her forehead. "Of course. Your family is over at Deja Brew. Didn't you get the message?"

"Deja Brew? What message?"

But a group of four had come in, and Cinder turned away from him.

Jonah shoved his two bags in behind the coatrack, then stepped outside. He looked across the street to Deja Brew. It looked closed. Was Cinder confused?

He jogged across the street and up to the entrance. He could see a few people through the window as he pushed open the door.

"*Surprise!*"

The shout startled Jonah. His family was all here—*all* of them, and Amy, too, of course. And Harper . . . and Kendal and Olivia?

They all watched him expectantly, as if they expected him to speak. "Why are you all here?"

"Because the Star is packed, duh," Amy said. She was wearing a pink prom dress, red cowboy boots, and thick red glasses. "Didn't you see them all? And Kendal said we could have it here. We're all friends now. It's a long story."

"It's not a long story," Kendal said. "We began to work more closely, and the people of the Lucky Star recognized my genius, and that was that."

"Wasn't *quite* like that," Amy said. "Plus he's dating her best friend."

Still, Jonah was confused. "But I thought—" He was hit with a force from the side and stumbled into the doorjamb. He knew instantly what had happened and threw one arm around his dog's huge body and buried his face in Truck's fur. Until Truck could stand it no more and started to try and lick him. Dodging Truck's dancing feet was little Lulu with her helicopter tail. Even Bob had come forward to greet him, and just behind Bob, another dog, white and furry, who was bouncing with excitement until it bounced headfirst into the wall.

"Mobley!" Harper cried, and hurried past Jonah to get the dog. "I haven't told you about Mobley yet." She pulled the dog away from the wall, then was suddenly in front of Jonah, her arms around his neck. "I wanted you to be surprised by everything. I'll explain, but first, I have to tell you how much I have missed you." She kissed him, hard and furious.

"Me too. Oh God, me too." He looked at everyone gathered, all of them grinning at him like he was in for a joke or something. Dad looked a lot better since the last time Jonah had Zoomed with him. His color was coming back, and Jonah's mother said he was in remission again. They were all here. His family, his aunt and uncle, Allen and Andy, Naomi and the baby. Even Paula, the morning server. Even the Little Stacy Book Club had come. "Why not?" said one of them. "We like a good party."

Robert and Lloyd had come, too, and were sitting in baskets, twisting this way and that, like two kids at a playground.

Jonah loved his work. He did. But as much as he liked looking into space, he liked being grounded in family, too. "It's so good to be home." They all came forward, their arms outstretched, hugging him, laughing at his surprise, at one another, at the dogs.

Oh, the laughter.

His mother was chattering about the new kitchen help that Burt had found in the Community First! Village. His aunt and uncle, Allen and Andy, and Naomi and Lena—she was crawling everywhere now—had come to visit and close on the sale of Marty and Belinda's house. The move to Chicago was complete. His dad said he was doing well, then pointed at Robert and Lloyd and said they were teaching him to play chess.

The book club presented him with a ceramic satellite they'd made in their pottery class. A joint project, he understood. He didn't see a satellite—he saw a ceramic ball with some stars cut into it. He was going to hang it near Roy Rogers.

And Harper. He couldn't stop looking at her. She was wearing jeans rolled up at the cuffs, and a pair of Chucks. She had on a T-shirt that said SAVE YOURSELF—HUG A DOG, and her hair hung loosely around her shoulders. But it was her eyes, her pale green eyes glittering at him, that made his heart swell and his pulse race. She looked so different and exactly the same and *hot*, and he couldn't wait to be alone with her.

"Mobley?" he asked, smiling down at her.

"I was going to tell you about her," she said. "But I didn't think she'd be around so long."

Jonah looked across the room. Mobley was following Bob very closely.

"She's blind, and it was supposed to be a weekend, but the ACC is overfull, and Bob really likes her, and you know, he doesn't like *anyone*. So . . . I kept her." She winced. "I know that's a lot of dogs—"

"There are never enough dogs, baby," he said, and kissed her.

"Come on, come on!" Amy was yelling at him and Harper. "Save that for later!" The group was moving outside.

Jonah and Harper followed them out to Deja Brew's lovely garden with the little umbrellas sparkling overhead. They had a cake, decorated with planets and stars and the message WELCOME HOME JONAS!

Confused, he looked at them.

"There was a little mix-up," his mother said, tugging on a gray curl.

Jonah laughed. "Let's eat Jonas's cake."

His mother grabbed a knife and started slicing.

Jonah looked around at the people he loved, at the dogs who had wandered out, Mobley following Bob by scent. Harper looking up at the lights, her skin glowing. She must have sensed his gaze on her, because she turned her head to him and smiled.

"You won't believe who drove me here."

"Who?"

"Amal."

Her eyes sparkled and she gasped with delight. "Was it a five-star ride?"

"That's the only kind of ride he gives, I've heard."

Harper laughed. "Can you believe that one ride would lead to so much?"

"It started with that ride."

"Actually, it started with a dog," she said, pointing to Truck. "Because I decided that whoever owned that dog was someone I had to know." She laughed. "I'm so glad you're home, Jonah. I can't wait to marry you."

"I'm so glad you're here, Harper. With me, and my family. This is where you belong."

She slipped her arm around his waist. "I know." She sighed with contentment, and Jonah thought there was not a better sound in the world.

Author's Note

My inspiration for the King Mutt competition came from the San Antonio Humane Society's annual El Rey Fido fundraising effort held in conjunction with the city's annual Fiesta celebration. San Antonio is unique in Texas in that the city honors the Battle of San Jacinto and the heroes of the Alamo every year with a week of events, parades, and even a day off school for the kids.

Many years ago, the San Antonio Humane Society began to hold the event for El Rey Fido as part of Fiesta to raise money for the dogs and cats that come through their organization. Any dog may be entered, and fundraising happens online or at sanctioned events. The dog who raises the most money for the society is crowned, and is accompanied by a royal court of the next four highest fundraisers. All proceeds go to support the cats and dogs that come into services through the San Antonio Humane Society.

Photo by Kathy Whittaker Photography

Julia London is the *New York Times*, *USA Today*, and *Publishers Weekly* bestselling author of numerous romance and women's fiction novels. She is also the recipient of the RT Bookclub Award for Best Historical Romance and a six-time finalist for the prestigious RITA Award for excellence in romantic fiction.